...ed

"Offering a clever twist on the tales of the Brothers Grimm, this debut historical cozy (and series launch) introduces an attractive, spunky heroine . . . and an entertaining, well-constructed plot that will satisfy fans of folklore and fairy tales." —*Library Journal* (starred review)

"Deliciously Gothic, intriguingly different, this story plunges us into the world of Brothers Grimm fairy tales, where the greed and evil are all too real, and everyone has something to hide." —Rhys Bowen, *New York Times* bestselling author

"[Chance's] lively debut, the first in a new cozy series . . . will whet the reader's appetite for Ophelia and Prue's next misadventure." —*Publishers Weekly*

Praise for

Snow White Red-Hand

Berkley Prime Crime titles by Maia Chance

SNOW WHITE RED-HANDED
CINDERELLA SIX FEET UNDER

Cinderella
Six Feet Under

Maia Chance

BERKLEY PRIME CRIME, NEW YORK

An imprint of Penguin Random House LLC
375 Hudson Street, New York, New York 10014

CINDERELLA SIX FEET UNDER

A Berkley Prime Crime Book / published by arrangement with the author

ISBN: 978-0-425-27163-6

PUBLISHING HISTORY
Berkley Prime Crime mass-market edition / September 2015

PRINTED IN THE UNITED STATES OF AMERICA

10 9 8 7 6 5 4 3 2 1

Cover illustration by Brandon Dorman.
Interior text design by Kelly Lipovich.

Penguin
Random
House

For Zach

Shams and delusions are esteemed for soundest truths, while reality is fabulous. If men would steadily observe realities only, and not allow themselves to be deluded, life . . . would be like a fairy tale . . .

—Henry David Thoreau (1854)

1

November, 1867
Oxford, England

The murdered girl, grainy in black-and-gray newsprint, stared up at him. Her eyes were mournful and blank.

Gabriel placed the chipped Blue Willow teacup beside the picture. His hand shook, and tea sloshed onto the newspaper. Ink bled.

Gabriel Augustus Penrose, although a bespectacled professor, hadn't—not yet, at least—developed round shoulders or a nearsighted scowl. Although, such shoulders and such a scowl *would* have suited the oaken desk, swaybacked sofa, towers of books, and swirling dust motes in his study at St. Remigius's College, Oxford. And at four-and-thirty years of age, Gabriel was certainly not given to fits of trembling.

But *this*.

He tore his eyes from the girl's. Was it today's newspaper? He glanced at the upper margin—*yes*. Perhaps there was still time.

Time for . . . what?

He didn't customarily peruse the papers during his four o'clock cup of tea, but a student had come to see him and he'd happened to leave *The Times* behind. The morgue drawing was on the fourth page, tucked between a report about a Piccadilly thief and an advertisement for stereoscopic slides. A familiar, lovely, and—according to the report—dead face.

SENSATIONAL MURDER IN PARIS: In the Marais district, a young woman was found dead as the result of two gunshot wounds in the garden of the mansion of the Marquis de la Roque-Fabliau, 15 Rue Garenne. She is thought to be the daughter of American actress Henrietta Bright, who wed the marquis in January. The family solicitor said that it is not known how the tragic affair arose, and that the family was unaware of the daughter's presence in Paris. The *commissaire de police* of that quarter has undertaken an assiduous search for her murderer.

Gabriel removed his spectacles, leaned forward on his knees, and laid his forehead in his palm. The murdered girl, Miss Prudence Bright, was a mere acquaintance. Perhaps the same might be said of Miss Ophelia Flax, the young American actress who had been traveling with Miss Bright when he'd encountered them in the Black Forest several weeks ago.

Mere acquaintance. The term could not account for the ripping sensation in his lungs.

Gabriel replaced his spectacles, stood, and strode to the jumbled bookcase behind his desk. He drew an antique volume from the shelf: *Histoires ou contes du temps passé—Stories or Fairy Tales from Past Times*—by Charles Perrault. He flipped through the pages, making certain a loose sheet of paper was still wedged inside.

He stuffed the volume in his leather satchel, along with his memorandum book, yanked on his tweed jacket, clamped on his hat, and made for the door.

Two Days Earlier
Paris

The mansion's door-knocker was shaped like a snarling mouse's head. Its bared teeth glinted in the gloom and raindrops dribbled off its nose. It *ought* to have been enough of a warning. But Miss Ophelia Flax was in no position to skedaddle. Yes, her nerves twanged like an out of tune banjo. But she'd come too far, she had too little money, and rainwater was making inroads into her left boot. She would stick to her guns.

"Ready?" she asked Prue, the nineteen-year-old girl dripping next to her like an unwrung mop.

"Can't believe Ma would take up residence in a pit like this," Prue said. Her tone was all bluster, but her china-doll's face was taut beneath her bonnet, and her yellow curls drooped. "You sure you got the address right?"

"Certain." The inked address had long since run, and the paper was as soggy as bread pudding by now. However, Ophelia had committed the address—15 Rue Garenne—to memory, and she'd studied the Baedeker's Paris map in the railway car all the way from Germany, where she and Prue had lately been employed as maids in the household of an American millionaire. "It's hardly a pit, either," Ophelia said. "More like a palace. It's past its prime, that's all." The mansion's stones, true, were streaked with soot, and the neighborhood was shabby. But Henrietta's mansion would dwarf every building in Littleton, New Hampshire, where Ophelia had been born and raised. It was grander than most buildings in New York City, too.

"I reckon Ma, of all people, wouldn't marry a poor feller."

"Likely not."

"But what if she ain't here? What if she went back to New York?"

"She'll be here. And she'll be ever so pleased to see you. It's been how long? Near a twelvemonth since she . . ." Ophelia's voice trailed off. Keeping up the chipper song and dance was a chore.

"This is cork-brained," Prue said.

"We've come all this way, and we're not turning back now." Ophelia didn't mention that she had just enough maid's wages saved up for one—and *only* one—railway ticket to Cherbourg and one passage back to New York.

Prue's mother, Henrietta Bright, had been the star actress of Howard DeLuxe's Varieties back in Manhattan, up until she'd figured out that walking down the aisle with a French marquis was a sight easier than treading the boards. She had abandoned Prue, since ambitious brides have scant use for blossoming daughters.

But Prue and Ophelia had recently discovered Henrietta's whereabouts, so Ophelia fully intended to put her Continental misadventures behind her, just as soon as she installed Prue in the arms of her long-lost mother.

Before Ophelia could lose her nerve, she hefted the mouse-head door-knocker and let it crash.

Prue eyed Ophelia's disguise. "Think she'll buy that getup?"

"Once we're safe inside, I'll take it off."

The door squeaked open.

A grizzle-headed gent loomed. His spine was shaped like a question mark and flesh-colored bumps studded his eyelids. A steward, judging by his drab togs and stately wattle.

"Good evening," Ophelia said in her best matron's warble. "I wish to speak to Madame la Marquise de la Roque-Fabliau." What a mouthful. Like sucking on marbles.

"Regrettably, that will not be possible," the steward said.

He spoke English. Lucky.

The steward's gaze drifted southward.

Ophelia was five-and-twenty years of age, tall, and beanstalk straight as far as figures went. However, at present she appeared to be a pillowy-hipped, deep-bosomed dame in a black bombazine gown and woolen cloak. A steel-gray wig and black taffeta bonnet concealed her light brown hair, and cosmetics crinkled her oval face. All for the sake of practicality. Flibbertigibbets like Prue required chaperones when traveling, so Ophelia had dug into her theatrical case and transformed herself into the sort of daunting chaperone that made even the most shameless lotharios turn tail and pike off.

"Now see here!" Ophelia said. "We shan't be turned out into the night like beggars. My charge and I have traveled hundreds of miles in order to visit the marquise, and we mean to see her. This young lady is her daughter."

The steward took in Prue's muddy skirts, her cheap cloak and crunched straw bonnet, the two large carpetbags slumped at their feet. He didn't budge.

Stuffed shirt.

"Baldewyn," a woman's voice called behind him. "Baldewyn, *qui est là*?" There was a *tick-tick* of heels, and a dark young lady appeared. She was perhaps twenty years of age, with a pointed snout of a face like a mongoose and beady little animal eyes to match.

"*Pardonnez-moi,* Mademoiselle Eglantine," Baldewyn said, "this young lady—an American, clearly—claims to be a kinswoman of the marquise."

"Kinswoman?" Eglantine said. "How do you mean, kinswoman? Of my *belle-mère*? Oh. Well. She is . . . absent."

Ophelia had picked up enough French from a fortune-teller during her stint in P. Q. Putnam's Traveling Circus a few years back to know what *belle-mère* meant: *stepmother.*

"No matter," Ophelia said. "Mademoiselle, may I present to you your stepsister, Miss Prudence Deliverance Bright?"

"I assure you," Eglantine said, "I have but one sister, and she is inside. I do not know who you are, or what sort of little amusement you are playing at, but I have guests to attend to. Now, *s'il vous plaît*, go away!" She spun around and disappeared, the *tick-tick* of her heels receding.

Baldewyn's dour mouth twitched upwards. Then he slammed the door in their noses.

"Well, I never!" Ophelia huffed. "They didn't even ask for proof!"

"I *told* you Ma don't want me."

"For the thousandth time, humbug." Ophelia hoisted her

carpetbag and trotted down the steps, into the rain. "She doesn't even know you're on the European continent, let alone on her doorstep. That Miss Eglantine—"

"Fancies she's the Queen of Sheba!" Prue came down the steps behind her, hauling her own bag.

"—said your mother is absent. So all we must do is wait. The question is, where?" They stood on the sidewalk and looked up and down the street lined with monumental old buildings and shivering black trees. A carriage splashed by, its driver bent into the slanting rain. "We can't stay out of doors. May as well be standing under Niagara Falls. I'm afraid my greasepaint's starting to run, and this padding is like a big sponge." Ophelia shoved her soaked pillow-bosom into line. "Come on. Surely we'll find someplace to huddle for an hour or so. Your sister—"

"Don't *call* her that!"

"Very well, Miss Eglantine said they've got guests. So I figure your mother will be home soon."

The mansion's foundation stones went right to the pavement. No front garden. But farther along they found a carriageway arch. Its huge iron gates stood ajar.

"Now see?" Ophelia said. "Nice and dry under there."

"Awful dark."

"Not . . . terribly."

More hoof-clopping. Was it—Ophelia squinted—was it the same carriage that had passed by only a minute ago? Yes. It was. The same bent driver, the same horses. And—

Her heart went lickety-split.

—and a pale smudge of a face peering out the window. Right at her.

Then it had gone.

On the other side of the carriageway arch lay a big, dark courtyard. Wings of Henrietta's mansion bordered it on two sides. The third side was an ivy-covered carriage house and stables, where an upstairs window glowed with light. The fourth side was a high stone wall. The garden seemed neg-lected. Shrubs were shaggy, weeds tangled the flower beds, and the air stank of decay.

"Look," Prue said, pointing. "A party."

Light shone from tall windows. Figures moved about inside and piano music tinkled.

"Let's have a look." Ophelia abandoned her carpetbag under the arch and set off down a path. Wet twigs and leaves dragged at her skirts.

"You mean spy on them?"

"Miss Eglantine didn't seem the most honest little fish."

"And that Baldy-win feller was a troll."

"So maybe your ma is really in there, after all."

Up close to the high windows, it was like peeping into a jewel box: cream paneled walls with gold-leaf flowers and swags, and enough mirrors and crystal chandeliers to make your eyes sting. A handful of richly dressed ladies and gentlemen loitered about. A plump woman in a gray bun—a servant—stood against a wall. A frail young lady in owlish spectacles crashed away at the piano.

"There's Eggy," Prue said. "Maybe that's the sister she mentioned." A third young lady in a lavish green tent of a gown sat next to Eglantine.

"Same dark hair," Ophelia said.

"Same mean little eyes."

"A good deal taller, however, and somewhat . . . wider."

"Spit it out. She looks like a prizefighter in a wig."

"Prue! That might be your own sister you're going on about."

"*Step*sister. Look—they're having words, I reckon. Eggy don't seem too pleased."

The young ladies' heads were bent close together, and they appeared to be bickering. The larger lady in green had her eyes stuck on something across the room.

Ah. A gentleman. Fair-haired, flushed, and strapping, crammed into a white evening jacket with medals and ribbons, and epaulets on the shoulders. He conversed with a burly fellow in black evening clothes who had a lion's mane of dark gold hair flowing to his shoulders.

"Ladies quarreling about a fellow," Ophelia said. "How very tiresome."

"*Some* fellers are worth talking of."

"If you're hinting that I care to discuss any gentleman, least of all Professor Penrose, then—well, I do not, I *sincerely* do not feel a whit of sentiment for that man."

"Oh, sure," Prue said.

Ophelia longed for things, certainly. But not for *him*. She longed for a home. She longed, with that gritted-molars sort of longing, to be snug in a third-class berth in the guts of a steamship barging towards America. She'd throw over acting, head up north to New Hampshire or Vermont, get work on a farmstead. Merciful heavens! She knew how to scour pots, tend goats, hoe beans, darn socks, weave rush chair seats, and cure a rash with apple cider vinegar. So why was she gallivanting across Europe, penniless, half starved, and shivering, in this preposterous disguise?

"Duck!" Prue whispered.

There was a clatter above, voices coming closer; someone pushed a window open.

Ophelia and Prue stumbled off to the side until they were safely in shadow once more. They'd come to the second wing of the mansion. All of the windows were black except for two on the main floor.

"Let's look," Ophelia whispered. "Could be your ma."

They picked their way towards the windows, into what seemed to be a marshy vegetable patch.

Ophelia stepped around some sort of half-rotten squash, and wedged the toe of her boot between two building stones. She gripped the sill to pull herself up, and her waterlogged rump padding threatened to pull her backwards. She squinted through the glass. "Most peculiar," she whispered. "Looks like some sort of workshop. Tables heaped with knickknacks."

"A tinker's shop?" Prue clambered up. "Oh. Look at all them gears and cogs and things."

"Why would there be a tinker's shop in this grand house?

Your ma married a nobleman. Yet it's on the main floor of the house, not down where the servants' workplaces must be." A fire burned in a carved fireplace and piles of metal things glimmered.

"Crackers," Prue whispered. "Someone's in there."

Sure enough, a round, bald man hunched over a table. One of his hands held a cube-shaped box. The other twisted a screwdriver. Ophelia couldn't see his face because he wore brass jeweler's goggles.

"What in tarnation is he doing?" Prue spoke too emphatically, and her bonnet brim hit the windowpane.

The man glanced up. The lenses of his goggles shone.

Holy Moses. He looked like something that had crawled out of a nightmare.

The man stood so abruptly that his chair collapsed behind him. He lurched towards them.

Ophelia hopped down into the vegetable patch.

Prue recoiled. For a few seconds she seemed suspended, twirling her arms in the air like a graceless hummingbird. Then she pitched backwards and thumped into the garden a few steps from Ophelia.

"Hurry!" Ophelia whispered. "Get up! He's opening the window!"

Prue didn't get up. She screamed. The kind of long, shrill scream you'd use when, say, falling off a cliff.

The man flung open the window. He yelled down at them in French.

"Get me off of it!" Prue yelled. "Oh golly, get me *off* of it!"

Ophelia crouched, hooked her hands under Prue's arms, and dragged her to her feet. They both stared, speechless, down into the dark vegetation. Raindrops smacked Ophelia's cheeks. Prue panted and whimpered at the same time

Then—the man must've turned on a lamp—light flared.

A gorgeous gown of ivory tulle and silk sprawled at Ophelia's and Prue's feet, embroidered with gold and silver thread.

A gown. That was all. That had to be all.

But there was a foot—mercy, a *foot*—protruding from

the hem of the gown. Bare, white, slick with rainwater. Toes bruised and blood-raw, the big toenail purple.

Ophelia's tongue went sour.

Hair. Long, wet, curled hair, tangled with a leaf and clotted with blood. A face. Eyes stretched open. Dead as a doornail.

Ophelia stopped breathing.

The thing was, the dead girl was the spitting image of . . . Prue.

2

The goggled man's yelling stopped, and he vanished.
He'd be summoning the law. Or maybe unleashing a pack of drooling hounds.

Ophelia managed to stagger away with Prue from that horrible . . . thing. Prue's whimpers inched into a hysterical register.

Ophelia lowered them both to a seat on the edge of a fountain. The fountain's black water mirrored the lights of the party still going full-steam ahead inside. Those fancy folk hadn't heard Prue's screams through the piano music.

"Calm yourself. It will be all right." Ophelia stroked Prue's hunched back. These were hypocritical words, since Ophelia was feeling about as calm as a nor'easter herself. But what else could you say to a girl who'd just laid eyes on her dead double? "We'll leave this place, Prue, just as soon as you're able to walk. How would that be?"

Prue panted through her teeth.

"And that girl," Ophelia said, "well, there must be some horrible mistake, or maybe—"

"How could it be a mistake? Them *holes* in her. The blood. The—"

"I don't know. But we'll leave, even if it means sleeping on a park bench, but first you must steady your breath, and—"

"My sister."

"Sister? Have you a sister?" In all the years Ophelia had known Prue, she'd never heard of a sister.

"Had. I *had* a sister. Now she's gone, and I never had a— had a—had a—" Prue crumpled into fresh sobs.

Her sobs were so noisy that Ophelia didn't hear the scrunching gravel behind them until it was too late.

"You two," someone said just behind them. "*Mais oui.* I might have guessed."

Ophelia twisted around.

Baldewyn the steward minced around the fountain. Even in the dim light, it was easy to see his pistol, aimed straight at Ophelia's noggin.

"You hold that gun just as prettily as a feather duster," Ophelia said, "but doesn't the hammer need to be cocked?"

"Forgive me," Baldewyn said. "I had been inclined to think I was dealing with a lady. Not"—he cocked the hammer— "a sharpshooter. I had almost forgotten that you two are not only derelicts, but Americans. Does everyone in that wilderness of yours fancy themselves a—how do you say?—cowboy? *S'il vous plaît*, rise and walk."

"Not on your nelly."

"What a quaint expression. Does it mean no? Sadly, *no* is not, at this juncture, a possibility. The marquis has informed me that you have been trespassing, and that there appears to be a corpse on the premises. On occasions such as these, it is customary to take invading strangers into custody."

"You aren't the police," Ophelia said.

"Oh, the *Gendarmerie Royale* has been summoned and the *commissaire* will be notified. You cannot escape. Now, I really must insist"—Baldewyn leaned around, pressed the barrel of the pistol between Ophelia's shoulder blades, and gave it a corkscrew—"that you march."

He prodded Ophelia with the gun across the garden to the

house, Prue clinging to Ophelia's arm all the way. They
reached a short flight of steps that led down to a door. Windows on either side of the door guttered with dull orange light.

"The cellar?" Prue said. "You ain't going to rabbit hutch
us in the cellar are you, mister?"

Baldewyn's answer was a shove that sent Ophelia and
Prue slipping and stumbling down the mossy steps. Bal-
dewyn followed. He kicked open the door, and bundled
Ophelia and Prue across the threshold.

The door slammed and a latch clacked.

They were locked in.

Prue had reckoned she'd gotten ahold of herself. A *slippery*
hold, leastways. But something about the sound of that latch
hitting home made her go all fluff-headed again. Another
scream bloomed up from her lungs, but it couldn't come out.
Her throat was raw now, wounded.

Wounded. Her sister. Those creeping dark stains. Her
poor, small, battered foot.

"Look," Ophelia said in the Sunday School Teacher voice
she always used on Prue. "Look. It's only a kitchen, see?"

Right. Only a kitchen. A mighty *dirty* kitchen.

"And," Ophelia added, "it's spacious. No need to feel
cooped up."

Half of the kitchen glowed from orange cinders in a fireplace. The other half wavered in shadow. Iron kettles on
chains bubbling up wafts of savor and herbs. Plank table
cluttered with crockery. Copper pots dangling from thick
ceiling beams.

And . . . little motions flickering along the walls. Prue
rubbed her eyes. The motions didn't stop. Black, streaming,
skittery—

"Mice!" she yelled.

In three bounds, Prue was on top of the table. Crockery
crashed. A chair toppled sideways.

Mice. *Uck.* Prue's skin itched all over. She disliked most
critters with feet smaller than nickels, and she *hated* mice.

Blame it on her girlhood, on the lean times spent in Manhattan rookeries.

"My sainted aunt." Ophelia righted the chair.

"Sorry." Prue crouched on the tabletop, arms hugged around her damp, muddy knees.

Ophelia, silent, stooped to collect shards of crockery.

Probably marveling at how she'd been dragged into yet another fix by Prue. Prue was fond of Ophelia, but she knew—or, at least, she powerfully suspected—that Ophelia looked upon *her* as a dray horse looks upon a harness and cart. A deadweight. A chafing in the sides.

Ophelia piled the crockery shards on the table. "Tell me about your sister," she said. "Did you never know her, then?"

"Only heard stories. Well, just one story. Ma only kept her long enough for the one story, see."

"What was her name?"

"Don't know. She is—was—a year or two older than me. Her pa took her off when she was only a new baby. I never got to *meet* her, Ophelia, I—"

"What else did your ma say?"

"That's all. That her pa was some hoity-toity French feller, and he hired a wet nurse and took the baby off to give her a better life. Didn't want his child raised by an actress. Do you think . . . maybe Ma married him, all these years later? Maybe this here's his house? But then, why is my sister lying dead out there in the weeds with those fine folks inside laughing and listening to piano songs and—"

"Shush, now. Don't work yourself up."

Prue patted her bodice. From beneath damp layers of wool and cotton came the comforting crackle of paper.

The letter. Her treasured secret. Proof that *somebody* in this wide world wanted her. Maybe.

Ophelia and Prue hunkered on stools at the kitchen hearth. They kept their wet cloaks and bonnets on. Their soaked boots steamed. Mice nibbled food scraps under the table.

From the rooms above came muffled voices, foot thuds,

door slams. Outside in the garden, men's voices rose and fell behind the spatter of rain on the windows. Lights shone and turned away like unsteady lighthouses.

More than an hour passed.

"Oh!" Prue's head bobbed up. "Someone's coming down the stairs."

Ophelia straightened her wig and stood. "Let me do the talking."

A person ought never show up to a murder wearing a disguise. Ophelia had realized *that* nugget of wisdom too late. The problem was that if one whipped off a wig and padded hips, say, shortly after a dead body was discovered, well, suspicions were sure to kindle.

Which meant there was no choice but to blunder forward in this absurd disguise.

Three men piled into the kitchen: the bald, egg-shaped fellow they'd seen tinkering with the screwdriver, and two young men in brass-buttoned blue uniforms. Police.

"Precisely *what* is the meaning of this?" Ophelia asked in her best Outraged Chaperone voice. "Locking us up like common criminals? I'll have you know this is the marquise's daughter, Miss Prudence Bright. Where is the marquise— where is Henrietta?"

The men gawked at Prue.

"I presume that your *extremely* rude staring," Ophelia said, "is due to the simple fact that the dead girl in the garden is—was—*also* Henrietta's daughter, and thus Miss Bright's sister. The resemblance is indeed uncanny, but that is not an excuse to gape at this poor girl as though she were a circus sideshow."

"Sister?" the egg-shaped man said. "Oh. *Sisters*. I see. I beg your pardon, *madame*. I have forgotten my manners. I am Renouart Malbert, the Marquis de la Roque-Fabliau. The master of this house."

Malbert wore an elegant suit of evening clothes that was fifteen years out of mode and frayed about the cuffs and collar. He was so short he had to tip his custard-soft chins up to look into Ophelia's face. His jeweler's goggles had been replaced with round, gold spectacles. His eyes blinked like a clever piglet's.

"*Et oui*, oh yes, *mon Dieu*," Malbert said, "Mademoiselle Bright does indeed resemble the girl—her sister, you say—in the garden, and also my dear, darling, precious Henrietta."

Henrietta was lots of things, but *dear*, *darling*, and *precious* were not at the top of the list.

"The girl in the garden, you say?" Ophelia frowned. "Then you do not know her name?"

"Why, no," Malbert said. "She is a stranger to me."

"A stranger!"

"Yet now that I see this daughter—Prudence, you say?—of my darling wife, well, now I begin to discern a family resemblance. Oh dear me." Malbert dabbed his clammy-looking pate with a hankie. "A most perplexing matter, troubling, macabre, even."

"I should say so," Ophelia said. "Perhaps the girl was searching, too, for her mother at this house."

"Are you a relation of dear Henrietta's, as well?"

"No, I am . . ." Ophelia cleared her throat. "I am Mrs. Brand. Of Boston, Massachusetts. Miss Bright could not, of course, travel without a chaperone. She is young, and quite alone. I encountered her by chance, degraded to the role of maid by an appalling series of events, in the scullery of an American family residing in Germany. I agreed to escort her, out of a sense of national duty and womanly propriety, to her mother here in Paris." Half-truths, and a couple of whoppers. But Ophelia couldn't very well say *she* was an actress, too, because that would mean revealing she was in disguise. Besides, she'd already had a mix-up with the police in Germany.

Speaking of which . . . Ophelia looked at the two officers. They had scarcely three chin hairs between them.

She could cow them. Easy as pie.

With Malbert translating, the two officers questioned Ophelia and Prue at the kitchen table. They had no identity papers, which caused a stir until Ophelia shamed the officers with a reminder that ladies needn't carry such vulgar documents, and that a lady's word was verification enough. She elaborated on the string of half-truths and whoppers, and summed up their discovery of the body in the garden.

"So," she said, "if you mean to arrest us for murder, I do hope you will be quick about it, for I do not think Miss Bright and I shall abide another hour—no, not another *minute*—in this shockingly inhospitable house. I would rather spend the night in jail, thank you very much."

Malbert translated.

Both officers' eyes grew round, and they muttered to each other in French.

"What rude men!" Ophelia said.

"They are surprised at your suggestion of arrest," Malbert said to Ophelia, "since the murderer has already been identified."

"Oh! And arrested?"

"Not yet. It seems the scoundrel eluded the police and he is still at large, but the *Gendarmerie* is out in full force and he is expected to be apprehended shortly."

"Who is he?"

"A certain vagabond, a useless, half-witted wretch who dwells in the alleyways and courtyards of this *quartier*, and who has been known to prey upon . . . ah . . . ladies of . . . ill-repute."

Prue gasped.

"You do not mean to suggest," Ophelia said, "that that poor girl—"

"I am afraid so."

It wasn't so scandalous, learning that Henrietta Bright's daughter was a fallen woman. The real wonder was that Prue had retained *her* virtue, given her upbringing and her beauty, a beauty that men wished to dig into like a beefsteak dinner.

"Why was the girl in the garden of this house?" Ophelia asked.

"The police tell me that her body and garments showed signs of having been dragged there," Malbert said.

Right. Her foot. Her bare, small, battered foot. What had become of her shoes? Had someone chased her through the night before shooting her? Is that how her toes had gotten so black and blue? "Do you mean to say that she was killed elsewhere?"

"Precisely. Her body was dragged from the street, through the carriageway, across the courtyard, and left in the vegetable patch."

"When?"

"Judging by the merely damp, rather than soaked, condition of her gown, she had not been out of doors for more than a half hour or so."

"If the murderer has been identified, were there witnesses to the crime?"

"Not precisely, but bystanders in the street reported seeing the murderer fleeing from the carriageway on foot, and he was recognized."

"What of the fine gown she wore?" Ophelia asked. "*That* was not such as ladies who haunt street corners are wont to wear." And—not that Ophelia could say it aloud—surely that girl's surpassing beauty would have protected her from walking the streets to find customers.

"She must have stolen the gown," Malbert said. "*Madame*, the unfortunate creature was placed by chance, and only by chance, in my garden."

"No, it is too, too great a coincidence," Ophelia said. "Placed by chance in her own mother's garden?"

"Forgive me for saying so, *madame*, but reality is . . . untidy. In reality, *la chance* plays the greatest role."

Ophelia's life had been just as pawed over by chance as the next person's, but being lectured by strangers didn't agree with her constitution.

The officers spoke with Malbert in French. Malbert looked at Ophelia. "They tell me that it would be wise for Mademoiselle Prudence to seclude herself until the villain has been arrested. And pray forgive me, dear ladies, for your inhospitable reception, and do consent to stay under my roof until the murderer has been arrested. It is clear, Madame Brand, that you are a lady of gentle breeding and that you are accustomed to better treatment. I shall reprimand my *majordome*, Baldewyn, and you and Mademoiselle Bright will be shown to the very best chambers in my home."

"But why must Miss Bright seclude herself?" Ophelia asked.

"Because she could be in danger. She bears such a resemblance to the murder victim, it is possible that if the murderer sees her he may believe that his victim did not, after all, die. He might attempt to kill again."

Kill Prue? Leaping Leviticus. *Where* was Henrietta? "I must insist upon being taken to the marquise this very instant!" Ophelia cried.

Malbert's cheeks trembled. "It is not . . . But you do not . . . the trouble is, Madame Brand, that the marquise, Henrietta, my darling wife, she is gone. Vanished. She has been missing since Tuesday."

3

Fourteen hours after Gabriel had first seen Miss Bright's morgue drawing in *The Times*, his train chuffed and screeched into Gare du Nord in the middle of a sodden gray Paris morning.

After leaving his study at St. Remigius's College, Gabriel had made a ten-minute stop at his lodgings to fetch a valise of clothing, don a greatcoat, and give directions to his house-keeper. Then he had gone directly to London. From Charing Cross, he'd ridden the South-Eastern Railway to Folkestone. He had boarded, just in the nick of time, one of the night ferries that trundled back and forth across the Channel between Folkestone and Boulogne. Once in Boulogne, it was a few hours' anxious wait for the first morning train to Paris.

Gabriel had had a surfeit of hours to mull over a plan. So it was with a brisk step that he alighted from his first-class railway car and into the steamy hubbub of the *gare*. He was deaf to the babble of porters and hawkers, to the hisses of long, gleaming, eel-black trains. He was blind to the glass vaults above the platforms. He scarcely smelled the coal smoke, the whiffs of sweat, musky perfume, fresh bread, cinders, roses.

His only thought was, after so many hours caged in railway compartments and trapped with his thoughts, that at last he could *act*.

Le Marais—"The Marsh"—on the right bank of the Seine, was a neighborhood that had been favored by blue bloods until about a century ago. Now its edges were tattered. The Roque-Fabliau mansion at 15 Rue Garenne was a grand private town house, what Parisians called an *hôtel particulier*, much to the confusion of British and American tourists. Hôtel Malbert was, by the looks of it, a seventeenth-century noble house in the style of Louis XIII. Pale yellow stone, rows of tall windows, steep slate roofs, Italianate pediments and cornices.

Gabriel rapped thrice upon the front door. The knocker was shaped like a mouse's head.

Poetic touch.

A prune-mouthed steward cracked the door several inches. *"Oui?"*

"Good morning," Gabriel said in French. "Is a young lady by the name of Miss Ophelia Flax within?"

"No, indeed, *monsieur*, there is not. I have never heard of anyone by that name."

Where was Miss Flax, then? Still in Germany? Returned to America?

"And the daughter of the house, the young American girl, is deceased as the newspapers claim?" Gabriel asked.

"Regrettably, yes." The steward shut the door an inch. "None of the family had ever made the girl's acquaintance, however, so although it was a great shock to discover a corpse in the garden, it was not felt as a *loss* as such."

Unfeeling wretch.

"I had hoped to locate the young American lady, Miss Flax, who had lately been traveling with the marquise's daughter. Alas, I fear she has journeyed elsewhere. No matter. I still wish to speak with the marquis."

"Oh, you *all* wish to speak with Monsieur le Marquis." The door closed another inch.

Gabriel wedged his foot in the remaining space. "You misunderstand. I am not a gentleman of the press." He drew a solid gold card case—a gift from his mother—from his inner jacket pocket and pushed his calling card through the crack.

The steward took the card. "Lord Harrington, is it? My, my. One is able to purchase *anything* these days, is one not?" He returned the card. "My compliments to your engraver. Beautiful work."

Another gentleman of Gabriel's station—his brother, for instance—would have cursed the steward, waved a cane about, made noisy demands. But Gabriel preferred more subtle tactics. He pulled his foot from the threshold. *"Merci, monsieur."*

The door thumped shut.

Gabriel was not in the habit of thinking a great deal about what one might term his heart. He had attained the age of thirty-four without anyone in particular stepping forward to claim that organ, and he was glad of it. His academic work consumed him utterly.

Yet, as he spoke to the driver of the hired cabriolet waiting at the curb, his heart constricted—or did it swell?—in his chest. Either way, it was behaving in a most uncomfortable and unaccountable fashion.

He climbed into the cabriolet.

What had he fancied? That he'd discover Miss Flax weak and weeping, that he'd drag her into his arms, rescue her like a knight errant?

Utter piffle. Miss Flax was not, by any stretch of the fancy, a damsel in distress.

His cabriolet rocked forward into the mist.

"Looks like they're changing the lock on the carriageway gate this morning," Ophelia said to Prue. "A locksmith is fiddling with it."

"Interesting," Prue said, and yawned.

"It *is* interesting." Ophelia peered through the trickling windowpane. Her—or, properly speaking, Mrs. Brand's—guest chamber looked down upon the mansion's rear courtyard. The chamber itself was an Antarctic expanse of creaking parquet, moth-chewed tapestries, furniture with chipped gold paint, and a lopsided canopied bed that smelled of mildew and mouse. However, its windows afforded a bird's-eye view. Ophelia preferred not to look at the matted vegetable patch, straight down, where they'd found that poor dead girl. But she could just see into the shadowy carriage arch, and a man with a toolbox was changing the gate's lock. "It's interesting for a couple of reasons. Prue—are you listening?" She glanced over her shoulder.

"Course I'm listening." Prue lolled on a brocade sofa. An ottoman-sized ginger cat lay in her lap. Prue popped a butterscotch drop into her mouth. "What's so mighty interesting about some locksmith?"

"Number one, when we went into the garden that night—"

Prue sucked harder on her butterscotch.

"—well, the gate was open. Not locked. Number two, the police said that they had identified the murderer—"

"Still haven't found him, though."

"It has been but two days."

"Feels like eternity. I got cabin fever, Ophelia."

Ophelia had cabin fever, too. But there was no use dumping kerosene on a fire. "Listen. The murderer was said to be a derelict who dwells in the streets here. So, he wouldn't have had a key to the gate."

"You're fishing for minnows."

"Something doesn't sit right." Ophelia turned to watch the locksmith some more. "I can't put my finger on it."

"I know you caught a murderer back in Germany, but that don't mean you ought to meddle again. Could be dangerous. Guess you ain't concerned about danger, though, on account of your nerves got all frazzled out in the circus, standing on them trick ponies."

"I cannot continue to twiddle my thumbs in this damp prison of a house while Eglantine and Austorga frisk about with their friends to the dressmaker's, the milliner's, lectures, concerts, lessons in—what did they say?—elocution, deportment—"

"Velocipede riding."

"Surely not! Dinners, soirées, the theater, the sweet shop—"

"Austorga *did* bring me a bag of butterscotch drops, and some nice orange jellies. And they're keen to find husbands so they need all them refinements."

"But they do not seem to care about that girl."

"My sister. *Their* sister, sort of."

"Yes. And your mother—it is as though she never existed. *'Oh, she'll be back!'* Malbert keeps saying, and your step-sisters look away." Ophelia had even searched Henrietta's bedchamber. It had been untidy, but it had offered up no clues as to her whereabouts. "The whole family is keeping things back, I'd wager. The servants, too."

"A spooky lot, that's for sure," Prue said.

Ophelia plopped onto the dressing table stool. She had been disguised as Mrs. Brand every waking minute for the last two days. Her scalp itched under the wig, her muscles ached from hefting around the rump and bosom padding, and her skin was dry and sore from the crinkly cosmetics. "And Malbert is downright peculiar."

"Looks like a mushroom that's lost its cap, don't he?"

"What does he *do* in that workshop of his? No one seems to know. Not his daughters. Not the servants. When I asked him last night at dinner, he behaved in a most evasive fashion— did you ever see so much blinking and stammering?" The only thing Malbert had confessed was that he was the student of some famous clockmaker, but that he did not make clocks.

Prue picked a loose blob of fluff from the cat and flicked it into the air. "Ma says *all* fellers is sneaky, and if you think they ain't you'd best be double careful."

What a distressing notion.

Ophelia got to work on her Mrs. Brand face. After that first night, she'd made certain to apply her greasepaint, and the flour paste that created the crepey effect, with a delicate hand so that it would stand up to close scrutiny. Heaven only knew how long she'd be stuck in this role, and now, well, there was no turning back.

Behind her, Prue began to snore.

When Ophelia had finished doctoring her face, she stashed her theatrical kit in the bottom of the wardrobe underneath a musty blanket. The housekeeper, Beatrice, had announced that no one would be cleaning their chambers, anyway, but Ophelia liked to be cautious.

She went to the sofa and jiggled Prue's woolen-stockinged toe. "Prue? Wake up, Prue. It's time to go down to breakfast." There was a hole in her stocking, at the heel. Poor Prue. Pretty as a princess, always in rags.

Prue snuffled awake and lifted her head. "Huh? What is it? Is Ma back?"

"No. Not yet. Are you coming to breakfast?" Ophelia's eyes fell again on Prue's stocking.

"What?" Prue asked. "What are you gawping at my foot for?"

"Merciful heavens," Ophelia murmured. There had been something familiar about the dead girl's foot, about the purple nails and that swollen jut on her big toe. "That is it. That is *it*."

Ophelia found Malbert hunched behind a newspaper at the breakfast table and demanded that he send at once for the police inspector. Malbert sent a note with an errand boy and returned to his newspaper.

Ophelia dug into her breakfast of coffee, buttery rolls, pungent cheese, ham, and hothouse oranges. Prue had probably gone back to sleep.

"I happened to notice a locksmith working on the carriageway gate this morning," Ophelia said.

Malbert slowly lowered his newspaper. *"Oui?"*

"Might I inquire why?"

"Madame Brand, you are most curious, *non*? What is it that they say about the cat and curiosity?" He blinked twice and raised his newspaper again.

Was that a threat?

Inspector Foucher, from the office of the *commissaire*,

arrived at half past eight. Ophelia and Malbert received him in a formal salon. Foucher was one of those fellows with twig legs and a barrel chest. Small brown eyes like chocolate drops peered out from a swollen face. He held a bowler hat.

"Madame Brand," he said in a weary tone, "I am a busy man. What is it?"

"Has the murderer been arrested yet?"

"Not yet."

"Ah. Well, I have made a most fascinating realization that might aid in your investigation. Her feet, you may recall—or, at least, the one that I saw—were in a most pitiful condition."

"The girl's feet were injured, *oui*."

"Both of them?"

"*Oui*, as the result of her body having been dragged to its place in the garden."

"I have a different theory. I propose that she was a dancer of the ballet."

Malbert shifted in his chair.

"The ballet!" Foucher chuckled.

"I do not jest, Inspector. The feet of ballerinas are subject to the most grievous ill-treatment and injury as the result of supporting their entire weight upon the very tips of their toes." Ophelia had seen it dozens of times, both in the circus and the theater. One dancer she'd known, Florrie, had had bunions like ripe crabapples.

Inspector Foucher frowned. "How, may I inquire, does a respectable lady like you know what the feet of a ballerina look like?"

"Oh, well." Ophelia smoothed her cuff. "In Boston, you see, I am a member of the Ladies' League for the Betterment of Fallen Angels."

"How charitable," Malbert murmured.

Ophelia leaned towards Foucher. "There are many *fallen angels*, you understand, employed in the theater."

"Ah, *oui*."

"I urge you, Inspector, to consider searching for the

deceased young lady's identity within whatever ballet theaters Paris possesses."

"You almost seem to know who the victim was."

"I do not. But it is worth investigating the ballet theaters, is it not?"

"Madame, I do understand that you are discomfited by this event. However, I must request that you do not intrude in police investigations. Indeed, I do realize that the gentle sex is prone to fancy, to making correlations where there are none—"

"Applesauce!"

"—but we officers of the police are trained to be *rationale*."

"What of the coincidence of the perished girl being placed in her own mother's garden? And what, for that matter, are you doing in the way of locating the Marquise Henrietta? I must most emphatically suggest that the two concerns must be related, even, perhaps, interlocking."

"Madame, I bid you good morning." Foucher made a stiff bow and dodged out.

Ophelia stared after him. Then she looked at Malbert sitting lumpishly in his chair. "It is an outrage!" she said. "It is almost as though—yes, it is as though the police are deliberately averting their eyes from any evidence that does not fit their theory. *Rationale?* Horsefeathers! That Foucher is a buffoon, or lazy. Or both."

"Madame Brand, I beg you to calm yourself. Come. Join me for a stroll in the garden. I would be most interested to hear of your charitable work in Boston."

Ophelia stared at Malbert. Did the recent presence of a corpse in his garden not trouble him in the *least*? All of a sudden, Ophelia made up her mind: it was time to take matters into her own hands. To Tartarus with the police! *She* would discover the dead girl's identity; *she* would learn where Henrietta had gone.

"No, thank you," Ophelia said to Malbert. "I've just remembered a most pressing engagement."

She hurried upstairs to her chamber. Prue was snoozing with the cat.

Ophelia cleaned her teeth at the washbasin. Then she dug the Baedeker and her reticule out of her carpetbag, tied on her black taffeta bonnet, and shrugged on her woolen cloak. Downstairs, she found an umbrella and trooped out of the house.

4

When Prue woke up, the ginger cat was purring on top of her, but Ophelia was gone.

Good.

She struggled to a seat. She seesawed her precious letter, Hansel's letter, out from under the cat and smoothed the puckers. Her eyes roved to the first troubling spot:

> *I do not wish you to suppose, dear Miss Bright, that when we last parted at Schloss Grunewald we had formed what one might call an understanding. That I hold you in the highest esteem goes, I daresay, without saying. But you are a very young lady, and until I have completed my medical studies and secured a living for myself, I could never presume to consider any lady, however our attachment might be felt or comprehended, as anything but free.*

Prue read this line for about the hundred and tenth time. She still wasn't exactly sure she'd caught Hansel's meaning. The line was so cluttered up with commas and genteel words, she didn't know if she had it by the head or by the slick tail. Was he saying they'd have an "understanding" *someday*, in the future? Or was this his way of telling her to scoot off?

Prue fluttered away tears, and reread the letter's second troubling spot:

> *Frau Beringer* (She was the landlady of Hansel's student boardinghouse in Heidelberg, Germany) *keeps such a spotless house, it is truly a marvel. I do not believe I have met with such a fine housekeeper before, and I hope someday to be the master of such a gracious and meticulous household.*

These lines pained Prue, fresh little heart stabbings each time she read them. Prue wouldn't be able to make a *doll's* house gracious and meticulous, let alone a real house. Ma had never taught her how.

Ma. Still missing. Her dead sister, gone forever. And Hansel acting just as sneaky as any other feller.

One fat tear plopped onto the letter. The ink of the word *spotless* blurred.

Ophelia may as well have been in Timbuktu, for all she knew about Paris. The Baedeker map had a crease straight through Le Marais, the streets ran higgledy-piggledy, and the rain was coming down in buckets. But she found her way to a bustling thoroughfare called Rue de Rivoli. She rechecked the map. Yes. It looked to lead straight to the Louvre. From the Louvre she could walk to Rue le Peletier, where the opera house was.

Because opera houses, Ophelia well knew, were where ballerinas were to be found.

She paid thirty *centimes* for an inside seat in a horse-drawn double decker. She had changed some of her hard-won German money for French at the train station the other day. Inside, the omnibus was entirely taken up by ladies' bobbing crinolines, which was probably why all the gentlemen fled to the open-air upper level despite the rain.

Ophelia rubbed at the foggy window with her fist, but she couldn't see much. Black carriages, black umbrellas, black hats, bare black trees. Tight-packed old buildings with shutters and awnings. Steep roofs, jumbly chimneys, dripping gargoyles.

A queasy half hour passed. When Ophelia saw the looming side of what she guessed was the Louvre, she piled off the omnibus with a bunch of other folks, snapped open her umbrella, and set off on foot.

The opera house, called Salle le Peletier (however you pronounced *that* one) was built of white stone, with rows of pillars and arches and a shining-wet paved square out front.

Ophelia soon discovered that all of the doors at the front of the opera house were locked. Well, they would be. It wasn't even ten o'clock yet. Even a matinee performance wouldn't start for hours.

She paused to look at a big, colorful placard behind glass. The placard said *Cendrillon*—not that she could read French—decorated with ornate scrolls and spirals, interlaced with rats, mice, and lizards. Pretty.

She set off again. Perhaps the stage door was unlocked. She hustled around the corner.

Blubbering over Hansel had worked up a hunger and thirst in Prue. She stuffed the letter down her bodice, tied on her boots, and repaired her hair. Downstairs, the breakfast salon was empty.

Crackers.

She poked around until she found the kitchen stairs. She tiptoed down.

The housekeeper, Beatrice, was bent at the waist, ramming a broom—*bang-bang-bang*!—under a china cupboard and muttering in a scalding whisper.

Prue coughed.

Beatrice spun around. Her jowls were flushed and wisps of gray hair sprouted from her bun. She was shaped like a church bell and she wore a soot-colored gown. A hefty ring of keys hung where her waist would've been. The mansion had only four servants: Beatrice, Baldewyn, the coachman, and the stepsisters' plump, spotty maid, Lulu. It turned out that Ma had fired all the other servants on account of they didn't speak English and they cost too much.

"Oh! Mademoiselle Prudence. You frighten me." Beatrice's accent was juicy. "These mice make me jump! How I hate them."

"Me, too." Prue scratched her suddenly itchy arms. "Is there mice under that cupboard?"

Beatrice curled her lip. *"Oui."*

A mouse sprinted out from under the cupboard and across the flagstones, and disappeared into a hole in the chimney corner. A portly cat, balancing on a stool at the hearth, watched the mouse's progress with idle interest.

"What is the matter with these cats?" Beatrice said. "I cannot think how it happens that the mice are never caught! I lay traps with the nicest, most fragrant *fromage* every day, and every day the *fromage* is gone, but the mice are not caught. I bring home cats said to be the fiercest hunters, from the fish market, from alleyways, and what do the cats do? Why, they grow fatter and fatter. *C'est répugnant.*" Beatrice glared at the cat. Then she glared at Prue. "Ladies must not be in kitchen! Go—go!" She shook the broom. Dust and cat hairs billowed up.

"I ain't a lady, ma'am. Look at me."

Beatrice looked at Prue's calico dress that was losing its dye at the elbows, the shiny-worn toes of her boots. "I have housework to do."

That was a snicker. By the looks of the kitchen, Beatrice didn't bother herself much with housework. A dead chicken, still in its spotted feathers, was draped over a chair back. Dirty dishes and pots filled a stone sink on the far wall. The floor didn't bear close scrutiny, what with all the cat fuzz, curls of potato peel, and tiny brown dots that Prue didn't fancy thinking too hard on.

"I wished to ask for a morsel to eat," Prue said.

"You did not eat breakfast?"

"Slept late." Prue's eyes fell on an apron, dangling from one of the wall hooks at the bottom of the stairs.

Hold it. Instead of idling away the days waiting for Ma to turn up, well, maybe Prue could learn how to keep a gracious and meticulous household, just like Hansel wished for. She could amaze Hansel—supposing she ever saw him again—with lavender-scented linens or a crispy-brown roast duck with those fancy fruits ringed around.

Beatrice had gone back to mashing her broom under the china cupboard.

"Would you teach me housekeeping, ma'am?" Prue asked. "How to cook up a nice roast fowl, say, or one of them soo-flay things? How to press linens?"

Beatrice screwed her neck around. Her mouth pooched. Skeptical. Yet her eyes gleamed, for some reason, with cunning. "Do you know how to cook?"

"No—but I might learn, and real fast, too. Matter of fact, ma'am, I was, up till just a couple days ago, a scullery maid."

"We *are* understaffed here, *malheureusement*." Beatrice twiddled her broom handle. "If I teach you to keep house, to cook . . . you will not tell Monsieur le Marquis?"

"Never. Only thing I won't do, I ought to mention, is work in that vegetable garden out there."

"*Bon.* The garden is nothing, the silly fancy of the *mademoiselles*, who thought it would be a lark to plant pumpkins."

"What's so funny about pumpkins?"

"Because this house . . . ah, no matter. You will start by cleaning the china cupboard"—Beatrice swept a hand—"from top to bottom."

"Really? Oh, thanks something fierce, ma'am!" Prue pulled the apron from its hook.

Gabriel stalked the ample-hipped auntie around the corner of the Salle le Peletier. The old dame plowed along like an ox.

After Gabriel had been barred from speaking with the Marquis de la Roque-Fabliau, he had directed his driver to wait one block from Hôtel Malbert. He had intended to follow the first member of the household who emerged, insinuate himself into his or her confidence, learn more about Miss Bright's death and, perhaps, gain access to the Marquise Henrietta. The marquise, of all people in Paris, might know of Miss Flax's whereabouts.

Gabriel did not like to admit to himself that his interest in Hôtel Malbert was not *entirely* restricted to Miss Flax and her whereabouts. Nothing in life was quite that simple, was it?

And it had been no easy feat following this auntie—Gabriel assumed that was what she was—from Hôtel Malbert, particularly after he had been forced to instruct his driver to deliver his luggage to his hotel, overpay him, leap onto the rear rail of an omnibus and ride, clinging to a handrail, for a mud-splattered half hour alongside a flock of smirking shop boys.

Auntie barged down Rue Pinon, which ran along the opera house's western side.

Ah. Perhaps she wasn't going to the theater after all; perhaps this was only a shortcut. To a tatting shop, perhaps, or a *pâtisserie* specializing in enormous chocolate *éclairs*.

Hold on a tick. Auntie was disappearing through a side door.

Gabriel followed and found himself in a simple, almost monastic passage. It smelled of damp plaster. The floorboards sighed.

Tallyho. There was Auntie. Trundling down the corridor, folded umbrella tucked beneath her arm.

What *could* the old game hen be doing?

Gabriel hurried after her, passing a gaggle of ballet girls with their hair scraped up in the tight buns only governesses and ballerinas wore.

Auntie launched up a flight of stairs. Piano music floated down the stairwell. A gentleman's voice bellowed rhythmically: "*Un! Deux! Trois!*"

Up went Auntie. Gabriel was four paces behind.

Tracked-in rainwater slicked the steps. Consequently, Gabriel was watching his feet, not the stair above him. Another herd of ballet girls stampeded down the steps—he heard their prattling—but he didn't realize that Auntie had paused on the stair to allow them to pass.

He crashed into her. She lost her balance. The ballet girls squealed. Auntie teetered, and then heaved forward onto a landing, breaking her fall with her hands. Her folded umbrella whipped upwards and caught Gabriel right in the wishbone.

"*Oof*" was all he could say. His mind wiped blank. He toppled onto Auntie.

The ballet girls slipped by, giggling, and hurried down the stairs.

"I *beg* your pardon!" Auntie squirmed beneath Gabriel.

He struggled to right himself. Auntie's enormous, wet, woolen cloak was tangled about his arms.

But—Gabriel froze. What was it about . . . that voice? "You are an American?" he asked.

Auntie went still. Slowly, she twisted her neck to see him.

Beneath that matronly bonnet, her gray hair was oddly askew. Gabriel found himself gazing into a pair of rather beautiful dark eyes.

"Professor Penrose?" she said. Her wig slipped another inch.

"Miss Flax." Gabriel grabbed the bannister and pulled himself to his feet. His wishbone still throbbed, but his astonishment overrode the pain. He helped Miss Flax to her feet, and though he wished to hold, perhaps, for a moment longer her cold, fine-boned hand in its damp glove, she tugged it free.

"What in Godfrey's green earth are you doing following me, Professor? I believed you were back in England."

"I was. Forgive me for saying so, Miss Flax, but you appear to be upholstered in not one, but two divans'-worth of cushions." The absurd disguise hid her regal form. Which was perhaps just as well. Gabriel had spent more minutes than he cared to count attempting to recall the precise arrangement of this young lady's limbs.

"Keeps the rain off," she said.

"Would it be terribly bothersome if I inquired what, precisely, you are doing backstage at the Paris Opera?"

She compressed her lips.

Miss Bright. Dead. Something to do with that.

"I beg your pardon," Gabriel said. "I quite—"

"Tell me what *you're* doing here, Professor. I thought I'd seen the last of you back in Germany. I was glad of it."

"Oh? I thought I spied a tear or two when we parted."

"Wishful thinking."

"Mm. Perhaps a trick of the light."

"Precisely."

"I must admit, *I* felt a pang when we parted."

"Did you?"

"Well, I thought I did. But perhaps it was only a touch of dyspepsia."

Her eyes narrowed. "You're meddling in my affairs. Again."

"And *you're* spitting fire, Miss Flax. I'd have expected to find you in a more"—Gabriel scratched his temple—"well, in a state of mourning, I suppose."

"Mourning! Why, the cheek! To think I'd be mourning *you*? Like some schoolgirl who'd lost her—her pet kitten?"

"I fail to grasp your meaning."

Miss Flax deflated. "Not . . . you didn't mean mourning . . . *you*?"

"Not at all. Though I must admit the notion is intriguing."

She shook raindrops off her umbrella with unwarranted vigor. "Oh, you believe Prue's bit it. Read it in the papers, came scurrying down from your ivory tower to see what all the fuss was about?"

"Miss Bright has not perished?"

"She's perishing from boredom in her mother's moldy old mansion, but other than that, alive and kicking."

"I seem to have quite missed the boat on this one."

"Sounds more like you missed the entire fleet."

They stood on the stair landing. Miss Flax told Gabriel how she and Prue had come to Paris looking for Henrietta and had stumbled upon the corpse of, evidently, Prue's long-lost sister. How Henrietta was missing, and how no one in the marquis's household seemed to mind. Miss Flax railed against the laziness of the Marais *commissaire*'s office and fretted over the weird coincidence of a daughter dead in her own estranged mother's garden. She wondered aloud why the carriageway gate's lock had been changed and described the dead girl's mangled foot.

"So you see," Miss Flax said, "something's fishy. And I'm here because Prue's sister wasn't a fallen woman. I suspect that she was a ballerina, and I mean to confirm it."

"Mightn't she have been *both* a ballerina and"—Gabriel cleared his throat—"a fallen woman?"

"You needn't look so grimacey, Professor. I'm an actress."

He studied her crepey face. "How could I forget?"

"Certainly I know that ballerinas—and lots of actresses, too—supplement their incomes with"—she glanced away—"the attentions of admirers. But the police made Prue's sister out to be some kind of common strumpet. They simply left it at that."

"So you came to the opera house in an attempt to learn her true identity."

"The police didn't even care about her name. Like she was just a—a *nothing*. Something chucked onto the rubbish heap. It's not right. Maybe they're even searching for the wrong murderer."

"Let's not get ahead of ourselves."

"Just as high-handed as ever, aren't you?" Miss Flax started up the stairs.

Gabriel scratched his head. In the past month or so, he had indulged in picturing what it might be like to meet Miss Flax again. But he had never pictured her so annoyed at him. Women were confounding. He gained her side. "I shall assist you. That is why I am here."

"You expect me to swallow that horse pill?" At the top of the stairs, Miss Flax looked left, then right. The piano music and rhythmic yelling was coming from somewhere to the left. She went left.

Gabriel went, too.

"You reckon I'll believe that you journeyed all the way from England only to assist me?" she asked. "And for no other reason?"

"I believed Miss Bright was murdered. I was concerned for your safety."

"And you followed me here from Hôtel Malbert."

"Yes."

"Tell me why you're *truly* here."

"The sightseeing here tends towards the vulgar."

"Not that."

"Everyone knows French cuisine is far too heavy on the butter."

She scowled.

"Although I must confess to a weakness for Bordeaux."

She stopped walking. "You, Professor, are as transparent as a windowpane. You've got a hidden motive."

"What have I done to be worthy of such prodigious distrust?"

"You didn't know it was really me when you followed me here!"

"The steward turned me away."

"Sounds like him. Baldewyn, he's called. Prue calls him Mister Lizard."

"I decided to follow the first member of the household who emerged and strike up a conversation. In order, you see, to discover *your* whereabouts, Miss Flax."

A half-truth. At this juncture, with Miss Flax careening so dangerously close to his secret, it must suffice.

Miss Flax fumed away down the corridor.

Gabriel touched the left side of his chest, felt the rectangle of the Charles Perrault volume nestled beneath layers of greatcoat, jacket, waistcoat, shirt. He shoved his hands in his greatcoat pockets and sauntered after Miss Flax.

5

Prue wiped her sweaty brow on her arm.

What had she signed on to, anyway?

The inside of the china cupboard, which Beatrice had commanded her to clean, turned her stomach: sticky cobwebs, mildew-blotted cookery books, chunks of something-or-other that was maybe bread but possibly cheese, judging by the reek of it. And an avalanche of mouse plops, both antique and fresh.

Beatrice had tied on her bonnet and cloak and taken a basket off to market, leaving Prue alone. Well, if the company of two tubby, dozing cats and mice playing peekaboo counted as *alone*.

Prue stacked the cookery books on the flagstones, swept rodent plops into a copper dustpan, and dumped the moldy whatsits in the rubbish bin outside the kitchen door.

Outside, she could just see the edge of that rotted vegetable patch. She still felt the coldness of her sister's body and she had to keep swiping the picture of her staring eyes away. Where was her sister now? Still laid out at some morgue? All of a sudden, Prue longed to attend her sister's funeral. To sew things up, maybe. But no one had said anything about a funeral.

On the sunny side, Prue was finally learning to be a housewife. For Hansel.

Prue's eyes fell on the topmost cookery book on the stack she'd made. The words, stamped in flaking-off gold on the loose cover, weren't in any language *she* knew.

She set aside her broom and dustpan and hefted the book. It was awfully thick, and it looked so, well, *serious*, as though the cookery or housewifing knowledge it held wasn't womanly twaddle, but honest-to-goodness Important Work.

Prue cracked it open. Dust puffed up, and she sneezed.

Page after page of thick, hand-lettered black script, in more of that mystery language. But there were plenty of pictures. Little, intricate, inky-black pictures of soup pots and turtles, bedsteads, stones, bees, carrots, flowers, boxes, pies, and brooms. Fascinating. Befuddling.

But it seemed that if one were to study the pictures with mighty care, all the magic of housewifery might be squeezed from this single, magnificent volume.

The china cupboard was forgotten. Prue, for the first time in her life, set to studying.

The opera house corridor was a buzzing hive of rehearsal and practice rooms. A trombone honked out scales, a violin spiraled through arpeggios, a soprano warbled and, mingled through it all, more of that man yelling: "*Un, deux, trois! Un, deux, trois!*" Then, "*Mon Dieu, Marie! T'es un éléphant! Encore!*"

All as familiar to Ophelia as the back of her own hand. Of course, the violinists in Howard DeLuxe's Varieties sounded much more screechy.

"Why are you still following me, Professor?" Ophelia asked. Encountering Professor Penrose, after months of scrubbing him out of her mind, made her heart flutter like a hatchling chick. And *that* was simply irksome. She felt angry at him, too, and embarrassed in his presence, and she was unsure how to behave. She figured she was missing a piece of her mind, a piece that other people had. The piece that allowed a person to do things like fall in love or believe in fairy tales.

Penrose drew something from his pocket and unfolded it. The morgue drawing of the dead girl that had appeared in all the newspapers. "You did not think to bring one of these along, did you?"

Drat.

"And I speak French," Penrose said. "I might be your translator."

"What's in it for you?"

"Nothing."

"You're a terrible actor. I know you've got better things to do."

"I may have *other* things to do, but they are not necessarily better."

Well. A translator *would* make snooping easier.

"Fine," Ophelia said. "But I'm in charge."

He smiled.

Ophelia peeked through an open door. A rehearsal room: high ceiling, tall windows, wooden floors, mirrors. Rows of lady dancers clung to wooden barres, kicking their legs like wind-up tin soldiers. They wore tulle skirts over tight linen chemises, white woolen stockings, and ballet slippers. In the corner, a gentleman in a waistcoat banged away at a piano, a cigar dangling between a moustache and beard. All the yelling was coming from a gentleman in a black suit. He was long and snake-narrow, with a pointy black beard. He paced between the rows of dancers, poking and prodding them.

"Who is that man?" Penrose asked Ophelia.

"A dancing master, I think. Dancing masters oversee the daily classes for the company, and the rehearsals and such." The dancing master in Howard DeLuxe's Varieties had *also* been a juggler of flaming sticks and a teller of bawdy jokes. Never mind that.

"Would he know every dancer in the company?"

"Yes."

Ophelia and Penrose waited for several minutes. The class ended. Sweaty dancers streamed through the doors, pulling knitted wraps around their shoulders and chattering.

Ophelia and Penrose went in.

The man with the pointy beard hovered beside the piano, going over something with the pianist.

"Would you show him the picture?" Ophelia whispered to Penrose. "Ask him straight out if she was a dancer here?"

Pointy Beard and the pianist glanced up in surprise as Ophelia and Penrose drew close.

"Oui?" Pointy Beard said, looking down his nose.

Penrose said something in French.

"Ah, you are an Englishman," Pointy Beard said. *He* had an American accent—Philadelphian, Ophelia would bet.

Peculiar.

"I do apologize for the intrusion," Penrose said, "Mister—?"

"Grant. Caleb Grant. And you are—"

"Lord Harrington."

"Ah." Grant dismissed the pianist with a shooing motion.

"I, and my"—Penrose glanced at Ophelia—"aunt, wish to confirm the identity of a young girl who was, most regrettably, found dead three days ago in Le Marais." He showed Grant the picture.

Grant barely glanced at it. "Sybille Pinet."

Ophelia's heart leapt. "She was a dancer in this company?"

"In the *corps de ballet*. Beautiful, graceful, if not particularly virtuosic or—"

"I knew it! Her feet, see—well, the police have not—the police don't know who she is. Why didn't you—"

"The police never asked, madam. If they had, I would most certainly have answered their questions."

"But," Ophelia said, "surely a *murder*—"

"L'Opéra de Paris, as you are doubtless aware, is an institution that must maintain a certain degree of, shall we say, discretion. The newspapermen would feast like carrion eaters if Sybille's death were linked to us. We cannot pack the seats with the dregs of a public that wishes to associate itself with sordid crimes when we count, particularly due to the current International Exhibition, great scientists, diplomats, important novelists, duchesses, even a prince of Persia, among our audience."

What a windbag.

"I beg your pardon," Penrose said, "but do you have any idea who killed the girl?"

Grant turned away and rifled through the stack of sheet music on the piano. "No."

"Have you ever happened to meet the Marquise de la Roque-Fabliau?" Ophelia asked, just in case.

"I cannot say that I have."

"She was—is—American, too. And she used to be on the stage."

Grant's nostrils pinched.

"Where did Sybille Pinet live?" Ophelia asked.

"I've no idea. Now"—Grant looked at his pocket watch—"I really must . . ."

"Of course," Penrose said.

"But—" Ophelia said.

Penrose drew her away. "Thank you, Mr. Grant," he said over his shoulder.

"What a slinky dog!" Ophelia whispered, once she and Penrose were in the corridor. "Not breathing a word to the police?"

"He was immediately forthcoming to us about the girl's name."

"Well, certainly. Because anyone else in this building could tell us the very same thing."

"True. Should we attempt to learn where Miss Pinet lived? I believe I noticed some sort of clerical office downstairs."

A cluttered room with wooden cabinets and shelves led off the downstairs corridor. Its frosted glass door was ajar. Inside, a sparrow-shouldered woman with faded blond hair and sagging, powdered cheeks sat at a desk. She wore a plain gown and, surprisingly, carmine paint on her lips.

Theater folk, Gabriel believed the term was. He glanced at Miss Flax in her preposterous disguise.

"Go ahead," Miss Flax said to him softly. "Ask her about Sybille."

"Excuse me, *madame*," Gabriel said to the clerical lady in French. "Did you by chance know Sybille Pinet, a young dancer in this company?"

"I keep the books. I know everyone. And I know, too"—the lady's eyes suddenly filled with tears—"of Sybille's death. Are you her uncle?"

"No. We are both her friends." Gabriel paused. "I beg your pardon, but why did you not suppose I am Mademoiselle Pinet's father?"

"You are too young, for one thing. And she said her father died five years ago."

"She knew Sybille," Miss Flax said in an excited whisper.

"Yes," Gabriel said. "And Miss Pinet's father died five years ago—or so she said."

"Ask her why the police haven't figured out who Sybille was, why nobody said anything to the police."

Gabriel translated.

"Sybille was a quiet girl," the lady said.

"But surely everyone knew her, still, and her picture was in half the newspapers in Europe, and surely every newspaper in Paris," Gabriel said.

The lady hesitated. "We, well, we decided to keep the connection between her death and the opera ballet . . . concealed."

"What's she saying?" Miss Flax whispered, impatient now.

"Who decided to conceal it?" Gabriel asked the clerical lady in French.

Miss Flax's umbrella poked Gabriel in the ribs. He winced.

The clerical lady glanced out into the corridor. She lowered her voice. "Monsieur Grant. The dancing master. He made an announcement to the company, and all the musicians and stage hands, too, that we should avoid speaking with the police."

"Whatever for?" Gabriel discreetly pushed Miss Flax's umbrella away.

"He said that the murderer had already been identified, that justice would prevail, and that, therefore, there was no need to drag our company's name through the mire through

association with a—a sordid crime. Because Sybille—oh!—I
believed her to be a *good girl*, but why, then, was she in that
costly gown that she had no business wearing, out in the night,
alone? Shot?"

"*Tell me what you're talking about,*" Miss Flax whispered. "This is *my* investigation, Professor."

"I haven't forgotten, Miss Flax, and neither have my ribs."
Gabriel told her what the lady had said.

"Everyone in the company agreed to silence?" Ophelia
said. "That's peculiar."

Gabriel said as much in French to the clerical lady.

"Yes, well, Monsieur Grant's word carries much weight.
He is not the impresario, but he *is* the head choreographer
as well as the dancing master. He is much feared. He alone
casts the roles and hires and dismisses dancers."

Gabriel passed this on to Miss Flax, who nodded. "Does
she have any notion why Sybille might have been in Le
Marais that evening?"

Gabriel translated.

"Oh dear me, no," the lady said. "Although . . . well, we
do try to protect the girls, but . . . now and again, one slips
through the cracks." Her eyes were distant. "I wonder . . ."

"She was extraordinarily beautiful," Gabriel said. "That
is sometimes dangerous."

"She was briefly employed as an artist's model, I was told,
a year or so ago, which *will* mix a girl up with the wrong sort.
And she had no protector. No family. She was a bit mysterious,
yet with something quite prim and proper about her. She had
grown up in an orphanage of some kind, where she had taken
dancing lessons, and she had demonstrated ability. She danced
for Monsieur Grant in one of our annual auditions. That was,
let me think . . . nearly two years ago."

Gabriel translated for Miss Flax.

"Ask her where Sybille lived," Miss Flax said.

Gabriel asked.

"In a boardinghouse in the Quartier Pigalle—"

"Pigalle!" Gabriel said. "Good heavens."

"Yes, well, that is where many of our girls live. It is fairly close by, and inexpensive." The lady rose, and found a card in one of the filing cabinets. "Sixteen Rue Frochot."

Outside, the rain had let up. Sunlight bounced off the wet square in front of the opera house. Carriages, delivery wagons, and omnibuses slopped by in the street.

"We ought to go to Sybille's boardinghouse," Ophelia said. "Surely someone there will know something about the night she died."

"Should you perhaps return to Hôtel Malbert? Won't you be missed?"

Ophelia rummaged around in her reticule. "You aren't going to do *that* old routine, are you? Nudging me in the direction of propriety?" She pulled out her Baedeker.

"Would it make a difference if I did?"

"No." Ophelia checked the index and flipped to a map captioned *Place Pigalle & Environs*. She scoured the map for Rue Frochot. "There. Ought to be an easy walk."

"It's well over a mile, surely."

Ophelia bookmarked the map with a red ribbon. "I used to walk three miles to the schoolhouse every morning as a girl."

"We'll hire a cabriolet."

"I *won't* have you paying for things." Ophelia turned in what she hoped was the direction of Place Pigalle.

She stopped. Once again, the fanciful placard decorated with mice, rats, and lizards caught her eye. She pointed it out to Penrose. "What does that placard say?"

"Good heavens. *Cendrillon.*"

"Sendry-what?"

He paused. "Cinderella."

Ophelia's jaw dropped. She swung on Penrose. "Cinderella? *Cinderella?* Why, you low-down, deceitful, double-crossing, two-faced scallywag! I knew it. I *knew* it!"

"I fail to grasp your meaning."

"Fail to—humbug! I knew you were fibbing about why you're here in Paris. And now"—she jabbed her umbrella at the placard—"I've got proof."

"That I've traveled hundreds of miles to take in a ballet?"

"That you're here on account of your everlasting, crumbly—and, might I add, downright *nutty* fairy tale obsession." Ophelia thought of Sybille in that dress, missing a shoe. In a pumpkin patch. "To think I swallowed that line about you coming here to help me. You're only in Paris on account of this ballet, and the way Sybille died." She barged off across the square. Pigeons scattered.

Ophelia hadn't believed for a second that the professor was in Paris because of her. But she'd *wished* to believe it. Ugh.

Penrose caught up and stopped her with a firm grip around her upper arm.

She *wouldn't* look at him.

"Miss Flax," Penrose said in a rough, low voice. "Please. Look at me."

Ophelia breathed in and out three times. She lifted her gaze. The professor's eyes, a clear, bright hazel behind his spectacles, looked like . . . they looked like *home*.

Madness. *Home* was four walls and a roof. *Home* couldn't be a man. And what was wrong with her to think for even a second that home *could* be a man?

She wriggled her arm from his grasp. "What was it you wished to say?"

"You have made rather a large leap of logic, assuming that this ballet has anything to do with the murder."

"But don't you see? Sybille's death *must* have had something to do with the ballet."

"Because she was a dancer within the institution in which a Cinderella ballet is being performed? That hardly seems—"

"Don't you know? Sybille, when we found her in the garden . . . she wore a fancy ball gown. Like Cinderella in the story. And there were squashes there, too—*pumpkins*, don't you see? I hadn't realized it until now, but . . . And her foot—well, she was missing her shoe."

"Good God."

"Quit pretending you didn't know. Like I said, your acting isn't exactly top rail." Why did everything she said come out so ornery? Ophelia found herself fidgeting with the umbrella handle.

"How could I have known? I saw but one report in the newspaper. It made no mention of what the girl wore. My interest in the murder stemmed solely from a concern for your safety. Pray, listen. Allow me to assist you, Miss Flax. I shall stay in Paris as long as it takes to locate the marquise."

"What of the university? Your students?"

"They'll barely notice I am gone. If the police are not searching for Henrietta, as you said, then finding her might be quite a simple task. We will check all the hotels in the city, check the steamship passenger lists for all of this week's sailings to New York—and elsewhere. She sounds like the sort who'd sail off to Bolivia."

"If she met the King of Bolivia, then yes. Why do you wish to help me?"

Penrose paused. He adjusted his spectacles and gazed past her into the street. "To be honest, I am not quite certain."

"Well, at least you're finally being aboveboard with me."

6

⚬⌇⚬

Gabriel could not convince Miss Flax to allow him to hire a carriage, so they walked all the way to Place Pigalle. Miss Flax kept her eyes on her Baedeker and the sights and left Gabriel alone with his guilt.

Why hadn't he told her the truth about the book and the house? She would have laughed, but that was surely no reason to lie. Gabriel was well accustomed to his research being scoffed at. And dash it all, what had possessed him to say he'd stay in Paris until Henrietta was found? It had been false, saying that he wouldn't be missed in Oxford. The dean would have his neck.

In the mile and a half between Salle le Peletier and the Quartier Pigalle, the buildings grew shabbier, the sidewalks thicker with pedestrians and alley cats and rubbish, and the street chatter grew more coarse. Quartier Pigalle, at the foot of Montmartre hill, brimmed with literary cafes and, up in the garrets, painters' studios. A disreputable class of women infested the quarter, although at this time of day such creatures were still sleeping off last night's wine.

Gabriel longed to whisk Miss Flax in and out of this

neighborhood, posthaste. Despite her colorful past, Miss Flax somehow retained an air of innocence.

"Here it is." She stopped at two large doors on Rue Frochot, painted a dingy yellow with the number *16* hanging on nails. She tried the rusty ring that served as a door handle. The door swung inward.

The boardinghouse's courtyard was tight, weedy, and reeking of sour waters. Rainwater mottled the plaster walls. A rawboned woman bent with a bucket over a rain barrel at the bottom of a gutter pipe.

"*Bonjour, madame,*" Gabriel said.

The woman straightened. She inspected Gabriel's gentlemanlike attire with approval, but she did not seem to be as impressed by Miss Flax's matronly appearance. "*Oui?*"

"Are you the landlady of this establishment?" Gabriel asked in French.

She nodded, wiping raw knuckles on her apron.

"She is the landlady," Gabriel said softly to Miss Flax.

"Good. Tell her we are here for Sybille's belongings—oh, and find out how long Sybille lived here."

"I am the uncle of Sybille Pinet," Gabriel said to the landlady. "I am here to collect her things."

"High time you did! I have already let her room, but she left me a box of trash. I was meaning to haul it to the rag and bone shop later today."

"I did not know my niece well," Gabriel said. "I had quite lost sight of her when I received a telegram from her place of employment at the opera house, informing me that she had been murdered."

"Yes, murdered." The landlady almost smiled.

"For how long did she let a room here?"

"Near two years—no, a year and a half. Would have been two years in the spring."

"Almost two years," Gabriel murmured to Miss Flax.

The landlady led them across the courtyard, through a low doorway, and into a murky room that was half office and half refuse heap.

"I remember Sybille as a meek young girl," Gabriel said.

"They always turn out that way from those convent orphanages. She grew up in one of those since the age of four, she told me. Mild as a little lamb she was, and always paid her rent on time and kept her room clean. Scarcely made friends with the other girls. Never a peep out of that one. No trouble at all. Well, until lately."

"Oh?" Gabriel said, ignoring Miss Flax's glare. She did not like being left out of things, but he sensed the landlady was in a hurry to be rid of them. He wished to learn all that he could from her while he had the chance.

The landlady dug through boxes and buckets on the floor. "In this month or so past, she stayed out past curfew several times. I insist upon a strict curfew. Even these ballet girls who work late can be in by midnight, and I will not have my establishment going to the dogs like *some*. Mademoiselle Pinet claimed to have lost track of time, but that was not *like* her, you see, and she also seemed, as of late . . . haunted."

"Haunted?"

Miss Flax pursed her lips with exasperation.

"*Wait*," Gabriel whispered to her.

"Nerves," the landlady said. "Almost on the verge of tears over her bread in the mornings, for no reason! And those dark circles round her eyes." The landlady clucked her tongue. "Mixed up in bad business, sorry to say. Ah. Here we are." She picked up a small wooden crate.

"Did you see her with any strange persons? Did she mention anything at all to you?"

"No. But it was as though all the color drained right out of her, and then . . . she was dead. Killed by a madman of the streets, I saw in the newspaper."

"What was the name of the convent orphanage from which Mademoiselle Pinet came?"

The landlady passed Gabriel the crate. "I do not quite remember, but I fancy it had something to do with stars."

"Stop keeping me out of the conversation," Ophelia grumbled to Penrose, once they were back on the street.

"She was anxious to be rid of us."

"What did she say?"

He told her.

This time, Ophelia allowed Penrose to hire a carriage. She was eager to look into the crate of Sybille's possessions. Also, her feet were sore, but she'd never admit to *that*.

Once they'd climbed inside a carriage, Penrose lifted the crate's lid.

A woman's garments lay folded in a stack. Threadbare gowns, dingy petticoats, darned stockings, and a sad little pair of button boots that had been resoled even more times than Ophelia's own. Beneath the clothes, a tarnished hairbrush and comb, a few stray ribbons and buttons, a tiny French prayer book, and a wooden rosary. That was all.

"Guess they don't pay the ballet girls much," Ophelia said. Sadness fell around her. Poor Sybille. Ophelia's life had been just as humble, but she had never been so desperately *alone*.

"There is nothing here to suggest that Miss Pinet had . . . admirers."

"No. She probably would have had finer things, wouldn't she? Wait. What's this?" A bit of paper stuck against the inside of the crate. Ophelia wiggled it loose. A lavish engraving of flowers and lettering—all in French—covered one side.

"A florist's trade card. It lists its name and address, here in Paris."

Ophelia flipped the card over. "Mercy."

The back of the card said, in a lady's hurried hand, *Howard DeLuxe's Varieties Broadway*.

"That's where Prue and I worked—where *Henrietta* worked."

"Is that Henrietta's handwriting?"

"I believe it is. What does this mean?"

"It suggests that at some point, Sybille Pinet met her mother."

Ophelia reckoned that riding about Paris in a closed carriage with a fellow was scandalous. But she knew that Penrose was an honorable gentleman. Besides which, her virtue was well-padded by the Mrs. Brand disguise. She asked Penrose to drop her two blocks from Hôtel Malbert.

"I ought not be seen alighting from mysterious carriages by any of the household," she said to Penrose as the driver handed her down. "And would you keep Sybille's things? I don't wish to explain the crate to anyone. I do wish I could attend the *Cendrillon* ballet." She paused. She detested asking for things. "Professor, perhaps you might go to the *Cendrillon* ballet—if you have the time, I mean to say—and inform me of any clues about the connection between Sybille's Cinderella getup and the ballet."

"Perhaps you would join me. This evening?"

Ophelia considered. "I might be able to pull it off. I'll meet you in the opera house lobby just before eight o'clock, if I'm able."

When Ophelia returned to Hôtel Malbert, it was nearing one o'clock. The stepsisters were holed up in their salon—Ophelia heard them bickering through the doors. Baldewyn was polishing silver in the dining room. He did not greet Ophelia when she looked in, although his face grew instantly blotchy.

Baldewyn hadn't warmed to Mrs. Brand.

Prue wasn't upstairs. Ophelia searched for her, but only caught the lady's maid, Lulu, trying on Eglantine's fancy slippers in front of a mirror.

Ophelia finally found Prue in, of all places, the kitchen.

"Prue!" she cried. Prue bent over the plank table, sleeves rolled, hair like a tumbleweed, scrubbing away. "Where is Beatrice? Did you clean this whole kitchen yourself?"

"Sure did. It's taken all morning. Beatrice went out to market hours ago but she ain't come back. I reckon I'm supposed to cook luncheon, only I don't know how."

"She's taking advantage."

"Not everyone in the wide world is trying to take advantage of little old me, Ophelia Flax. Matter of fact"—Prue lifted her chin—"I'm learning housewifing. I wish to be useful for a change."

"Anything that keeps you in the house and out of mischief is grand." Ophelia told Prue how she'd encountered Professor Penrose.

"Penrose!" Prue glanced at Ophelia. "Yes. You look right rosy and giddy."

"I'm wearing this sludgy face paint."

"The giddy shines through. I *knew* he'd crop up again."

"Bunkum."

Ophelia told Prue everything she had learned about her sister, Sybille, and how Sybille had had Howard DeLuxe's name scribbled on the back of a card amongst her things.

"I'd bet my boots Ma was sending Sybille to go work for the Varieties," Prue said. "She was always sending girls to Howard. Howard paid her a finder's fee for the good ones."

"Your mother wouldn't take a finder's fee for her own daughter!"

"Maybe."

"Why would Sybille wish to go to New York?"

"Don't know. Clean slate, maybe?" Prue kept scrubbing.

Once Gabriel was established in an elegant suite of rooms in the Hôtel Meurice, he sent a note to Lord and Lady Cruthlach with a messenger boy. If anyone knew about a murder connected to "Cinderella," it would be that ominous, fairy tale relic–collecting pair. Although Gabriel did not count Lord and Lady Cruthlach as friends, he had done business of sorts with them before, and their Paris address was recorded in his notebook.

While Gabriel waited for his answer, he enlisted the hotel concierge to make discreet inquiries as to whether a lady fitting Henrietta's description was registered in any of the finer hotels in Paris. He also requested that the concierge make a similar investigation into the passenger lists of steamships that had sailed from France in the last week. Henrietta could have left by rail or coach, but there was no way to check on that.

Then there was the matter of the convent in which Sybille Pinet had been schooled. The landlady had said its name had something to do with stars. He requested a list of every convent orphanage in Paris.

These inquiries would come at great expense to Gabriel, but he did not much care. He had inherited his father's vast estate along with his title, and having neither a wife nor any costly vices, he was somewhat at a loss as to how to spend it.

Next, Gabriel walked several blocks to the florist's shop of the trade card found in Miss Pinet's crate. The fashionable shop was perfumed by blooms that glowed like sickbed dreams in the cold, gray afternoon. It was warm inside, and thick with smartly dressed ladies. The shopkeeper merely laughed when Gabriel asked if he could recall a lady matching Henrietta's description. Customers were blurs to persons in such trades. A dead end, then.

When Gabriel returned to his hotel from the florist's shop, the messenger boy had his answer: Lord and Lady Cruthlach would gladly receive him. Immediately.

Lord and Lady Cruthlach's mansion would have done rather nicely as an illustration in a gothic horror novel: pointed black turrets, leering monkey gargoyles, leaded windows, evil-looking spires. Up on the roof, crows bobbed up and down, cawing.

Gabriel rapped on the front door. When it opened, a red-haired ogre of a manservant filled the doorway. Hume. Gabriel had met him before, unfortunately. Hume's scarlet livery coat could have fit a bull. His knee breeches terminated in gold braid, and white silk stockings encased his Highland clansman's calves. His feet were shod in scarlet satin, Louis-heeled slippers as big as soup tureens.

"Good afternoon, Hume," Gabriel said.

"His Lordship and Her Ladyship await, Lord Harrington," Hume said in a gravelly Scots accent.

In the upstairs sitting room, draperies shut out the day. Upholstered furniture, carved tables, and sumptuous rugs clogged the stifling hot chamber. The throbbing, orange fire threw everything into velvety silhouette.

"He comes," a creaky voice said. "Wake up, my love, he comes."

Hume took up a post against the wall.

Gabriel approached the fire. Two forms slumped side by side on a sofa.

"Lord and Lady Cruthlach," Gabriel said. "How delightful to see you." He *had* hoped never again to lay eyes on this accursed pair. "How long has it been? Two years? Three?"

"Three, dear Lord Harrington, three." Lady Cruthlach tipped her undersized head and smiled, revealing teeth as perfect as a little child's.

Ivory teeth, surely. Not . . . a little child's.

Lady Cruthlach's too-bright eyes sunk into her crumpled face. Her sparse yellowed hair was dragged back from an aristocratic, high forehead and fastened with jeweled hairpins. The jewels emphasized the shining flesh of her scalp.

Gabriel forced himself to kiss her mottled hand.

"*Why,*" Lord Cruthlach wheezed beside her, "why does he stand? Rohesia, why? He blocks the light. He blocks the warmth. My bones ache from the *cold*, Rohesia, oh!"

Legend had it that Athdar Crawley, Lord Cruthlach, had once been one of the tallest, proudest gentlemen in the Scottish peerage. Heaven only knew how long ago *that* had been, for now he resembled nothing so much as a suit of clothes abandoned on the cushions.

"Rohesia, they pain me again. My veins, they pain me. Oh, why does this blackguard block the warmth?"

"Drink?" Lady Cruthlach crowed to Gabriel. "And please, *do* sit."

Gabriel sat. Sweat beaded beneath his arms and at the small of his back. "A drink would be splendid."

Hume poured out tiny glasses of something at a sideboard. His bulky back concealed his operations.

Three drinks were brought forth on a tray.

Normally, Gabriel wouldn't dream of accepting a drink from the Crawleys. He had heard whispers of foes found, necks snapped, at the base of Castle Margeldie's battlements. Of a snooping Cambridge scholar sunk forever out of sight in a bog on their Highland estate. Of a nosy marchioness taken fatally ill after ingesting a slice of chocolate cake at their winter solstice dinner party in 1861.

Gabriel sipped. Putrid, medicinal sweetness, and it scalded all the way down. The four of them seemed to silently count together ten ticks of the mantelpiece clock. Gabriel did not topple to the carpet in convulsions.

Good, then.

7

Ophelia devoured two apples, a wedge of cheese, nearly half a loaf of bread, drank three glasses of water, and felt her spirits perk up. She left Prue in the kitchen—Prue would not be pried away from her scrubbing—and went upstairs to her chamber. She took the back staircase she'd discovered. Better not to let the entire household in on her comings and goings.

She set to work on a note to Inspector Foucher, using paper, envelope, fountain pen, and ink she kept in her carpetbag. The paper was crumply and the ink flaked. She described with as much detail as possible what she had learned about Sybille Pinet at the opera house and the boardinghouse.

A scream rang out. Then another, and another.

Ophelia dropped her pen. She followed the screams down to the stepsisters' salon. She burst through the doors.

The screams stopped. Several pairs of eyes stared at Ophelia.

"Is everything quite all right?" Ophelia asked.

"Madame Brand," Eglantine said. "Is it not the fashion to *knock* in Boston?" Eglantine stood upon a dressmaker's stool. She was flushed, and she clutched a ripped piece of paper to her chest. Her pink moiré silk skirts half concealed two seamstresses who knelt at the hem, stitching.

"I beg your pardon, but I grew alarmed at the sound of screams."

"That was Austorga," Eglantine said.

Austorga sat on a sofa. Her sturdy shoulders rose and fell. Like her sister, she clutched a ripped piece of paper. In her other hand she held a large, square envelope.

"Was the screaming not Austorga, Mademoiselle Smythe?" Eglantine asked.

Miss Seraphina Smythe was the frail girl in owlish spectacles who had been playing the piano when Sybille's body had been discovered. She sat beside Austorga on the sofa and she had just bitten into a chocolate bonbon. At Eglantine's question, her jaws froze. She nodded.

"Screaming?" Mrs. Smythe, Seraphina's mother, said in a vague voice, from the opposite sofa. She looked up from the pages of a book. "*I* did not hear anything." Mrs. Smythe had also been in attendance at the stepsisters' soirée on the evening of the murder. She was a stout lady with bleary blue eyes, attired in a smart visiting gown.

"You never *do* hear anything, Mother," Seraphina said.

Mrs. Smythe did not seem to have heard. She resumed reading.

Mr. Smythe, Ophelia had been told, was some sort of diplomatic attaché from England. Seraphina and her mother, who had met Eglantine and Austorga at a public concert, spent a great deal of their time in the company of the stepsisters. Mrs. Smythe served as chaperone, and the stepsisters always spoke English in the presence of the Smythe ladies.

"Madame Brand," Austorga said, "we have just been apprised of some most stimulating news." She waved her piece of paper.

"Madame Brand does not wish, you uncouth twit, to hear of all the dull details of the, well, *you* know," Eglantine said.

"It is not dull," Austorga said. "You said yourself you thought you might swoon—"

"Oh, for pity's sake, you ninny!" Eglantine shouted. It was unclear if she was speaking to her sister or to one of the seamstresses.

The company of Prue's stepsisters was intolerable. Ophelia had dined enough with them in the past few days to be convinced of it. However, she had questions to ask.

She sat down next to Mrs. Smythe. Mrs. Smythe did not look up from her book. Ophelia glanced at the top of a page. *Pride and Prejudice.*

"Oh!" Seraphina cried. "Do be careful of Réglisse."

"Réglisse?" Ophelia said.

A roly-poly black cat yawned beside Ophelia on the sofa.

"Good heavens," Ophelia said. "I had taken him for a cushion. He is quite . . . well-fed."

"Surely, Madame Brand," Eglantine said, "*you* are able to sympathize."

"So I can," Ophelia said. "So I can. My dear, I have been meaning to ask, is there any news in the disappearance of your stepmother, Henrietta?"

"No," Eglantine said.

"And no arrest of the murderer?"

"*Must* we speak of this?" Seraphina whispered.

"No arrest," Eglantine said.

"And no more news of the dead girl's identity?"

"What do we care of that little tart?" Eglantine said.

Seraphina gasped.

"I do wish you had not torn the letter!" Austorga shouted to Eglantine.

"It would not have torn if you had simply let *go*, as I instructed!" Eglantine shouted back.

Seraphina cowered. Mrs. Smythe turned a page of her book.

"*He* knows that I adore cream-colored paper," Eglantine said, adopting a dreamy tone. "I told him last week when we sat in his box at the opera."

"I said that *I* adored cream-colored paper, too!" Austorga said. "I said that cream was my very favorite color for theater programmes."

"You said that *Don Carlos* was the dullest opera you had

ever attended. You said it made you feel as though you were coming down with paralysis of the mind."

"Not to *him*."

"*I* believed you already *had* paralysis of the—"

"Pray tell," Ophelia said, "of which gentleman do you girls speak?"

"No one," Eglantine said.

"Prince Rupprecht," Austorga said. "Simply the most handsome, cleverest gentleman in all of Europe."

Mrs. Smythe suddenly looked up from her book. "*Quite* the eligible bachelor." She threw an accusing look at her daughter.

"Everything the prince says is so marvelous," Austorga said, "or so absolutely, hilariously funny that one must simply giggle and giggle and one cannot *stop* giggling."

"You sounded like the parrot at the zoological gardens, when he was here for our soirée," Eglantine said.

Prince Rupprecht had attended their soirée? He must've been either the strapping towhead with all the medals and ribbons, or the burly fellow with the lion's mane.

"I had so hoped that we would not have to spoil sweet, *precious* Prudence's stay in our household," Eglantine said, "for you see, she will not be able to attend the ball on Saturday. It is a private event. If you must know—because I beg your pardon, Madame Brand, but you *do* seem to pry into our family affairs—"

The little snot.

"—a most fascinating missive came in the post today."

"An invitation to the ball?" Ophelia asked.

"No, no," Austorga said. "We were invited to the ball ages ago, and Mademoiselle Smythe, too. It is—"

"*Today*," Eglantine said, "we received a supplement of sorts to the invitation, to the effect that Prince Rupprecht will make an important announcement at the ball."

Austorga made a seal-like bark.

"He writes," Eglantine said, "that his announcement will be of particular interest to the young ladies in attendance—"

Austorga muffled another bark in her palm.

"—but that is all."

"The prince loves surprises," Austorga said. "He adores them!" She bit into a chocolate bonbon, and cried out in pain.

"What is the matter?" Ophelia asked.

"It is my teeth." Austorga kept chewing, but her eyes brimmed with tears. "They are terribly sore."

"It is because of all that vinegar you have been drinking," Eglantine said. "Everyone knows vinegar weakens one's teeth."

"But Mademoiselle Smythe said every English rose drinks vinegar to slim herself," Austorga said.

Ophelia looked at Seraphina. Seraphina said nothing, and her expression was bland.

"I must be slim for the ball," Austorga said, taking another bite of bonbon. "I *must*."

"Oh, do shut *up*!" Eglantine flailed her thin arms for emphasis. One of the seamstresses, still stitching Eglantine's hem, tumbled backwards. Eglantine muttered something waspish.

The seamstress crawled around the carpet, picking up pins. She was delicate, with a waxen complexion, lank blond hair, and blue half circles under her eyes.

"Is your seamstress well?" Ophelia asked Austorga. The seamstress glanced over. Had she heard? Could she understand?

"Josie is always a miserable little thing," Austorga whispered. "Do not mind her. She is only one of Madame Fayette's assistants."

"Is the other seamstress over there Madame Fayette?"

"No, no, Madame Fayette is our dressmaker. Surely you know of her, for I have heard tell of American ladies traveling all the way to Paris to have their trousseaus made at Maison Fayette."

"New England ladies always stitch their own trousseaus," Ophelia lied.

"Well, Madame Fayette does not pay house calls. Only her seamstresses do."

Mrs. Smythe looked up from her book. "Madame Fayette and her seamstresses are ever so busy, since every young lady of quality wishes to appear to the utmost advantage at the ball on Saturday. Or"—she threw her daughter another accusing glance—"*almost* every young lady."

"Ah," Ophelia said. Then, since everyone fancied she was a nosy old dame anyway, she said, "Why is it, I wonder, that the carriageway gate lock was changed this morning?"

"Was it?" Eglantine said in an airy tone.

"On account of the murder," Austorga said.

"Oh?" Ophelia leaned closer. "How so?"

"Because the gate was left open that night, you see, and the murderer dragged that girl's body in through the gate, and only after the police arrived did Beatrice notice that the carriageway gate key, which she always keeps on a little hook at the bottom of the kitchen stair, was missing."

"Good heavens!" Ophelia said. "But the murderer is a derelict with no connection to the house. How did he obtain the key?"

"No one knows."

"Beatrice must have lost the key," Eglantine said. "She drinks like a fish when she plays cards with her friends behind the marketplace. Lulu told me so."

"Is there only one key?" Ophelia asked.

"Two," Austorga said. "The one kept in the kitchen, which Beatrice uses to open the gate for tradesmen's deliveries, and the one kept by the coachman, Henri. But Henri said he still has *his* key."

"Perhaps the murderer dragged the body through the gate behind the coachman," Ophelia said.

"Surely Henri would have noticed something," Eglantine said sharply.

"Yes, Henri would have noticed," Seraphina said in a small voice.

"Seraphina!" Mrs. Smythe exclaimed. "Pray do not speak of the servants."

Seraphina took a sullen bite of bonbon.

"I *must* insist that we discuss something more pleasant," Eglantine said. "Mademoiselle Smythe—are you simply *dying* with envy over my ball gown?"

"Oh yes, quite. Dying," Seraphina said, chewing. She nudged her enormous spectacles upwards.

"I traveled to Paris after reading an astonishing report in *The Times* of a murder in Le Marais," Gabriel said to Lady Cruthlach after interminable and antiquated pleasantries. "I wished to meet you, to learn what you know of the matter and, perhaps, to propose another . . . exchange."

"Oh yes, Lord Harrington," Lady Cruthlach said, treacle-sweet. "Our last trade was *most* beneficial."

For *her*, perhaps. The Tyrolean black wolf's tooth they had given him, in exchange for a rare specimen of Siberian *Amanita muscaria*, had been a fraud.

"However, I know not of the astonishing newspaper report to which you refer," Lady Cruthlach said.

"You did not notice the report of the girl found murdered in the garden of a house in Le Marais?"

"We do not worry ourselves with the rush and stew of the present day. You know as well as we do that the *past* is everything and all."

Lady Cruthlach didn't know about the house, then. Gabriel could continue to guard the secret. On the other hand, she might know something that he did not.

Gabriel drew the Charles Perrault volume from his jacket. He slid out the loose sheet, and unfolded it.

"Well?" Lady Cruthlach said. "What is this?"

Lord Cruthlach wheezed softly.

"My notes," Gabriel said. "A transcription, rather, of an excised passage from Perrault's 'Cendrillon.'" There was actually more than one passage, but he would begin with this one.

"Excised passage?" Lady Cruthlach licked the corner of her mouth. "I knew not of such—such treasure. How did you come by this?"

"I stumbled upon it a few years ago, quite by chance, whilst researching 'The Sleeping Beauty' in a rare first-edition housed in the Sorbonne."

"Well? Come now, don't be a tease. Read it aloud. My eyesight is no longer good."

"The excised passage was appended to the moral at the end of the tale. It denotes the address of the Cendrillon house—the house, that is, in which Cinderella dwelled with her father, stepmother, and stepsisters. The address was removed from subsequent editions of the volume, no doubt in order to protect the privacy of the Roque-Fabliau family."

"Roque-Fabliau? Of Hôtel Malbert? You must be mistaken. That pitiful little marquis, up to his fat chins in debt? His two daughters were thrust upon me at a lecture on Pliny the Elder not long ago. Ugly, grasping creatures. Surely *they* cannot be descendants of Cinderella."

"If the manuscript is to be believed, then they are not descendants of Cinderella, but descendants of Cinderella's father and stepmother."

Lord Cruthlach's mouth opened and shut like a carp fish.

"What is it that you know?" Gabriel asked.

"Know?" Lady Cruthlach smoothed the blanket on her knees. "We know nothing, my dear."

"Perhaps, then, it would be best if we forego any trades in the future." Gabriel replaced the sheet of paper in the book and snapped it shut. He stood.

"No!" Lady Cruthlach cried. "Stay. I shall tell you. I shall tell you! You are the most diligent, the most resourceful and *adventurous* collector that we are acquainted with, Lord Harrington. I *would* so hate to see the last of you."

Gabriel remained standing, and he tucked the book into his jacket.

"We have heard tell, for many years past, of a most *extraordinary* relic hidden in the Cendrillon house," Lady Cruthlach said. "The queen mother of all other fairy tale relics."

"I don't quite follow."

"My lord Athdar is dying, Lord Harrington. Surely that is apparent. But there is something hidden in the Cendrillon house that will change that. Something of such fantastical power that my lord will be restored. And he will live. Yes, he will *live*."

"What is the nature of this relic?"

"We know not." Lady Cruthlach's eyes glittered. "Yet."

Had Miss Flax been present, she would have doubtless remarked that Lady Cruthlach wasn't a very fine actress.

Gabriel gave Lady Cruthlach his card with the name of his hotel written on the back. He left the mansion with the uneasy sense that he had somehow revealed too much.

8

Ophelia had never laid eyes on the Malberts' coachman,
who the girls had called Henri, because she had never
ridden in their equipage. She did know that Eglantine and
Austorga kept him busy day and night with their chock-full
social calendars and that he must, then, be always at the ready.

She slipped away from the ladies in the salon, donned her
cloak, and went out into the rear courtyard through a pair of
doors in the library. The mansion formed two sides of the
courtyard, and the ivy-covered carriage house and a high wall
formed the other two sides. Beside the large, curved carriage
doors was another, smaller door. Ophelia knocked on the
small door.

Rustling and footfalls sounded within, and the door
opened. A fine-looking young man stood before Ophelia.
He was not very tall, but he had well-formed muscles, a
proud bearing, and floppy brown curls. He wore shirtsleeves
and a coachman's shiny boots. "Madame Brand, *bonjour*,"
he said in a calm, deep voice.

"Do you speak English?" Ophelia asked.

"*Oui*, yes, a little, please only." His dark eyes twinkled.

"Madame la Marquise, she keep all servants only who speak English."

Ophelia fancied Henrietta had kept Henri on for reasons quite unrelated to his English-speaking abilities. And it was no wonder the three young ladies were so quick to spring to Henri's defense. He would've caused a sensation on the dramatic stage.

"How did you know my name?" Ophelia asked.

"Baldewyn, he always tell me name of guest, *oui*? So that I might be, how you say, polite. Good servant." His winning smile hid something sly.

"Well, I simply wished to ask you, Henri, about the carriageway key."

"Ah, *oui*? It is kept locked always, *madame*, for we are in city very big."

"No, no, I do not wish to go *through* the gate. I merely wished to ask if it had been left open, by you, on the night that, well"—Ophelia lowered her voice—"that the poor girl was dragged into the garden."

"*Non*. I tell police. I never forget of locking gate. Never. That evening, *aussi*, I stay in. Here, in carriage house, *parce que* the *mademoiselles* entertain at home."

"You were here."

"*Oui*. And I have key in waistcoat pocket always."

Ophelia glanced at his waistcoat. A button fastened the small pocket at the front. "Then did you notice anything? Hear anything?"

"Only when *la jolie mademoiselle*, the daughter of marquise, begin screaming. I was sleeping."

"Oh, I see." Ophelia peered past Henri into the dim carriage house. She saw straw on the floor, and smelled horse. His quarters would be upstairs.

"Is there a groom?" she asked.

"I do all the work. Horses, everything, and harnesses *aussi*."

"And is there any way to reach the courtyard through the carriage house? From whatever street or alleyway lies behind, I mean."

"*Non*. The carriage house was built without doors other

than these." He patted the doorjamb. "To keep family safe, *oui*? City very big all around."

"Thank you, Henri."

Ophelia went back inside. If Henri was telling the truth, then there was only the key that had gone missing from the kitchen to wonder about. Someone had stolen it. Either the murderer, or someone aiding the murderer.

Ophelia returned to her chamber, finished writing her note to Inspector Foucher, and took it downstairs to Baldewyn. She asked him to have a delivery boy take it to the *commissaire*'s office.

"Very well, *madame*," Baldewyn said.

She gave him a few coins.

Baldewyn looked insulted, but kept the money.

Ophelia waited about an hour, and Baldewyn brought her Inspector Foucher's reply. She read it in her chamber.

Madame Brand: Thank you for your message with regards to the identity of the murdered girl. Although your fortitude and resourcefulness are to be commended, your efforts are entirely misplaced, and I would be obliged if you would not continue to misuse the valuable time of the police. Mademoiselle Pinet's identity has been duly noted but, as I informed you this morning, her identity is not relevant in this case, as the murderer has been identified. I will reveal to you, to put your evidently nervous mind at ease, that the murderer was spotted near the Pont Marie this morning, and we expect to apprehend him at any moment.

M. Foucher

Sybille's identity wasn't *relevant*? Ophelia crumpled the note and threw it into the fireplace. It caught fire on a smoldering coal and quickly turned to ash. Sybille's identity would have been relevant had she a family, or position in society.

Ophelia felt a kinship with Sybille. Ophelia had no family, no position in society, either. Her mother was dead, her father had scarpered when she was only four, and her brother, Odie, well, she'd lost sight of him after he'd enlisted during The War Between the States. In her heart of hearts, she knew Odie was a goner, but that never stopped her from picturing him walking through a door one day with a big smile on his face.

Ophelia looked up Pont Marie in her Baedeker. Her stomach sank. It was a bridge a mere five or six blocks from Hôtel Malbert. If the police *were* after the right man, he was lurking close by.

Beatrice had shown up just long enough to slap together luncheon for the upstairs crowd, and then she ankled it out of the house again.

Prue got to work sprucing up the broom closet beneath the kitchen stairs. Maybe if everything was shipshape when Beatrice returned, she'd show Prue how to cook something Hansel might like.

When Prue darted outside the kitchen door to dump yet another dustpan full of mouse berries into the rubbish bin, she saw the man.

He was bulky. Uncommonly bulky, carrot-topped, and wearing drab, patched workman's clothes, a woolen cap, and leather boots that fit snug around hamlike calves. Peculiar, too: it seemed, somehow, that Prue laying eyes on him startled him into motion. As though he'd been waiting for her to come out.

Prue dumped the dustpan and went back inside. Before she could slam the door, the man called out, "Wait." In English. Not French.

Prue stayed by the door. She waited until the man arrived at the top of the kitchen steps.

The police had warned her to stay out of the sight of strangers. But surely it wouldn't hurt to find out what the man wanted. Besides, he spoke English, and the murderer was French. Wasn't he?

"You are a servant of this house, miss?" the man asked. He spoke with a funny kind of accent, not American or English. It reminded Prue of the dockworkers in New York.

"No," Prue said. "I mean, yes. Well, in a manner of speaking. Doing servants' tasks and such, but I ain't being paid."

"Not paid? How could you be held here, thus, like a slave?"

"No! It ain't . . . I'm just helping out Beatrice. The housekeeper. She's giving me lessons, like."

The man peered over Prue's shoulder. "Is Beatrice within?"

"She's at market."

"Ah." A pause.

Prue clung to the door handle. The sky overhead churned dark. It hit her now, how alone they were. And how much this feller resembled an ogre in a pantomime.

"I must go inside," Prue whispered.

"Of course." The man bowed and set off towards the carriageway gate.

Prue went inside. Her fingers shook as she fastened and refastened the latch.

Something didn't tally up right. That feller's words, his gestures, had been gentlemanly in spite of his scruffy duds. He hadn't said why he'd been in the garden. He hadn't carried a parcel or a crate, as a deliveryman would. And how had he gotten past the carriageway gate?

One thing was certain: Prue couldn't mention that she'd spoken to a stranger to Ophelia, or Beatrice, or *anyone*. She was supposed to stay sealed up tight in the house, like a pickle in a jar.

If Ophelia was to attend the ballet, she required something to wear. Her Mrs. Brand bombazine was not the crispest, to say the least. And something told her that muddy boots wouldn't go over too well at the Paris Opera. She had fretted over it all through luncheon—a mysterious greenish soup and cold, tough meat—and the only place she could think of from which to borrow a fancy gown was Henrietta's bedchamber.

Once Ophelia was in the bedchamber, she decided to have a more thorough look-see for clues before choosing a gown.

Henrietta wasn't what you'd call a fastidious lady. Certainly, she was an expert on the authenticity of gemstones, and she could discern the name of a gentleman's tailor with the briefest glance at his jacket lining. Still, her chamber was in more disarray than Ophelia ever recalled her dressing room at the Varieties having been. However, there was no blood anywhere, nor anything broken. No train ticket stubs, no letters, no photographs of a dashing gentleman who wasn't her husband.

Wait. *Here* was something Ophelia had overlooked the first time around: a small book on the dressing table, underneath a bottle of rosewater complexion tonic. *How to Address Your Betters*, by A Lady. Ophelia flipped through. Nothing but advice on kowtowing to European blue bloods, with some bits about which fork to use and when *not* to use your hankie thrown in. On the title page, someone had scribbled a dedication: *May you use this in good stead.—Arty.*

Arty? Just like Henrietta to have some fellow involved.

Ophelia replaced the book under the bottle and kept searching. A jumble of shoes on the carpet, withered roses on the mantel—aha. A half-burned letter in the grate. Ophelia crouched and shook off ash from the remnant of envelope. Nothing remained but a return address:

M. T. S. Cherrien (Avocat)
116 Avenue des Champs-Élysées

Avocat? Ophelia only knew a handful of French words, but *avocat* looked an awful lot like *advocate*.

A lawyer.

Knowing Henrietta, a lawyer reeked of one notion, and one notion only: divorce.

Ophelia dusted off the remaining ash, folded the bit of envelope, and slid it up her cuff. She got to work choosing an opera gown.

* * *

After stashing the borrowed gown in her own chamber, Ophelia went to visit Prue in the kitchen. Prue was sleeping at the table, head on her arm.

"Wake up," Ophelia said.

Prue lifted her head. "What time is it?"

"Three thirty, more or less."

"Rats. I need to get going with those turnips." She pointed to a heap of purple turnips on the table.

"I've heard from Inspector Foucher, Prue, and he says that the man the police suppose is the murderer, well, he was sighted only a few blocks from here. Please be careful."

"I *am* being careful."

"Even more so, then."

"You said the flatfeet was after the wrong feller."

"I believe they may be. But we cannot be too careful— *you* cannot be too careful."

"Sure." Prue poked at a turnip. "Whatever you say."

When Gabriel caught sight of Miss Flax at three minutes till eight, his heart once again performed that peculiar squeezing-and-swelling feat.

Miss Flax paused just inside one of the opera house lobby doors. Gabriel, with a stab of self-reproach, did not immediately go to her. She wore a sumptuous, midnight-blue velvet mantle—where had she gotten that?—the standing collar of which framed her anxious face.

Here, at last, was the face he had been dreaming about these many weeks past, the face that had been obscured that morning by her wretched matron's disguise. A pure oval face, dark, darting eyes like the centers of poppies, a gleam of honey-brown hair swept back into knots—

Miss Flax's eyes lit on him.

He pretended to adjust a cufflink.

She smiled a little and started towards him.

* * *

By the time Ophelia reached Professor Penrose, he no longer looked like he'd just been punched. He'd probably had too much cream sauce with his dinner. The French were heavy-handed with the cream sauce.

"Good evening, Professor." Ophelia forced herself to employ a calm and friendly tone. She had given herself a talking-to on the way to the opera house, concluding that if being with Penrose made her feel as nervy as a human cannonball, well, that wasn't *his* fault.

"Miss Flax. You look lovely."

"It's Henrietta's cloak and gown. And reticule."

"You had no trouble leaving the house for the evening?"

"None at all." A lie. Ophelia had squeezed out of Hôtel Malbert through a cellar window that opened onto the side pavement. Even if Malbert and his daughters were out, she couldn't sashay out the front door in Henrietta's gown and her own cosmetics-free face. Baldewyn might see, or Lulu or Beatrice. "The family has gone out, only"—Ophelia glanced around the thronged lobby—"I suspect they might have come here."

"But they would not recognize you without your matron's armor. Might I assist you with your mantle?"

"No!" Ophelia said, a little too loudly.

"All right. Shall we go in?" The professor held out his arm. Ophelia took it.

Henrietta was a few inches shorter than Ophelia, so the gown Ophelia had borrowed didn't quite make it to the floor. Worse, Henrietta's dainty satin slippers were an inch too small, so Ophelia's toes were crunched-up balls of agony. But the main conundrum was that Henrietta was bountifully gifted in the bosom territory, whereas Ophelia was, regrettably, not.

Luckily, the velvet mantle covered up that territory. Just so long as Ophelia kept it on.

She leaned towards the professor as they followed streams of people up a swooping staircase. She told him what the stepsisters, Miss Smythe, and Henri, the coachman, had said about the carriageway gate key. "So you see, if the murderer was indeed that derelict, as the police claim, he still would've required help from someone *inside* the house. Members of the household, or the party guests, or people who had *help* from members of the household or party guests."

"Is it possible that Miss Pinet's body came from inside the house?"

"Yes, I've thought of that, but the cast of suspects would remain the same."

"Cast of suspects? How theatrical. Miss Flax, you aren't attempting to collar Miss Pinet's murderer, are you?"

"Of course I am. And I must find Henrietta, too. Oh yes— and that's the other thing I've found. I reckon Henrietta is safe and sound somewhere, and that she wished to initiate a divorce from Malbert." Ophelia showed Penrose the bit of charred envelope that she'd brought in the reticule.

"*Avocat* does indeed mean *solicitor*, and that happens to be a very good address."

They found their seats, plushy red, in the first row of a balcony curving around the theater. Four tiers in all, carved and gold-painted, reached up to a ceiling painted like cherub-plagued heavens. An enormous chandelier blazed over the orchestra-level seats.

How peculiar that she, Ophelia Flax of Littleton, New Hampshire, was here. Gussied up in borrowed finery. Seated next to an earl. Confabulating about murder.

"I do not wish to alarm you, Miss Flax," Penrose said softly, once they were settled in their seats. "However, I feel I must point out that even if the Marquise Henrietta had initiated a divorce, that does not preclude the possibility that she . . . that something unfortunate befell her."

"If something unfortunate befalls a lady who wishes for a divorce, I reckon that the one doing the befalling is her husband."

"Does Malbert seem capable of violence?"

"He's an odd duck. He seems *weak*, but he's awfully secretive and he's always holed up in his workshop, building what, no one knows. He mutters things about his 'inventions' if one asks. Oh, yes—and he did remind me that curiosity killed the cat."

"Good Lord."

Ophelia also described Inspector Foucher's dismissive note—with its mention of the madman sighting near the Pont Marie—and then the chandelier dimmed and was cranked up on a chain to clear the view. The audience grew hushed, the orchestra tuned, the conductor emerged and bowed, and then the overture began.

Halfway through the overture, Ophelia was so hot and steamy under the velvet mantle that she had no choice but to fan herself with the programme.

The professor leaned close. "Are you well, Miss Flax? May I take your—"

"*No!*" she whispered.

9

The ballet's first act was a wonder. In the circus and the variety hall, *if* you could see anything through the cigar smoke and hear anything past the men's hoots (or the trumpeting of elephants), the quality of the production might've been found lacking. However, the *Ballet de l'Opéra de Paris* pulled out all the stops. The dancers jumped and twirled, no tripping. The orchestra hit all the right notes, which was the first time Ophelia had heard *that*. The pit musicians in Howard DeLuxe's Varieties read the newspapers down there, and some of them even drank beer.

The really breathtaking thing about the ballet was the stage scenery.

"Are those flowers growing?" Ophelia whispered to the professor. They watched a scene in which Cinderella lamented (gracefully, with hand-clasping) the wicked stepsisters' shoddy treatment of her, out in the garden. The garden set had started out simple enough, but as the scene progressed the flowers and insects grew bigger and more colorful until they were the size of Cinderella herself.

"Marvelous, isn't it?" Penrose said softly. "Ah. I nearly

forgot." He dug into his breast pocket and produced a pair of opera glasses. "Here. Borrowed them from my hotel."

Ophelia peered through. "Gimcrackery indeed. Those flowers are made of painted metal—they're mechanical."

"The set quite upstages the dancers, does it not?"

After a few minutes, Ophelia allowed the opera glasses to drift away from the stage—despite those mechanical wonders—to the balconies. Row after row of togged-up ladies and gents. Swaying fans, bent heads, bloated gowns, sparkling jewels.

Oh, *drat*. There was Austorga! One tier up. And there was Eglantine beside her, frowning and fanning herself, and the Smythe ladies. Mrs. Smythe read a book. Light bounced off Seraphina's spectacles. No Malbert, though.

Austorga had opera glasses glued to her eyes. She wasn't viewing the stage; she was viewing the opposite balcony. Ophelia trained her own opera glasses on the spot where she fancied Austorga was looking.

Aha.

Ophelia passed Penrose the opera glasses. "Up there, first balcony on the right, second tier. That towheaded gentleman in the white jacket was at the party in the mansion that night, and so was that lion-looking fellow next to him, with the hair down to his shoulders."

Penrose looked.

"I fancy one of those gentlemen might be a fellow by the name of Prince Rupprecht," Ophelia said. "The stepsisters were raising a ruckus over him just this afternoon. He's giving a ball on Saturday, and seeing as he's the apple of every Parisian debutante's eye, it sounds as if it's to be the biggest to-do of the year. What's more, it seems he's making an important announcement at his ball."

"Of a matrimonial nature?"

"I reckon so."

"Well, if he and that other chap were in attendance at the Roque-Fabliau mansion the night Miss Pinet was killed, I must go and speak with them. One of them is, quite possibly, a murderer."

"*We* will go speak with them."

At the first interval, Penrose sent along his card with one of the ushers. The usher returned with an invitation for Lord Harrington to join Prince Rupprecht in his box for the remainder of the ballet.

"You do wring every last drop from that title of yours," Ophelia said.

"I try."

As soon as they had pushed through the curtains at the back of Prince Rupprecht's box, Ophelia wrinkled her nose. The box reeked of cigar smoke, brandy fumes, and some other scent that called to mind dark dens and musky fur.

Four gentlemen occupied the box.

"Lord Harrington!" the towheaded gentleman said. "Come in, come in!" He had some sort of exotic accent. Ophelia couldn't put her finger on which one, but it smacked of the far frontiers of Europe. He lounged in a chair near the front railing, where he'd propped up both of his glossy-booted feet in order, presumably, to better enjoy his brandy and cigar. Epaulets, gold braid, and colorful medals bedecked his white evening jacket, and a scarlet sash cut diagonally across his chest. His pale hair contrasted with his flushed complexion. "I made the acquaintance of your brother—Edgar is it?—in Wiesbaden last year. Is he still preoccupied with horses? But how rude of me—*gauche*, these frogs like to say. I am Prince Rupprecht of Slavonia."

Penrose drew Ophelia forward. "Monsieur le Prince, may I present to you Miss—ah—Miss Stonewall. My cousin, visiting from America. Her first time in Paris."

"Any *mademoiselle* is welcome here," Prince Rupprecht said with a leer, "but sometimes we take issue with the *madames*. May I introduce Monsieur Garon, Count de Griffe?"

The Count de Griffe was the galoot with shaggy, dark gold hair. His barrel body strained the seams of his black evening suit, his collar appeared to be stained, and his jaw hadn't met with a razor in a few days. When he spied Ophelia, his tawny eyes lit up.

Oh, golly.

"And this," Prince Rupprecht said, gesturing to a third gentleman, "is Monsieur Apollo-Aristede Colifichet, the toast of Paris."

Colifichet was a narrow, praying mantis sort of fellow in a mauve waistcoat and gray evening jacket. He perched on the edge of his chair, legs crossed, spine straight as a broomstick. His hair was scraped back with Macassar oil.

Colifichet barely glanced at Ophelia as they were introduced.

"That little scamp over there at the end," Prince Rupprecht said, "is Pierre, Colifichet's little delivery boy and apprentice, here to view the fruits of his master's labors, to learn, to dream, yes?"

Pierre, who was well within earshot, looked over. His expression was dark; he must've understood everything, which meant he spoke English. Purple shadows circled his eyes. His blond hair was cropped close, and he had extraordinarily large ears. He was about Ophelia's own age—far too old to be referred to as a little scamp.

"Fruits?" Penrose said. "Labors?"

"Why, I believed that was why you sent up your card," Prince Rupprecht said. "To make the acquaintance of the gentleman who designed those stupendous stage sets. Mechanical, every last bit. Much more of a spectacle than pasteboard props moved around by ropes and pulleys, would you not agree?"

"They are indeed stupendous," Penrose said to Colifichet.

"Yes, wonderful," Ophelia said.

"They are not perfect, *non*, yet I did my utmost."

"Are you a regular designer for *l'Opéra de Paris*?" Penrose asked. "I did not realize they—"

"I am an *employee* of no one." Colifichet twiddled bony fingers.

"Of course not!" Prince Rupprecht said, spilling brandy on his lap. "Spilt drink. Rain is on the way."

"I daresay the rain has already arrived," Penrose said.

"Are you superstitious, Prince Rupprecht?" Ophelia asked.

"It is what comes of having peasants for nursemaids. They

filled our heads with magic and tales." Prince Rupprecht stared down at the droplets on his lap with a creased brow. Then he looked up at Penrose. "Lord Harrington, I have heard tell that you are afflicted with superstitions of your own. That you hunt down relics of a most peculiar nature, yes?"

"Good heavens," Penrose said in a mild tone. "Who told you such nonsense? I am a professor."

Colifichet said to Penrose in an impatient tone, "I have a shop on Rue des Capucines. Colifichet and Sons. Perhaps you have heard of it?"

"Finest clockwork toy shop in all of Paris," Prince Rupprecht said.

"*Toy* shop," Colifichet said, flushing, "is not the term I prefer. I invent and create automata. My grandfather built the shop, but in those days it was strictly a clockmaker's."

Ophelia tried to think why *clockmaker* rang a bell.

"My grandfather once made an engraved pocket watch for Napoleon Bonaparte," Colifichet said.

"How remarkable," Ophelia said, attempting to remember when Napoleon Bonaparte had lived.

"Not really. Bowing down before aristocrats was never what I wished for myself. I wish to create more. More beauty, more ingenuity, even the semblance, *oui*, the poetic semblance of life itself. Life, indeed, perfected."

"Life, I daresay," Penrose said, "at least, judging from that garden in Act One, made fantastical. Phantasmagorical, rather."

"If only I could make clockwork ballerinas, too," Colifichet said. "Did you see that wretched display in scene two? Like a troupe of dromedaries."

Prince Rupprecht grunted his agreement.

"I work so hard, so very, very hard," Colifichet said, "and those girls destroy it all with one cumbersome arm out of place. My work, my sweat, my blood!" He curled his lip. "Wasted. I would like to kill those girls, sometimes."

Ophelia and Penrose traded glances. "Pardon me, Monsieur Colifichet," Ophelia said, "but is the Marquis de la Roque-Fabliau a student of yours? A student of clockwork inventions?"

"*Oui*, my only student. The marquis is eager to learn, and, well, how could I say *non* to such passion?"

Sounded like Malbert paid handsomely for his lessons in clockwork.

Meanwhile, the Count de Griffe had lumbered close to Ophelia.

Ophelia had always had a way with animals. For starters, she'd spent her girlhood on a farmstead where her mother had been a maid-of-all-work. Ophelia had fed the chickens, milked the cows, and in the summertime, supervised a bratty herd of goats as they foraged along sloping green meadows. Later, when she'd joined P. Q. Putnam's Traveling Circus, she'd been not only a trick rider, but assistant to a poodle who leapt through hoops.

For some reason, this all came to mind as she regarded Griffe and his lionlike aspect.

"Mademoiselle Stonewall," he said with a gruff French accent, "I beg of you, what is your given name? I shall perish, perish like the buffalo of your American soil, if you do not consent to bestow upon me that small morsel."

He was a regular Lord Byron, wasn't he? Well, surely there was no harm in telling him her real given name. "My name is Miss Ophelia Stonewall."

Griffe kissed her hand. "*Merci*, ah, *merci*! Mademoiselle Ophelia Stonewall. Like an angel's name, no?"

Ophelia yanked her hand from his grasp. "I've always thought it sounded a little forbidding."

"I fall at your feet in shame, please, if I have offended you. Please, where are you from?"

"From? Oh—"

"Ohio? I have heard of it."

"Yes. Ohio. Cleveland, Ohio."

"I, myself, am from the Périgord, a most beautiful region to the south. Cleveland. Your family has been settled there long?"

"Not terribly. My father is a—a soap manufacturer. Tallow, you know."

"A soap and tallow heiress? *Magnifique*."

"Heiress? Well, I . . ." Ophelia *was* wearing a gown and

mantle that had probably cost more than most folks' yearly wages. The mantle, by the by, had become stifling. She was going to have to bite the bullet and take it off. "Yes," she said, sliding it from her shoulders, "Papa has met with good fortune." She sighed in relief as cooler air flowed over her neck and shoulders.

Griffe's eyes were glued to her bodice. Pinning it hadn't helped, so Ophelia had had no choice but to stuff it full of rolled-up stockings. The result was the sort of hourglass shape one only saw in fashion plates.

"Perhaps, Mademoiselle Stonewall, I might call upon you at your residence tomorrow?"

"Oh. Well. Not tomorrow."

Mercifully, the lights dimmed and the second act overture began. Ophelia edged away from Griffe to a seat at the front railing.

The professor sat beside her. "Have you and the Count de Griffe much in common?"

"Not a drop." Ophelia willed her bosom to deflate.

"Did you accuse him of murder?"

"Certainly not. I don't know why, but I simply can't believe he would hurt a fly."

"Really." Penrose's eyes slid sideways, lit for a fraction of a second on her bosom, and then met her gaze. "You didn't . . . give anything away, did you? About our inquiries?"

The professor wasn't going to mention her faux bosom, then. He'd seen her real, beanstalkish shape in everyday garb back in Germany.

"I'll give away whatever I please," Ophelia said, warm with embarrassment.

The ballet's second act was even more marvelous than the first. The centerpiece was an enormous, orange-painted mechanical pumpkin. When the music escalated and Cinderella's fairy godmother waved her wand, the pumpkin contraption slowly unfurled like an enormous blossom and the middle of it rose up. The pumpkin had become a glistening golden coach.

Oooooo, the thousands of people in the audience breathed. *Ahhhhh*.

Ophelia glanced at Colifichet. He looked mighty pleased with himself. The apprentice Pierre rested his chin in his hand, elbow on the railing, frowning. The prince and the count were helping themselves to more brandy.

The music swirled and the fairy godmother transformed rats, mice, and lizards into footmen, a coachman, and horses. With a last wave of the wand, sky-high violin trills, and a poof of fake smoke, Cinderella's rags fell away to reveal a gorgeous ball gown.

Ophelia started. "Professor, pass me the opera glasses, would you?"

He passed them.

Ophelia leaned forward and peered through the glasses. "Good gracious," she whispered. "It's the same gown Sybille was wearing. Yes, the same gown exactly, except shorter. Same ivory tulle, same embroidery."

Penrose spoke in low tones, so the other men in the box wouldn't hear. "Whoever made the girl's gown must have seen that costume. Are you certain it's identical?"

"Fair certain, but perhaps we ought to go backstage after the ballerina changes and have a closer look."

They waited. The act dragged on. Ophelia tapped her throbbing toes. At last, Cinderella appeared onstage once again in her raggedy costume.

"Let's go," Ophelia whispered.

"Please excuse us," Penrose murmured to Prince Rupprecht. "My cousin requires a bit of air."

Prince Rupprecht nodded without taking his eyes from his gold opera glasses. The Count de Griffe sent Ophelia an ardent glance as she and Penrose slipped by.

10

Ophelia found the backstage entrance handily, through a door around the corner from the lobby.

Backstage, no one paid them any mind. Tight stairs and meandering corridors brought them to the busy rooms adjacent to the stage. The music sounded muffled. Dancers chatted or stretched. Men in shirtsleeves rushed about, moving bits of scenery. Ophelia led the way through tables covered with stage properties and into a corridor lined with doors. Each door had a brass nameplate.

"The dressing rooms," Ophelia said. "What was the prima ballerina's name?" She stopped before a door at the end of the corridor, just before a corner. "The one dancing the role of Cinderella."

Penrose drew the programme from his breast pocket and scanned it. "Polina Petrov."

"That's what I thought. Look." Ophelia tapped the nameplate on the door: *Polina Petrov, étoile*. She looked left and right. The corridor was, for the moment, empty. For good measure, she looked around the corner.

Her breath caught. She nipped back around the corner.

"Austorga!" she whispered. "Prue's stepsister. What is *she* doing back here?"

"Indeed. She is, presumably, a young lady of gentle breeding."

Ophelia nodded. Well-bred ladies never ventured backstage. Well-bred *gents*, certainly, but not the ladies.

Ophelia looked around the corner again. Many paces away, Austorga was speaking to a thin, elegantly dressed woman of about forty years, with striking black eyebrows and a pointy nose. The woman appeared to be annoyed, and Austorga was getting worked up.

"Can you hear what they're saying?" Ophelia asked.

"No. And we might consider hurrying if you wish to investigate that costume before the end of the second act."

They darted inside Polina Petrov's dressing room and shut the door.

Polina Petrov's dressing room was catawampus and smelled of greasepaint and talcum powder. Gas globe lamps hissed softly on either side of the dressing table mirror. Jars of face powder, hairbrushes, curling tongs, and rouge were scattered across the top. A sagging divan overflowed with garments, and a folding screen concealed a corner of the room.

Penrose held a battered ballet slipper up by its ribbon. "Good lord, this smells like my brother's basset hound."

Ophelia went straight to the garment rack. She pulled out one of the costumes. "Here it is. Yes. It's exactly like the one Sybille was wearing in the garden. Sybille's was longer, and not quite as—as decorated-looking, I suppose." She touched the silver and gold embroidery on the skirt.

"What could she have been mixed up in?" Penrose said. "Playing at Cinderella. Why?"

"What if she was some sort of understudy for the role in the ballet? Or what if she wished, for some mad reason, to *be* Cinderella? Wait a moment." Ophelia frowned. "I know why this costume looks more decorated—it's the bodice. Sybille's bodice was much simpler, just plain, ivory-colored silk. It hadn't got *this* thing on it." She ran her fingertips over a large, triangle-shaped panel on the front of the bodice. The panel sparkled with crystal beaded flowers stitched on with gold thread.

"A stomacher."

Ophelia glanced up at Penrose. She'd heard a faint note of excitement in his tone. "That's right. A stomacher. In the Varieties, we always had them on our Shakespeare costumes. Old-fashioned, they are."

"In the Charles Perrault version of 'Cinderella,'" Penrose said slowly, "the elder wicked stepsister wears red velvet with French trimming, and the younger a gold-flowered cloak and a diamond stomacher."

"But this isn't the stepsister's costume."

"True. But the more pressing concern is, if Miss Pinet's gown was identical to this costume, with the exception of the stomacher—and you're certain they are identical?"

"Positively."

"—then the question is: what happened to the stomacher on Miss Pinet's gown?"

"I know what's happening here, Professor, and I can't say I fancy it."

"I cannot fathom what you mean."

"Your eyes have that glow about them. Tell me what's so intriguing to you about the notion of a stomacher."

"You'll laugh."

"What of it?"

"Very well. It came to my attention, when reading a rare first edition of Charles Perrault's 'Cendrillon'—he's the chap from the seventeenth century who penned many of these well-known French fairy tales—"

"Cooked them up, you mean."

"Not precisely. More, well, committed them to paper and ink, shall we say. At any rate, although the standard versions of the tale assign the diamond stomacher to one of Cinderella's stepsisters, in that rare first edition, Cinderella *herself* wore the stomacher when she attended the prince's ball."

"What are you angling at? That whoever designed this costume somehow had read that version of the tale?"

"Does it not appear to be the case? Although I have, in all my years of scholarship, never met anyone else who has encountered that version of the tale. The volume was in a forgotten box in a storeroom of a library at the Sorbonne—a university here in Paris. It looked to have been untouched for decades. Although, it *was* a few years ago that I myself examined it."

When the professor started rambling about universities and old books, Ophelia felt like a sinking stone. It was easier to make light of his fairy tale obsession. Then the mean little voice in the back of her head couldn't say, *He's too fine for the likes of you.*

"There is more," Penrose said. "According to that version of the tale, Hôtel Malbert was Cinderella's home—her father's home, where she lived with her stepmother and stepsisters before she married. Her father was a Marquis de la Roque-Fabliau. The current marquis Malbert, and the Misses Eglantine and Austorga, are direct descendants of a son borne by Cinderella's stepmother, so they count both the wicked stepmother and Cinderella's father among their forebears."

Ophelia burst out laughing.

"Laugh all you wish. It is historical fact. Cinderella's name was Isabeau d'Amboise. She married a minor prince and lived in his château in the Loire Valley for the rest of her days. I have visited her grave."

"No, no, it's only, well, if you *met* the Misses Malbert, you'd reckon they were simply your garden variety wicked stepsisters with nothing else mixed in."

Ophelia and Penrose inspected the costume. Its stitches were so tiny a mouse might've made them. Inside of the bodice they found a white label with embroidered words:

> *Maison Fayette*
> *Couturière*
> *Rue de la Paix*
> *Paris*

Ophelia pointed to the word *Couturière*. "What is a—?"

"Dressmaker—a rather grand one, not simply a person who stitches. A designer of garments, really, along the lines of the famed Charles Worth."

"Now that I think of it—Madame Fayette is the lady who designed the ball gowns for Miss Eglantine and Miss Austorga."

"Do you suspect there is a connection?"

"Probably not. I've been told that every Paris debutante worth her salt is having her gown for Prince Rupprecht's ball made by Madame Fayette. The funny thing is, this is just a theater costume, so why was it made by some fancy dressmaker? Most theaters have their own costume masters and mistresses and they sew all the costumes right inside the theater. This is so finely made, too. It needn't to be so fine. No one in the audience could tell the difference—they're too far away. And dancers tend to perspire right through their costumes. The gaslights up there are hot. This delicate gown's not going to last a fortnight."

A woman spoke loudly in French, in the corridor. Ophelia and Penrose locked eyes. The voice was just outside.

Penrose grabbed Ophelia's hand and pulled her behind the folding screen. They crouched. Ophelia's buoyant crinoline and skirts nearly knocked Penrose sideways.

The door creaked open.

The silk panels of the folding screen were old and stained, and there was a rip in one. Ophelia squinted through the rip.

She saw a lady's legs clad in white dancing stockings. Polina Petrov, most likely. She bent before the dressing table and poked around in a drawer, muttering to herself in Russian.

Housewifery, it turned out, was a tedious business. Maybe that's why Ma had never taken a shine to it.

Beatrice had gone off again, leaving Prue to watch an iron cauldron of water. When it boiled it would help take the burned food bits off the dinner pots. Beatrice's cooking made a lot of burned bits.

Prue crouched on a stool at the hearth, gazing into the twinkling cinders. Her eyelids drooped.

A thud on the kitchen door made her eyes fly open.

Another thud.

Just to be on the safe side, Prue picked up a heavy stone pestle as she passed the table.

When she cracked the door, the first thing she saw was a wide expanse of scarlet cloth, white ruffles, brass buttons. Her gaze roved up—*way* up—to the face.

"Oh." Prue's shoulders sagged. "It's you. I near didn't recognize you in that getup. What're you doing, going to a fancy-dress ball?"

It was the ogrelike feller from that afternoon. His smile was, if not exactly *kind*, leastways the first smile Prue had been given all day.

"Would you come with me, miss?" he said.

"Why, no." Behind the door, she hefted the pestle in her hand. "I got work to do, mister. What's it you want? Beatrice? Because she's off somewhere."

"No indeed, not Beatrice. My lord and lady wish to speak with you."

"Me?" Prue edged the door closed.

The man put out a hand and stopped the door. "I must insist."

"No, siree." Prue shoved the door harder. "What do some lord and lady want *me* for? I'm just a—a nobody. Ain't even from around here. I'm from New York. You got me mixed up with somebody else."

She was fair certain she knew who she'd been mixed up with: her dead sister. Sybille.

"There has been no mistake." The man butted the door wide with a big, scarlet satin knee. Prue staggered back and plopped down hard on her rump. Pain shot up her spine. The door crashed against the inside wall and the stone pestle rolled away.

Before Prue could take a breath, the ogre slung her over his shoulder. She tried to scream but just like in a nightmare, nothing came out.

The Russian ballerina continued to rummage about her dressing room, searching for something. Miss Flax watched her through the rip in the folding screen. Gabriel, for his part, watched Miss Flax. He was unable to tear his eyes away from a small section of the side of her neck where her smooth skin met her elaborately twisted hair.

What would it be like to kiss that spot?

The ballerina slammed a drawer and padded out of the dressing room.

"Miss Flax," Gabriel said.

She turned her head.

They were still crouched behind the screen. Miss Flax's capacious skirts oozed around them, and her obviously padded bodice was lopsided. Quite absurd. He must put an end to this, *all* of this, before he forgot himself. There was the impropriety of it, of course, and the question of Miss Flax's innocence. And then there was the matter of *impossibility*.

"Miss Flax, I . . ." Gabriel paused. "I wished to tell you that, during these weeks past, I did think of you. I thought of you more than I wish to admit, and although I am not certain *why* I—"

"Well, we really ought to go." Miss Flax struggled to her feet.

"No, please. I must finish." Gabriel stood. He was surprised by the coolness of his own voice as he said, "I feel it is only right that I tell you, I have an understanding of sorts with a young lady in England." An understanding *of sorts* was accurate. He had never in fact proposed to Miss Banks, although the thought had clearly crossed Miss Banks's mind on several occasions.

"How pleasant for you," Miss Flax said. "I reckon she is a most wondrous young lady indeed to have won your esteem. Is she a duchess? A countess, maybe?"

"Miss Ivy Banks is not a noblewoman, although she comes from a very good family."

"Oh, right. Good family. Those are simply *indispensable*, I hear. I suppose she's as lovely as—what do they say?—as the sunrise."

"Miss Banks is quite a beautiful young lady, yes, but more importantly, she is very well-educated. She reads Latin and Greek, not to mention being fluent in Italian, German, and French. She is working her way through translating an ancient manuscript for me."

"How clever."

The translating bit was a stretch. Ivy had elbowed her way into Gabriel's study one day and demanded a way to, as she put it, *help.*

"Miss Banks is an avid collector of scientific specimens," Gabriel said stiffly, "particularly botanical, although she has of late taken an interest in fossils—"

Ophelia wasn't really sure what fossils were. Something to do with caves. That was it—caves and teeth. Or was it ferns?

"—and she has impeccable penmanship. In my line of work, that, and a certain retiring and ladylike nature, are two indispensable qualities in a wife."

"Oh, I do agree." Miss Flax smiled, too sweetly.

Gabriel's neck began to sweat as they went out into the backstage corridor. "I would quite understand if you did not wish to see me again."

"No, no, it's hunky-dory." Miss Flax walked so quickly Gabriel was compelled to lengthen his stride. "It is quite logical—I fancy Miss Banks enjoys logic immensely? Yes? Well. You'll be wanting to find the missing stomacher. That's pretty clear. And I wish to locate Henrietta. Since these two problems are, by the looks of it, tied up together, we may as well continue to assist each other."

"Oh. Quite."

"To that end—to the end, that is, of a certain arrangement that is of mutual benefit in a strictly businesslike sense, for I would not wish to in any way do *anything* that might give Miss Banks cause for . . . What I mean to say is, tomorrow, perhaps, you might accompany me to the lawyer's office, and translate for me if need be when I ask him what he knows about Henrietta, and then, well, we might go to Maison Fay-ette and inquire about the two gowns and the stomacher."

"Yes. A capital plan. Shall I collect you round the corner of Hôtel Malbert at, say, nine o'clock tomorrow morning?"

"Sounds fine."

11

꧁✕꧂

The ogre had carried Prue from the kitchen, up the steps, clear across the nighttime, earthworm-smelling garden, through the wide-open carriageway gate, and out to the street. Prue heard clopping hooves, the creaks of harness and wheels. He pitched her like dirty laundry onto a carriage seat and slammed her inside.

The carriage rolled away with her shut up inside it. Prue fumbled in the blackness for the door handle. One of her fingernails ripped.

"Do not be afraid, little one," someone said just by her ear. "We will not harm you. Not *you*, of all people, darling girl, no, no, no."

Stale breath, that of an ancient person rotting on the inside first. Prue wedged herself in the seat corner.

"We turned down the lamps because we did not wish to attract any attention from the house. We only wished for *you*, you see."

"It ain't me you want," Prue said. "I told that to your—your footman feller. The cheek of him, too, *hauling* me like so!"

"We instructed Hume to convey you to us using whatever

means necessary. You mustn't be angry with him. He is a most faithful servant. Hume, the lamp."

He was in here? Sweet sister Sally.

A lamp sizzled up and Prue blinked. When she could see right, she took in silken black on the ceiling, black velvet curtains, black leather seats.

Across from Prue sat an old fogey. He must've been skinny as a rake, because for all the world it looked like he was an empty frock coat draped across the seat with a shriveled monkey face under a top hat.

The ogre—Hume—sat beside the fogey. His huge knees in the scarlet britches were close to his chin.

Prue slid her eyes sideways. Next to her sat a lady as shrunken as the gent, but with a bit more life in her face. She wore a glossy black fur and an old-time black bonnet. Her dark eyes shone. "I am Lady Cruthlach," she said, "and this is Lord Cruthlach."

"Pleased ever so." Prue licked her lips. "Where're you taking me?"

"Oh, we are only going for a little journey about the block, my lovely. No need to fuss. We merely wished to *see* you. You are indeed quite as lovely as Hume reported." Lady Cruthlach took a lock of Prue's loose hair between a gloved thumb and forefinger and held it up to the light. Greasy and tangled though Prue's hair was, Lady Cruthlach cooed. "Like ripe flax! Such a *folkloric* color, I have always thought. One rarely sees flaxen hair anymore. Girls these days seem faded, somehow. Is it all the photography, do you think, drawing the life out of them? Because girls *will* endlessly sit for their photographic portraits, will they not, despite what everyone knows about energy fields and camera lenses."

Prue had never heard of *that* one. Not that she was up to snuff on scientific notions.

"Just look at her gown," Lady Cruthlach said to the fogey. "Practically in tatters."

The fogey made a rustling-tissue sound with his throat.

Lady Cruthlach fingered Prue's sleeve. "Oh my, is this"— she drew a shuddery breath—"are these *cinders*, girl?"

"Could be," Prue said, tugging her arm away. She folded her arms.

"The music box," the fogey wheezed. Then he coughed into a hankie held by Hume.

Lady Cruthlach clapped her hands. "Yes! The music box! You are correct, dear Athdar. Oh, I *had* so hoped you might be able to see her. Shall we bring the music box to the sitting room when we return home? We have not enjoyed it for many months."

"Listen here," Prue said. "It's come pretty clear that there's a mix-up happening. I reckon, see, you got me mixed up with my sister."

Silent staring. The carriage bumped along.

"My dead sister," Prue said. "I suppose you saw it in the newspapers? She was near a mirror image of me—as far as I could tell. But she's dead, see, and I'm—well, like I said, I'm just nobody."

"Nobody!" Lady Cruthlach tittered. "How delightful!"

Prue eyed the door handle. Looked like it would lever open nice and easy. Only problem was, Hume was eyeing *her*. He would grab her before she could say, "Bob's your uncle."

"I suppose you haven't received an invitation to the prince's ball, have you?"

"Me? A prince? No prince ever heard of *me*, I'm sure."

"Tell me," Lady Cruthlach said, "does your mother look just like—like *this*, too?" Her eyes took to ant-crawling all over Prue again.

"Ma? Naw, Ma don't look like me and—and my sister at all. Ma's got chestnut hair, and—"

All the interest drained from Lady Cruthlach's eyes.

But Prue *was* interested in Ma, so she went on yapping anyway, because it had been a while since she'd been able to talk of Ma's disappearance, what with Ophelia off on her sleuthings all day. "I'm practically an orphan, now."

"There, there." Lady Cruthlach stroked Prue's arm. This time, Prue let her. The gesture held a tiny germ of comfort. "An orphan, you say? Lord Cruthlach and I know about orphans, all about indeed. Our own young ward, Dalziel, was an orphan, too, until we took him into our household and raised him as our own. But poor, poor Dalziel will once more become an orphan. We are dying, you see. Lord Cruthlach has slipped farther beneath the waves than I, but I shall follow him shortly to the grave."

"Are you ill, ma'am?"

"These modern doctors tell us that so many generations of cousins marrying cousins has weakened the Cruthlach blood. Weakened! There is no value, anymore, placed upon purity, is there? Our blood, girl, is as pure as the driven snow. Its very purity leaves us vulnerable to the assails of this rude, modern world."

"Awful sorry you're ill, ma'am. Might I get out of the carriage, now?"

"No!" Lady Cruthlach twisted Prue's sleeve so tightly it pinched. Prue cried out. "Not until I make you understand that *Dalziel will become an orphan* if you do not help us."

"Help you with what?"

Lady Cruthlach let go of Prue's sleeve.

Prue rubbed her pinched arm.

Lady Cruthlach rummaged for something in her bodice, under heavy furs. She drew out a locket, chained about her neck with fine-wrought gold. She snapped the locket open and pressed it towards Prue.

The locket held a miniature painting of a beautiful young man. Dark hair, dark eyes, grave expression, a dusky tint to his complexion.

"That is Dalziel." Lady Cruthlach snapped the locket shut. "The young gentleman who will become, like you, an orphan, cast out into the nightmare dark of the world, shivering, alone. Unless you help us."

"Dalziel looks nice," Prue said. "Sure wouldn't want him to be cast out into the nightmare dark of the world and what you say. But it ain't clear to me how I can help, ma'am."

Lady Cruthlach signaled to Hume. Hume thumped the ceiling. The carriage stopped. Hume reached over the fogey, jerked open the carriage door, and gave Prue a shove.

Prue screamed. She tumbled out and splashed on all fours

into a cold puddle. She looked up. The carriage was rolling away into the night and—she looked around—she was in front of Hôtel Malbert.

Only when Prue was drifting to sleep in her bedchamber, arms around the fat ginger cat, did it hit her: those old folks, and Hume, too, had never asked what her name was.

For some reason, her name was of no consequence.

Ophelia crawled back into Hôtel Malbert through the cellar window, which she'd left ajar. She groped through the darkness to the door between the cellar rooms and the kitchen. She peeked through. Empty. She tiptoed in. A fading fire glowed and mice swarmed on top of the table, nibbling the remains of a tart. Dirty china filled the sink. A stone pestle lay on the floor. Ophelia picked it up and set it on the table. A mouse with quivering whiskers looked at her.

Ugh.

Well, she wasn't hungry, anyway. For some reason, her belly had been in knots ever since the professor had told her about Miss Ivy Banks, of the ladylike, retiring nature and impeccable penmanship. Well. Ophelia refused to be envious of any lady, and indeed, perhaps the existence of Miss Banks could be considered a relief.

Yes, that's what it was.

Ophelia lit a taper and stealthily searched the pantry until she found a tin of bicarbonate of soda. She mixed a spoonful into a glass of water, drank it down, washed the glass in the sink, and crept upstairs the back way.

But the soda and water did nothing. It seemed the pain wasn't in her stomach, after all. It clung higher up, around her heart.

She looked into Prue's chamber and saw her asleep with the ginger cat.

In her own chamber, Ophelia shucked off Henrietta's clothing and wrested her crushed toes from the slippers. She washed at the basin and then pulled her theatrical case from its place in the bottom of the wardrobe. Her skin was still chapped from the Mrs. Brand cosmetics. She needed her calendula flower salve.

She opened the case. Something was different. The light wasn't good—she had only the one taper—but . . . the crumbly sticks of greasepaint, in their paper wrappers, were not in their customary order. Yes, one stick, a carnation pink for lips and cheeks, was missing.

Someone in the house knew she was an actress.

Gabriel did not usually take port before bed. More often than not, he fell asleep over his reading or writing. Yet tonight he ordered a bottle of aged Colheita to be brought to his suite.

The combination of a guilty conscience and acute excitement would require at least two full glasses of port to still them.

The guilt was a simple matter. He had lied to Miss Flax. It was for her own good, though, and he'd not seen any pain in her eyes at the news of his understanding—well, his understanding *of sorts*—with Miss Ivy Banks. He had been foolish to suppose Miss Flax had any interest in his attachments.

The excitement was an altogether separate affair.

Cinderella's stomacher. Gabriel had never seen it illustrated. Who would bother to illustrate what was believed to be a detail from a wicked stepsister's gown? Still, he could quite easily envision it. Although delicate, it would possess an unnatural weight, and the glints from those diamonds would pierce the eye. It would be intricate, too, with a pattern that seduced one into deeper and deeper labyrinths of luster.

Gabriel took a deep swallow of port. The stomacher must be the relic Lady Cruthlach had spoken of. It had even been made, perhaps, by the mysterious woman called Fairy Godmother. But the stomacher was not hidden somewhere in the Malbert mansion, as Lady Cruthlach believed. No, it had vanished off Sybille Pinet's corpse in the foul hands of a murderer. And he, Gabriel, would find it.

12

"Good morning, Professor Penrose," Miss Flax said, settling into the carriage seat.

"Good morning, Miss Flax. The rain has stopped, for now at least."

The carriage moved forward. The solicitor's office would be the first stop.

"Oh, indeed. Nice to have a break in the rain."

There. Gabriel adjusted his spectacles. This was better. Polite. Formal. None of that bickering and bantering. He'd been right to mention Miss Ivy Banks last night because now, for perhaps the first time since Gabriel had met Miss Flax, he was able to enjoy a placid conscience. No more fretting about their discordant stations in life. He could even observe her, this morning attired in her own plain cloak and bonnet, her cheeks smooth and rosy, without even the *faintest* stirring of desire. Yes. Miss Ivy Banks was the solution to the problem.

The Avenue des Champs-Élysées was broad, with rows of bare chestnut trees and buildings of pale stone and fanciful wrought iron. In the third-story reception room of Monsieur T. S. Cherrien (*Avocat*), a toad of a secretary manned a mahogany desk. "Might I be of assistance?" he asked in French.

Gabriel introduced himself as Lord Harrington and said that he wished to speak with Monsieur Cherrien.

The secretary looked at Miss Flax in her simple attire. He twitched a faint, knowing smile. "A settlement, perhaps?" he said in English.

Miss Flax sucked in an affronted gasp.

"No," Gabriel said coldly. "I—*we*—wish to speak with Monsieur Cherrien regarding the disappearance of the Marquise de la Roque-Fabliau."

"We believe she is one of Monsieur Cherrien's clients," Miss Flax said.

"We never discuss our clients, *monsieur et mademoiselle*. And I regret to say that Monsieur Cherrien is at present occupied, and I expect that he will be occupied for many, many, *many* hours. Please do make an appointment." The secretary spread open an appointment book and flicked through several pages—mostly empty pages. "Ah. He does have an available time on the fifteenth of January."

"January," Gabriel said. "This is November."

The secretary looked up. "Do you wish for the appointment, or no?"

Miss Flax leaned over the desk and, cheeks flaming, said, "I have a mind to go straight into Monsieur Cherrien's office this minute."

"You will be sadly disappointed. He keeps the door locked. Shall I summon the police?"

"Good morning, *monsieur*." Gabriel led Miss Flax out of the office.

"Stonewalled," Miss Flax said, as they went down the stairs.

"We'll go to see Madame Fayette, the *couturière*, next, but it occurs to me that you ought to have a cozy chat with Malbert later. Perhaps he'll divulge something about Henrietta wishing to divorce him."

"Malbert is about as liable to divulge secrets as a suet pudding. But I reckon it's worth an attempt."

* * *

Maison Fayette was a mile or two away, in a fancy shopping street called Rue de la Paix. Marble pillars flanked its carved door, and sparkling windows on either side displayed nothing but mauve velvet draperies.

"A waiter at my hotel told me fantastical tales of Madame Fayette," Penrose said. He pressed the doorbell. "Evidently she is a sorceress with needle and thread, and he said that ladies swear she works magic on their figures."

"Magic? No doubt she's got her hands on some extra strong corset laces, then."

The door opened and a maid led them inside. Penrose gave the maid his card and she scurried away, leaving them in a waiting room decorated with mirrors and urns of roses.

Ophelia caught sight of herself in one of the mirrors. She'd done her best to sponge her traveling gown and cloak, but she still looked as shabby as a church mouse next to the professor. Oh, well. Nothing to be done about it except stand up tall. No need to ponder how well Miss Ivy Banks probably looked next to him.

"When you speak to Madame Fayette alone," Penrose said, "ask her if she made the gown and the matching ballet costume. When it comes to the stomacher, be as subtle as you are able."

"Why am I to speak to her alone?"

Penrose didn't answer.

"Welcome, Lord Harrington!" A tiny, chubby woman floated towards them, arms outstretched. "I am Madame Fayette." Her voice was fluting and French-accented. She was between grass and hay—sixty years old, maybe—clothed in an expertly darted black silk gown. Her silver hair was swept up beneath a Spanish lace cap, and a diamond bracelet shimmered at her wrist. "I made your cousin Eliza's wedding gown last year. To what do I owe the honor of your visit?"

"My American cousin, Miss Stonewall"—Penrose drew Ophelia forward—"is in need of a few gowns. She lost her trunks somewhere between Cleveland and Paris, I'm afraid, and has been forced to borrow her maidservant's attire. Do you suppose you might have a visiting gown and—what do you ladies call your coats these days?"

"A paletot?" Madame Fayette said.

"Yes, a paletot, made up for Miss Stonewall by tomorrow, and a ball gown and another gown in the next few days?"

"*Tomorrow?* Oh dear. I do have sixteen seamstresses, *oui*, but we are quite busy, Lord Harrington. *Quite*. Prince Rupprecht's ball is in but three days' time, so—"

"I would compensate you for the rush. Miss Stonewall is rather desperate."

"Oh, very well. I may have a few half-made gowns that could be altered. Please, do sit, Lord Harrington, and the maid will bring you tea. Come along, Miss Stonewall."

The walls of Madame Fayette's inner sanctum were hung with mauve and cream stripes and edged with plasterwork like thick, white cake icing. Three plum-colored velvet dressmaker's stools stood in front of three huge, gilt-framed mirrors. Flowery chandeliers burned with gas bulbs. The room was unoccupied.

"Please." Madame Fayette gestured to a folding screen in the corner. "I shall go and fetch Josie. We have just enough time before my first appointment, if we hurry."

Ophelia stripped down to her unmentionables behind the screen. Her chemise and petticoats were gray-tinted from age and hand-laundering, and her corset had never been quality.

Madame Fayette reappeared with a delicate, blond-haired young lady.

Ophelia recognized her as Josie, the seamstress who had been hemming Eglantine's ball gown yesterday. The one who had spilled her pins. Ophelia had been disguised as Mrs. Brand then, so Josie wouldn't recognize her. Knock on wood.

"Josie," Madame Fayette said. "Your notebook." Madame Fayette addressed Ophelia. "Mademoiselle Baigneur is my chief assistant and most skilled seamstress. She speaks English, too, which helps—so many of my customers come not only from England, but New York, Boston, and Philadelphia as of late. But you are my first"—her brows lifted—"from Cleveland."

"Fancy that."

Madame Fayette took Ophelia's measurements every which way and murmured numbers in French. She moved quickly, and her bracelet slid up and down her arm. The bracelet was hefty, with a braided design crusted all around with diamonds. And for some reason, it looked awfully familiar to Ophelia.

Josie scribbled away in a notebook.

"For the visiting gown," Madame Fayette said to Josie, "the forest green crepe we were working on for that Italian princess who ran off with the painter—I do not suppose *she* will return. With three rows of black velvet ribbon along the hem—*oui*? The matching paletot to wear over. Black velvet. With a hood, for this dreadful weather, and a small, flat hat of the green crepe to tie under your pretty chin. *Très jolie.* And the ball gown, ah, *oui*, the ball gown of eggshell blue that was meant for that courtesan with the smelly little dog. She is a gambler. I would likely never be paid anyway. Oh! But I beg your pardon, Mademoiselle Stonewall. I should not speak of such things in front of a young lady."

Did she say *lady* with an ironic lilt?

"I told my cousin, Lord Harrington, that I must come to your shop," Ophelia said. "I have seen such lovely gowns that you've made. Even, I'm sorry to say, on a dead girl."

Madame Fayette glanced up. "Dead?"

"Surely you've heard—it's been in the newspapers. It was—it was simply *horrid*."

Madame Fayette continued to measure. "Ah, *oui*. The girl in Le Marais. You were a . . . witness?"

Josie's eyes were on her notebook, but she seemed to be all ears.

"Yes. At a party given by the Misses Malbert. There was a lot of screaming and a lot of . . . blood."

"You wore your maid's gown to this party, I presume?" Madame Fayette said.

"Yes. Of course." Drat. "Well, the dead girl's gown—ivory

silk and tulle, with silver and gold embroidery—the funny thing is, it looked exactly like the prima ballerina's costume that you made for the Cinderella ballet I saw last night."

"How do you know I made that costume?" Madame Fayette stopped measuring. "My name does not appear in the programme."

"I saw a label—Maison Fayette, it said—stitched into the costume, when I went backstage to congratulate the ballerina." A true lady wouldn't venture backstage. Hopefully Madame Fayette would chalk it up to Miss Stonewall's American rearing. "Why does a ballet costume need a label?"

Madame Fayette narrowed her eyes. "We are all very proud of the work we do at Maison Fayette."

"Did you not tell the police you made the dead girl's gown? It could be a clue."

"What makes you believe I did not tell them?"

"Because if you had, they'd know more about her. Her name, for instance."

"I assure you, I know nothing of the murdered girl."

Was she fibbing? Hard to say. Just because someone had the chubby cheeks of a two-year-old didn't mean they had the conscience to match. "But how is that possible? Surely she came in for fittings, just like I'm doing now."

"I maintain the utmost discretion when it comes to my customers."

Discretion? Hardly, if Madame Fayette's comments about the Italian princess and the gambling courtesan were any indication. "Then I don't suppose you'll tell me if the Marquise de la Roque-Fabliau is one of your customers," Ophelia said. "She's missing, you know."

"If my customers request that I keep a secret, why, then I keep a secret," Madame Fayette said. "Surely, *Miss Stonewall*, you must appreciate this. One does not sew garments for empresses if one is a—how do you say?—blabbermouth." She looped her measuring tape around Ophelia's waist, and squeezed.

Ophelia winced.

"I would be fascinated to discover precisely why it is that you have taken on the duties of an officer of the police,"

Madame Fayette said. "Now, if you will excuse me, I must go fetch a few samples for you to view." She whipped her measuring tape free and hurried out.

Ophelia was left alone with Josie.

As soon as Madame Fayette disappeared, Josie whispered, "*Madame* does not ever admit to it, but she was, years ago, the costume mistress at *l'Opéra de Paris.*"

"Indeed?"

"I believed you should know this, because you seem so interested in those gowns. The way they were the same. *Madame* knows people at the opera house. Many people."

"She knew the murdered girl, then?"

"*Non.* She designed that gown based upon measurements given to her by a customer. She never measured or fitted the girl in person. None of us did."

"But who was the customer?"

"I know not." Josie pushed a wisp of hair from her eyes. "Is the murderer not . . . caught?"

"No. And I reckon the police are after the wrong murderer. I wonder if the marquis—the father of the Misses Malbert—is mixed up in this. Because his wife, his *missing* wife, perhaps desired a divorce, and he's so secretive about whatever he does in that funny workshop of his." Ophelia clammed up. Josie was so mild a presence, she had been thinking aloud. But she ought not be so trusting.

Ophelia studied Josie. She would've been pretty as a picture if she hadn't appeared so unwholesome. Her ears seemed too large for such a hollow face, and her lips were bloodless, as though she hadn't enough sleep or enough to eat. But surely Madame Fayette paid her employees a good wage. They were highly skilled workers.

"Would you tell me, Josie . . . the Marquise de la Roque-Fabliau—did she patronize this shop?"

"*Non.*" Josie lowered her voice still more. "The murderer is not caught? Then I must—I must tell you, Mademoiselle Stonewall. It is something so odd, but Madame Fayette, she will deliver a parcel to a gentleman today."

"To whom?"

"I know not. The note I saw from him, it was anonymous, but the penmanship was that of a gentleman. His note—*bonté divine!*—I saw it by mistake as I was bringing it to *Madame*—his note said it was urgent that he collect a *certain parcel* that *Madame* has in her possession. I fear he is the customer who ordered that poor dead girl's gown."

"He will come here, to the shop?"

"*Oui*, today, at twelve o'clock. But please, do not ask me anything more. Poor *Maman* in the country, she is almost blind from the sewing, and she depends upon the wages that I send. *Et* my dear brother, he is so mistreated by his master and must leave his place of work. If *Madame* knew I was speaking of our customers—"

The door swung open. Madame Fayette bustled in, arms piled high with garments. "Now, Miss Stonewall, should we decide upon the ball gown?"

Ophelia breathlessly recounted to Penrose all she'd learned, as soon as they were outside and walking along Rue de la Paix. More people were out now, mostly fashionable ladies in complicated hats. Shop windows brimmed with perfume bottles, feathered fans, jewelry, furs, and bolts of gorgeous cloth. The street may as well have been a stage set, it all seemed so dreamlike.

"Hold your horses." Ophelia stopped in front of a hatmaker's window and frowned up at Penrose. "Your eyes have got that *glow* about them again."

"I can't think what you mean." Penrose pushed his hands into his greatcoat pockets. "Oh, do look at that tilbury hat. I haven't seen one of those in years."

"You suspect it's the stomacher in the parcel, don't you?"

"Is that far-fetched? It was, according to you, at any rate, missing from Miss Pinet's gown when you discovered her in the garden. The murderer perhaps removed the stomacher. It would be rather valuable, both as an antiquity and as an assemblage of precious metal and gems. Now, this mysterious customer who ordered the gown—the gown that incorporated the *real* diamond stomacher—wants the stomacher back."

"But if Madame Fayette has the stomacher now, that means *she* shot Sybille."

"Not necessarily. But it would seem that she is deeply involved."

"Do you suppose Sybille was killed on account of the stomacher?"

"It is possible. As I said, it would be valuable in more than one respect."

"Surely no one but you, Professor, cares about the stomacher's fairy tale history."

"No? Then why was the stomacher sewn onto a gown that matches, specifically, a Cinderella costume? Like it or not, Miss Flax, the fairy tale *is* a part of this."

"Then Sybille knew a person, was *murdered* by a person, who is as nutty about fairy tales as you are."

"You are assuming the gown was sewn expressly for Miss Pinet. That Miss Pinet did not, as the police claim, simply steal the gown from its true owner."

"But Sybille doesn't sound like a thief, and she wasn't a strumpet."

"How can you be certain on either point?"

Ophelia sighed. She couldn't be certain. She only *hoped* that Sybille wasn't a strumpet or a thief but the truth was, Sybille had likely been wearing the stomacher for some reason. "What I wish to know is, why didn't Madame Fayette go to the police with the name of this customer?"

"She's either covering up for someone else, or for herself," Penrose said. "Shall we have a walk about the Louvre? It is nearby and dry inside, and at twelve o'clock we could return to spy on Maison Fayette and discover the identity of the gentleman customer."

13

∼✦∽

The ogre Hume showed up while Prue was working on the breakfast dishes. He burst into the kitchen, hauled her out, flipped her into a waiting carriage, and fastened the door from the outside.

After fifteen, maybe twenty minutes, the carriage stopped in front of a house with witch-hat towers and mean little slits for windows.

Hume dragged Prue inside, up some stairs, and into a stuffy, dim, parlor sort of room that stank of woodsmoke, cough medicine, and ancient folks' morning breath.

"Ah, the beautiful little orphan who nobody wants." Lady Cruthlach was all bundled up on a sofa. "Dear Lord Cruthlach is abed, I am afraid. Such a pity, for he did so enjoy seeing you last night."

Hume shoved Prue down onto a chair. He retreated to a post against a wall.

"My name's Prue. Prudence Bright. And somebody does so want me."

"Oh, but your mother shan't ever return."

Why did Lady Cruthlach sound so certain? "She *will*,"

Prue said. Tears prickled. "But anyway, I ain't talking about Ma. I'm talking about my—my friend. Hansel. He's to be a doctor, and maybe we'll marry someday."

"You? Marry a doctor? Oh, good gracious, no!"

"It ain't so tough to think of! I'm learning housewifing, and—"

"No, no, my dear, the fates have other things in store for you. Tell me. This *Hansel* person—is he in Paris?"

"Well, no. He's in Heidelberg. Studying, like I said."

"Then he abandoned you, too. Just like everyone else has."

Prue's throat swelled. "He's waiting for me. He—he writes me letters. Or, leastways, he used to." She had sent along her mother's address to Hansel, but she'd yet to receive a letter from him in Paris.

"Now, you see? He has already forgotten you. My advice to you, my lovely, is to forget Hansel. He is nothing. You, however, *you* are something quite, quite extraordinary. Now. I wished to ask of you a favor. Not especially for my sake, you must remember, or Lord Cruthlach's, but for Dalziel. You liked Dalziel's picture in my locket, yes? You would not make him an orphan?"

Something thawed inside Prue. "No, ma'am."

"Good. Sweet?" Lady Cruthlach held out a dish heaped with orangey-red candies with white dots.

Uck. Looked like poisonous mushrooms. "No, thank you," Prue said.

"Come, now." Lady Cruthlach shoved the dish closer. "I shan't take no for an answer."

Prue took one.

"Go on, then. Try it."

Prue's stomach turned, but she bit. Marzipan. Only marzipan, though sickly sweet and with a hint of dust.

"Now, then." Lady Cruthlach replaced the dish on a side table next to a music box with a golden crank. "I need you to bring me—bring *us*—something from Hôtel Malbert."

Prue stopped chewing. "Steal something for you, ma'am?"

"It wouldn't be *stealing*, heavens, no. The item does not rightfully belong to anybody in the house. It belongs to me, and to my husband. And we mean to have it. It is a book. A book of great age, written in Latin. It must be quite thick, for all the wondrous secrets it holds."

"Pardon me, ma'am, but there are hundreds, maybe thousands of books in the house. I saw a whole library chockablock with them."

"But *this* book will appear to be different. Special. Alluring, even, to all but the dullest mind. It will likely have pictures."

Prue swallowed dry marzipan.

"You've seen it!" Lady Cruthlach lurched forward.

"I—"

"Tell me! *Tell* me what it looked like!"

"Well, there's a sort of cookery book I found in a cupboard down in the kitchen, in some peculiar tongue—"

"Latin, you beautiful little dullard. *Latin.*"

"—and it's got all kinds of receipts and household hints and whatnot."

"Bring it to me."

"Some of them soups and stews in there don't look too appetizing, if you don't mind me saying."

"Not *soup*, you nincompoop . . ." Lady Cruthlach's words dribbled off, because someone had opened the door.

"I beg your pardon," a youthful, British-accented voice said. "I did not know, Grandmother, that you were entertaining a visitor."

"No, no, Dalziel, please! Please come forward, into the light. Come, closer—that's it!—closer, meet our charming young visitor."

Dalziel strode closer and stood with his back to the fire.

A quick, bright energy bounced off of Dalziel, and his expression, though grave, had a sweetness to it. He was about twenty years old, dressed in a subdued, tailored black wool suit, a white linen shirt, and a gray silk waistcoat and cravat.

He glanced at Prue. Then his eyes flew to Lady Cruthlach. "But she is—Grandmother, what have you *done*?"

"It is a sister, Dalziel. Only a sister."

It? That was the first time Prue had been called *it*, and she'd been called lots of not-nice things.

"She knows of the book, Dalziel—she works as a scullery maid in the house."

"House?"

"We found the *house*."

"I beg your pardon, miss," Dalziel said to Prue. "What is your name?"

"Prue. Prudence."

"Forgive me, Miss Prudence. I was taken by surprise. You do so resemble your sister—her morgue picture so tastelessly published in the newspapers—that I quite forgot my manners. You are a young lady in mourning, too, so—well, do you forgive me?"

Prue gazed into Dalziel's melting-dark eyes. "Sure," she whispered. "Sure I forgive you. That's the first anyone has said a peep about me being in mourning. I don't even know where Sybille's buried or *nothing*." If such a nice young man was the kin of Lord and Lady Cruthlach, maybe they weren't as monstrous as she had supposed.

Lady Cruthlach made an impatient little bleat.

"Sybille was her name?" Dalziel said.

"Yes." Prue brushed away a tear. She turned to Lady Cruthlach. "I will bring it to you. The book, I mean. But only if, after that, you leave me be."

"Yes, yes," Lady Cruthlach said. "Leave you be."

"Because I won't be kidnapped again!" Prue found herself on her feet, fists balled. "Do you *promise* you'll leave me be?"

"I am a lady, dear girl. No need to exact promises. Sit down."

Prue stayed on her feet. Standing made her feel like she had at least a little control over things. "Hume will take me back?"

"Of course."

"Will you tell him not to throw me in the gutter this time?"

"Grandmother!" Dalziel cried.

"If you insist," Lady Cruthlach said to Prue. She waved a knobby hand. "Take her back, Hume. And wait in the carriage until she emerges again with the book."

"Grandmother," Dalziel said, "I really must insist that—"

"Quiet, child."

"I reckon it might take some doing," Prue said to Lady Cruthlach. "Beatrice will be back and she'll set me to my chores, and it might not be so easy to—"

"Hume is patient," Lady Cruthlach said. "Hume will wait as long as necessary."

At noon, Gabriel and Miss Flax sat silently in a hired carriage parked across the street from Maison Fayette. Raindrops smacked on the roof. Traffic splashed by. Miss Flax watched the shop in silence with her folded umbrella across her lap. Gabriel watched Miss Flax.

The Louvre had been a bit of a debacle, because Gabriel had not sufficiently considered in advance the quantities of nude Classical statues on the premises. After her initial surprise, Miss Flax had kept her gaze strictly on the "Museums" chapter of her Baedeker whenever Gabriel was near. Although he *had* noted her, from afar, viewing *Psyche Revived by Cupid's Kiss* with interest and a somewhat high color in her cheeks.

Miss Ivy Banks, although well-versed in ancient Greek texts, was a staunch advocate for fig leaves on statuary.

"Look!" Miss Flax whispered. "Someone's at Maison Fayette's door! He's ringing the bell. Is that—? Why, that's the dancing master from the opera house."

"So it is," Gabriel said. "Caleb Grant."

"If he killed Sybille, well, that explains why he told the entire opera house to keep mum about her identity. He wasn't covering things up to save the opera house's reputation. He was covering up to save his own skin."

"This is merely a theory, you do realize."

Miss Flax rolled her eyes.

The shop door opened. They caught a glimpse of the maid, and then Grant disappeared inside. In less than a minute he was back out on the sidewalk, opening his umbrella. A small, brown paper-wrapped parcel was tucked under his arm.

"He's got something," Miss Flax said. "If it's the stomacher then, well, he's the one who ordered the gown to be made from measurements. *That* would be something to tell Inspector Foucher."

Gabriel bounded out of the carriage, instructed the driver to follow Grant, and leapt back in. They were off. But only one block later, Grant got in line to board an omnibus.

"Dash it," Gabriel said. "Come on." He helped Miss Flax out, paid the driver, and they climbed onto the packed omnibus just before it reeled forward.

"There he is," Miss Flax whispered. "He's going upstairs." A curved flight of steps at the back of the omnibus led to the open-air level.

"Good, then. He won't see us, and we will be able to see him exit if we keep watching the stair."

The omnibus traveled a few blocks, made a turn, and then lurched and stopped all the way down the Rue de Rivoli until they had almost arrived in Le Marais. But it turned again and passed over the Seine and alongside Notre Dame, and then they were in the Latin Quarter.

At the Rue Saint-Séverin stop, Grant hurried down the omnibus stairs and into the street. Gabriel and Miss Flax followed.

The streets here were narrow and the old, mismatched buildings somehow suggested a child's toy blocks. Cramped shops displayed dingy wares, and cafes emanated cigarette fumes and bitter coffee. Presently, Grant pushed through a pair of chipped blue doors.

Miss Flax stopped. Rain dripped from her bonnet brim onto her nose. Gabriel ignored the urge to wipe the drop gently away.

"If this is where Mr. Grant lives," Miss Flax said, "why, we might be waiting here all day for him to come back outside."

"Perhaps we might learn the number of his apartment. That would be a start."

"A start to what? You don't mean you would house-break?"

"I prefer to call it reconnaissance. And I seem to recall

that you, Miss Flax, are not entirely ill-disposed towards the practice yourself."

The doors weren't locked, and they went into a dark little vestibule that smelled of mildew and garlic. An iron railing marked the foot of a staircase.

A squat lady, hands on her hips and her back to them, was bickering with a man. She was doubtless the concierge. Parisian concierges were like dragons guarding the mouths of caves, only instead of breathing fire, they breathed gossip. Luckily, the concierge was too consumed by her tirade, and the man was too frightened of the concierge, for either to notice Gabriel and Miss Flax.

"What's she going on about?" Miss Flax whispered.

"Something about burst pipes."

Gabriel was prepared to wait and then simply ask the concierge where Caleb Grant's apartment was located. But Miss Flax disappeared through a doorway on the other side of the vestibule and returned a few moments later. She tugged his sleeve, saying, "I've got a notion."

"Not another one."

"Don't be such a curmudgeon."

Gabriel hid his smile and followed Miss Flax through the door. A dank flight of stairs led to a cellar cluttered with mops, buckets, and rags, lit only by one high window. Cobwebs swagged the corners. Water pooled across the floor.

"What are we doing down here?" Gabriel asked. "Not everything need be so very theatrical, you realize."

"I'm not being theatrical. We cannot very well rap upon Mr. Grant's door and announce that we've followed him all the way across the city, that we suspect him of murder, and that he'd better hand over his parcel."

"I had conceived a somewhat subtler plan, but I do see your point."

Miss Flax pulled some sort of filthy garment from a peg on the wall.

"You don't mean to disguise yourself," Gabriel said.

"No. I don't need a disguise, because Mr. Grant only saw me dressed as Mrs. Brand. I mean to disguise *you*."

* * *

Two minutes later, Gabriel's Savile Row suit was covered by a damp, gray workman's smock that smelled of either underarms or overripe Gruyère, and baggy drawstring trousers. He had changed from his own gleaming shoes into muddy-soled boots, and stashed his kidskin gloves, felt hat, and greatcoat in an empty crate.

"Are you able to see without those goggles, Professor?"

"Goggles? Oh. I suppose so, but—"

"Good." Miss Flax removed Gabriel's spectacles and slid them into his smock pocket. "I don't fancy they go with the plumber's costume." She passed him a wooden toolbox. Then she reached up, mussed his hair, and smudged some grease from a pipe joint on his cheeks.

Gabriel attempted not to enjoy her efficient touch.

They went upstairs.

Miss Flax loitered in the background while Gabriel spoke to the concierge. He convinced her that Caleb Grant had sent for him to look at the pipes under his lavatory sink, and that Miss Flax was his assistant. The concierge didn't appear the least bit surprised about any of this—although Gabriel had never heard of a lady plumber's assistant—and led the way to the topmost floor.

When the concierge rapped on the door, there was no answer.

"Must have gone out," she said in French. "No matter. I have my keys right here. I shall just let you in. *Sacredieu*, I am sick to death of these pipes." She left.

Inside, a quick survey confirmed that indeed, no one was home.

"He must've gone out again while we were in the cellar," Gabriel said.

"Well, let's see if he took his parcel with him."

Grant's apartment was the shabbily elegant variety favored by artists and writers. Threadbare carpets of wild arabesque designs overlapped on stained parquet floors. Windows were draped in mismatched silks. The furniture ranged from

Oriental lacquered to Chippendale, littered with books, over-flowing ashtrays, primitive pottery, and half-empty wine goblets. There was no kitchen, only a copper teakettle hanging from a small marble fireplace. Watercolors of stage scenery designs filled one wall. Grant had probably gotten those from the opera house. A tiny lavatory lurked under the eaves.

"Ah," Gabriel said, setting the toolbox down. *"La vie de bohème."*

"What's that?"

"The artist's life."

"Oh. Not all it's cracked up to be."

"I'm rather enjoying my stint as an actor."

"Well, we'd better hurry up or it could be your last."

A tall, skinny Siamese cat slunk down from a shelf, yowling.

"Here kitty, kitty," Miss Flax said. The cat galloped to-wards her.

"Animals seem to like you," Gabriel said, scanning a jumbled bookshelf.

"I've always had a way with animals." She stroked the cat.

"So I've noticed." An image of the loutish Count de Griffe rose, unbidden, in Gabriel's mind. He moved to the mantel. Dust-coated miniatures, wax-caked candelabras, and a brass mail rack cluttered the ledge. "Here's the post."

Most of the envelopes were addressed to *M. Caleb Grant*, but a few were addressed to *Mme. Clara Babin*.

"A lady lives here?" Miss Flax said. "How very French."

Gabriel cleared his throat. Of course, now that Miss Flax knew about Gabriel's understanding (of sorts) with Miss Ivy Banks, speaking of these indelicate kinds of things did not bother him.

He flipped through the envelopes. Bills, bills, bills, invita-tions to lectures, soirées, art exhibitions. No passionate letters. No blackmail notes. He replaced the envelopes in the rack.

14

❦

Ophelia looked through curtains into an alcove. A lumpy, unmade bed sat under the sloped ceiling. Petticoats were flung over the bedframe. Books towered up on the nightstand and the air was headachey with patchouli.

A large oil painting filled one wall. It depicted a long-limbed woman lounging on a chaise. Her back was turned to the viewer and bare all the way down to her bottom, which was, blessedly, swathed in diaphanous green. Her profile displayed a pearl drop earring, upswept mahogany hair, flower-stem neck, striking black eyebrows, pointy nose.

"Professor," Ophelia called.

Penrose appeared. He followed her gaze and then coughed.

He had been doing an awful lot of coughing and throat-clearing today, starting at the Louvre.

"It is only that the French, Miss Flax, have rather different views on, ah, states of undress than those found in the Puritan regions of America and in—"

"Not *that*. Doesn't this painted lady look an awful lot like the lady Miss Austorga was speaking with backstage at the opera house last night?"

"I had but the briefest glimpse of her, but I suppose she might be the same."

"I'd wager it's the lady to whom those letters on the mantel are addressed." Ophelia preferred not to take a crack at pronouncing *Babin*, so she left it to the professor.

"Madame Clara Babin," he said.

Sounded like the noise a French sheep would make. "Right. Not many ladies would cotton to having such a great quantity of another lady's bare back dangling over their bed."

"I suppose not. This, then, connects Austorga to Caleb Grant, via this lady."

"How peculiar." Ophelia frowned. "Austorga is a deep one. Between the two sisters, she seems by far and away the more forthright one. The nicer one, too, if a bit of a, well, dingbat."

"There is always the possibility that she simply found herself lost backstage at the opera house."

"On an expedition to the powder room? I reckon that's possible, but it's a little too coincidental for my palate. If Mr. Grant killed Sybille, he would have needed help from someone inside Hôtel Malbert. Austorga was inside. *She* could have easily stolen the carriageway key to let Grant through to place the body. What if Austorga and Mr. Grant—and Madame Babin, too—were in cahoots?"

"We still cannot account for why Grant would have placed Miss Pinet's body in the Malberts' garden. And have you any theory as to why Miss Austorga would wish to do away with Miss Pinet?"

"Well, if Austorga knew Sybille was her stepsister, maybe she was, I don't know, envious?"

Penrose smiled. "Envious of her beautiful stepsister? Perhaps Prince Charming preferred her?"

"You don't have to put it like *that*."

"Don't I? I have another theory: if Austorga did indeed help to kill Miss Pinet—"

"Which, I allow, is hard to picture."

"—she did it for the stomacher."

"Why?"

"Because the stomacher—if it indeed exists—would be a precious family heirloom."

It made sense—just so long as you believed that flapdoodle about Cinderella being a real lady. Ophelia hated to believe that. It went against every particle of common sense she possessed.

"Would you ask the Mademoiselles Malbert if they know of the stomacher?" Penrose said.

"I'll add it to my list."

They searched the apartment high and low and they did not discover the brown paper parcel, although they found one more Siamese cat under the bed.

"All right then, we ought not tempt fate," Penrose said. "Should we go?" He held open the apartment's front door.

Ophelia made one last rummage through the pockets of a greatcoat that hung by the door. "Wait. What's this?" She pulled out a small, black-bound book. She flipped through it. Minute penciled handwriting filled ten or twelve pages. "Look. Lists of names."

"Gentlemen's names."

"Wait. No—not exactly. Look. For every gentleman's name there is at least one girl's name in the second column. See? *Duke of Strozzi*, and then, *Adele* and *Diana*."

"*Duke of Strozzi*. English. I assume this is Grant's book, then, and not Madame Babin's."

"The girls haven't got surnames. That's funny."

"I do not suppose it's really very humorous."

Ophelia glanced up. "You've got that sickly grimace on again. The one that says you're afraid of tarnishing my innocence and you might start coughing."

Penrose didn't answer. He'd taken the notebook. "I don't see Sybille listed anywhere." He scanned the rest of the pages, squinting because he didn't have his spectacles on. "Ah," he said. "Here is a gentleman I am acquainted with. Lord Dutherbrook."

"You know him?"

"Unfortunately, yes."

"He's matched up with someone by the name of Clotilde."

Penrose slid the book back into the greatcoat pocket. "I believe Lord Dutherbrook haunts the Jockey Club."

"Jockey? A shrimp, is he?"

"Quite the contrary. No. The Jockey Club is merely a gentleman's club that, among other things, has rather equine propensities."

"I've been thinking—what if Caleb Grant is Sybille's father?" Ophelia said, once Penrose had crept back down to the cellar to change and they'd gone back outside to the street. "He *is* an American."

"But she grew up in an orphanage. And didn't you say that Sybille's father was a French diplomat?" Penrose smeared grease off his cheeks with his handkerchief.

"Well, that's what Henrietta told Prue. But Henrietta isn't known for her sterling word. And if he's Sybille's father, then he'd know Henrietta, too—even though he said he didn't when I asked him yesterday. What if Henrietta looked him up when she arrived in Paris, and something went wrong?"

"I suspect that learning precisely what Grant was doing, matching gentlemen's names with girl's names in his notebook, will shed a good deal of light on the matter. I'll speak to Lord Dutherbrook. From what I recall, he rarely stirs from his chair in his club."

"Do you reckon he's there now?"

"Very likely. He's a bit like a beached whale. However, Miss Flax, the Jockey Club is no place for a lady."

"Oh, I don't mind. I'm not known for my retiring and ladylike nature." How had *that* slipped out?

"No, what I mean to say is, ladies are not allowed inside the club."

"Oh."

"I shall send a note along to you—to Madame Brand— and apprise you of anything that I learn at the club. Now— shall I hire a carriage to take you back to Hôtel Malbert?"

"No, thank you." Ophelia had already dug out the Baedeker from her reticule, and she popped open her umbrella. "I'll walk."

As soon as Ophelia had tumbled through Hôtel Malbert's cellar window, bent her umbrella back into shape, and dusted herself off, she went in search of Prue. Once again, she found Prue scrubbing away—this time at a dented copper pot—in the kitchen. Beatrice was nowhere to be seen, so Ophelia crept in.

"Still at your housewifing then?" Ophelia said.

Prue shrugged.

"Are you well, Prue? You look a little peaked. Should you take a rest?"

"Too much to do. Sleuthing with the professor again?"

"Yes."

"Learn anything?"

Ophelia told her about Madame Fayette and the stomacher, but Prue seemed distracted. "Prue, the kitchen work is not your responsibility. Where *does* Beatrice take herself off to, anyway?"

"Market, she says. Course, she smells like a saloon every time she comes back, and one time she clean forgot to even buy any food. Are you hungry? There's cold beef in the pantry, and a nice onion tart I helped make."

"Sounds lovely." Ophelia was ravenous; she hadn't had a bite to eat since breakfast. Although she and the professor had passed countless cafes and bakeries today, she hadn't suggested they stop to eat. *That* would have led to him paying for things.

Ophelia sat at the table and dug into the food Prue brought. The onion tart was surprisingly tasty, and only a little burnt. Prue even served her a cup of tea. Sitting here in the kitchen without the Mrs. Brand disguise was risky, but Ophelia was too hungry to care.

"Well, I do hope you'll come upstairs, come dinnertime,"

Ophelia said to Prue, once she'd washed her fork, plate, and teacup.

"Not in these dirty duds. My stepsisters would turn up their noses at me."

Ophelia tiptoed up to her chamber the back way. The first thing she did was write a note to Madame Fayette requesting that she cancel Lord Harrington's order for the gowns. Ophelia would rather have a tooth pulled than accept handouts. She remembered to sign the note *Miss Stonewall*, and sealed it in an addressed envelope. Then she hurried into her Mrs. Brand disguise. She meant to locate Malbert and have a cozy chat with him, as the professor had suggested. She just might be able to squeeze something from him about Henrietta and divorce.

Ophelia was just replacing her theatrical case in the wardrobe when a rap sounded on her door.

She shut the wardrobe. "Enter."

The stepsisters' maid, Lulu, cracked the door. "Mademoiselle Eglantine wishes to speak with you in the salon."

Ophelia looked hard at Lulu. Lulu was spotty, true, but had her cheeks always been so pink? So . . . *carnation* pink?

Yet Lulu gave no hint that she knew about Ophelia's theatrical case. Her face was guileless.

"Very well, Lulu. You may go."

Downstairs in the salon, Eglantine sat on a sofa, rubbing at her upper lip. When she saw Ophelia, she kept her fingertips on her lip. "Madame Brand, there you are. Lulu and Baldewyn have been searching the house up and down for you for *hours*."

"I must take frequent walks, my dear. My digestion is simply not what it used to be."

"Well, if you are free this afternoon, might I beg of you to act as chaperone for Mademoiselle Smythe, my sister, and me? We had so hoped to attend an exhibition, but Madame Smythe is abed with a sick headache."

An afternoon in the company of that particular trio could give anyone a sick headache. However, it would present an opportunity to quiz Austorga about her backstage chat with Madame Babin, and at least one of the sisters about the stomacher.

"Allow me to gather my bonnet and gloves, dear," Ophelia said. She'd send the note to Madame Fayette with an errand boy, and her cozy chat with Malbert would have to wait.

Just as Ophelia was going upstairs to fetch her bonnet and gloves, a rap sounded on the front door. Baldewyn sighed loudly and answered it. Ophelia saw Pierre, Monsieur Colifichet's apprentice, pass Baldewyn a large parcel wrapped in brown paper and twine.

Probably some sort of delivery for Malbert and his mysterious clockwork hobby.

"Good gracious, what has happened to your lip, my dear Miss Austorga?" Ophelia asked, once they were rattling along in the carriage towards the exhibition hall.

Austorga's fingers flew to her red, swollen upper lip. "Oh! Nothing at all."

Ophelia looked at Eglantine, beside her sister. Eglantine still covered her own lip. Seraphina, next to Ophelia, had an upper lip as calm and white as a daisy.

"Miss Smythe," Ophelia said in a stern voice. "Did you suggest to the Misses Malbert that they should apply hot beeswax to their lips?"

"I simply *cannot* have hair on my lip at the prince's ball," Austorga said.

"It is *swan's* down, dear," Ophelia said in soothing tones.

"Hair!" Austorga yelled.

"Oh, do shut up," Eglantine muttered.

Seraphina blinked behind her spectacles and stared out the carriage window.

Once the young ladies and Ophelia had gone off in the carriage, the coast was clear. Henri the coachman was driving the carriage, and Beatrice was out tippling.

Prue carried the housewifery book upstairs. Baldewyn the Lizard snored away, bolt upright, on a dining room chair. She went out the front door. Sure enough, Lord and Lady Cruthlach's carriage stood across the street. Two ebony horses shifted from foot to foot. She crossed the street and the carriage door swung open.

Hume put out a hand and snatched the book.

Fine by Prue.

She turned, but fingers hooked her collar and she was lifted up like a stray kitten and tossed into the carriage. The door slammed, and the carriage rumbled forward.

"This routine is getting a little worn out, mister." Prue righted herself on the seat.

No answer.

"You might do me the nicety of looking me in the eye next time you kidnap me."

Stony silence.

When Hume corralled Prue into that infernal parlor, Lady Cruthlach cried, "Do you have it?"

Hume did have the book, tucked under a meaty arm.

"Oh, yes, I see it, I see it! Bring it closer. Come! Hurry, hurry!"

Prue stayed by the door. "You promised to leave me alone!"

Lady Cruthlach ignored her. Hume placed the book on a low table before Lady Cruthlach. Lady Cruthlach dove to her knees and opened it.

How could the old dame's knees take it? Her joints must be as crackly as a boiled fowl's.

Lady Cruthlach pored over the pages, flipping and looking, flipping and looking. "Oh, 'tis the one! 'Tis the one indeed!" Her face went back and forth from gleeful to serious, like an actor practicing in a mirror. She let out a chirrup and pointed to a page. "This one, Hume. This one will make a fine start."

"Yes, Your Ladyship." Hume bowed, took up the open book, and carried it off.

Prue had been forgotten. She turned to sneak off, but then

thought better of it. She should make sure the Cruthlachs were going to leave her in peace, now that they had their moldy book. She cleared her throat. "Lady Cruthlach, I don't suppose it would be forward of me to make questionings into why exactly you've had your ogre kidnap me again."

"Oh, good heavens," Lady Cruthlach said. "I had quite forgotten about you—it is so thrilling to at last be in possession of that volume, you understand. Well, no, of course you do *not* understand. You are but a simple girl, born into the cinders, no? But all of that will change, and soon, too, as soon as Athdar and I have regained our strength. We have *just* enough time, I think."

No doubt about it: Lady Cruthlach was a little misty in the attic. "I'll just be going, then."

"No!"

"Sorry, but I really ought. I got work to do." Prue opened the door.

Hume hulked on the other side.

"Good boy, Hume," Lady Cruthlach said. "Take Cendrillon to the chamber Marguerite prepared."

Sendry-on? Who in tarnation was *that*?

Hume pinched Prue's wrists together at her back.

"I ain't Sendry-on!" Prue shouted over her shoulder. "I'm Prue! Prue Bright!"

"Lock her up, Hume," Lady Cruthlach said.

15

⁓

The International Exhibition had had Paris in a lather since April. Eglantine and Austorga told Ophelia all about it during the carriage ride. Seraphina kept aloof. Exhibits from dozens of nations displayed artworks, handicrafts, the latest scientific and industrial inventions, ancient relics, and even entire Japanese and Chinese houses. The center of everything was an enormous building that enclosed a pavilion and gardens.

Their carriage crunched to a stop on a packed drive. Henri handed them down one by one. Seraphina ignored Henri, but Eglantine and Austorga both treated him to a simper.

Henri's brown eyes twinkled. He did not seem to have noticed any rashy red upper lips.

In the packed exhibition hall, the echoing chatter was deafening. Some folks pushed and others, their faces buried in catalogues, tripped. The crowds around the daises were so thick that Ophelia couldn't really see the newfangled steam-powered mechanisms on display.

"Mademoiselle Smythe is mad for velocipedes, Madame Brand," Austorga said in Ophelia's ear. "Her father has given her two of them, but her mother won't allow her to ride them anywhere but in their back garden."

Ophelia stood on tiptoe to observe the steam velocipede. It did not have pedals to turn the wheels, as a usual velocipede had. Instead, it glistened with a large brass canister, pipes, and tubing.

"It looks dangerous," Ophelia said.

"Well, yes, but Papa always says that danger is the price one pays for scientific advancement."

"Does he, now?" Danger. Interesting. Were the clockwork inventions in Malbert's workshop dangerous? "Miss Austorga, I have been meaning to ask you—do you have a great interest in the ballet?"

"I do enjoy attending the ballet, yes. As well as the opera and the theater—I do so enjoy beauty and spectacle, as well as opera chocolates, and, well, the society." She blushed.

Gentlemen's society. "I see. And do you happen to know a great many persons who work at the ballet?"

Austorga glanced away. "Work there? Why, no."

"You have never been backstage at the opera house?"

"*Mais, non!* A lady would not go there. Why do you ask me such things, Madame Brand?"

"Oh, because the Boston Ladies' League for the Betterment of Fallen Angels wishes to extend their ministry to Paris—and it occurred to me that *you* might make a splendid president of—"

"My days are *ever* so full . . ."

Ophelia patted Austorga's arm. "Fine, dear, fine. Perhaps, also, you are too young for such a post."

They moved with a noisy clump of people to the next display. Austorga receded into the crowd, and Ophelia found herself next to Eglantine.

Eglantine studied her exhibition catalogue, dark eyebrows furrowed.

"When I was a girl, I did so love to read stories," Ophelia said in the rambling fashion people expected of matrons.

"Ah, indeed?" Eglantine didn't look up from her catalogue.

"Magical stories, mostly. You know—fables and romances and fairy tales. *Particularly* fairy tales." In fact, when Ophelia was little she'd enjoyed, more than anything else, the no-nonsense hints in the *Farmer's Almanac*.

Eglantine's gaze snapped up. "Fairy tales?"

"Oh, yes. At any rate, I meant to say that once, I cannot recall precisely when or where—perhaps in my uncle's library in Concord, because the old dear was *such* an avid collector of rare books—once, I read a different version of the 'Cinderella' tale. It was only *slightly* different, but I do recall that in that version, the tale provided the address of Cinderella's home."

Eglantine slitted her eyes.

"Yes, my dear," Ophelia said. "Fifteen Rue Garenne. *Your* house."

"What a fine memory you have."

"How true! I simply *cannot* be defeated at that charming game called 'I'm Going on a Picnic'—"

"We do not speak of this," Eglantine said, lowering her voice. "Our family has our privacy to think of, but yes, Cinderella dwelled in our house. I never heard of this knowledge printed in a version of the story, however. It is simply something we *know* in our family. I must confess, Madame Brand, that I find it not a little alarming that you know this family secret when you only *happened* to meet Prudence in Germany."

"Ah, yes, but as your own father, the marquis, told *me*, in life it is *la chance* that plays the greatest role. Oh, yes, I've just remembered the other difference in the tale." Ophelia watched Eglantine carefully as she said, "The diamond stomacher belonged, not to one of the stepsisters, but to Cinderella."

Something like panic shone in Eglantine's eyes.

"*Is* there a stomacher, Miss Eglantine? A real one?"

"It is forward of you, Madame Brand, *very* forward to quiz me in this manner!"

"Nosy Posy—that is what my sisters used to call me."

Eglantine looked like *she* wished to call her something

a sight more potent. "Very well. I shall satisfy your curiosity, Rosy Fosy—"

"Nosy Posy."

Eglantine sniffed. "There is a stomacher, a family heirloom, that has been passed down for almost two hundred years."

"Made for Cinderella."

"Perhaps. Or for one of her stepsisters—I myself suspect that if Cinderella did indeed wear it to the ball, she had *stolen* it from her stepsister."

"Goodness!"

"Yes. Cinderella was a conniving creature, or so my grandmother told me—and *she* heard it firsthand from her father, who heard it from *his* grandmother. Cinderella was her great aunt, you see."

"And . . . where is this stomacher now?"

Eglantine lifted her brows.

"Because, you see, I simply adore antiquities with these wonderful tales attached to them."

"It was always kept in the house until several years ago, when Papa decided it was best to keep the family jewels in a locked box at the bank."

"It is there?"

"Yes."

"Who might unlock this bank box?"

"Only Papa." Eglantine looked as though something was eating her.

"What is it, my dear?"

Eglantine tossed her head. "Nothing, only, well, I wished to wear the stomacher on my gown at Prince Rupprecht's ball. The stomacher . . . when you touch it, you see, and *wear* it, well, it makes one feel so beautiful and strong—"

Sounded like hocus-pocus to Ophelia.

"—but then Austorga said that *she* wished to wear it— she must always *ruin* things, she always has—and she caused us to bicker so fiercely that Papa said neither of us should have it."

"Your poor thing," Ophelia said, and *tsk*ed her tongue.

* * *

Gabriel had not thought it decent to explain to Miss Flax the precise nature of the Jockey Club de Paris. The club had been founded, thirty-odd years ago, as a "Society for the Encouragement of the Improvement of Horse Breeding in France." But like any gentlemen's club populated by aristocratic and wealthy men with too much time and money on their hands, the Jockey Club was less about racehorses and more about—so to speak—fillies. The club held permanent boxes at the opera house, and Gabriel had heard rumors of club members having special after-hours soirées with the most admired members of the *corps de ballet*.

The club was housed on the main floor of the magnificent Hôtel Scribe on Rue de Rabelais. The smoking room, every inch polished wood, gilt, crimson damask, or voluptuous marble nudes, was silent. Four or five men lounged here and there, cradling drinks, gazing blearily at newspapers, puffing at cigars, and pondering clouds of smoke. Two waiters flitted.

"Ah! Penrose old boy!" Anselm Pickford, Lord Dutherbrook said. "Told the concierge to send you right in! Said you were welcome in the good old club any day."

"Pickford." Gabriel dropped into a leather armchair. "How long has it been? Three years?"

Pickford grunted. "Lost count. After the scandal with that saucy little charwoman, I won't go back to England. An entire nation of Goody Two-shoes." Pickford was a corpulent fellow with a boyish face, straw-straight hair, and a prominent bald spot. He had evidently insisted that his tailor not take into account his inflating anatomy. Everywhere one looked, one saw straining threads and flesh bulging behind fine woolen cloth. He held a goblet of pink *glacée* in one hand and a silver spoon in the other.

"Never go back? What a pity," Gabriel said.

"Well? Still at the musty books and whatnot? No one, you realize, understands why you insist upon spending your days and nights swotting when you might lead a life of utter leisure."

"I'm afraid I wouldn't be any good at that. I must have work to do. As it happens, Pickford, I was very pleased to learn that you were residing in Paris and that you are a member of this club."

"Learned from who?"

"From, ah, who was it? That fellow from Eton, the one with the, ah, the nose and the—"

"Right ho. St. John, was it?"

"Quite right. St. John. Jolly chap."

A waiter appeared.

"Whiskey," Gabriel said to the waiter. He turned back to Pickford. "As I was saying, I was pleased to learn of your presence here, because I am looking into a small matter regarding a gentleman by the name of Caleb Grant."

Pickford's spoon hovered. Pink *glacée* plopped onto his lap.

"You have made Mr. Grant's acquaintance, then," Gabriel said. He fished out his handkerchief—still stained with the pipe grease Miss Flax had smeared on his cheeks—and passed it to Pickford.

"Yes, I know him, but Penrose, old boy, I never thought you were one to chase skirts." Pickford blotted his trousers. "Grant picks them out just so. Couldn't be better at it." He passed the handkerchief back.

"I understand that Grant is the head choreographer and dancing master at the opera ballet. But he—?"

"He's the dancing master, indeedy-o. Runs those little teases through their courses, makes them keep their figures. Never allows a plain one through his doors. You wish to enlist his services? Sample a little French fare?"

The waiter arrived with Gabriel's whiskey. Gabriel took a grateful swallow. He wasn't a prude, nor was this by any means the first time he had shared company with a gentleman of such habits. Yet since Gabriel had met with Miss Flax, the notion of theater girls making extra monies on the side made him feel at once guilty and, oddly, angry. Although precisely with whom he was angry—Miss Flax? Himself? Men who regarded such women as mere trinkets?—he did not know.

"Yes, I would very much like to enlist the services of this Grant fellow," Gabriel said. "Tell me, how does it work?"

"Simple, really. One of us—one of his clients—will make an introduction, usually at the ballet."

"In a box."

"Yes, of course. Heavens, I don't believe I have ever sat in one of those—those seats of the hoi polloi. Oh, good heavens, no. Although one *might* meet a more willing class of girl than one does when sitting with all those stuffy little society debs with nothing but matrimony on the brain. Yes, Penrose old chap, that is a fine notion that you've had."

"It was not—"

"I'll sit in the orchestra seats next time."

"Returning to Grant's services," Gabriel said.

"Ah, yes. Well. I'll just introduce you, and you'll explain to him the sort of girl you wish to meet."

"Sort?"

"This isn't the London marriage mart, old boy. Grant's got a big stable, with fresh ones coming and going all the time. You choose. Brunette or blond. Gazelle or ripe peach. Saucy or stupid. Put in your order—even have a look-see through your opera glasses—and he'll arrange the rest."

"For a small fee."

"His fee is not precisely *small*—but I happen to know that you, Penrose, need not worry yourself with such vulgar things as money. How I *do* detest vulgarity in any form." Pickford shoveled in more *glacée*.

"What if the girl of my choice is not willing?"

"They're all willing, old boy. Every woman in Paris has got her price."

"Should we meet tonight at the ballet, then?" Gabriel stood. "I shall be in Prince Rupprecht's box."

"Good, good. Prince Rupprecht I've not yet met, but I've heard he's a fine fellow. New to Paris, only six months or so here. Tired of the old homeland, they say, and he's come to savor a bit of culture, what? Yes. Perhaps you and I and our little treats might dine afterwards—if Grant is able to immediately procure what you are searching for."

"Capital." Gabriel made his escape.

Before he left, Gabriel stopped to speak with the club's doorman. He slid a banknote into the doorman's hand. "Would you tell me if the Marquis de la Roque-Fabliau is a member of this club?"

The doorman made one grave nod.

Ophelia, the stepsisters, and Seraphina continued to view the steam-powered marvels, along with droves of other folks. None of the three young ladies seemed terribly interested in the exhibit and Ophelia was just wondering why they had been so eager to come, when she saw her answer.

Prince Rupprecht. She should've known. He stood on the other side of a dais that displayed a steam-powered submersible ship. He wore a black greatcoat and a silk top hat, and so did the Count de Griffe next to him.

Before Ophelia could duck out of sight, Griffe saw her. His face lit up. But . . . surely he did not recognize her. They had met last night when she'd been in Henrietta's stuffed gown, and now she was frumped up as Mrs. Brand.

Griffe and Prince Rupprecht wove their way over through the mob.

"How did you know Prince Rupprecht would be here?" Ophelia asked Eglantine.

Eglantine's fingertips fluttered on her red upper lip. "I had not the slightest notion."

And Ophelia's name was Saint Nick.

Eglantine got to Prince Rupprecht first, but Austorga was just behind her. Seraphina lurked in the background, seemingly content to be left out of the whole thing.

Poor Eglantine and Austorga. Ophelia wasn't a coquette—that sort of trickery was for ladies of a less practical bent. But she *did* know that pushing and shoving your way into a fellow's notice wasn't the best way to conduct matrimonial business. Fellows were like cats: getting the cold shoulder only made them that much more keen.

Or, so Ophelia had thought. Because the peculiar thing

was, Prince Rupprecht seemed mighty taken with the step-sisters. Both of them.

"Ah, *mademoiselles*!" Prince Rupprecht boomed. "What an unexpected delight to find you here!" He spoke English, Ophelia figured, on account of Seraphina, although *she* was staring at the submersible steamship, not at the prince. "Mademoiselle Eglantine, your bonnet—how charming! And Austorga, yours, too. What are those—pheasant feathers? Delightful!"

The stepsisters tittered and preened.

"Such a shame that your delightful soirée last week was ruined in such a fashion," Prince Rupprecht said. "Your home is superb, one of the oldest of such houses in Paris, I am told. I would very much enjoy another visit."

"Indeed, Prince Rupprecht," Eglantine said, "and we would be most obliged if you *would* visit again."

"Most obliged," Austorga said, giggling.

Ophelia happened to see Eglantine stomp on her sister's foot.

"Soon, perhaps?" Prince Rupprecht's blue eyes glinted. They were only the tiniest bit bloodshot from last night's brandy.

"*Oui*," both stepsisters breathed in unison.

16

Ophelia reckoned it was odd that Prince Rupprecht took such an interest in the stepsisters. Eglantine and Austorga didn't appear to have much in the way of funds. Prince Rupprecht certainly didn't need their family name. And from what Ophelia had heard him say about the dancing girls at the ballet last night, Prince Rupprecht was a bird fancier. Yet he did not seem put off by their plain looks or their forward ways. *Or* by their rashy upper lips.

While Ophelia chewed this over, the crowd somehow jostled her forward to the red velvet rope that surrounded one of the daises. At last she could view one of the contraptions up close. She could not read the plaque, but it looked to be some sort of steam-powered digging machine, as big as a stagecoach, with wheels and cogs, a few sets of exposed gears, and a large shovel with sharp-looking teeth. The shovel was poised midair, and just as Ophelia was noting how the shovel was quaking from the vibrations of the throng, she felt a hard shove against her Mrs. Brand rump padding. She stumbled forward, over the top of the velvet rope. Just before she collapsed onto the dais, a strong hand caught her arm and pulled her upright.

The shovel hit the dais with a metallic clang.

The crowd gasped and a lady squealed.

"Ah, *c'est dangereux, madame*," a husky voice said in Ophelia's ear, "to stand so close to such a machine, *non*?"

"I beg your pardon," Ophelia said, looking up at the Count de Griffe. "I do not believe we have been introduced. And kindly remove your hand." Her heart pounded and the crowd seemed to swim. She could have sworn she'd been deliberately pushed. But by whom? Surely not Griffe.

"I beg your pardon a thousand and one times, *madame*." Griffe swooped her hand to his lips. "I am the Count de Griffe. You must be the young *mademoiselles'* chaperone, eh?"

"Yes. Quite." Ophelia ripped her hand from his grasp.

"*Et* you are *une Americaine*?" Griffe studied her face and her gray hair, just visible beneath the brim of her bonnet.

Ophelia fought the urge to hightail it. Had he recognized her—or, rather, had he recognized Miss Stonewall?

She made a mental note not to ever, ever juggle two disguises again. Better yet: once she'd straightened out all this Henrietta and Sybille business, no more disguises at all.

"I am American, yes," she said. "Mrs. Brand, of Boston Massachusetts. Although I grew up in Cleveland, Ohio, where many of my mother's family still reside."

"Ah! That is why you so much resemble *la belle* Mademoiselle Stonewall."

"My niece. Yes. She is also visiting Paris at present."

"Your niece! Ah! She is like a prairie wildflower, *oui*? So simple, so fresh. Forgive me for saying so, *madame*, but the ladies of your family are very handsome." Griffe gazed at Ophelia's crepey, greasepainted face with frank appreciation. "*All* of the ladies."

The rest of the visit to the exhibition passed without incident, although dodging the Count de Griffe's earnest, poetic speeches had been taxing. Evening was falling, drizzly and cold, when they dropped Seraphina at her home across the river. When Ophelia and the Misses Malbert arrived at the mansion, Baldewyn assisted them with their cloaks and bonnets, informed them that dinner would be ready shortly, and then passed Ophelia an envelope.

"Delivered for you, *madame*," he said in a disgusted tone.

The envelope was addressed to Madame Brand.

Ophelia tore it open in her chamber.

Interesting news. I shall look for you in the opera house lobby at ten minutes until eight.—G.P.

News!

Ophelia forgot all about how she was exhausted, hungry, and footsore. She even forgot to check on Prue—who was surely at her drudgery down in the kitchen. Ophelia burned the note in the grate and set out for Henrietta's chamber to borrow another evening gown.

This time, she had the sense to choose a gown made of gauzy green silk that could be pulled tighter across an uninspiring bust, and a green mantle. The matching slippers would be agonizingly snug.

She loaded the lot in her arms. As she passed by the dressing table, she stopped.

The book—*How to Address Your Betters*, by A Lady—was gone.

She frowned, and then hurried out. Probably Lulu had taken it. Lulu seemed to have secret aspirations that had nothing at all to do with being a maid.

Prue huddled on a numbingly cold stone floor in the dark.

It had been hours since Hume had dragged her along stone corridors, up stairs, around more corners than a granny's quilt, and locked her up in a dim chamber.

At first, Prue had been too flabbergasted to cry. Then she was furious with herself for letting this lot get the better of her for the third time. Then the sobs came, heavy and hard. Now she was just parched and bone tired. She didn't even have the gumption to inspect the chamber, only barely lit now that evening had fallen outside. She just lay there on the floor, waiting to see what Fate had up her dirty sleeve this time.

The door latch rattled.

Prue held her breath.

When the door opened, it wasn't Hume. Dalziel looked in, holding a candle.

Prue pushed herself up into a mermaid's pose (well, that's what Howard DeLuxe had called it when they'd put on *The Lusty Whalers of Nantucket*). "I don't know what you folks is planning for me," she said, "but I—I'll—"

"I shan't harm you, Miss Prudence." Dalziel stepped into the chamber and shut the door. "I am ashamed of them, and ashamed of myself for not having realized sooner how much Grandmother's mind has decayed. I have been busy with my studies, and I assumed that everything was as well as it could be—despite Grandfather's health, but that has been failing for many years now. Hume, of course, is little more than a trained bulldog, and he does Grandmother's bidding slavishly. . . ." He swept a loose hank of black hair from his eyes. "Forgive me. I ramble." He stepped closer.

Prue shrank back. "You look like a nice enough feller, Mr. Dalziel, but for all *I* know your whole family means to sup on me tonight."

"I shan't come a step closer. You are frightened. You do not understand." Dalziel knelt on the floor, a funny sight with him in his fine clothes. He placed the candleholder on the stone floor and nudged it between Prue and himself.

"All I know is that I got to leave this house," Prue said.

"I shall take you. But we must wait until later tonight. If you wish, we might visit your sister's grave, too."

"Her grave! How do you—"

"It troubled me when you said that you knew nothing of her burial place. I took the liberty of visiting the morgue today, on the Île de la Cité. That is where all the unidentified or unclaimed deceased are brought and where, I knew, the newspaper artist must have seen her laid out—forgive me for my bluntness. I discovered that Sybille's earthly remains, after the police agreed to her release, were taken away by nuns from the Pensionnat Sainte Estelle. That is a convent not far from here."

Prue nodded. "Nuns. Ophelia—that's my friend—told me that my sister had grown up in a nunnery."

"I called upon the convent. I was told that Sybille was buried in the Montparnasse Cemetery yesterday."

"I missed it." Prue's voice wobbled.

"I might take you there this evening, before I return you to your home."

"Ain't much of a home." Going to the graveyard after dark with a strange feller? Even Ma would've balked at that one. Prue didn't care, though. Her whole life was already in the spittoon. Besides, Dalziel was offering her a free ticket out of this hellhole. "Sure."

"Good. I shall return soon. The cover of darkness will allow us to elude Hume and our wretched *domestique*, Marguerite. Grandfather is abed and Grandmother never looks out of the windows. She cannot bear sunlight, or even intense moonlight."

"Why do you call her Grandmother? She told me you was her ward. An orphan."

"I am, from a legal vantage point, a ward, yes."

Prue waited for more, but Dalziel only stared into the candle flame.

Prue's breathing ironed out. "Why do they want to keep me here? Is it because of that book she had me nick? Because I can't even *read* that consarned thing! Hume can read it, I warrant, since he took it off to the kitchens to cook up one of the receipts she found. Soup, most like."

"I don't believe it is soup that Hume will prepare."

"One of those medicine receipts, then? Hold it—you don't think they meant to, I don't know, give their medicines a tryout on me, do you?"

Dalziel didn't answer.

"They planned to make me some kind of medicinal what-you-call-it?"

"An experiment? No. I suspect that Grandmother wishes to keep you here for other reasons altogether. Reasons that might have nothing at all to do with that receipt book. Stand up, Miss Prudence, and have a look about this chamber."

Prue frowned. "I ain't saying changing up the topic now and then don't keep a conversation *fresh*"—Ma had taught her that—"but that's a mighty sharp roundabout you're making."

"I enjoy the way you speak, Miss Prudence."

"Beg your pardon?" No one had *ever* complimented Prue on her grammar, pronunciation, elocution, or poetical whats-its. Not even Hansel.

"Go," Dalziel said. "Take the candle. Look."

Prue took the candle and stood. Her bones were rattled and her head felt light.

The chamber was not large, but its corners and ceiling were swallowed in shadow. It held a canopied bed and pieces of dignified, dark wood furniture, all cluttered up with bric-a-brac. Two windows, draperies mostly shut.

Prue finished a loop around the chamber. "All right, then. I've had a look-see. Nothing peculiar, as far as my knowing of grand Continental houses goes."

"You did not look closely enough, then." Dalziel sprang to his feet and led her to a chest of drawers. "Hold the flame close. Closer."

Candlelight bounced off small statues—a dozen or more of them—all lined up. Some of them were made of porcelain, others metal, wood, or even what looked to be ivory. But they all had one thing in common: they were all doll-sized like-nesses of a yellow-haired girl in a shimmering ivory gown.

"Cendrillon," Dalziel said. "Cinderella. And they all re-semble, to an uncanny degree, *you*."

Prue smeared her nose on her cuff. "Not me. My sister."

"Very well, then, your sister. But to Grandmother, you must understand, there is no difference. To her, the important thing is that you—and your sister—look like Cinderella."

Dalziel picked up one of the doll-things. Its face and hands were porcelain, just like any old doll, its yellow hair swept under a tiara. The doll wore a tiny, gauzy-skirted dress embroidered with silver and gold.

"Geewillikins," Prue whispered. "That's—that's just like

the dress my sister was wearing in the garden. Except her bodice didn't have this thing on it." She poked the sparkly triangle decorating the doll's bodice.

"Stomacher." Dalziel turned the doll over. A little golden crank poked out of its back. He wound it up—*scritch-scritch-scritch*—crouched, and placed it on the floor.

With a whirring sound, the doll spun in a figure-eight pattern over the stones. Its little porcelain arms waved gently, and its smiling-blank face tipped from side to side. Gradually, the doll slowed and then came to a stop. It toppled over sideways.

"Uck," Prue said. "Who'd want a creepy little thing like that?"

The lobby of Salle le Peletier swarmed with gaudy colors. Professor Penrose was easy for Ophelia to spot: he was taller than most of the other men by inches.

Ophelia waded through the crowd towards him. Her feet already had blisters from Henrietta's slippers.

"Miss Flax," Penrose said. "Good evening."

Ophelia couldn't help noticing that he didn't really look at her. Probably daydreaming of that paragon Miss Ivy Banks. *She* probably had feet as tiny as mole paws.

"I've got to keep my head down," Ophelia said. "At dinner, the Misses Malbert convinced their father to chaperone them to the ballet this evening."

"Again?"

"I fancy it's not the ballet they wish to observe, but Prince Rupprecht."

"Ah."

Ophelia told Penrose about her excursion to the steam-powered conveyance exhibition: how Austorga had lied about being backstage, what Eglantine had said about the stomacher, and how Prince Rupprecht had been so gallant towards the stepsisters.

"Only Malbert has access to the bank box in which the stomacher was locked?" Penrose asked.

"That is what Eglantine claimed."

"I am certain the employees of the bank would not allow just anyone to unlock the box."

"Not even a daughter? Or a wife?"

"Well, perhaps, given the proper amount of bribing."

"I wonder if Eglantine got the stomacher out of the bank, and then she lost it. Or someone stole it."

"Sybille stole it, perhaps? And Eglantine took it back?"

"Maybe." Ophelia told Penrose how the Count de Griffe had rescued her from a gory mishap with a steam shovel.

"He *rescued* you," Penrose said. "You must be jesting."

"The count didn't push me! If it even *was* a push—and now I'm beginning to wonder—it might have been one of the stepsisters, or Miss Smythe. Neither of the stepsisters enjoyed my quizzing them, and Miss Smythe is a sneak."

"Stay away from Griffe. He's a brute."

Better to steer the topic into a new channel. Something about the count nettled the professor. "What is the interesting news that you mentioned in your note?"

Penrose spoke in low tones, and the buzz in the lobby made their conversation private. "Caleb Grant, for a fee, ah . . . unites members of the *corps de ballet* with gentlemen of the Jockey Club."

"Mercy. I was afraid of that. I suppose he got his hooks into poor Sybille, then. I reckon a convent upbringing makes a girl stupid about fellows."

"Lord Dutherbrook means to introduce me to Grant this evening."

"*Formally* introduce, you mean—you spoke to him at the ballet class."

"Yes. I can only hope that does not impede the plan. Grant might be suspicious of me. If I am able to convince him, despite our first meeting, that I am a potential client and obtain something in writing regarding the transaction, that might be something to take to the police. Unlike the knowledge we gleaned by unlawfully entering Grant's apartment today."

"Do you think Inspector Foucher will care what Mr. Grant does? Is it illegal?"

"Grant merely makes introductions, and there are innumerable ways he could mask financial transactions. I would assume he simply takes cash. Still, it will be something. I am to meet Lord Dutherbrook in Prince Rupprecht's box."

"I suppose once again it's no place for a lady?"

"Yes. Well. I purchased a ticket for you." Penrose passed Ophelia a yellow paper ticket. "I shall join you back here at the first interval."

"Why am I here? I might have stayed in and kept Prue company."

"Because I wished to speak to you of this matter in person. It would not do to send detailed messages about these sorts of things. Anyone might read them. Which reminds me—I asked the concierge at my hotel to make inquiries regarding Henrietta at hotels and steamship offices."

"And?"

"Nothing. Which is meaningless. Henrietta could have used any sort of alias, and she *is* an actress, so if she wished to remain anonymous she could have easily done so. If she left Paris, or even France, she might've gone by railway or stagecoach. She could be staying at one of the myriad less reputable hotels and boardinghouses in the city, which the concierge did not check. Or she might"—Penrose *ahem*ed—"have taken up residence with another, ah, gentleman. I could not discover, either, a convent orphanage that is named something to do with stars. Miss Pinet's landlady must have been mistaken on that point."

Ophelia stared at the ticket in her gloved palm. She suddenly felt weary and irritable, and the notion of that Miss Ivy Banks, perched at home in England somewhere, embroidering hankies or painting china bunny rabbits, or whatever it was that a *real* lady did, made her feel as cross as two sticks. "I don't like charity."

"The ticket is not charity, Miss Flax. I was under the impression that you dislike being left out of things. We are aiding each other in a joint investigation, as it were."

"That does sound better than gallivanting about in Paris with a person you don't know from Adam."

She knew she'd really irked him, because a lock of hair had come lose over his neatly combed hairline. "Miss Flax," he said in a rough voice, "what I—"

"Oh, do look!" Ophelia twiddled her fingers. "The Count de Griffe!"

Griffe plowed his way through the crowd, his gaze fixed on Ophelia. When he drew close, he ignored Penrose and swept up Ophelia's hand for a juicy kiss.

"Mademoiselle Stonewall," he murmured, "how ravishing you look in green. Like a budding plant, eh?"

Ophelia said hello, batted her eyelashes, and gently laughed in the coy way she'd perfected for her role in *The Serpent's Sting: A Melodrama*. As she did so, she happened to notice that Penrose had crumpled his ballet programme in his fist.

17

Ophelia viewed the ballet's first act by herself from the lowest balcony. Penrose had lent her the opera glasses and, after escorting her to her seat, had curtly left. He was jealous of the Count de Griffe, all right. However, he'd given her a box of chocolate-raspberry opera bonbons.

How did he know raspberry was her favorite?

Cendrillon was just as jaw-dropping as it had been last night, but Ophelia's mind was on Sybille Pinet and Caleb Grant. If Grant had matched up Sybille with a gentleman admirer or two, then that could explain why the boarding-house landlady had said Sybille had seemed haunted lately. Being a quiet girl from a convent orphanage, maybe Sybille had had qualms about the business. Then, Sybille somehow met her mother—either Henrietta looked her up, or saw her dancing at the opera house, or maybe Sybille discovered Henrietta herself. Either way, Henrietta might've offered Sybille a ticket out of Paris in the form of a prospective job at Howard DeLuxe's Varieties.

And then what? Had Grant killed Sybille because he knew she wished to leave for New York? That seemed excessive. His black-bound book indicated he had a slew of other girls from whom to reap a profit. What about Henrietta? Might Grant have killed *her*?

If Grant had killed Sybille and dragged her body into the garden, glaring questions cropped up. How had Grant gotten the carriageway gate key? Could he have gotten it from Austorga, with Madame Babin somehow mixed up in it, too? Why would Austorga have helped him commit murder? And why in land sakes had Sybille been togged up like Cinderella?

Ophelia worked her way through the entire box of bonbons without even tasting them. The lights went up for the first interval. She checked the corners of her mouth for chocolate and went down to the lobby to meet the professor.

On the stairs, she narrowly missed an encounter with Malbert and his daughters. Not that they would recognize her without her Mrs. Brand accoutrements, but they might recognize Henrietta's gown. However, the stepsisters were too busy bickering, and Malbert was blinking too rapidly behind his spectacles, to notice Ophelia slip by.

When Penrose found Ophelia he said, "No go. Lord Dutherbrook never arrived—probably snoring in his chair at the club—and so I was not introduced to Grant."

"No matter. Grant's just over there." Ophelia gestured with her chin.

Grant stood across the lobby, wearing evening clothes. His black hair and pointy beard shone with pomade. The shoulders of his greatcoat glittered with raindrops, and he held a top hat.

"He's just arrived from out of doors," Ophelia said.

"Yes, and looking quite as much like a hearse driver as the last time we saw him. That looks like the greatcoat in which we found his notebook."

"He seems nervy." Ophelia frowned. "And so does Madame Babin on his arm."

Grant and Madame Babin had their heads bent together in urgent conversation. Grant looked angry, but Madame Babin seemed frightened. Her shoulders were hunched, and her eyes flicked about. She, too, had just come in from out of doors; her purple cloak and ribboned hat were wet.

"Let's go eavesdrop," Ophelia said.

"Miss Flax, I really don't—"

"No time to dillydally. Mr. Grant might be a murderer."

The crowd was dense, so they were able to position themselves just behind Grant and Madame Babin without being noticed. They strained their ears.

If pressed, Gabriel would have had to admit that Miss Flax's innocent face was convincing. He knew better now. Although she didn't seem entirely experienced in, say, the ways of the birds and the bees, she was a first-class trickster.

Grant and Madame Babin were still murmuring to each other, but the hubbub was too thick to make out a single word. It appeared that a crinkly envelope, held by Madame Babin, was at issue. She gesticulated with the envelope. Grant made a swipe at it. Then Madame Babin stuffed it in her reticule.

Miss Flax tugged Gabriel's sleeve.

"Yes?"

She threw a significant look towards the reticule. The crinkly envelope protruded halfway.

Gabriel whispered, "You cannot even *begin* to think that you are going to steal that from—"

In one liquid motion, Miss Flax plucked the envelope from the reticule and swayed off.

Grant and Madame Babin hadn't noticed a thing.

Gabriel shouldered into the throng after Miss Flax.

"How did you learn to do that?" he asked.

She stopped behind a pillar and pulled a sheet of paper from the envelope. "Played a pickpocket on the stage once."

"Once? It looked as though you've done that a thousand times."

"It was a long-running show." Her eyes were on the sheet of paper. "Are you suggesting I've withheld choice morsels regarding my past? I can't read this. It's in French."

Gabriel's neck was itchy and hot beneath his collar. Each and every time he managed to convince himself that Miss Flax was a naturally demure young lady who'd simply had a trying time of it, she proved otherwise. She wasn't demure. She was downright audacious. And the very idea of that perishing Count de Griffe looking at her like—like—

Penrose snatched up the paper. There were only a few lines, which said in French:

> *Meet me in the wardrobe between La Sylphide and Le Papillon at nine o'clock, or you will pay for the stomacher with your life.*

Gabriel translated it for Miss Flax.

"By golly, it's a death threat!"

"That does appear to be the case," Gabriel said. "*Garderobe*—wardrobe—well, I cannot fathom how it is they intend to kill someone inside a piece of furniture."

"Who's it for? Who's it *from*?"

"There is no indication."

"But it was in Madame Babin's reticule."

"The envelope was already opened."

"Not exactly—it had never been sealed." Miss Flax held up the envelope.

"Therefore, we do not know if the note was coming or going."

"But look." Miss Flax poked the page. "That is a lady's handwriting, isn't it?"

Was it his fancy, or did Miss Flax pronounce *lady* with a touch of sourness?

"It is a markedly feminine hand," Gabriel said.

"Which means that Madame Babin wrote it, and she's on her way to deliver it to whomever it is she plans to top off." Miss Flax, on tiptoe, scanned the crowd. "Look! There they go, both of them. We must hurry! It's near nine o'clock now!"

Gabriel looked over just in time to see Grant and Madame Babin duck out of sight around a corner.

Miss Flax hitched up her skirts and barged after them.

"Where are you going?" Gabriel called after her. "We really ought to take this matter to the police."

A dignified lady in pearls threw Gabriel a shocked glance. He closed his mouth. Miss Flax escaped.

For once, Ophelia was one step ahead of Professor Penrose. It felt marvelous. He had been confused by the theater jargon in the note, but Ophelia knew exactly what it meant. *Garderobe*, or wardrobe, didn't refer to a piece of furniture; it meant the backstage chamber where costumes were stored. And Ophelia just happened to know that *La Sylphide* was the name of a ballet, because Howard DeLuxe's Varieties performed ballets from time to time. After a fashion. *Le Papillon* was most likely the name of another ballet.

Grant and Madame Babin intended to murder someone between the garment racks where the costumes for those two ballets were stored. And it was up to her, Ophelia, to save their next victim.

Gabriel considered following Miss Flax. She had gotten a good start, however, and he couldn't begin to think of what she was doing.

Because, surely Miss Flax did not suppose that Grant or Madame Babin were off to *deliver* a note to someone threatening action at nine o'clock when it was in fact—he glanced at his pocket watch—mere minutes to nine o'clock already.

"Lord Harrington!"

Gabriel turned to see Prince Rupprecht. "Ah. I was just about to return to your box."

Brandy fumes emanated from Prince Rupprecht's very pores. "Come on then, old man, yes? I've got a new box of cigars that are from Spain but taste like they are from paradise."

"Splendid." Surely Miss Flax would go straight to the prince's box to find him, once she realized her folly.

*   *   *

Ophelia followed Caleb Grant and Madame Babin back-stage, but she lost sight of them when they passed by the stage right wings. Too crowded. Dancers in costume rushed around, finding their Act Two positions onstage or in the wings. From beyond the closed curtain came the sound of the orchestra sailing through the second act overture. Onstage, stagehands were making last-minute adjustments to the mechanical garden set. Ophelia recognized the big pumpkin-coach contraption.

From beyond the curtain came applause, and the huge, red velvet curtains rolled open. Act Two had begun.

Ophelia knew the wardrobe would be somewhere in the more remote regions of the theater. She only hoped she could find it in time.

Except—she stopped in her tracks.

Except that *there* was Madame Babin, hands on hips, in one of the wings. She was scolding one of the ballerinas in French. The prima ballerina Polina Petrov, as a matter of fact, in her raggedy Cinderella gown. Caleb Grant was no-where in sight.

Ophelia crept closer and hid herself behind one of the curtains that formed the wings.

Dancers in flower and mouse costumes twirled across the stage. Madame Babin's voice pierced the sounds of the orchestra. Polina was silent.

Ophelia peeked around the curtain. Polina was in costume. She would soon dance the scene in which the fairy godmother magically transformed her rags into finery. This meant that her costume looked like rags on top but had a version of the embroidered ivory tulle ball gown underneath.

Madame Babin lunged for Polina and lifted her ragged gown to expose the ball gown costume.

The stomacher flashed in the brilliant stage light. Was it the false, beaded stomacher of the ballet costume? Or was it, for some unfathomable reason, the real, *diamond* stomacher?

Polina tried to tug herself free, but Madame Babin would not stop pulling on her.

Ophelia's heart sped.

Madame Babin wanted the stomacher. She was prepared to *kill* for the stomacher. There was no choice in the matter.

Ophelia sprang from her hiding place and found herself in the midst of a three-lady tussle. Madame Babin spat French words that didn't sound too nice and left off tugging at Polina in order to claw at Ophelia instead. Polina got away; Ophelia caught a glimpse of her taking one last horrified glance over her shoulder before leaping onstage to a spatter of applause.

Madame Babin was all elbows and hisses and nipping fingernails.

"Get off me, you wretched critter!" Ophelia whispered. She *felt* like yelling, but she'd hate to ruin the show.

Madame Babin grabbed a handful of Ophelia's coiffure and gave it a hard twist.

"That one has got legs like a chicken," Prince Rupprecht said. He pointed to one of the ballerinas down on the stage. The second act had begun only moments earlier, yet Prince Rupprecht had already evaluated the dancers as efficiently as a farmer at a livestock auction.

"Ah, *oui*," Griffe said, studying the girl in question through opera glasses. "But a breast like a hen, *non*?"

For God's sake. Gabriel raked a hand through his hair and continued pacing at the back of the box. As soon as he'd reached Prince Rupprecht's box, Gabriel had sent an usher backstage to summon Caleb Grant. He'd told the usher that Grant was perhaps to be found in a room with a wardrobe—although he still couldn't understand what that was supposed to signify.

Surely Grant would come. This was a bally *prince's* box. Then Gabriel might be able to discern what that note had meant.

The audience sucked in a collective gasp.

"*Mon Dieu.*" Griffe rose halfway in his chair, opera glasses glued to his eyes. "It is Mademoiselle Stonewall!"

Gabriel froze, mid-pace. "I beg your pardon?"

"Ah, how sweet she is in green!"

"Give me that!" Prince Rupprecht snatched the opera glasses from Griffe. "Indeed, it is she!"

Gabriel fancied his neck was in danger of exploding. "Miss Fl—Miss Stonewall, my cousin, onstage?" He strode to the prince, grabbed the opera glasses, and scanned the stage. "Oh dear God. It is."

Dancers dressed as mice and flowers crowded the stage, while Cinderella pirouetted before the footlights.

But . . . *there*.

Miss Flax, in her green evening gown, crawled on all fours towards the wings. A mouse hopped over her.

"Why the deuce is she onstage?" Gabriel muttered.

"She *has* got rather nice ankles," Prince Rupprecht said.

"She is a lady," Gabriel said coldly. "Pray do not speak of her in that fashion."

Prince Rupprecht turned to Griffe. "She is onstage to impress *you*, you must understand. Wishes to stand out in your mind as a daredevil—and to show off her fine stems and flower petals, too." He chortled.

Gabriel was just weighing the cost of cuffing a prince on the nose—and perhaps a count, too—when Miss Flax crawled out of sight into the wings.

The usher poked his head through the curtains at the rear of the box and gave a tactful cough.

All three men swiveled around.

"I regret to say," the usher said, "that Monsieur Grant is dead."

18

❧

Gabriel found Miss Flax in a backstage corridor surrounded by a ring of dancers and theater workers, all
berating her in French. She caught sight of Gabriel.

"Get me out of this, won't you?" she called.

Gabriel strode through the ring of people, grabbed Miss
Flax's hot, gloved hand, and pulled her away through the still-
yelling group—they were all going on about her ruining the
performance, with a few accusations thrown in that she was
some sort of anarchist or else a saboteur sent from the ballet
company in London.

"Where are we going?" she asked as he whisked her along.

"I'm taking you home. What were you *thinking*?"

"It wasn't my fault! I was pushed onstage! I was trying
to save that ballerina! And did she demonstrate even the
smallest bit of gratitude? No!"

"Caleb Grant is dead."

"What?" Miss Flax stopped walking.

Footsteps clattered towards them, and a harried little
fellow in side-whiskers and two uniformed gendarmes burst

around a corner. Gabriel and Miss Flax pressed themselves against the wall so the men could pass.

Miss Flax's eyes met Gabriel's.

"No," he said.

"We've *got* to."

"I cannot continue to enable your harebrained schemes—"

"Hurry, before it's too late. And I'm *not* harebrained, if you don't mind. Merely resourceful."

"Resourceful?" Somehow, Gabriel found himself following Miss Flax as she hurried down the corridor after the men. How precisely did she convince him, against his better judgment, time after time? "You are not simply *resourceful*, my dear. I daresay you will stop at nothing."

They followed the clattering footsteps of Side-Whiskers and the gendarmes, and caught sight of them in the dressing rooms corridor. The performance was still going onstage, so dancers darted here and there.

The men did not stop there, but continued down a twisty flight of stairs into the bowels of the theater.

The three men didn't notice Ophelia and Penrose, following at a distance. They spoke in low, anxious tones. They came to an open doorway. Beyond lay a huge, dim room filled with costume-stuffed racks. The three men went inside.

Ophelia and Penrose hid themselves just outside the doorway.

"The wardrobe," Ophelia whispered. "In the theater it's a *room*, not a piece of furniture."

"Ah."

They looked in.

The three men stood between two rows of garment racks straight ahead, looking down at a heap of something on the floor. No, not a heap of something. A heap of some*one*. Of Caleb Grant.

"They are saying that he has been shot in the heart," Penrose whispered to Ophelia.

One of the gendarmes whipped out a handkerchief, crouched, and picked up something.

"He says that is the murder weapon," Penrose whispered.

The gendarme held up a small, silver-colored pistol. The cylinder flopped open and a bullet clinked on the floor.

"We had better go," Penrose said.

Truth be told, when Prue escaped the Cruthlach mansion it wasn't the first time she'd snuck out a window. But the first time had been with Hansel, and she'd been in love. Seemed it wasn't exactly right to go sneaking out windows with a feller you *weren't* in love with. Or—wait. Did that rule only apply when the feller was sneaking *in*?

Dalziel had placed a ladder outside—it seemed he was as capable as a soldier—and then he'd come to the chamber where Prue was locked up and helped her down to the murky courtyard. A carriage was waiting in the street. Dalziel handed her up.

"That was as easy as falling off a log," Prue said, breathless.

Dalziel stepped up into the carriage beside her and slammed the door. The carriage started forward. "I've had a bit of practice."

"You don't say so!"

Dalziel smiled in the dark. "Grandmother has always desired to keep a close watch on me, ever since I was a baby. She said she was afraid the fairies were going to steal me back."

Fairies?

The drive to the cemetery took only ten minutes or so. Prue had just nodded off when the carriage stopped and Dalziel said, "We are here."

"It is a lady we want," Professor Penrose said.

Ophelia and Penrose stood in the shadows on an uneven cobbled sidewalk. Across the street, the opera house blazed with light. Only a few carriages rolled by. Overhead, the moon floated behind quick, silvery clouds.

"Because of the lady's handwriting on the death threat, you mean," Ophelia said.

"Yes. We are able to rule out the derelict the police are after, for surely he doesn't have the foresight to write letters in a feigned hand, let alone deliver them."

"The police said that man preys upon ladies of ill-repute, too. Which Mr. Grant wasn't."

"We are also able to rule out Madame Babin and Polina Petrov . . . Miss Flax, you are shaking. Might I lend you my greatcoat?"

"I've got my mantle. Well, Henrietta's mantle." Ophelia held it up. "It's only nerves. I always used to get nerves onstage, too, whenever I had a big role. It'll pass." She blotted the lumpy shape of Caleb Grant's corpse from her mind, along with the notion that if she hadn't gotten sidetracked by Madame Babin in the wings, she might've prevented his death. "It looked like a lady penned the death threat, but couldn't a lady have written it out *for* a gentleman murderer? Or couldn't a gentleman have pretended a feminine hand?"

"Yes. Although it is noteworthy that Grant was shot with a lady's pistol—did you see how dainty it was? I believe I even glimpsed floral décor carved on the barrel."

"A gentleman could shoot a lady's pistol."

"True. Did you see how the cylinder fell open to the right when the gendarme held it up?"

"I'm no crackerjack sharpshooter, Professor."

"It was a left-handed pistol."

"Oh."

"The cylinder opens on the right because the shooter holds the gun and pulls the trigger with the left hand, and loads with the right."

"So the murderer is a southpaw."

"Perhaps. Or simply a person who possessed, for some reason, a southpaw's gun."

The professor's accent made *southpaw* sound like the name of a fancy aperitif.

"One thing is certain," Ophelia said. "The murderer is killing because of the stomacher."

"It does seem so."

"Do you think Henrietta is dead?"

Penrose studied her, concern shining in his eyes. "Perhaps," he finally said. "She might have gained access to the stomacher herself at one point, and paid the price."

Ophelia hugged Henrietta's mantle and caught a faint whiff of Henrietta's perfume. If Ophelia *could* have cried, now would've been a fine time. But she hadn't shed a tear for longer than she could remember.

She must've made a face, though, because Penrose frowned. "Miss Flax, perhaps it would be wise if you ceased poking about in this affair."

"Now is the time to buckle down and go at it even harder."

"You might place yourself in unnecessary danger."

"I'll be the judge. I'm not a child."

"The police—"

"They're incompetent. Stubborn. Blind! I told you what Inspector Foucher wrote about our discovery of Sybille's identity. He ought to be a circus sideshow: The Insensible Man. No. I've undertaken to figure out what happened to Henrietta, and I'm not about to stop now simply on account of the water's gotten higher."

"And finding this—this murderer, of *two* people now, if it is indeed the same culprit, that will bring you to the solution of Henrietta's disappearance?"

"Looks that way."

Penrose gazed at Ophelia for such a long moment, she wondered if she had chocolate somewhere on her face. At last, he said, "I told you that I would help you, and so I shall. I must have time to think of what is the wisest course."

"*We* must have time to think."

He smiled a little. "*We*. Now, won't you please allow me to hire a carriage to return you to Hôtel Malbert? Then you must rest. The past two days have been fatiguing for you. I see it in your face."

Ophelia wasn't what you'd call a vain lady. Years of

experience in the circus ring and on the stage had taught her that beauty is an illusion, as fleeting as a magic lantern show. But still, did she really look *so* tuckered out?

"I'll walk."

"At this time of the evening?"

"Can't be more than two miles." Ophelia's pinched toes, in Henrietta's tiny slippers, cursed her.

"Then I shall walk with you. A murderer is afoot, my dear."

Yes, and Ophelia's feet were murder.

A high, moon-sheened stone wall surrounded the Montparnasse Cemetery. Dalziel instructed the driver to wait. He led Prue through iron gates that hung, half open, from thick pillars. Beyond the gates sprawled gravestones, tombs, and statues, glowing pale against the shadows.

Wind rippled. Bare trees rattled. The air smelled of fresh-dug dirt—or was that just Prue's fancy? She shivered, despite the shawl that Dalziel had brought for her. Or maybe *because* of the shawl, which stank a little of camphor and probably belonged to Lady Cruthlach.

"I confess I took the liberty of visiting here earlier, after I called upon the convent," Dalziel said. His voice was carried off by a twirl of wind. "Her grave is along this way."

"All right," Prue said. She swallowed. "Sure."

She stuck close to Dalziel all the way along a cobble-paved avenue, and then down a smaller, sandy path that sliced through rows of graves like an aisle in a shop. Moonlight brightened the sky and bounced off the statues—mostly of dead bodies and cherubs and such. She nearly jumped out of her boots when a cat skittered across the way.

A few raindrops started smacking down.

"Here," Dalziel said softly. He slowed, and pushed his hands in his pockets.

A big, stone rectangle lay between two others, piled around with fresh, black dirt. A bunch of lilies drooped on top. The headstone said—Prue could see it clearly in the moonlight—

Ici Repose
Sybille Pinet
1846–1867

"She must have been beloved by the sisters in the convent," Dalziel said. "This is a costly grave."

Prue nodded, numb. Now it felt—what? More real? That couldn't be it. Nothing had felt more real than Sybille's chilly, rained-on skin in the garden that night.

"It's the end," Prue said. "I never got to meet her, and now it's the end." Cold tears dripped down her face along with the rainwater.

Dalziel wrapped his arms about her and although he was not a large fellow, he felt wiry and strong under the soft wool of his greatcoat. He smelled a little like cinnamon, too. Prue started sobbing. For herself, but also for her missing ma, and for Sybille, forever lost.

After a few minutes, the sobs left off and Prue opened her eyes. Her breath caught. "*Someone's here*," she mumbled against Dalziel's shoulder.

He spun around, placing himself in front of Prue.

A figure with an umbrella stepped out from behind a marble angel. Something white flashed around the face.

By gum, it was a nun. A nun in a flowing black habit and a white—what was it? Oh, yes—a white wimple. Once in Howard DeLuxe's Varieties, Prue had been one of a whole chorus line of naughty nuns who favored red stockings. But surely *this* nun wouldn't be caught dead in anything but soot-black socks.

The nun drew close and spoke briskly in French. Her eyes fixed on Prue's face. Sourness puckered her mouth, yet her eyes were kind.

Dalziel turned to Prue. "She says her name is Sister Alphonsine, of the Pensionnat Sainte Estelle. She came here to lay flowers upon the grave and hid when she saw us coming. She asks if you are the twin sister of Sybille, because she prepared Sybille with her own hands for burial, so she knows that she is truly dead. Shall I tell her that you are her sister?"

"Sure. Tell her everything." Everyone trusted nuns, right?

Sister Alphonsine gripped her umbrella hard as she spoke with Dalziel, and her eyes kept darting back to Prue.

"She says you are in danger," Dalziel said.

"Danger! Does she know anything about my ma?"

"No. I asked her. But she says that because you look so much like Sybille, the murderer could strike again."

"That's what the police said. Wait. Ask her why she didn't tell the police who Sybille was."

Dalziel asked her. Sister Alphonsine did some more sharp talking.

"She says that she wrote to the police, to someone called Inspector Foucher, and informed him of Sybille's identity, but he never replied. She begs that you stay at the convent, where you will be safe, until the murderer is caught."

"Bunk in a convent?" *How Ma would laugh at* that *one.* "I'll be just fine—as long as your grandmother and Hume leave me be."

Sister Alphonsine looked like she wished to say more, but after a long hesitation she crunched away on the path. She stole one last look over her shoulder before she swished out of sight around a tomb.

"Are you ready to go?" Dalziel asked. "Her talk of murderers has made me feel wary. I ought not keep you out any longer."

Prue gazed one last time at Sybille's headstone. "I'm ready."

19

Dalziel ordered the driver—a hired driver, not Lord and Lady Cruthlach's—to go to Hôtel Malbert by way of the Pensionnat Sainte Estelle.

The nunnery was on a corner: a tall, spiked iron fence and bare bushes, with a blocky stone building behind.

"If the occasion should arise that you needed to know of its location," Dalziel said.

"You ought to train to be a lawyer," Prue muttered.

"I intend to, once I have completed my studies at the Sorbonne." Dalziel smiled.

His smile was too fetching, and Prue flicked her gaze out the window. She had no business admiring Dalziel's beautiful black eyes and white teeth. She was in love with Hansel. Wasn't she?

Ma had always said, *A bird in the hand is worth two in the bush*. Well actually, she'd said a *man* in the hand (and then she'd trill with laughter). Was Prue's admiration for Dalziel proof that she was becoming . . . just like Ma?

When Prue knocked on the front door of Hôtel Malbert because there was no other way to get in, Baldewyn opened it. Lucky he never asked questions. He only looked a little shirty. Prue bolted upstairs.

Sleep came hard. Prue shivered, even with the fat ginger cat purring like a locomotive on top of her and a nice coal fire winking in the grate. She couldn't stop seeing Sybille's headstone, all mixed up with the jerky motions and pearl-tooth grins of a dozen windup Cinderellas.

Gabriel bade Miss Flax farewell and watched her crawl through a sidewalk-level window into the cellar of Hôtel Malbert. He would have liked to help her, but she insisted upon doing it herself. There was a thump—had she fallen?—and then she lifted up a hand to the window in farewell.

No other lady in the world was quite like Miss Flax.

Gabriel turned up the collar of his greatcoat and began the long walk to his hotel.

Ophelia propped her feet on the grate in her bedchamber. The heat relieved her cold, crunched toes. It was near midnight, she estimated, but sleep would not come. After she'd clambered back through the cellar window (it had been most humiliating to have the professor watch her do *that*), she had checked on Prue and the ginger cat—both sound asleep—and readied herself for bed. She'd heard Malbert and the stepsisters noisily arrive. After that, the house fell silent.

Malbert and the stepsisters had been at the opera house tonight. Each one of them might have a reason to kill for the stomacher. After all, it was their family heirloom. Ophelia was only a little comforted by the notion that the murderer wouldn't do Prue or her any harm, since it was the stomacher the murderer was after. Still, being under the same roof as that bunch was downright eerie.

Ophelia mulled things over. There had to be something she'd missed, some crucial ingredient that would make it all firm up and set, like calf's-foot jelly in fruit preserves.

There was the lawyer. They hadn't been able to speak with

him, and Ophelia had never managed to have a cozy chat with Malbert in order to extract any divorce secrets. But other than that, all of this business about the ballet and the Cinderella stomacher? Befuddling.

Except.

Except Malbert always seemed removed, as though the events around him did not quite touch him. But what if he were really the center of it all? Henrietta, after all, was *his* wife. Sybille's corpse had been found just outside *his* workshop. The stomacher that everyone was so interested in belonged by rights to Malbert, and had come from *his* bank box. Malbert had even had the opportunity, perhaps, to shoot Caleb Grant at the opera house tonight.

Ophelia sat forward. What was it Austorga had said at the exhibition this afternoon? Something about Malbert and inventions? Oh, yes: something like, *Danger is the price one pays for scientific advancement.*

Danger. Sybille had met with danger, and so had Caleb Grant.

Yes. It was high time Ophelia took a gander at Malbert's workshop.

She lit a taper, drew on her shawl, and tiptoed though dark corridors and stairs to his workshop. She knocked softly on the door, but there was no reply. Good thing, too, since she wasn't in her Mrs. Brand disguise.

She twisted the knob. It gave.

Well. Surely if Malbert stored diabolical things in his workshop, he'd keep the door locked.

Inside, wet wax extinguished her taper. Smoke and darkness filled her eyes. She should've brought spare matches.

She blinked. Her eyes adjusted. The draperies were open, admitting fragile moonbeams that glinted off bits of metal on the table. When Ophelia had spied upon Malbert through the window last week, her impression had been of piles of mechanical disarray. Now she saw that the piles were sorted: springs in one, bolts in another, and so on. She squinted. There certainly *could* be the makings of a pistol in there—a *left-handed* pistol—but she couldn't be sure. She picked up a box, like the one Malbert had been tinkering with the other night. It was a hollow metal cube, big enough for a large apple to fit inside, and one end was open. Peculiar.

Ophelia noticed a wooden cabinet against the wall. One door was wedged open a few inches. She replaced the metal cube on the table.

She went to the cabinet and opened the door. The hinges squeaked.

Once her eyes adjusted to the gloom, she saw that the cupboard's shelves were bare, except for—

A sob of horror fell out of her mouth.

Except for a glass jar the size of a small butter churn, filled with brownish liquid like a brining jar. Except there weren't any gherkins or dills in this jar. No. In *this* jar, two fair, dainty feet bobbed inside. A lady's feet. In a brining vat.

Ophelia slammed the cupboard door. She couldn't breathe.

Henrietta. Were those Henrietta's feet? Had she requested a divorce, and Malbert had retaliated with—with what? Murder? Or was Henrietta held captive somewhere, missing her feet?

Ophelia's guts heaved. She hustled out of the workshop as fast as her own blessedly attached feet could carry her.

Gabriel breakfasted early in Hôtel Meurice's dining room. His night had been a torment of tangled bedclothes and twisting thoughts. He felt like he'd had too much wine but the truth was, he'd had too much Miss Flax.

Telling her of Miss Ivy Banks *had* seemed a brilliant antidote to the distraction that she, Miss Flax, posed. Obviously, Gabriel could not even begin to think of *marrying* Miss Flax (the very idea!) and he refused to become like that repulsive Lord Dutherbrook and take an actress for a mistress. Which, of course, was an utterly laughable idea in itself. Although Miss Flax was bold beyond all comprehension, she would never be any man's mistress. Of that, Gabriel was certain.

However, Miss Flax's antics yesterday had done nothing

to ease the tug Gabriel felt towards her. The antidote had, somehow, already worn off.

When the waiter arrived with more coffee, he deposited two envelopes on the tablecloth.

"These were delivered to the front desk," the waiter said. He poured coffee from a silver pot, and left.

One envelope was stark white, with a tidy, clerical hand that read *Lord Harrington*. The second envelope was damp and slightly crumpled. *Professor Penrose*, it read, and Gabriel recognized Miss Flax's uneven handwriting.

There. You see? She even had flawed penmanship. Better to think of Miss Ivy Banks's hand, which might've been in a schoolroom primer.

Gabriel tore open Miss Flax's envelope with the butter knife.

Strange developments. Must speak with you. Will be waiting in the Place des Vosges at ten o'clock.—O.F.

Place des Vosges was a small park a few blocks from Hôtel Malbert. Miss Flax had doubtless looked it up in that Baedeker she was forever lugging about. He was somewhat alarmed at her message, but surely if it was an emergency she would have said so.

Gabriel sliced open the second envelope.

An excessively grand letterhead, with a scrolled design of waves and dolphins, declared *M. T. S. Cherrien (Avocat) 116 Avenue des Champs-Élysées*.

Ah. Perhaps Cherrien had found a spare moment before January, then.

The note was in English.

Lord Harrington,

I expect your presence at my office this morning at nine o'clock, regarding a most pressing matter. Your discretion is necessary.

—M. Cherrien

Oh-ho! He *expected* Gabriel's presence, did he? Gabriel was accustomed to persons, if not scraping before him, at least addressing him as a respected equal. This Cherrien chap deserved to have his insulting summons crumpled and abandoned among the bread crusts.

Yet curiosity trumped pride. Gabriel glanced at his pocket watch. Eight thirty-seven. He downed the last of his coffee and stood.

Ophelia had been up since the crack of dawn. Once she'd sent off the note to the professor at his hotel, she'd fallen to pacing and fretting in her chamber. The vision of those white feet bobbing in the brining vat was just about enough to make her pack up Prue and their carpetbags and put them on the first train to *anywhere*.

But Ophelia had never been one to run from problems. They usually caught up to you again, anyway. And Henrietta was yet to be found.

Ophelia looked through the window into the sky. Gray clouds bulged. Another rainy day. She glanced down into the garden, and averted her eyes from the vegetable patch.

Motion caught her eye, over by the carriage house.

Good gracious. There was the coachman Henri, standing in the carriage house doorway. He spoke with a lady whose back was turned. A slim lady in a hooded cloak. Eglantine, maybe?

Ophelia watched. Henri's exchange with the lady was brief. His shoulders hunched, and the lady kept glancing over her shoulder. Then Henri went inside and the lady hurried towards the house.

Her hood fell back in her haste.

It wasn't Eglantine. It was Miss Seraphina Smythe.

She disappeared through the carriageway arch.

Ophelia checked the mantelpiece clock. Almost nine o'clock. She went to fetch Prue.

Prue was still abed.

"Prue? Prue, wake up. Don't you want breakfast?" Ophelia wiggled Prue's shoulder.

The fat ginger cat on the pillow yawned and stretched a foreleg. Prue muttered something, rolled over, and went back to sawing gourds.

Petered out from all that house drudgery. Ophelia would leave her to sleep. She went downstairs to the breakfast room.

Ophelia's stomach lurched at the sight of Malbert's bald head gleaming above a newspaper at the head of the table. Eglantine and Austorga slumped across from each other, eating in silence. They both wore irritable expressions, and each had a peculiar oily sheen to her face.

Where was Miss Smythe?

"Good morning, everyone!" Ophelia said, forcing a cheery, matronly tone. She plopped down next to Eglantine.

Malbert peeped over his newspaper but said nothing.

Those pickled feet. *Ugh*.

"Good morning, Madame Brand," Austorga said. She took a bite of pastry—holding it, Ophelia noted, with her right hand. Not her left. A few pastry flakes clung to her oily cheeks.

"Mm," Eglantine sighed, stirring her coffee. She held her spoon with her right hand. Not her left.

Beatrice plodded in. She brought the coffeepot from the sideboard and poured Ophelia a cup. Greasy hairs hung loose from her bun, and she smelled faintly of soured wine. She flung a pastry on a plate in front of Ophelia, and left.

The family crunched and sipped in silence. Malbert turned a page of his newspaper. With his right hand, not his left.

"Did you enjoy the ballet yesterday evening?" Ophelia asked.

Malbert's newspaper froze. Eglantine sputtered on her coffee.

Austorga said, "Oh! Most exciting. There was a murder! It was the same murderer as the girl in the garden, too, and the police have caught him."

"Indeed?" Ophelia carefully placed her coffee cup in its saucer. Still, it rattled. "The madman of the streets?"

"Yes. He was seen by several people fleeing from the opera house—with blood on his hands, and raving about someone paying him to kill! Quite mad."

Ophelia frowned. Perhaps she'd been wrong in thinking the madman was innocent. Perhaps he *was* a killer . . . for hire.

"Someone caught him and held him until the gendarmes arrived," Austorga said. "Who was it that caught him, sister dear?"

"The apprentice lad from Monsieur Colifichet's shop," Eglantine said. "*Must* we speak of this?"

"Pierre," Malbert said.

They all stared at him; it was the first word he'd said.

"The apprentice is named Pierre," Malbert said.

"Yes, well, Pierre caught the murderer—he frequents the opera house because Monsieur Colifichet, his master, designed the sets for *Cendrillon*—and he is being treated as quite a hero by the police."

"It is good, Madame Brand, *oui*?" Malbert blinked at Ophelia. "The murderer is caught. We will sleep soundly tonight."

"But what of the Marquise Henrietta?" Ophelia asked. "It wouldn't do to forget her."

"She will return," Malbert said. He raised his newspaper.

"Oh! Réglisse!" Eglantine shrieked. *"Non!"*

A rotund cat had leapt onto Eglantine's lap and was licking her oily cheek. *"Non! Vilain! Vilain chat!"* She shoved Réglisse. He thumped to the floor and licked his lips.

Eglantine wiped her face with a napkin.

"What has Miss Smythe told you this time?" Ophelia asked.

"Nothing," Eglantine snapped.

"Beef lard face pack," Austorga said. "For a dewy complexion. Only two more days till the prince's ball."

"Dewy complexion?" Ophelia said. "My dear girls, I'm afraid beef lard will give you nothing but spots."

Baldewyn appeared and announced something in French. Ophelia only understood *Mademoiselle Smythe*.

Ophelia bolted to her feet. "Excuse me," she murmured.

Eglantine looked quizzical. Ophelia patted her stomach in explanation. Didn't dignified matrons always suffer from digestive afflictions?

Ophelia rushed past Baldewyn and intercepted Seraphina in the corridor.

"Good morning, Miss Smythe," Ophelia said.

"Mrs. Brand. Good morning." Seraphina's spectacles were fogged. "Are the Misses Malbert ready? We are going to the shoemaker's to fetch our dancing shoes for the ball. Mother is waiting in the carriage."

Ophelia lowered her voice. "I won't beat around the bush, young lady. Why were you speaking with the coachman a few minutes ago?"

"Did my mother instruct you to spy upon me?"

"I happened to notice your rendezvous with Henri from my window, and I demand an explanation for your subterfuge."

"It was hardly a rendezvous, and I assure you there wasn't a jot of subterfuge. I do not owe you explanations of any kind, Mrs. Brand, but since you are a dotty old woman with a passion for prying—Miss Eglantine was quite right about that—I shall tell you. I was simply asking Henri if he had found a dropped glove of mine in the carriage."

"Oh." Ophelia swallowed. "Well. The Misses Malbert are still at the table. I shall accompany you there."

20

The stepsisters left the house with Seraphina a few minutes later, and Ophelia was alone with Malbert at the breakfast table. She wished to be alone with this doughy little monster like she wished for a splinter in the eye.

"My dear Monsieur Malbert, I am so glad we are at last able to speak in privacy."

The newspaper lowered. *"Pourquoi?"*

Ophelia knew *pourquoi* meant *why*. In the circus, Madame Treminskaya had always asked her customers *pourquoi* over her crystal ball, in order to figure out what their fortunes ought to be.

"Why? Because I have two important questions to ask you." Ophelia took a deep breath. "First, did the Marquise Henrietta ever see the diamond stomacher you keep in your lockbox at the bank?"

To Ophelia's surprise, Malbert's face dimpled in a smile. "Did my daughters tell you of the stomacher?"

"Indeed they did."

"And I suppose one of them—Eglantine?—enlisted you to convince me to allow her to wear it to the ball?"

"If you must know . . . yes."

"But what does my dear, darling Henrietta have to do with it?"

Ophelia thought fast. "It occurred to me that perhaps you had given the stomacher to Henrietta and that it was no longer truly in the bank box, and that is why you will not permit either of your daughters to wear it."

"No, no, the stomacher is still in the bank. *Oui*, I showed it to Henrietta, but she preferred to keep for herself different, more fashionable pieces of jewelry instead."

"When was this?"

Malbert blinked rapidly. "I cannot recall. Three or four months ago, perhaps?"

"Did Henrietta have a key to the bank box?"

"No, but I share everything with my dear wife."

Mighty interesting.

"That was the last time you laid eyes on the stomacher?" Ophelia asked.

"*Oui.*"

"Monsieur Malbert, I don't know quite how to put this, and I do realize it is *indelicate*, but as I have taken it upon myself to look after Miss Bright until her mother has been found, well, might I ask, did Henrietta wish for"—Ophelia lowered her voice to a whisper—"*a divorce?*"

"Good heavens, no! We were only married last spring! And we were—are—deeply *amoureux*."

"Yes, I suppose you love everything about Henrietta, such as . . . her feet."

"What a strange thing to say, Madame Brand." Up went the newspaper.

Well, that was the end of their cozy chat, then.

"Thank you for your punctuality," Monsieur Cherrien said to Gabriel across a gleaming expanse of desk. "My time is valuable."

Cherrien spoke in French, and his voice was only just past the yodeling stage. If Gabriel had seen him on the street, he would have gauged him to be not more than twenty years old. Yet that couldn't be right. Not unless he had taken up studying the law while still in short pants.

"Please"—Cherrien gestured to a chair—"sit."

Gabriel sat. The chair had evidently been constructed for an elf, because once seated, Gabriel found that his chin was scarcely higher than the edge of the desk.

"Now then." Cherrien steepled his hands. "I suppose you are wondering why I have summoned you here this morning."

"The thought has flitted through my mind, yes. But first—your secretary did tell you that I called here yesterday morning? Yes? Good. I wished to speak with you regarding the Marquise de la Roque-Fabliau. She is a client of yours, I have been led to believe, and she wished for a divorce—"

Something flashed in Cherrien's eyes. Alarm? Then it was gone.

"—and now, as you are doubtless aware, she is missing. What do you know of this affair, Monsieur Cherrien?"

"Know? Nothing."

He was lying. But Gabriel had no means to make him talk.

Cherrien waved his hand. "I do not have much time. Now. I have learned through certain avenues that you are well aware of the existence of a certain . . . item. An item that holds great significance as a historical relic, a significance that surpasses even its monetary value, which is not to be sneezed at, as I believe you English are fond of saying."

"Are we?"

Cherrien made a chilly little smile. "Cendrillon's stomacher. I see in your face that you know of it. My client wishes to have it."

"And your client is—?"

"That is confidential."

"But your client is aware that it is a priceless relic. That it belonged to Cendrillon, and that some say it is imbued with magical powers."

"As a gentleman of the law, it is beyond my capacity to assess the *magical* attributes of items, although I am willing to believe that it did indeed belong to a real lady who came to be known as Cendrillon. My opinion on the matter is neither here nor there. My client wishes for the stomacher, and it is my job to procure it for—"

Gabriel held his breath, waiting for Cherrien to slip up and say *him* or *her*.

But Cherrien caught himself. After a pause he said, "I require you to perform the legwork in locating the stomacher. I am a very busy man, and I understand that you are experienced with such things."

"Who told you that?" Lady Cruthlach. This had to be her doing.

"Bring me the stomacher by no later than ten o'clock on Saturday morning."

"Why Saturday?"

"Do not worry yourself with details."

"Why would I do this for you? Or for your client?"

"Because if you do not, I will be forced to go to the police and inform them of an American actress who has, in an exceedingly bizarre fashion, insinuated herself into the household of the Marquis de la Roque-Fabliau. It has a certain—what is it?—a romantic element, does it not? The actress and the earl, scheming to steal Cinderella's diamond stomacher. Alas, my client grows impatient."

Gabriel stood. "Good day, Cherrien." He went to the door.

"Get me the stomacher, Lord Harrington," Cherrien called after him, "or I shall be forced to have your little confidence trickster of an actress arrested."

Gabriel attempted not to slam the door as he left.

Just as Ophelia was gathering her Baedeker and reticule— it was almost time to go meet Professor Penrose—there was a knock at her bedchamber door.

She expected Prue (not that Prue usually knocked). But it was Baldewyn, holding an enormous, flat paperboard box fastened with twine.

"A delivery for you, *madame*," he said with undisguised contempt.

"Oh, Baldewyn, you *are* an old pet!" Ophelia gathered the box to her padded bosom and closed the door with her foot.

She placed the box on her bed. A small tag dangled from the twine: *Madame Brand: Enjoy!—Madame Fayette*.

Ophelia unfastened the twine and opened the box. She peeled away layers of tissue. A lovely plaid silk gown.

Her hands shook as she put the lid on the box and shoved it under the bed.

How could this be? The tag on the box said *Madame Brand*, but Ophelia had told Madame Fayette that her name was Miss Stonewall. She had also taken care to sign the note cancelling the order *Miss Stonewall*, and she had not included a return address with that note. Madame Fayette must have bribed the courier boy yesterday. And the order had not been cancelled, despite that note.

Not only was Madame Fayette wise to Ophelia, she was *taunting* her.

Noble mansions of red brick and yellow stone looked down upon Place des Vosges from all four sides. Tall windows, each with dozens of small, square panes, reflected a blank white sky. Bare linden trees dripped and the fountains didn't gurgle. No children romped in the grass. Pigeons paced on sandy paths and perched on the statue of Louis XIII on horseback.

When Gabriel caught sight of Miss Flax on a bench near the statue, he breathed a sigh of relief; she wore her matron's disguise. He would not be in danger of forgetting himself today, then.

She jumped to her feet when she caught sight of him and came hurrying down the path, umbrella in one hand, dumpy reticule in the other.

"Miss Flax, you look pale. At any rate, I *suspect* you look pale beneath all that muck."

"I don't even know where to begin," she said, out of breath.

"What has happened? Your note said—"

"Oh, my word. The *feet*."

"I beg your pardon?"

She told him what she'd seen in Malbert's workshop. "I tell you, Malbert's a fiend. A foot fiend! He chops ladies' dogs off and—and *brines* them."

"The first explanation that comes to mind is that the feet are medical or scientific specimens of some sort. Medical training does, alas, include a certain amount of . . . dissection."

"Malbert's no medical man."

"I have also heard of more than one example of the bound foot of a deceased Chinese lady being preserved in fluid for all posterity to inspect."

"Ugh."

"I do agree. At any rate, perhaps you stumbled upon the marquis's cabinet of curiosities—which is rather like a circus freak show in miniature."

"I have a better theory: how about Malbert is the murderer?" Miss Flax listed Malbert's opportunities, peculiar behaviors, and possible motives.

"I did not yet mention this to you, Miss Flax, but Malbert is a member of the Jockey Club."

"Indeed! I allow, it's hard to picture him taking up with a ballet girl."

"No? He took up with Henrietta."

"True. But when Henrietta sets her sights on a fellow, he doesn't have much choice about what happens next."

Miss Flax also told Gabriel how the police had arrested the derelict, who'd been caught with blood on his hands and raving about being paid to kill. "Do you reckon the madman's some sort of hired killer?"

"Quite possibly. I must visit the *commissaire*'s office and endeavor to speak with this man."

Finally, Miss Flax told Gabriel how Madame Fayette had discovered her two disguises. "She was mighty suspicious of me when I went in yesterday morning. I don't believe she bought the story that I was your American cousin for a minute."

"Madame Fayette? Now that is rather interesting." Gabriel told Miss Flax about Cherrien's demand for the stomacher, and his threat to hand Ophelia over to the police if they failed.

"The rat! Wait. You say the client desires the stomacher by Saturday? Saturday is the day of Prince Rupprecht's ball."

"I hadn't thought of that. Yes."

"Who do you suppose the client is?"

"Someone who desires the stomacher."

"The *murderer* desires the stomacher."

"Yes. And maybe the murderer is Madame Fayette."

"What are you saying?"

"If Madame Fayette knows that Mrs. Brand and Miss Stonewall are, for lack of a better word, frauds, and Cherrien's client *also* knows—"

"Then it follows that Madame Fayette is his client." Miss Flax nodded. "But Madame Fayette is an awful gossip. She might've let slip what she knows about me to someone else."

"We really must pay her a call."

"We ought to turn over this Cherrien fellow to the police."

"If you do so, Cherrien will surely share *your* secrets with the police," Gabriel said. "Do you wish to risk exposing yourself in that fashion?"

"I'll hazard it."

"If you are jailed, Miss Flax—"

"I'm innocent!"

"Not of deceiving everyone as to your true identity. You could be jailed merely on suspicion. As a foreigner, your legal status is somewhat hazy. You could not attempt to locate Henrietta from jail. You could not look after Miss Bright from jail."

"Then what are we to do?"

"Locate the stomacher. If we accomplish that, then we will, one way or another, unmask the murderer."

"Then we'll go see Madame Fayette."

"Yes. Madame Fayette, and two other people of my acquaintance who also have an ardent interest in the stomacher."

Prue chiseled at egg yolk crusted on breakfast plates and had a good, long think about Hansel and Dalziel. The checklist Ma had always used for measuring up fellers wasn't the slightest help. Hansel and Dalziel were *both* handsome. Both of them were European blue bloods, and while neither had pots of brass, both of them probably would someday. The main difference was that Hansel seemed to have plum forgotten about Prue, while Dalziel had been so very sweet. Ma's checklist didn't include *sweet*.

There was a rap on the kitchen door.

The plate slipped silently under the water.

"Alors?" Beatrice shouted from the broom closet, where she was routing out mice with a rolling pin. "Open it! It must be Baldewyn locked himself out again, silly old *cancre*."

Prue smeared her wet hands down her apron and went to the door.

Only a hump-backed old woman in a raggedy gown, a shawl, and a brown kerchief. She cradled a large, gorgeously colored box in her arms. "Bonbons?" she said in a raspy voice. She was missing a couple of her choppers.

Candy? Well, Prue *had* finished the orange jellies and butterscotch drops Austorga had given her.

"Non!" Beatrice came up behind Prue, making shooing motions with her rolling pin. *"S'en aller!* How did you get past the gate, you old witch?"

"Bonbons *délicieux*." The crone stroked the top of the candy box with a boot-leather hand.

"Close the door, Prue," Beatrice said. "We do not allow peddlers, and Henri must have left the gate open again, the fool."

Quick as a wink, the crone dropped the candies and drew a revolver from the folds of her shawl. She cocked it—the gun looked too big for her rickety body—and aimed it at Prue.

Prue's lips parted. A gurgle came out.

"Sacre Dieu!" Beatrice screamed. She dropped her rolling pin.

The crone grabbed Prue and half pushed, half pulled her across the kitchen, meanwhile aiming her revolver at Beatrice. The crone herded Beatrice—squeaking in fright—into the broom closet and latched it shut.

Beatrice pounded on the closet door. Her cries were muffled.

With a steely grip, the crone dragged Prue out the door and as far as the carriageway—where the gate stood wide open. When Prue saw Lord and Lady Cruthlach's carriage in the street, she made up her mind: she'd rather take her chances getting shot than go like lambykins to slaughter in that carriage.

She wrenched her arm from the crone's grasp and started running.

A gunshot cracked the air. Prue kept going.

Prue had been a street rat as a tyke. Ma had given her free reign to roam the streets of their neighborhood, since Ma was usually too occupied to do mother-type things. And New York street rats were *mean*. Prue didn't have the fighting spirit, so she'd preferred to dodge, not tussle with, other ragamuffins.

The trick to a successful dodge was to make lots of turns. If you kept running in a straight line, your pursuer could just catch up and collar you. But clever urchins on the run made sudden turns, twists, and switchbacks, and survived, just like rats, with a zigzag kind of cunning.

Prue found a place to turn. And then she turned.

When Ophelia and Penrose arrived at Rue de la Paix, only a few delivery vans and errand boys were about. The door of Maison Fayette was shut tight.

"Too early," Ophelia said.

Just as they were turning away, the door cracked open.

"Josie!" Ophelia exclaimed without thinking. Josie had met Miss Stonewall, not Mrs. Brand.

Josie peered up at her with puzzled eyes. *"Oui, madame?"*

Drat. Ophelia resolved to keep her trap shut.

Penrose said, "Is Madame Fayette within?"

"Non, monsieur. We do not expect her at the shop today. She is quite overcome with fatigue as of late."

"But you, *mademoiselle*, are working?"

Josie appeared to be on the brink of nervous exhaustion. Her eyes were sunken, and bloodred cracks extended past the corners of her lips.

"I have been working all night. The prince's ball, you see. . . ."

"Ah. Gowns to be finished."

"Oui, monsieur."

"Would you be so kind as to tell me the address of Madame Fayette's private residence?"

"Oh, *non*! I could never—"

"Please," Ophelia said. "It's most urgent. It concerns the gentleman's death at the ballet last night—did you hear of it?"

"Oui . . . but you do not suppose *Madame* had anything to do with that poor gentleman's death?"

"I do not wish to upset you," Penrose said, "but yes, I'm afraid she might."

Josie's eyes darted up and down the sidewalk. She looked behind her, into the shadows of the shop's foyer. She leaned close. "Eighty-six Rue Vaneau." She clamped the door shut.

Rue Vaneau lay on the left side of the river, a genteel avenue of apartment blocks with iron balconies and steep slate roofs.

Penrose and Ophelia got past the building's concierge by using his Lord Harrington calling card. They climbed three flights of stairs, and Penrose rapped on Madame Fayette's door.

A maid answered, and she and Penrose held a whispered confabulation in French. Then Penrose passed the maid another one of his calling cards.

"Madame Fayette is abed," Penrose told Ophelia as they hiked back down the stairs. "I told the maid we will return in an hour. In the meantime, we aren't too terribly far away from the old acquaintances of mine that I mentioned."

"Old, as in longtime? Or old, like ancient?"

"Both."

21

⟶⟲⟵

Twenty minutes later, Ophelia and Penrose's carriage stopped in a gnarled side street. A soot-streaked mansion rose up, with pointy turrets, mullioned windows, and grinning monkey gargoyles.

"Looks like a witch's house," Ophelia said. They climbed the front steps.

"You're frightfully close to the mark." Penrose knocked on the front door. "Lord and Lady Cruthlach believe they possess . . . uncanny blood."

"And why exactly might they be Cherrien's clients?"

"Why? Because they believe in fairy tales, my dear."

Oh, my.

After a minute or so, a bulky, ginger-haired footman opened the door. He was stuffed into crimson satin livery, high-heeled shoes, and—oddly enough—a white apron. "Lord Harrington," he said in a Scots accent.

"Hume. I must speak with Lady Cruthlach."

"Yes, Your Lordship."

Moments later, Ophelia and Penrose were led into a stifling, dim sitting room. Hume positioned himself against a wall.

An old lady sat on a sofa before the fire. "Lord Harrington," she creaked. "What a pleasure. And who is this with you?"

"Mrs. Brand, my American aunt."

"Goodness! America? How *sad*. A nation singularly lacking in magic."

"Where is Lord Cruthlach?" Penrose asked.

"He is not well, I am afraid. And a pity, too, for he would so enjoy speaking with you. Please, sit."

Ophelia and Penrose sat side by side on a sofa.

"You and I, Lady Cruthlach, have known each other for many years," Penrose said. "Indeed, from time to time we have taken care with each other's secrets. I feel, then, that I may be perfectly blunt. Have you enlisted a solicitor by the name of Monsieur Cherrien to force me into locating the Cendrillon stomacher?"

"A solicitor? Good heavens, no, Lord Harrington. Why, if I wished to *force* you to do anything, as you say, I would simply do it myself." She twittered. "A stomacher, you say? Belonging to Cendrillon?"

"Pray, do not attempt to persuade me that you are ignorant of this matter." Penrose's voice grew hot. "I had deduced that this was the relic from Hôtel Malbert that had piqued your interest so much the last time we spoke."

"Then you deduced incorrectly."

Hume drew close, carrying a tray of glasses filled with something chokecherry red. Ophelia, Penrose, and Lady Cruthlach each took a glass. Hume placed the tray on a side table and positioned himself in front of the table. He was so near to Ophelia, she heard him breathing.

"*Do* drink, Mrs. Brand," Lady Cruthlach said.

Ophelia pretended to sip. Her eyes floated sideways to Hume. Some kind of object sat on the table behind him, next to the tray. A cream-painted box with glimmers of gold—

Hume made a side step, concealing the object.

He was hiding that thing.

"Of course, Lord Harrington," Lady Cruthlach said, "if you were to tell me *more* about this stomacher, what it looks like, for instance . . ." She began prying and wheedling. Penrose fended her off.

Ophelia took a gulp of the red cordial and, as she'd hoped, it made her cough. And cough.

"Good heavens, Mrs. Brand, are you well?" Penrose asked, half rising.

"Fine." Ophelia wheezed, with a pinch of dramatic flair. "It's just a bit like"—she staggered to her feet—"like turpentine."

"Turpentine!" Lady Cruthlach sounded affronted. "I have this shipped to me from Italy, from the only region the bull berry grows."

"Too . . . strong." Ophelia coughed some more and pounded a palm on her chest. She toppled sideways against Hume. *"Oof,"* she said as her padded hip struck Hume's thigh.

Hume was built like a brick chicken coop, but he staggered to the side. Ophelia reached out for the table. She knocked it over. The thing Hume had been hiding went flying and crashed on the floor. It tinkled a half measure of music, and fell silent.

Lady Cruthlach said nothing. Hume panted. Penrose, who had leapt to Ophelia's aid and had his hands on her shoulders, froze. All four of them stared.

The thing on the floor was—or *had* been—a music box. The cream-and-gold wooden base was splintered along one edge and the lid had opened to expose a mirrored inner lid and a little porcelain girl. Her yellow-haired head had snapped off and lay a few feet away. Real human hair on the head, by the looks of it, and a tiny, rosy, flawless little doll face.

"Looks just like Prue," Ophelia whispered.

Hume grunted.

"Sue?" Lady Cruthlach said. "Who is *Sue*?"

And the body. Well, the body of the doll, still affixed to the inside of the music box, was dressed in a miniature ivory gown, embroidered—of course!—in silver and gold, the bodice decorated with a tiny, silvery stomacher.

"Pick it up, Hume," Lady Cruthlach snapped. "Why are you standing there like an ox?"

Hume obeyed.

"*That*, dear Lady Cruthlach," Penrose said, "is what the stomacher looks like. Where did this music box come from?"

"I simply cannot recall."

"*Where did you get it?*"

Hume tensed, an attack dog waiting for the signal.

"Ah yes, I recall now. From that dear little trinket shop in Rue des Capucines. What is it called? Oh, yes. Colifichet and Sons."

stage sets

"We'll go to Colifichet's shop directly." Penrose handed Ophelia up into the carriage and jumped in beside her. "Colifichet has seen the stomacher." The carriage jerked forward.

"And Hume was trying to *hide* the music box."

"Yes—I haven't yet had a chance to congratulate you on your rather stunning sleight of hand. Or, I should say, sleight of hip."

"Prue shouldn't be left all alone at Hôtel Malbert. I've got a bad feeling about this." A sickening thought hit Ophelia. "Lady Cruthlach—and her husband, too—they're collectors, right? Fairy tale collectors, like you?"

"Yes."

"What if . . . do you think Lady Cruthlach might try to, well, *collect* Prue? Because she looks like her Cinderella music box?"

Ophelia wished with all her might that the professor would laugh off the notion. But to her dismay, his eyes grew troubled. "It is not inconceivable."

"Might we take Prue along with us today, then? She could stay in the carriage. She's able to take naps anywhere, and I'm certain she won't complain if we give her some penny sweets."

"Very well. I'll instruct the driver to go first to Hôtel Malbert."

Penrose waited in the carriage. Baldewyn appeared to have been awoken from a snooze when he opened the front door. Ophelia rushed past him without a word.

Prue wasn't in her bedchamber. But then, why would she be? It was nearing luncheon time.

Ophelia hurried downstairs. As she passed through the entry foyer, the stepsisters and Miss Smythe were just returning from their outing. Their arms were piled high with parcels. Only Miss Smythe noticed Ophelia rushing past. Behind her owlish spectacles, her glance was sharp.

Ophelia heard the thuds and shouts as soon as she was on the kitchen stairs. She raced down. The thuds were coming from the closet under the stairs.

Ophelia fumbled with the latch and flung open the door. Beatrice staggered out, begrimed and sweaty, with flyaway hair.

"Where is Prue?" Ophelia cried.

"Oh, that woman, that old woman with the gun!"

Ophelia's heart shrank to a pebble. "What woman?"

"A peddler woman, old. A hunchback. Selling sweets."

Sweets? Prue would follow a pointy-tailed demon if he lured her with sweets.

Ophelia tore out the kitchen door and through the courtyard. The carriageway gate stood open.

"Miss Flax!" Penrose cried when he saw her.

"She's gone! Someone has taken Prue."

Ophelia insisted that they drive straight back to Lady Cruthlach's mansion. She had a mad, sickening hunch that somehow Lady Cruthlach was mixed up with Prue's disappearance. That horrible little music box . . .

The traffic thickened and slowed, and Ophelia fought panic. She held her elbows tight in cupped hands. The professor sat in tense silence.

The carriage hadn't quite stopped in front of the mansion when Ophelia leapt out and ran up the steps. Penrose was just behind her. They both pounded on the door.

No answer.

Ophelia tried the door handles. Locked.

"What about another door?" Ophelia stepped back to scan

the façade. She had just spied an archway off to one side, when the front door opened.

Hume.

Penrose grabbed Ophelia's hand. "Please excuse us," he said. Hand in hand, they raced up the stairs and burst into the stifling sitting room.

Lady Cruthlach slept upright on the sofa where they had left her.

"Shall I wake her?" Penrose asked.

"No. Let's search the house."

For once, the professor didn't argue.

Ophelia and Penrose raced through the mansion, room by room. In one chamber, they saw Lord Cruthlach asleep in a huge sleigh bed. They saw rooms filled with rich furnishings, empty rooms, and rooms cluttered with trunks and broken chairs and bric-a-brac.

But no Prue.

"The cellar," Ophelia said. She stopped in the corridor, half bent, panting. "We must check the cellar."

They clattered down a stone stairwell and found the kitchen.

Bitter-smelling steam clouded the kitchen. A huge iron pot sputtered on the stove. The table was a hodgepodge of bottles and bowls, heaps of green leaves, and paper boxes. A small, brownish-green turtle wandered across.

"What's cooking?" Ophelia said. "Witch's brew?" She picked up the turtle. "You poor thing. I won't allow them to boil you."

The turtle shrank into its shell.

Hume emerged from an arched stone doorway near the stove. He held a big wooden spoon like a bludgeon. "I suppose you didn't find what you were looking for?"

"The girl," Penrose said.

"No girl here."

"Where is the serving woman?"

"No serving woman here."

"Don't tell me you do all the work yourself."

"I am the most loyal of servants."

"Would you kill for your master and mistress?"

"If they instructed me to do so."

"Did you kill Sybille Pinet and Caleb Grant?"

Hume's eyes flicked to something on the table and back to Penrose.

A thick, age-splotted book lay open on the table amid the jars and bowls and funny ingredients. That's what Hume had glanced at. Only a receipt book, surely. But then, why did Ophelia have the sense that all of Hume's attention, all the fibers in his bulky body, were fastened tight to that book?

"What's in the book?" Ophelia asked.

Beside her, the professor tensed.

When Miss Flax said *book*, Gabriel recognized in an instant all that he had overlooked. Lord and Lady Cruthlach had never desired the stomacher. What they desired was this book.

Gabriel had read of it, once. *Mediocris Maleficorum*. What a layman might simply call the Fairy Godmother's spell book. It had been Gabriel's understanding that the book—*if* it existed—was either an originary text of unimaginable power, or an intricate hoax.

Gabriel leaned over the book.

A thrill, almost painful, coursed up the nerves of his fingers and straight to his heart, which pumped still faster. Handwritten. Latin. Small, woodcut illustrations. The receipt at the top of the page read: *Elixir Vitae XIII*. An elixir of life.

Then, a sharp crack at the base of Gabriel's skull. Hume's spoon. Pain vibrated. Gabriel staggered forward and Hume whisked the spell book off the table just before Gabriel went sprawling across the top. Miss Flax cried out. Glass and porcelain vessels crashed. Something splatted on Gabriel's cheek.

Hume strode towards a doorway with the spell book tucked under his arm.

"You really don't think, man, that you'll bring those two corpses back to life?" Gabriel yelled after him.

But there was no answer. Hume was gone.

* * *

"Don't panic, Miss Flax," the professor said as they swung out the front doors of the Cruthlach mansion. He was still wiping a slimy green smear from his cheek with his handkerchief.

Ophelia *was* on the verge of panic. She was sweating under her wig and she clutched the turtle to her chest. "I had it fixed in my head that this was where we'd find Prue. If she's not here, she could be *anywhere*." Oh dear Lord, Prue couldn't, *couldn't* be hurt. "Is your head all right, Professor? Shall I have a look?"

"Quite all right," Penrose said quickly. "We've two more obvious possibilities—at least, if we are still operating under the assumption that the stomacher is central to the question of every death and disappearance."

"Maybe Henrietta whisked Prue away—couldn't that be it? Couldn't she be safe and sound with her mother somewhere?" Ophelia heard the shrill edge in her own voice.

Penrose gingerly rubbed the back of his head, where Hume had conked him with the spoon. "Yes. Yes, that would certainly be—"

"You don't think Prue is—that she's a goner, do you?" Fury suddenly bubbled in Ophelia. "I'll find who took her, and I'll—I'll make them sorry!"

"We'll go to visit Colifichet in his shop. That is the first order of business. He has evidently seen the stomacher. He knows, because of the ballet, that the stomacher is related to the story of 'Cendrillon.' And most important, at one point or another Colifichet must have encountered Sybille Pinet."

22

C OLIFICHET & FILS, the gilt lettering on one of the arched windows read. The carriage stopped at the curb.

"Are you ready, Miss Flax?" Penrose asked.

"Do you think he'll be all right?" Ophelia gently touched the turtle, who she'd placed on the seat. "The little fellow hasn't so much as glanced out since I picked him up in that kitchen."

"You rescued him from certain death. Perhaps he requires time to recover his equilibrium."

They got out. Lustrous teal velvet lined Colifichet's display windows. Toys of gilt, enamel, silk, colored jewels, brass, and human hair nestled in the velvet. There were monkeys in jesters' costumes, a doll seated at a tiny harpsichord, a crouched tiger, several grinning acrobats, a rabbit with a drum, and a donkey in a three-piece suit. But no Cinderellas—although there *was* a Wicked Wolf, covered in what looked like real dog's fur, attired in Granny's nightgown and cap.

"I'd never give one of those things to a child in all my livelong days," Ophelia said.

"They would surely inspire nightmares," Penrose said. "And you haven't yet seen them wound up and whirring about."

Inside, the shop smelled faintly of the grease P. Q. Putnam's Traveling Circus had used to slick the carousel gears. A portly shopkeeper in a green coat was helping a lady at a display case. The shopkeeper placed a tiny camel on the countertop. Slowly, and with a soft clicking, it walked across the counter.

The shopkeeper said something in French to Penrose.

"He says he will assist us in a moment," Penrose said to Ophelia.

They waited.

A slim form emerged from the rear of the shop.

Pierre, Colifichet's apprentice. He appeared to be searching for something behind one of the counters.

Ophelia made a beeline for Pierre. His eyes flared. "Just the gentleman I wished to see," she said in an imperious tone. "Or, *one* of the gentlemen—pray tell, boy, where is your master, Monsieur Colifichet?"

Pierre's jaw drooped, sullen.

"Where is Monsieur Colifichet?" Ophelia repeated. "I know that you speak English—Lord Harrington here told me as much."

"Monsieur Colifichet is working," Pierre said. His eyes darted to the shopkeeper, still nattering to the lady customer, then back to Ophelia. "Why is it, *madame*, that you wished to see him?"

Ophelia ignored Penrose's warning glance. With Prue missing, this was no time to mince words. "It concerns the matter of a stomacher. Cinderella's stomacher, to be precise. Oh yes—and two disappeared ladies, and two murders."

"A stomacher? Murder?" Pierre cocked his head. "*Mais oui*, that sounds precisely the sort of thing in which my master would be interested."

Ophelia and Penrose exchanged an amazed look.

Pierre lowered his voice. "I have, in truth, noticed a stomacher in Monsieur Colifichet's workshop."

"Hidden?"

Pierre nodded, and leaned closer. "In a cabinet. Locked up. Is it important?"

"Very," Ophelia said.

"I shall bring you to my master, but I am certain he will not admit to possessing the stomacher."

Pierre beckoned them behind the counter and through a curtain. The shopkeeper didn't notice. Pierre led them down a gloomy corridor and paused in front of a closed door.

"I must warn you, Monsieur Colifichet has not slept in two days. The special project he has been working on is not going as well as he would like. There have been a few small, unforeseen problems." Pierre opened the door.

"*Allez-vous en!*" Colifichet screamed.

Go away!

Colifichet perched on a tall stool at a draughtsman's table, hunched with a pencil and ruler.

He held his pencil in his right hand, Gabriel noted. Not his left.

Tidy workshop benches stored tools and glimmering little metal things. Weak white light slanted through tall windows. In the far corner, black cloth shrouded four or five tall, bulky forms.

"What is the meaning of this interruption?" Colifichet asked in French. He got down from his stool, fists balled, jaw unshaven, shirt untucked. "I told you that I was not to be disturbed under any circumstance. You again, Lord Harrington. Is this your nursemaid, perhaps?" He sent a scornful glance to Miss Flax in her dumpy disguise.

"Allow me to do the talking just this once," Gabriel murmured to Miss Flax.

Miss Flax, uncharacteristically silent, nodded.

"They insisted upon coming to see you," Pierre said to Colifichet. "They pushed me aside and forced their way in. I attempted to stop them."

"That is not precisely the way I would describe it," Gabriel said. Why was the apprentice lying? "It is about a trinket I happened to view today."

"Trinket?" Colifichet massaged his eye sockets. "Pray, do not call the fruit of my labors a *trinket*."

"A music box, then. In the house of Lord and Lady Cruthlach. Its toy dancer was in the form of Cendrillon, dressed in a miniature costume precisely like that in the ballet playing at the opera house."

"Lord and Lady Cruthlach commissioned that music box—and, I must add, they are both quite, *quite* senile. I simply built it to their specifications."

"Oh, indeed? When was this?"

"A year ago or more. I cannot recall. In fact, it was Pierre who built all but the interior mechanism of that piece."

"Were either of you at all surprised when the ballerina's Cinderella costume happened to be identical to that of the doll on the music box?"

Pierre's eyes were empty.

Colifichet sniffed. "I pay no attention whatever to ballet costumes. My work concerns the stage sets. The rest—mmn!—it is women's rubbish."

"What of the fact that the music box figure resembles, to an uncanny degree, the murdered girl Sybille Pinet? I was told she worked as an artist's model at one point. Did she model for you?"

"No. I do not use models."

"That is rather difficult to believe."

"Believe whatever you wish, Lord Harrington. I do not much care. As for the Cinderella figure on the music box, well, it possesses an insipid sort of beauty. A beauty with every distinguishing characteristic quite refined out of it until all that is left is a rather bland perfection. A living girl, with all of a living girl's flaws, simply cannot compete with the cool perfection of art."

"A pretty speech, Monsieur Colifichet, but quite beside the point. I'll ask you directly: did you send a woman to steal a young lady from the house of the Marquis de la Roque-Fabliau today?"

"*Mon Dieu*, your accusations grow more and more curious. Do I appear to have any interest whatsoever in young ladies? Now, if you do not mind, I must return to my work. And you, Pierre—stay. We must get that leg just so. You, *madame et monsieur*, may show yourselves out—and perhaps peruse the shop before you go, hmn? You might find an automaton to amuse you—because you must be *ever* so bored if you are intruding in police business. *Bonjour."*

Ophelia started down the gloomy corridor towards the front of Colifichet's shop, but Penrose touched her arm and beckoned her in the other direction. A door at the end led out to a tight rear courtyard. Moss clotted the paving stones. Yellow walls rose five stories high, and clotheslines drooped from windows. Penrose studied the buildings.

"Do you mind letting me in on the big secret?" Ophelia whispered. "I don't even know what Mr. Colifichet *said* back there."

"I shall tell you in a moment. But first—I'll be returning later. I must learn of all possible points of entry. This place is a bit like a fortress, unfortunately—although there does seem to be a gate at the back."

Ophelia squinted up at the windows and clotheslines. "Oh, we'll find our way in."

"We."

"Goodness, Professor, surely you aren't so elderly you require an ear horn." Ophelia bustled back inside.

Madame Fayette's residence was next. During the carriage ride, Penrose told Ophelia what Colifichet had said.

Ophelia, holding the turtle on her lap, said, "If Monsieur Colifichet has the stomacher, as Pierre claimed, then *he* must have killed Mr. Grant last night. But what does it have to do with Prue?"

"I do not know."

"How will we ever find her?"

Penrose didn't answer at once, and Ophelia didn't fancy his grim face one bit. Finally, he said, "It seems to me that we must continue to pursue the stomacher. If we do indeed find it in Colifichet's workshop tonight, we must bring it to the police, along with a report of the lawyer Cherrien's demands."

"You'd give up a fairy tale relic like that?"

"Prue is far more important. Meanwhile, it is still necessary to speak with Madame Fayette. If she is Cherrien's client, then she desires the stomacher."

"I don't *care* about the stomacher! All I care about is Prue."

"We *will* find Prue. I give you my word."

"You cannot give me your word."

"The stomacher will lead us to her. And as I believe you well know, Miss Flax, there is much to be said for steely determination."

Ophelia stared out the carriage window as they bumped along. Never had the Paris streets seemed so alien. "I feel as though everything is slipping through my fingers like sand. Henrietta gone. Now Prue." Ophelia couldn't say it aloud, but she wondered how she'd ever live with herself if she never saw Prue again.

This time, Madame Fayette's maid told them that her mistress was awake and expecting them.

Madame Fayette's entry foyer was a little, airy space done up in shades of lemon and periwinkle. The maid led Ophelia and Penrose down a narrow, lofty corridor scented with dried lavender and into a light-filled parlor. Oil paintings, framed sketches, and watercolors filled the walls, and side tables and shelves displayed busts and baubles. Yellow roses overflowed from crystal vases. An ornate brass birdcage stood on a stand. Inside, a canary hopped.

"Good morning," Madame Fayette said. She wore a gown of green silk with more ruffles than a flustered goose. She poured coffee from a graceful silver pot, and her diamond bracelet sparkled. "Lord Harrington and—?"

"Mrs. Brand, my American aunt."

"Ah, indeed?"

Ophelia watched Madame Fayette closely. If she knew that Miss Stonewall and Mrs. Brand were frauds, and if she was the one who'd enlisted the lawyer to put the screws on Penrose, she didn't show it. Maybe she hadn't sent that boxed gown addressed to Madame Brand, after all. But if she hadn't, who had? Funny, too, that Josie had said Madame Fayette was suffering from fatigue, because she appeared rosy and well-rested.

"Please, do sit," Madame Fayette said. "I was most surprised when my maid told me that you called at such an early hour but I must admit, my curiosity is piqued. Coffee?"

"Thank you," Penrose said.

Ophelia nodded. She'd made up her mind to let the professor do the talking. *All* of the talking. No point in giving her disguise away.

They sat. Madame Fayette passed cups of coffee and gestured to the cream and sugar. "Does this concern Miss Stonewall's garments, Lord Harrington? Josie has not been herself as of late—she is the seamstress who finished those gowns—so I do apologize if the garments were not sewn to your young cousin's taste."

That was rich. Madame Fayette lolling about in splendor while poor Josie worked her fingers to the bone?

"It is to do with murder," Penrose said. He was staring at a watercolor painting on the wall. "And a young lady called Prudence Bright who was taken against her will from Hôtel Malbert this morning."

"Taken?" Madame Fayette touched her throat. Her diamond bracelet slid towards her elbow. "Who is the girl, precisely?"

Penrose began to describe Prue's disappearance.

Ophelia stopped breathing. Mercy. That bracelet, with its braided design and thick crust of diamonds, had seemed familiar before, when Madame Fayette had taken her measurements at Maison Fayette. And now Ophelia knew why: the last time she'd seen that bracelet it had been on *Henrietta's* wrist, back in New York. It had been a gift from one of her gentleman suitors.

"Excuse me, *madame*," Ophelia said, interrupting Penrose's ramblings. "I can't help admiring your bracelet."

They all looked at the bracelet.

"Where did you get it?" Ophelia asked.

Madame Fayette laughed, but her eyes were hard. "You Americans and your simply *charming* informal—"

"That bracelet belonged to the Marquise Henrietta. You *do* know her, and she *was* one of your customers. Why did you lie about it when I asked you?"

"I never said that I did not know the marquise. I merely refrained from engaging in gossip. Either way, this is not her bracelet—what a fantastical suggestion! It is mine. I have owned it for years. And, do you not mean to say, Madame Brand, why did I lie to *Mademoiselle Stonewall*?"

A heavy silence. Penrose scratched his temple.

"I shall not even attempt to understand the meaning of your various and absurd disguises, Madame or Mademoiselle Whoever-you-are," Madame Fayette said.

"How did you know?" Ophelia asked.

"I measured you. Every inch of you. I recognize the turn of your wrist and the set of your shoulders. And you, Lord Harrington. I cannot begin to fathom why a gentleman of your standing would consort with this—this actress thing—"

"Now see here," Penrose said.

"—but I *am* somewhat intrigued as to why the two of you have undertaken to play at officers of the police." Madame Fayette picked up a little silver handbell and jingled it.

With her left hand.

Madame Fayette was a southpaw!

"If, that is," Madame Fayette said, "you are able to explain your charade before my maid arrives to show you out."

"You're a lefty, Madame Fayette," Ophelia said.

"Pardon?"

"You rang the bell with your left hand."

"Ah," Penrose said.

"I cannot think why that is of any interest to you, but, *oui*, I do use my—"

"I'm *interested*," Ophelia said, "because Caleb Grant— and maybe Sybille Pinet, too—were shot with a lefty's gun. A *lady* lefty's gun."

"Are you accusing me of murder? Good heavens, you *are* an audacious creature. Where are your manners? But wait— I do not suppose they teach those on the musical stage or wherever it is you have come fr—"

"I'll save you some puff and cut this short," Ophelia said. "Did you do it?"

Madame Fayette's face flushed. "If I *had* murdered anyone, why would I confess it to *you*?"

Good point. "To get it off your chest?"

"If you must know, I owned a small pistol specially made for me once for a journey through the mountains. There were tales of bandits at the time, and I wished to protect myself. But that pistol was stolen."

"Stolen!" Ophelia said, glancing at Penrose. But he was staring at that watercolor painting again. "When was it stolen?" Ophelia asked. "Was it stolen from this apartment?"

"That is quite enough, you impudent little morsel. I did not intend to mention it, but . . . how could anyone be fooled by that wig you have on?" Madame Fayette rang the bell again, furiously this time. "It appears to have contracted mange."

Ophelia scowled. She'd paid a pretty penny for this wig.

"I allow, your application of cosmetics is remarkably cunning," Madame Fayette said. "But that bust? Those padded hips? Laughable!"

"I reckon if it's your calling in life to measure busts and hips, then you might discern a—"

"My *calling*, you vicious little impostor, is to create works of art that may be worn—"

"Sure. On ladies' busts and hips."

Madame Fayette's face turned a shade of puce.

Ophelia felt Penrose's eyes on her. She wouldn't look at him. Surely the ladylike, retiring Miss Ivy Banks would never, ever say *busts and hips*.

But it turned out that Penrose had his mind on something else.

"Madame Fayette, this watercolor"—he gestured to the painting he'd been staring at—"it is a stage scenery design, no? With rather a distinctive style to the trees."

"That dingy little thing? I mean to be rid of it. It doesn't go at all with the rest of the décor."

"I saw many quite like it at the apartment of the late Caleb Grant. These are at times quite valuable, I understand—"

"No, no, that is only a cheap reproduction. And I must protest that this *interrogation*, in my own home no less, is quite impermissible!" Madame Fayette stood. "If that will be all, I really must ask that you leave—ah, Odile! There you are. Where have you been?" She scolded the maid in French and kept at it even when Ophelia and Penrose were walking out the front door.

23

"You're certain that bracelet belonged to Henrietta?" Penrose asked Ophelia as they trotted down the stairs.

"If not, then one just like it."

"If Madame Fayette received Henrietta's bracelet in exchange for keeping a secret . . ."

"I'd reckon it had to do with a fellow. With Henrietta, it *always* has to do with a fellow. And you're certain that watercolor painting was like those in Mr. Grant's apartment?"

"Yes. Which in itself would not be strange, because surely they both could own paintings by the same artist, particularly by a scenery designer from the opera house where they were both employed at one time."

"Except Madame Fayette said it's only a cheap reproduction. Which sounded like a tall tale to me, because nothing in her apartment looked cheap."

Penrose nodded.

"Do you suppose Madame Fayette is a blackmailer?" Ophelia asked. "Finds out her customers' secrets and then squeezes them for jewelry and paintings and things?"

"It certainly seems a plausible conjecture."

"Maybe she knew why Mr. Grant had that gown made for Sybille, and took a painting or two to stay mum."

They reached the bottom of the stairs and hurried through the black-and-white marble vestibule and out into the street. They paused on the sidewalk. Pedestrians streamed around them.

Ophelia raised her voice over the clamor of traffic. "All right, then, let's make a list. Madame Fayette blackmails her customers—maybe. She knows plenty about the stomacher since she designed the ballet costume and the gown, and the stomacher was even in her shop yesterday morning, before Mr. Grant took it away. Madame Fayette is a lefty, and she even admitted to having owned a lefty's pistol. Does that mean she's the murderer?"

"What of a motive? And opportunity?"

"Motive? The stomacher."

"She voluntarily handed the stomacher over to Grant, remember—"

"But then he was shot that very night, maybe for the stomacher."

"Why would Madame Fayette devise such a maneuver? Giving the stomacher to Grant only to kill him for it the same day?"

"It's peculiar, I allow. As for opportunity, well, Madame Fayette must know her way around the opera house if she was once the costume mistress. She could've gotten into Hôtel Malbert's garden because she knows the stepsisters. She is their dressmaker. Remember, too, that Austorga was backstage—"

"Which brings us right back round to Caleb Grant and Madame Babin." Penrose pushed his hands into his pockets and gazed thoughtfully at Ophelia. "By the by, that was a tremendous performance up there, Miss Flax."

Ophelia sighed. Here he went with the stick-in-the-mud act again. "I beg your forgiveness if I made you *uncomfortable*, Professor—"

"No, no. I meant to say only that, well, your disguises— your quite frankly *absurd* disguises—and your, ah, loquacity, shall we say—"

"If you're saying I'm mouthy, you aren't the first one."

"Yes, well, *no*, I mean . . ." Penrose adjusted his spectacles. "Your methods are effective. Remarkably effective. Impressive, to be perfectly honest." He smiled.

Confusion knocked over Ophelia's thoughts and sent them scattering. "I guess there are a few advantages to not being ladylike and retiring, then." Drat. Why had she said that?

Penrose looked at her curiously. "Whatever do you mean?"

"Oh. Well. Only that your betrothed, Miss Ivy Banks, possesses a retiring and ladylike nature—you said so—and I was only pointing out that the likes of me have strong points, too."

"The likes of you, Miss Flax?" Penrose's eyebrows knitted and his eyes shone with warmth. "There is only one of you, but I do agree, you possess strong points. Multitudes, in fact, and I daresay there is a turtle waiting in that carriage who would heartily concur."

Ophelia wasn't sure what the professor was getting at. She glanced away. Just when she thought she was done with that nervy, human cannonball feeling when she was with the professor, he had to go and stir it up again.

Well, *this* was an unexpected turn of events.

Miss Flax seemed to be, oddly enough, envious of Miss Ivy Banks. Or, rather, envious of the idea of Miss Ivy Banks. And that might mean that Miss Flax, well, *cared* about him, Gabriel.

She'd turned her face away so he could see nothing but her homely taffeta bonnet and a curve of crepey cheek. And, by God, that cheek suddenly seemed a beautiful sight.

He was further gone than he'd thought.

Suddenly, a large-wheeled velocipede jerked up the curb and onto the crowded sidewalk several paces off. A slim figure in a dark suit pedaled the velocipede furiously, jacket flapping wide. The figure wore a black highwayman's mask and a shoved-down bowler hat.

Ladies screamed. Gentlemen shouted. A dog reared up on its hind legs and yapped.

Miss Flax hadn't noticed the velocipede. She frowned out into the teeming traffic, apparently lost in thought.

The velocipede careened towards her. The cyclist hunkered forward to heave more weight into the pedals. Three yards off, close enough for Gabriel to see the glint of a pistol tucked inside the cyclist's jacket. Then two yards, one—

Gabriel grabbed Miss Flax's arm and pulled her back. The velocipede whizzed by. Miss Flax sagged into Gabriel's arms with a cry. The velocipede bumped down the curb and zigzagged out of sight behind an omnibus.

Gabriel considered himself quite the opposite of what one termed *a romantic*. Yet he'd somehow managed to sweep Miss Flax into his arms quite like a pose from one of those perishingly self-serious Wagner operas.

Her eyes stared up at him with their melting darkness (never mind the faux crow's feet). Her chest, beneath all that padding, rose and fell. Gabriel's chest rose and fell, too. Her lips, too wide to be considered truly beautiful and yet, suddenly fiercely beautiful to *him*, parted—

"My toe," Miss Flax whispered. "Oh golly, he crunched my toe."

"Oh. Yes. Rather. Your toe?" Gabriel returned her to a perpendicular position. "Are you quite all right?"

"Not exactly." She tried to put her weight on her right foot and winced. "He did it on purpose!" She glared up the street in the direction the velocipede had gone. Nothing but a steady stream of traffic and the hissing clatter of dozens of wheels and hooves against wet stones. "Did you get a good look at him?"

"He wore a mask and a bowler, and—well, on that velocipede, his entire appearance was really quite farcical." Not as farcical, of course, as Gabriel *himself* felt at that juncture. He ran a finger under his collar.

"Might it have been a lady?" Miss Flax asked.

"A lady? On a velocipede? In a bowler hat?" The cyclist *had* had a slight build.

"Miss Smythe—you remember, the friend of the Misses Malbert—is supposedly mad for velocipedes. I was told she owns two of them."

Gabriel handed Miss Flax up into the carriage. "But why, for pity's sake, would Miss Smythe attempt to mow you down in that fashion? And how might she have known where to find you?" He glanced at the driver, and then said to Miss Flax, "Where are we going next?"

"To see Madame Babin about Mr. Grant's watercolor paintings." Miss Flax checked on the turtle, still hiding in its shell. She bent to touch her foot and winced again.

Gabriel directed the driver and climbed up into the carriage. They wedged into the stream of traffic.

"I'm awfully sorry, Professor, but I've got to take a look at my foot." Miss Flax began to unlace her boot.

Gabriel looked away. If the sight of a lady in a padded matron's disguise unlacing a boot that appeared to have gone through the wars seemed fetching to a chap, well, what precisely did that say about him?

He feared that he knew the answer.

Although it felt distressingly intimate to do so in front of the professor, Ophelia shimmied off her boot. The little toe of her right foot had already swollen to the size of a grape. She had no doubt that beneath the black woolen stocking it was also the purplish hue of a grape, too. And it hurt like the dickens, with that noisy, throbby kind of pain.

"That looks frightful, Miss Flax. We ought to go directly to see a doctor. I am certain they will send for one at my hotel if—"

"No, no, it's nothing." Ophelia was acutely aware of the large hole in her stocking. She tried to stuff her foot back into the boot. No go. Too swollen. She loosened the laces, and tried again. This time she got it in—barely. Splendiferous. Now her feet—or at least one of them—were even *bigger*. "I didn't mention it before, because it didn't seem too important, but this morning I saw Miss Smythe out in the garden, speaking with the coachman, Henri. I couldn't hear, because I saw them from my window and they were outside by the carriage house, but they seemed . . . familiar."

"Arguing?"

"Not exactly."

Penrose *ahem*ed. "Embracing?"

"No. But it seemed sort of secretive and urgent. Miss Smythe said they were merely conversing about a lost glove and I put it out of my mind but now I wonder . . . what if it was Miss Smythe on that velocipede? She could have followed us to Madame Fayette's if she'd set her mind to it. She could be following us still."

"On a *velocipede*?"

"The traffic is certainly moving slowly enough."

"I don't wish to alarm you, Miss Flax, but whoever the cyclist was, he—or she—was carrying a gun."

The funny thing about a nunnery was, it didn't matter if you were pretty or plain, bony or plump, or even if you had a burn scar across your cheek as big as a hand. Which, as a matter of fact, someone in the Pensionnat Sainte Estelle *did* have, and it was a pity, too, because that dark-haired novice would've been a right looker without that scar.

Except.

Prue dropped her gaze down to the damp dirt of the garden plot and hurried up ripping out more dead plants. Except being a looker didn't matter. *Shouldn't* matter. She had figured that out already, and she'd only been hunkered down in the nunnery for—what was it?—three hours? It felt like longer. The nunnery was so quiet and cool, and everything smelled like beeswax and clean laundry. Time seemed gentler.

When Prue had finally found the Pensionnat Sainte Estelle, across the river from Malbert's mansion, and, hopefully, miles away from that crone and her revolver, she'd been wheezing for breath and sweaty. She'd rattled the nunnery gates. When a nun came and opened up, it was as though they'd been expecting her. The nun had led her to Sister Alphonsine.

Prue had gulped water, taken a hot bath, dressed up in clean, nunnish togs, and devoured a big meal. Then Sister Alphonsine had set her to work in the herb garden out back.

The nunnery felt safe. No mice in sight, either, although Prue missed the fat ginger cat.

The only snag was, Prue didn't know what she was going to do next. Ophelia would be worried sick about her. But how could she tell Ophelia where she was without risking telling the wrong people, too?

24

When Ophelia and Penrose alighted from the carriage in the Latin Quarter, Ophelia indulged in a quick glance about the street. A peddler wheeled a handcart piled with onions. Ladies in kerchiefs chattered out second-story windows. A violinist screeched away on the corner, hat at his feet. Two students, already drunk—or still drunk—stumbled into an inn. Nothing seemed unusual.

It was silly to think a person might've followed them all this way through the city on a velocipede.

Madame Babin was at home. Her mahogany hair clung to her slack cheeks. A wrinkled, saffron silk dressing gown drooped to her ankles. *"Oui?"*

"Madame Babin, we would be most obliged if we could have a brief word with you," Penrose said in English.

Surely she understood English; she had been living with the American Caleb Grant.

A Siamese cat curved around the doorjamb. Clara scooped it up. "Who are you?" she asked in throaty English. Her eyes flicked to Ophelia. "Who is this old river barge?"

Ophelia drew herself up. "I am his aunt, Madame Brand."

"His aunt? You might buy a nicer bonnet, then. You resemble a charwoman."

"How rude! Did—"

"Madame Babin," Penrose said quickly, "it is urgent that we speak with you regarding Monsieur Grant's death."

"What does it matter? He is gone and the murderer was arrested. And why do you care one way or the other?" Clara stroked the cat. Hard.

Ophelia said, "We care because two ladies, the Marquise de la Roque-Fabliau and her daughter, are missing. We believe their disappearances are related to Monsieur Grant's demise."

"Go away." Clara, still holding the cat, nudged the door shut with her shoulder.

"Our questions also concern the Cinderella stomacher and a certain letter you could describe as a death threat," Ophelia said.

The door stopped.

"We *had* supposed the wisest course was to go to the police with the matter," Ophelia went on, "but I suspected that you would not especially enjoy being questioned."

Clara's voice fell to a hiss. "How do you know about the letter?"

"You must have dropped it in the opera house lobby."

"Bah!" Clara threw a hand up. "Very well, then, very well. What do I care?" She left the door open and stalked into the apartment. Her dressing gown wafted. The cat glared over Clara's shoulder at Ophelia.

"Well done," Penrose murmured in Ophelia's ear, and Ophelia smiled in spite of herself.

They followed Clara into the sitting room. It was cluttered, as before, with the addition of half-filled wine bottles, goblets, brimming ashtrays, and tasseled pillows on the carpet. Acrid smoke drifted in the air.

"I could not sleep." Clara crouched on a stool and picked up a cigarette that had been left burning in an ashtray. The cat leapt away. "I was waiting for him to come and shoot me, too. And I was thinking of Caleb, laid out on a slab at the morgue. To be sure, he *always* seemed to be laid out on a morgue slab, even in life." She took a long inhale from her cigarette. The skin about her lips puckered. "But still."

"You suppose the murderer is a *him*?" Ophelia asked.

"I *know* the murderer is a him, and he was arrested!"

"Come now, Madame Babin," Penrose said. "You know as well as we do that the police have not arrested the true culprit."

"The madman had blood on his hands!"

"He was probably paid to kill," Ophelia said. "What raving lunatic would have the foresight to write that death threat and feign a lady's hand in the bargain?"

"We believe Monsieur Grant's death was somehow related to his little enterprise of procuring ballet girls for wealthy gentlemen," Penrose said. "What might you be able to tell me about that?"

Clara squinted at Penrose through a stream of smoke. "Lord Harrytown, you said you are called?"

"Harrington."

"Yes. A lord. You look just the sort who would pay for Caleb's services."

Penrose's jaw tightened. "You confirm that there was indeed such an enterprise?"

"Does it come as a great shock? Those girls parade half unclothed onstage every night. None of them come from respectable backgrounds."

Penrose shifted in his chair, and Ophelia knew he was thinking of how *she* was just such a young lady. She sat even straighter.

"The girls all desire—and need—the money," Clara said. "And the men? Bah! To hell with all of them!"

"Did Madame Fayette blackmail Monsieur Grant?" Ophelia asked.

"Blackmail? No. Why would she?"

"Did Madame Fayette write the death threat?"

"We did not know who wrote it. Someone slipped it under the door here, yesterday afternoon. I told Caleb to leave it alone, but he insisted upon confronting whoever it was. If I had not been waylaid by an insane woman in the stage wings

when I was scolding that careless Russian ballerina for stain-
ing her costume, he might still be alive."

Ophelia fought the peculiar urge to cry. "Are you an employee of the opera house, then?"

"Yes. I look after the costumes. Why would Madame
Fayette blackmail Caleb? We only knew her slightly. She
left her position as costume mistress years before Caleb
moved to Paris and took the position at the opera house."

"He came from America?" Ophelia asked.

"Yes. Philadelphia. But the Americans are philistines
who would not know real art if it smacked them in the face.
So Caleb left."

"Was Monsieur Grant Sybille Pinet's father?" Ophelia
asked.

"Good heavens, no."

"Speaking of art"—Penrose gestured to the wall behind
Clara, the wall filled with watercolors of stage scenery
designs—"I noticed a watercolor quite like these in Madame
Fayette's home. I have reason to believe she received it in
exchange for keeping quiet about something. Something to
do, perhaps, with Caleb's enterprise and the stomacher. Did
Caleb have the stomacher in his possession when he died?"

Clara sucked her cigarette and nodded.

"If he gave the murderer the stomacher, why was he
shot?" Ophelia asked.

"How would I know?"

"Do you know what the stomacher means?"

"Of course I know."

"Because of the ballet costume."

"Stupid woman. *You* do not know."

Ophelia lifted her brows. "Know what?"

"Who I am."

"No, not exactly."

"Not merely the mistress of Caleb!" Clara twitched her
shoulders. "My God, everyone believes that! How much I
gave up! And for what?"

Ophelia and Penrose exchanged a glance. Ophelia said,
"I'm sorry, I don't quite follow."

Clara tapped ash into a vase full of withered flowers. "I am the Marquise de la Roque-Fabliau."

Ophelia's breath caught. "You are Miss Eglantine's mother? And Miss Austorga's?"

"What a *curious* old auntie you are. Did no one ever warn you that curiosity killed the cat? Yes. Babin is my maiden name."

"And Malbert?"

"Their father. Odious little fungus."

"And you are still married?"

"In the eyes of the church and the state."

"What about Henrietta?"

"Puh! Henrietta! A grasping vixen, that one. She is quite, quite welcome to the putrid slug. Not for a single minute have I ever wished to have Malbert back. I left him many years ago, once our daughters were old enough to do without a mother. I was never very fond of those two, anyway. Ugly creatures. Eglantine is devious, too, and Austorga has a slow wit. She finds me at the opera house now and then, and attempts to engage me in mother-daughter repartee. Disgusting."

Not exactly a mother hen, was she? But this explained what Austorga had been doing backstage that night.

"As the Marquise de la Roque-Fabliau," Penrose said, "—and I suppose you are not lying about that?"

"Why would I lie? It makes me ill to admit it."

"All right then. As the marquise, you must have been aware of your husband's family's rather unusual claim to share an ancestor with the lady called Cinderella."

Ophelia tapped her toe. How did the professor always manage to steer the ship into the fairy tale channel?

"Isabeau d'Amboise," Clara said. "Yes. I never heard the end of it. But they always left out the bit about being descended from the wicked stepmother, too."

"Then you were also aware of the provenance of the diamond stomacher," Penrose said.

Clara picked up a half-empty wineglass and sniffed it. "Yes."

"Surely you noticed that the bodice of the ballet costume replicated the stomacher."

"I did. But I thought nothing of it." She polished off the wine.

"Why not?"

"Does it surprise you that I do not much care about that foolish tale and that dreary old stomacher? If you wish to know why the ballet costume replicated the stomacher, you must go and ask Prince Rupprecht. He commissioned the ballet, you know. Caleb told me that he took an inordinate interest in all of the scenery and costume design."

Ophelia leaned forward. "Really? Prince Rupprecht?"

"Would you please leave, now?" Clara rose from her stool and stretched out on the sofa. "I am tired, and weary of this game. Go and play detective somewhere else."

"Well, scratch the notion of Henrietta wishing to divorce Malbert," Ophelia said, once they were back in the hired carriage parked in the street. "Because a lady can't divorce a fellow she's never been married to."

"Perhaps Henrietta had enlisted the lawyer for other reasons entirely."

"You mean, maybe *Henrietta* is the lawyer's client?"

"She is connected to him somehow, judging by the half-burned envelope bearing his address in her grate."

"But what would Henrietta want with that stomacher?"

"It is valuable."

"But she's got no right to it, no legal right, since she's not really Malbert's wife. Besides, if Henrietta is the lawyer's client, that would make her the murderer, right? And I can't see it. Henrietta would double cross anyone, but she wouldn't *kill* anyone. Especially not her own daughter."

"If Henrietta was not legally married to Malbert, the Misses Eglantine and Austorga, and Malbert himself, do not have credible motives for doing away with Henrietta. They were not bound to her in any way."

"You mean to say, they could have simply kicked her out."

"Yes. And now they are keeping it quiet."

"Why?"

"Because it is shameful in more than one way. Bigamy.

Cruelty. And then Henrietta's daughter found dead in their garden soon after."

"I can't help thinking about those feet, Professor." Ophelia bent to look at the turtle on the seat. He'd peeked out of his shell, and his curved snout and beady eyes were somehow comforting. "Where is Prue? We aren't getting any closer to finding her."

"I believe we are. Prince Rupprecht commissioned the ballet. He may know why the ballet costume resembled Sybille Pinet's gown and why it incorporated a replica of the stomacher."

"He might know all right, but there's something in the air. Everyone's lying like dogs on the floor. Do you know where the prince lives?"

"No. But I suspect that the Misses Malbert do."

Hôtel Malbert was quiet when Baldewyn let Ophelia in the front door. Penrose was waiting in the carriage since they had no way to explain his presence.

"*Madame*," Baldewyn muttered as he stalked away.

"Are the *mademoiselles* at home?" Ophelia called after him.

"*Non, madame.*"

"What of Monsieur le Marquis?"

"I could not say, *madame*." Baldewyn disappeared through the library door.

Ophelia thought fast. She had once seen Eglantine writing letters at a desk in the ladies' salon. Perhaps she kept an address book of some kind there. She hurried to the salon.

Empty. The remnants of a ladylike repast littered the coffee table. A mouse sat on its haunches beside a half-filled coffee cup, nibbling a pink macaron. Another mouse went at a chocolate bonbon. An obese cat dozed on a nearby chair.

Ophelia hurried to the dainty writing desk and opened it. Little compartments, lined in yellow silk, were stuffed with papers and envelopes, pens, and bottles of ink. Ophelia rifled through. Everything was in French, but she could read the names on the envelopes. In her haste, a few envelopes drifted to the carpet. She left them. *Wait!* Here was that addendum to the Prince's ball he'd sent a few days ago—it was the same large, square envelope, and yes, there was a Paris return address—

Someone behind her made a dry cough.

Ophelia held her breath. She straightened and turned.

Malbert stood in the doorway. His bald pate shone. So did the large, squared-off meat cleaver he held in one hand. In his other hand he held Ophelia's battered theatrical case by its handle. "Baldewyn told me that you were back. He is a good servant, Baldewyn."

"Monsieur Malbert!" Ophelia said, overdoing the imperious matron's voice just a touch. "I have misplaced an important missive that I—"

"You may cease the ruse, whoever you are." Malbert's eyelids fluttered like a fly's wings.

"Who*ever* I am? Why, what do you—"

Malbert adjusted his grip on the meat cleaver. He took a step forward.

Ophelia tried to swallow. Her throat stuck.

"At first, I did not believe it when Lulu told me of your theatrical case."

Lulu. She'd *known* it was Lulu.

"But then, *oui*, I began to see how peculiar you really do seem, *madame*. Or are you a *mademoiselle*? You came to my home under false pretenses. Disguised. Lying at every turn. What do you want?"

"I want to find Prue. To protect her."

"Surely that did not require continuing with your ridiculous disguise." He came still closer.

The meat cleaver didn't look especially sharp—thank the heavens for Beatrice's incompetent housekeeping. But it looked heavy.

Ophelia pressed herself back against the desk. "Why did you kill Henrietta? Was it on account of your bigamy?"

That stopped Malbert. His moist lips parted.

"That's right. I know you're still married to Clara Babin. Did Henrietta find out? Is that why you got rid of her?"

"I would never have harmed my darling, precious Henrietta."

"Do you mean to hack off my feet?" Ophelia's voice shook. "Just like you did to Henrietta? Hack them off and pop them in a pickling vat?"

Malbert's eyes fell to Ophelia's large, worn boots, just visible below the hem of her bombazine gown. "Hacking off *your* feet would indeed be an undertaking."

Ophelia flicked her eyes around the room. Malbert stood in the path to the door—the only door—but there were the tall windows overlooking the street. She could make a side step and take her chances with the windows.

Only—she glanced back to Malbert—only he had her theatrical case. Her trusty theatrical case that she'd carted around with her from circus to variety hall and all the way over here to Europe. True, the greasepaints, wigs, and false muttonchops in there had gotten her into a fair amount of trouble. But they'd also gotten her *out* of trouble.

Malbert edged closer.

It was now or never.

Ophelia folded the prince's envelope in half and stuffed it into her bodice, sideways between two buttons. She lunged towards Malbert.

He swung the meat cleaver high.

She snatched the theatrical case from his weak grip and darted to the side. She fancied she felt the breeze of the whizzing meat cleaver behind her. She ran to the windows and swept aside the draperies. There. The latch. She fumbled with it but her fingers were for some reason like clumsy sausages.

"I will not allow you to go!" Malbert said behind her. Thumping footsteps coming closer, and she'd bet the farm that he was still brandishing that cleaver.

Ophelia hefted the theatrical case and bashed the window. Glass shards showered down. She climbed onto the low sill, hugged her theatrical case to her chest, and jumped. Her skirts poofed like a parachute. She landed on two feet on the sidewalk, hip pads bouncing.

Penrose was halfway out of the carriage. Shock slackened his face as he watched her galloping towards him, but he said nothing. He bundled her and then himself into the carriage and slammed the door. They jostled forward.

Ophelia couldn't breathe or speak. Her heart raced. She looked out the carriage window just in time to glimpse Malbert staring out the shattered window. She pulled the folded envelope from her bodice and waved it. "I've got Prince Rupprecht's address," she said, panting.

25

By the time they reached Prince Rupprecht's house, Ophelia had straightened her wig and, since she had her theatrical case right there on her lap, she had done some repairs to her face. Professor Penrose had watched the proceedings with interest and, Ophelia fancied, slight alarm.

Prince Rupprecht resided in a stately, white stone mansion behind spiked iron gates. The drapes were all drawn.

"You need not come in, Miss Flax," Penrose said. "Perhaps you should rest after your ordeal with the—"

Ophelia was already halfway out the carriage door.

"At least allow me to ask the questions of Prince Rupprecht," Penrose said. "He strikes me as the sort who only feels regard for gentlemen's conversation."

"You're right about that."

The front gates were ajar, and a dignified manservant answered their knock on the door.

Penrose said something about the prince in French and passed his card. He *had* to be running low on those cards by now. He passed them out like show bills.

The servant led them into a foyer and disappeared.

"Looks like we've come just in the nick of time," Ophelia whispered. She pointed to the pile of traveling trunks at the base of a lavish marble staircase. "He must be setting off for his château."

"I am, I am!" a voice boomed above them. Prince Rupprecht trotted down the stairs. "Lord Harrington! What a charming surprise." He reached the foot of the stairs, and surveyed Ophelia in her matronly disguise. "Good afternoon, *madame*," he said in a bored voice.

Penrose once again introduced Ophelia as his aunt. "I would very much like to have a word with you, Prince Rupprecht, if you have the time."

"I am just about to set off for Château de Roche, but certainly, certainly. Come this way."

Prince Rupprecht led Ophelia and the professor down a wide corridor filled with chandeliers and statues of voluptuous ladies, and through tasseled curtains into a sitting room. He went straight to a sideboard and poured out two brandies. He passed one to Penrose—completely ignoring Ophelia—and fell into a thronelike chair.

Ophelia and Penrose sat.

Penrose laid aside the brandy and leaned forward, elbows on knees. "I shan't waste your time. I was told you commissioned the ballet *Cendrillon* at the opera house. Why?"

"Why?" Prince Rupprecht swirled his brandy. "I am a newcomer to this city, Lord Harrington. My land, Slavonia, is thought to be backward by the Parisians. Provincial. Some even say barbaric. I wish to make France my home, however, and so, to earn the respect of the people here, I commissioned the ballet. At great expense, true, but it proves, I think, that Prince Rupprecht of Slavonia belongs here, at the center of the civilized world. Not in a backwater."

And Ophelia thought *she* was touchy about being a bumpkin.

"Why do you ask, Lord Harrington?"

"I was considering commissioning a ballet myself, as it happens."

What a tall tale! But Prince Rupprecht seemed to buy it; he nodded.

"Another fairy tale ballet, I fancy," Penrose said.

Prince Rupprecht grunted what sounded like approval and finished off his brandy. He placed the glass on the carpet and lounged back in his chair.

"'The Sleeping Beauty,' perhaps," Penrose said. "I enjoyed that tale as a lad. But I must get the sets and the costumes just so, and I was told that you, Prince Rupprecht, took great care over the costumes and scenery of *Cendrillon*."

"Who told you that?"

"I cannot recall."

"I paid some attention, yes. If a man sinks that much money into something, he must see it through, yes?"

"The detail of that ballet! Colifichet's scenery is simply stupendous, and the costumes." Penrose paused. "How is it that the ballerina's costume has a stomacher that resembles to a startling degree an heirloom stomacher belonging to the Malbert family?"

"Does it?" Prince Rupprecht had drawn a small object—a coin—from his pocket, and he tossed it into the air and caught it, over and over. "I did not design the costumes, Lord Harrington." He chuckled, his eyes strained. "I wished for the costume to be particularly beautiful, of course, so I commissioned Madame Fayette—have you heard of her?—to design and make it. No cheap theatrical rags, yes?"

That explained why the ballet costume was so unnecessarily fine, then.

Up went the coin, and Prince Rupprecht caught it. And again, and again.

Ophelia glanced at Penrose. He made a slight shake of his head: *no*. She ignored it.

"Prince Rupprecht, whatever are you throwing that coin about for?" Ophelia asked.

He caught the coin and tucked it in his pocket. "My nursemaid told me, when I was a boy, that you must keep a coin in your pocket to appease the ghosts you meet."

"Ghosts! Have you ghosts in your house?" Ophelia asked.

"One never knows." Prince Rupprecht snatched his empty glass from the floor and lumbered—unsteadily now—back to the drinks table.

"I ask about the stomacher," Penrose said, "because in my academic work I happened to have come across an old version of the tale that assigns the stomacher to Cinderella's ball gown. Not the younger stepsister's."

Prince Rupprecht brought his sloshing-full brandy glass back to his throne and thumped to a seat. "That is but a silly bit of lore, is it not? I heard it from the mouths of the mademoiselles Malbert. They claim kinship with Cinderella and claim their house was the setting of the tale. Rubbish."

"Rather," Penrose said.

Ophelia frowned. Prince Rupprecht had been so attentive to the stepsisters at the exhibition, but now he seemed contemptuous of them. As she thought this over, her gaze floated around the chamber. Another chamber opened out behind the prince, beyond a pair of satin curtains held open with golden cords. She saw a statue of a fryer-hipped Venus, an enormous Turkish divan bursting with pillows, and an oil painting of frolicking nymphs—in their birthday suits—over the fireplace.

Prince Rupprecht caught her staring. He stood and, rambling to the professor about ballet costumes and scenery designs, went to the curtains and shut them.

"Well, we won't keep you any longer, Prince Rupprecht." Penrose stood, and Ophelia did, too. But she kept trying to see through the crack the prince had left in those curtains. "I do hope your ball is a success."

"You must come, Lord Harrington. There will be far too many ladies, and I cannot dance with them all."

"Perhaps I shall. I have heard rumors of an important announcement. You won't tell me who the fortunate lady is, will you?"

Prince Rupprecht smiled, and tapped the side of his red nose. "It is to be a grand surprise."

* * *

"He was hiding something in that alcove," Ophelia whispered as she and Penrose swung through the prince's front gate. "I'm sure of it."

"He merely wished to hide all of those"—Penrose cleared his throat—"all of his artworks, Miss Flax. He wished to protect your ladylike sensibilities."

"No. I can't believe it." Prince Rupprecht, of all the gentlemen Ophelia had ever met, was one of the least likely to give a fig about a lady's feelings.

"What is next?" Penrose asked. They paused beside their carriage, waiting at the curb.

Ophelia pressed her lips together. Amid all that hullabaloo with Malbert and the meat cleaver, she hadn't exactly planned things out.

"You cannot return to Hôtel Malbert," Penrose said.

"Not if I want to keep my feet on."

"Stay at my hotel."

All the air gusted out of Ophelia's lungs. "Oh. I—"

"In your own suite, of course." Penrose glanced past her, looking flustered. "I am thoroughly aware that you have your pride, Miss Flax, and are perhaps about to condemn my offer of assistance as a *handout*, but at this juncture you really haven't anywhere else to go."

"I've got money." Ophelia jutted out her chin. The plain truth was . . . if she spent even five more francs, she could bid her steamship passage to America good-bye. *Then* what would she do? Become a cancan dancer?

"You worked a great deal for that money, as a *maid*, for pity's sake," Penrose said. "I shan't allow you to spend it all. You need it."

This was too, too humiliating. When Ophelia was traipsing around with the professor, spying and quizzing people, well, she felt they were just about equal. But once money got into the mix, it poisoned things. He was an earl. She was an unemployed actress who was probably wanted by the Paris police by now.

"Miss Flax. Please. We'll go to my hotel and have luncheon—surely you are famished by—"

"*Mercy*," Ophelia hissed. "Professor! Look!" She pointed over Penrose's shoulder. He swung around.

The masked velocipede rider pedaled behind a delivery wagon. The rider turned his—or her—head. The eyeholes in the highwayman's mask were shadowed by the brim of the bowler hat. The rider reached inside the flapping jacket, pulled out a revolver, aimed at Ophelia—

Penrose pushed Ophelia behind their carriage just as a shot cracked out.

"Are you all right?" he whispered, pressed against her.

"Think so."

Penrose pulled something from inside his jacket. A revolver.

Their driver yelled at Penrose in French. Penrose signaled the driver to crouch down. He cocked his revolver. Slowly, he peered around the carriage, revolver poised. He watched for several seconds, breathing hard.

He turned to Ophelia. "He's gone. Let us go, before Prince Rupprecht emerges and asks questions." He said something to the driver, and the driver shook his head and waved his hands.

"He refuses to follow the cyclist," Penrose told Ophelia.

"We could follow on foot."

"He's had too much of a start. Besides which, I won't expose you like that, Miss Flax. That cyclist is mad."

"That settles it," Ophelia said, once the carriage was moving. "Someone's trying to pop me off. That's the third time! First at the exhibition hall, then two times with that creepy velocipede rider." *pushing her*

Penrose nodded, his mouth grim.

"The only people possessing the slight build of the cyclist who were at the exhibition hall were Miss Smythe and Miss Eglantine," Ophelia said.

"Are you really able to picture either of those young

ladies on the loose in the city, dressed as a gentleman, shooting a pistol?"

"If she were desperate enough, sure."

"Why would someone choose to follow us, shoot at us, from a velocipede rather than a closed carriage? They risk being identified, and it is wildly inefficient."

"Not everyone is able to afford a carriage."

"You suggest that the cyclist is short of funds?"

"Perhaps. Young ladies like Miss Smythe and Miss Eglantine, while their wants are taken care of by their parents, do not always have money of their own to spend."

"I hadn't thought of that."

"Or it might be someone who is really and truly penniless."

"That does not match the description of, say, Madame Fayette, or Monsieur Malbert, or Monsieur Colifichet—all persons who I wouldn't blink an eye if you told me they wanted to harm us, but all who have sufficient funds to hire not only an assassin, but a carriage for their assassin."

They made a detour to the Le Marais *commissaire*'s office. This time, Ophelia stayed behind in the carriage with the turtle. After her confrontation with Malbert, Inspector Foucher was the last person she wished to see, but the professor hoped to take a stab at speaking with the madman who'd been arrested last night.

Penrose slammed himself back into the carriage in fewer than five minutes.

"Did Inspector Foucher tell you to hit the trail?" Ophelia asked.

"After a fashion, yes."

Hôtel Meurice, Professor Penrose's hotel, stood across from the Tuileries Gardens. Penrose booked Ophelia into a suite of rooms while she dawdled at his elbow, feeling mortified but at least reassured that, in her Mrs. Brand disguise, no one would take her for a disreputable lady. She held her reticule sideways in both hands because the turtle was inside, on top of the Baedeker.

They planned to meet at nine o'clock in the evening to go to Colifichet's shop. Penrose left her at her door.

The suite's windows overlooked a busy thoroughfare. Across the street sprawled the Tuileries Gardens: bare rattling branches, puddly walks, statues of wild beasts, and a large fountain in the distance.

The suite was staggeringly grand and Ophelia was afraid to sit down lest her mud-stained skirts soil the rich brocade. The four-poster bed was huge and downy-looking. Delicious heat, all for her, radiated from a coal fire. The lavatory taps would pump endless hot water, and a brand-new bar of lemon blossom soap, still wrapped, sat in a crystal dish.

She'd never experienced such luxury. It gave her the jitters.

But she took a hot bath and scrubbed away the face paint. Pity she couldn't scrub away the guilt. Guilt at having this, enjoying this, while Prue was missing. Not to mention the green-at-the-gills fact that Professor Penrose was footing the bill.

After she dried off, she filled the bathtub again with cool water and let the turtle have a swim. While he did so, Ophelia inspected her run-over toe. Still swollen, purple, and shiny. She might've broken it. She dug through her theatrical case and rubbed some of her calendula flower salve on her foot. She really could've used a cup of the birch bark tea her mother used to boil, but this was Paris, not the New Hampshire hills.

Presently, a waiter rolled in a trolley piled with enough food for ten people: roast chicken, buttery potatoes and yellow beans, bread, more butter (this was, after all, France), fish and greens and salads and gelatin molds and chocolate cake, strawberries, and iced cream. She placed the turtle on the carpet next to the table and offered him greens and strawberries. He liked both.

Clean, warm—a little too warm—and stuffed like a Christmas goose, Ophelia curled up on the bed. She was practically in a stupor, she was so exhausted from the last few days. She'd just have a little shut-eye . . .

When she woke, night had fallen. The trolley and all the dishes and silver domes were gone. The turtle sat in the corner, and it was past nine o'clock.

Ophelia tied on her boots, pulled on her black bombazine gown, black bonnet, and cloak, but did not bother with the Mrs. Brand face. She went downstairs.

26

❧

"I believed you had a plan," Ophelia whispered to Professor Penrose. They huddled over the handle of the door in the rear courtyard of Colifichet & Fils. The door was locked. A fine mist twirled through the dark air, and Ophelia's heart thudded.

"Have faith, my dear." Penrose pulled a pointed bit of iron from his inner jacket pocket and fitted it into the lock.

"Professor!"

"You've seen me pick a lock before, Miss Flax. Have you forgotten?"

"I reckon I blotted it out."

"Mm."

The lock caught and tumbled. But when Penrose pushed, the door did not give.

"It's bolted from the inside." Penrose scanned the windows at first-story height.

So did Ophelia. They were all barred.

"We'll find another entrance," Penrose said. He slipped his lock-picking tool in his pocket and started across the courtyard.

"Hold your hat on. Look. That window above this door is ajar—and it hasn't got bars."

Penrose looked up at the window, then threw a glance down at Ophelia. "You do realize that that window is at least twelve feet above us."

"Sure. But *that* one isn't." She pointed to another window, on the opposite side of the courtyard.

"Miss Flax." Penrose sounded impatient. "That window is *not* ajar and, furthermore, as it is on the other side of the courtyard, there could be any number of locked doors inside the building that would impede our progress to the workshop. No, we must—"

"Oh, just button it and *listen*."

Penrose lifted an eyebrow.

He'd probably never been told to *button it* in his life.

"Here is what I'm thinking," Ophelia said. She pointed to the window across the courtyard. "You could help me get up onto that windowsill. Then I might cross over this clothesline there"—she traced its sagging length with a pointed finger—"that leads straight to the open window. I'll climb through the window, go downstairs, and unbolt the door from inside."

Penrose stared at her. "You'll walk on the clothesline?"

"It's a circus trick. Tightrope. Heard of it?"

"Yes. But this clothesline is anything but tight."

"But I'll have that other clothesline to hold on to—see?"

"And if it were to collapse? Those two clotheslines, in addition to being flimsy and possibly decayed, are weighted down with what appears to be three weeks' worth of some rather large infant's nappies."

"I guess you'll have to catch me, Professor." Ophelia hurried across the courtyard.

Penrose grumbled something, but he followed her. He hoisted her up by having her step into his hooked-together hands. After a few tries—with crashing and flailing—Ophelia got her boot-toe wedged onto the windowsill. With a last heave, she had both feet on the sill, and then—with a mighty stretch—both of her hands were wrapped tight around the upper clothesline.

"Steady now," Penrose whispered.

Ophelia bit her lower lip, and with great care stepped her left foot onto the lower clothesline. The line sagged under her weight and swung from side to side.

"I have never attended a circus, I allow," Penrose said below her, "but I gather that tightropes do not typically swing like hammocks."

"Do you wish for me to attempt this, or not?"

"I suppose it is worth—"

"Then *shush*. I must concentrate." Ophelia brought her right foot up the clothesline, too. The upper clothesline hung at about rib-height. The lines wobbled, but she told her body to stay at once relaxed and springy, in the manner she'd always used while trick riding. The clotheslines went still.

Ophelia edged along, stepping carefully around wooden clothespins and flapping laundry. It would be a shame to mess up some poor lady's work. Her crinoline swayed like a big bell and her injured little toe pulsed.

She reached the center of the courtyard, which was the droopiest, swingiest point of the clothesline. She lost her balance. Her feet, on the bottom clothesline, went one way. Her hands, clinging to the top clothesline, went the other. She squawked.

"Miss Flax!" Penrose exclaimed.

Her skirts sagged, pulling her. Her muscles strained.

"I'll catch you." Penrose opened his arms.

"I'm *not* going to fall." With a great heave, Ophelia got herself vertical again. She inched forward. She breathed hard, and sweat trickled from her hairline. Her corset stuck like glue to her damp middle. However, she reached the window.

She went through headfirst, and her hands hit the floorboards. Her ankles and feet stuck up into the air, and her skirts puffed around her hips. It was too dark for the professor to see anything, wasn't it?

She collapsed on the floor, sat up, and looked around. Weak moonlight illuminated piles of crates. This was some sort of storeroom.

She gathered herself up and hurried to the door. Unlocked,

thank goodness. She groped along a corridor, lit dimly from the storeroom window behind her, and found a flight of stairs leading downward. Once the stair hooked around a landing, the darkness was so thick she had to feel along the wall. At the bottom, she felt for the courtyard door.

The door seemed to be fastened with three sliding bolts and a latch. *Bang-bang-bang-clack.* She opened the door.

"Brilliant." Penrose slid inside. They left the door open for light, and crept to the workshop door.

Penrose peered at the four brass locks on the workshop door. "These are moving combination locks, I'm afraid."

"Afraid?"

"One cannot pick them."

Cripes.

"These small dials—with letters, see?—twist about," Penrose said. "You've got to line up the correct sequence of letters on the lock, and then it falls open."

Ophelia peered closely. Tiny carved letters went around each of the dials. The top two locks had only three dials, but the third one had six, and the fourth had five. "But there are five or six letters on each dial. It looks impossible."

"That is precisely the point. However, there are certain things to be observed about these locks."

"Like what?"

"First, they appear to have been made—or at least, designed—by Colifichet himself. Do you see how finely they are wrought? In addition, he chose to make the dials with letters rather than numbers."

"What's the difference?"

"None, from a mechanical standpoint. Yet, from the standpoint of cryptography—code breaking—letters are, or I ought to say, *might* be, more easily broken than numbers, because letters suggest that the locks spell out words. My suspicion of the existence of words is further augmented by the irregular number of dials on the locks—three, three, six, and five."

"*How* is it you know about all this?"

"The cavalry," Penrose said vaguely. He fiddled with the top lock. "There is, of course, the question of language.

Colifichet is a Frenchman." He tried a few combinations: *MOI, CLE, ECU*. The lock held fast. "But he also speaks English." *AGE, RID*. No go.

"On the other hand," Ophelia said, "Monsieur Colifichet is not only a Frenchman, he's a snob."

"What do you mean?"

"Well, do you fancy he knows Greek or something?"

"Latin," Penrose murmured. He tried a few combinations that Ophelia could not read, and then there was a gratifying, sighing *snap*, and the top lock fell open.

"What does *that* mean?" Ophelia squinted at the winning combination: *ARS*.

"Art. Colifichet does indeed hold his art—or industry— in the highest esteem."

"By golly, he does. What's next? Beauty? Science? God?"

"It's another three-letter word. If it is a sentence, I suppose the next word would be a verb of some kind." Penrose tried a few words, and then—snap!—it was open. *EST*. "That means *it is.*"

"Art it is?" Ophelia frowned.

"Well, there are considerations of syntax." Penrose studied the third lock, the one with six letters. He fussed and twirled. Ophelia stood; the crouching was too much for her tender toe. She limped around, peered over the professor's shoulder, and anxiously out into the courtyard—

Another *snap*.

She darted over. "You've got it!" The dials spelled *CELARE*.

"To conceal." Penrose was quickly turning the dials of the last lock.

"You know what it says?"

"Yes. A common saying." Penrose positioned the final dial on *M*. The lock spelled *ARTEM*. "*Ars est celare artem*. It is art to conceal art."

"Art to conceal . . ." Ophelia's eyes narrowed. "Aha. Quite the jokester, that Colifichet. He made these locks— they are artworks, in a sense—to conceal the artworks in his workshop."

"Precisely." Penrose pushed into the dim workshop. "Well,

Miss Flax. After all is said and done, we make rather a fine housebreaking team, do we not? Or, I ought to say, *shop-breaking*."

Ophelia hurried through just behind him.

The workshop felt bigger than it had before. Light seeped through tall windows, but the ceilings and corners disappeared in shadow. They picked their way towards the draughtsman's table. Whatever it was that Colifichet had been laboring over was no longer there. When they inspected the workbenches, there was no sign of any finished projects, or even works in progress. Only delicate hand tools lined up in neat rows or hanging from brackets on the walls.

And those big, shrouded shapes in the corner.

Penrose headed for them.

From somewhere behind her, Ophelia heard an *almost-*sound. Like another person's breath in the dark, or the faint rustle a sleeve makes when it brushes against one's side. She froze and strained her ears.

Nothing. Only Penrose's soft footfalls and her own wheezy pulse.

Ophelia hurried to Penrose's side, feeling sheepish.

The shrouded shapes—there were four of them—stood about as tall as Ophelia. Drop cloths covered them from top to bottom. Behind them was a cupboard.

Penrose took hold of one of the drop cloths and pulled.

Something clicked, followed by a soft, rhythmical gear-grinding. The drop cloth swished to the floor.

They stood face-to-face with a man. Ophelia stepped back. No, not a *man*, exactly. A sort of mechanical person, with ivory-white skin, a curly white wig, and knee breeches. In one hand it held a bottle and in the other a tray with a champagne glass. It grinned, its eyes shifted back and forth, and it lifted and lowered the champagne bottle.

"I don't fancy the look in his eye," Ophelia said.

"It's merely a charming trifle." Penrose unveiled another of the shrouded shapes.

This automaton was meant to resemble, Ophelia fancied, a man of Chinese extraction. It wore a toggle-buttoned blue suit, a round, pointy hat, and a droopy black moustache. It held a long-stemmed pipe. With that grinding-gears hum, it brought the pipe to its lips.

"Ingenious," Penrose murmured. "Human-sized automatons. Now I understand what Colifichet was suggesting when he said he'd like to replace the ballerinas with mechanical dancers." He reached for the third shrouded shape.

"Why don't you leave the other two alone, Professor?" Ophelia swallowed. "We don't know how to stop them. Colifichet will know we've been here."

"I'm certain there is a crank or something that will quickly send them back to sleep." Penrose unveiled a third automaton.

Ophelia took another step back.

A bear stood on its hind legs, claws outstretched, teeth bared, eyes rolling. It lurched forward.

"It's on wheels," she said. "And I think that's a real bear hide. And real claws and teeth—watch out!"

Penrose dodged to the side just as the bear bent and took a chomp at the air where Penrose's shoulder had been.

"Behind you!" Ophelia cried. The footman had wheeled up behind Penrose, holding the champagne bottle high. It brought the bottle down with a jerky swing, narrowly missing Penrose's skull.

Ophelia heard a sinister little chugging next to her. She spun. The Chinese automaton had rolled close, puffing some kind of steam from its pipe. Ophelia coughed. She took another breath, and suddenly felt woozy. Things went slow and sideways.

"There's something wrong with this smoke," she said, doubling over. She could feel the Chinese man's eyes on her. But how could that be? A mechanical contrivance couldn't *see*. Could it? She coughed again, and her eyes streamed.

Penrose drew up his lapel to cover his face and darted around the bear—which was still chomping and tearing the air—and tried the cupboard doors. They didn't give, and so Penrose rammed his shoulder against them two, three, four times. Wood splintered, and the doors opened. Penrose reached in and rummaged around.

His back was to the footman automaton. The footman had somehow turned around on its wheels so it was just behind Penrose, holding its champagne bottle high.

Ophelia screamed. It came out like a rasp.

The bottle came down with a sickening crunch on Penrose's skull. He collapsed.

Ophelia staggered forward, away from that sickly puffing smoke, around the clawing, snapping bear. But she reeled too close to the bear and its claws sliced into her shoulder. Pain sang out like a soprano. "Get off, you monster!" she yelled. She shoved the bear over and it crashed to the floor. She crouched down beside the professor.

He was half upright already, blinking and coughing, with some kind of parcel clasped against his chest. He gave her a crooked smile. "I sincerely regret unveiling this lot," he said.

"The stomacher. You've found it!" Ophelia said. The smoke was dissipating. She could think more clearly now.

"Put that down," someone said behind her, "or I shall shoot."

Penrose sprang to his feet. Ophelia twisted around.

A slim form was silhouetted in the workshop doorway: legs bowed, back hunched, a large revolver aimed at Penrose.

The figure prowled closer. The hand holding the gun shook a little.

"Colifichet," Ophelia whispered.

"Don't be foolish, Colifichet," Penrose called. "Put the gun aside."

"I am quite aware, Lord Harrington, that you are accustomed to giving orders. But the Revolution has come and gone in France, and I need not do as you say. And, in point of fact, you must do what *I* say." Colifichet adjusted his grip on the gun. "The police are already on their way. Pierre told me you would be here, you see. He is a loyal lad. Now just put that parcel aside like a good boy—*oui*?—and no one will be shot."

Penrose looked at Colifichet. He looked down at the parcel in his hands and tore off the paper.

"Stop!" Colifichet cried.

"What in hell?" Penrose muttered. He held up, not a diamond stomacher, but a white, rectangular piece of cloth. One of the diapers from the clothesline in the courtyard. Penrose threw it aside.

"Fitting, given your childish meddling, *non*?" Colifichet said. "I shall shoot the girl, first, mmn?" He took aim.

Penrose lunged in front of Ophelia.

BANG.

Ophelia screamed. Penrose was sprawled facedown on the floor.

"Professor!" Ophelia cried.

Penrose rose to his knees, but something dark was streaming down his cheek. He reached inside his jacket. He stood.

"Pardonnez-moi," Colifichet said. "I had meant to get the girl—who is she, anyway?" He aimed again.

Penrose aimed the revolver he'd drawn from his jacket. "Put it down, Colifichet."

"I told you that I do not take orders fr—"

In four long strides Penrose had crossed the room and collared Colifichet with one hand. With his other hand, he pressed his revolver to Colifichet's temple. He shoved him against a workbench. Table legs screeched and tools clattered to the floor. "Where is the marquise's daughter, Colifichet?"

"You will not get away with this, you—"

"Where is she?" Penrose twisted his collar.

Colifichet choked for air.

Ophelia's mouth hung open. She had never seen or heard Penrose like this.

"I told you," Colifichet said, "I do not know of the gi—"

"And the stomacher?"

"The police will—"

"The stomacher." Penrose pressed the pistol barrel deeper into Colifichet's temple.

"I know not! I know not! I only came here tonight because Pierre said you meant to break in and steal my work."

"Why would I wish to steal your work?" Penrose growled. "Toys and trinkets are not to my taste." He glanced over his shoulder. "Miss Flax. Go, by way of the courtyard."

"But I—"

"Go!"

Ophelia decided it was best, for once, not to argue with the professor. Some fellows transformed into frogs, but he had somehow transformed into a beast.

27

Gabriel wished for nothing more than to extract a full and detailed report from Colifichet. The little weasel knew more about the stomacher. He *had* to know more; he'd dressed that frightful little music box doll in a tiny stomacher.

But there was no time.

Penrose swiped Colifichet's pistol from his trembling hand, removed his own pistol from Colifichet's temple, and dashed after Miss Flax.

"You will not get away with this!" Colifichet screamed.

Gabriel and Miss Flax's hired carriage raced past the darkened front of Colifichet & Fils. A police wagon was just rolling to a stop, two horses prancing, and four gendarmes piled out.

And then their carriage had passed.

Ophelia glanced out of the corner of her eye at the professor, bumping along on the carriage seat beside her. She felt a little wary of him after his beastly performance with Colifichet.

Penrose touched the side of his head and winced.

"Oh!" she said. "I'd clean forgotten he'd shot you. Allow me to look."

"It's only my ear." Penrose dug his handkerchief from his jacket and held it over his ear.

"But it's bleeding all *over*—look at your collar! Are you certain it's only your ear? We ought to find a doctor—did you say they'd call a doctor to your hotel? Come on, turn your head so I might see."

Penrose turned his head to the side. Ophelia leaned close and peered through the dim light. "Merciful heavens. It *is* only your ear—but the bullet has removed a bit at the top."

"One doesn't really have need for a complete ear." Penrose turned his head. Now their faces were merely inches apart. His eyes shone, dark and liquid. "Does one?"

"Well, that depends upon lots of things." Ophelia swallowed. "On the style of hats one favors, to begin with."

"I have never owned, and never shall own, one of those fur monstrosities with the ear flaps."

"Well then, there is also the consideration of music."

"Music?" Penrose touched Ophelia's cheek with a gentle pressure that seemed, more than anything else, curious. He left his fingertips there.

"Well, yes, because if one were inclined to attend the symphony, perhaps having one's ear not all of a piece might interfere with the quality of the sound."

"I have attended the symphony on occasion, but I am not so much a connoisseur that a missing bit of ear would make a difference. In fact, I once had a piano instructor, as a small boy, who informed me that I have a tin ear."

"If you had a tin ear, this would not have happened."

"I am rather glad that it has." Penrose's hand slid to the back of Ophelia's neck.

Time seemed to float. The knocking and clatter of the carriage receded. Here they were at the center of things, with every detail sharpened into more-than-real: the half-hidden glow of the professor's eyes, the white of the handkerchief still pressed against his ear, the weight of his hand at Ophelia's neck, her own breathing, his curved mouth so very close to her own. And the peculiar urge—no, *longing*—to simply get closer to him in order to understand what exactly made him, well . . . *himself.*

So Ophelia did what she fancied she'd never, ever do. She leaned in the last couple of inches and touched her lips to his.

When that snoozing Beauty of the fairy story was roused by the kiss of Prince Charming, his lips broke through all the languor, dreaming, stiff joints, and crusted eyes of one hundred years. Ophelia had never liked that tale. It had seemed laughable to think that a simple kiss could carry so much weight. But then, she'd never had a kiss. Not a *real* one, anyway, one not rehearsed with greasepainted and booming actors who, as they kissed her, were surely pondering what to eat for supper.

In the brief moment—three seconds at the most—during which their lips touched, understanding gleamed. *This* was what everyone was always going on about! This—what was it?

Penrose drew away. "I must not," he murmured.

"Oh. Right." *Miss Ivy Banks.* "I—well, I beg your pardon, Professor Penrose." Ophelia edged away down the carriage seat.

"No, I beg *your* pardon. The blame falls entirely upon my shoulders. I should not have taken such liberties, and I assure you it shan't happen again." Penrose turned away to look out the window.

The few minutes it took to reach the hotel were just about the longest of Ophelia's life.

Later, Ophelia lay curled in a tight ball on the grand four-poster bed. On the floor beside the bed, the turtle swam gently in the washbasin of water Ophelia had set down for him. She'd propped the Baedeker and a cushion against the washbasin as a sort of stairway for the turtle to get in and out.

The smooth bed linens smelled of laundry soap, starch, and geraniums. Ophelia's toe throbbed quietly. The deep scratches the mechanical bear had made on her shoulder were red and stingy, but nothing serious. She'd washed them with soap and water and applied calendula flower salve.

If one could not be on speaking terms with one's self, well, that's what she was right now. She'd kissed another lady's betrothed. And now she lay in this impossibly plushy hotel suite that had been paid for by that same man, which made her . . . what?

Well, it made her one more actress kept in luxury like a pampered cat.

They were looking for Prue, she kept reminding herself. Prue and Henrietta. But the reminding didn't help, because there was that confounded kiss. Her mind wished to roost on the memory, to nestle into it, to return to it again and again like a bird flying home.

It took hours to fall asleep.

The whole caboodle of nuns walked two blocks to mass every morning. Prue had no choice but to go along with them. They walked in a line like ants, eyes cast down to the paving stones. Prue was accustomed to having fellers stare at her on the street. Staying invisible in her borrowed nun's habit was a relief.

The church was big and blocky, with huge red doors. Inside, incense swirled through air stained red by the windows. Sad-eyed Mary statues gazed down, oversized baby Jesuses on their hips. Off to one side, hundreds of candles flickered on brass stands.

The nuns silently filed into pews. At the back, Prue copied what the other nuns did and knelt, but she wasn't sure what came next. She'd never really been to church before.

"*Psst*," someone said behind her, just as she was folding her hands.

She tried to ignore it.

"*Miss Prudence.*"

Prue swiveled around. Dalziel stood halfway behind a huge marble pillar to the back of the pews. He crooked a finger.

Prue glanced around at the nuns. All busy praying. She hoisted herself off the kneeler and tiptoed over to Dalziel.

"What in tarnation are you doing here?" she whispered. "How did you find me?"

"You forget that I was present when Sister Alphonsine told you of the pensionnat."

"Oh. Right. Well I can't talk now. We're churching."

"You must come with me."

"Not on your nelly!"

"Miss Prudence, please listen to me. I am the only soul in all of Paris who knows where you are."

"That's the notion, clever-boots."

"But I feel responsible for you. And you must leave this place. You aren't a nun."

"I could be if I set my mind to it."

"Miss Prudence!"

"I thought you wished for me to be safe. I'm safe with the nuns, so why would I leave them?"

Dalziel didn't answer at once, but his aching eyes said it all. He wanted to take Prue away from the nuns because he wanted her for himself.

Prue knew what Ma would say: *Splendid work, sugarplum! Now reel him in! Easy does it—don't allow him to slip the hook.*

"If you stay with me, Miss Prudence, I shall take care of you," Dalziel said. "You require someone to take care of you."

Prue thought of Hansel. *He* didn't seem to reckon she required care. She stole a glance at the nuns, black domed shapes in rows. "Will you help me go to my friend, Ophelia? Take me in a closed carriage, maybe? I've been trying to figure how to get hold of her without being seen or having some spy of a messenger boy read my note—not that I've got any money for a messenger boy, anyway, and I'm not sure if I could find the Malbert mansion again even if I tried—"

"Yes."

Prue sighed with relief. "Then let's go."

Ophelia dressed that morning in her Mrs. Brand disguise. The bombazine gown was, of course, the only one she had at this point. She'd stitched up the rip the mechanical bear had made the best she could, with a needle and thread from her theatrical case. But she didn't *need* to wear the Mrs. Brand cosmetics. She was no longer camped out at Hôtel Malbert.

"And anyway," she said to the turtle, "everyone and their grandma seems to have caught on to my disguises."

The turtle munched lettuce on the rug.

The real reason Ophelia was wearing the complete Mrs. Brand disguise was that she required something to hide behind after that shameful kiss in the carriage last night.

She went down to the front desk in the lobby and somehow made it understood that there was a small turtle occupying her suite, and that neither he nor his washbasin were to be disturbed.

The clerk smiled and nodded, but as Ophelia was marching away he muttered, "*Dame folle.*"

Didn't sound too flattering.

Penrose's eyes widened when Ophelia plopped down in the chair opposite his in the hotel dining room. He set aside the newspaper he'd been reading. He looked clean and pressed and combed, and he had a plaster on the top of one of his ears.

"Seems like we're back to square one again," Ophelia said.

"Square one? What do you—ah. You refer to the stomacher. To Miss Bright."

"What else could I be referring to?" Ophelia knew *exactly* what else she could be referring to, but she'd made up her mind to pretend it had never happened. "This is a fine scenario, isn't it? Here we are dining in a hoity-toity hotel while Prue and her mother are who knows where, and a mad velocipede rider might pedal in at any moment, bandying a revolver about, or the police might come rushing in to arrest me, supposing Malbert—or Madame Fayette or that nasty lawyer—told them I'm an impostor, or the police might come for *you*, Professor, after our interlude in Colifichet's workshop last night—"

"We will tend to each obstacle as it arises."

How could he be so calm?

"I have given it some thought," Penrose said, "and I feel I must visit the lawyer Cherrien again. Alone. Perhaps at his home."

"You mean to squeeze something out of him?"

"No one is talking—or if they do, I fancy they're lying. The police are useless. Yet Henrietta and Miss Bright are still missing, and learning the identity of Cherrien's client seems to be the key to it all. By the way . . . Mrs. Brand again?"

"Would you please pass the butter?"

"You needn't keep yourself in such a state of discomfort."

"One never knows who one might meet." Ophelia's eyes fell on a large form lumbering towards them. "You see?"

"Lord Harrington!" the Count de Griffe said.

Penrose stood. "Please, join my aunt and me," he said to Griffe. He threw Ophelia a dark look.

Ophelia took Griffe's proffered hand. "Count! How delightful to meet you again."

"And you, *madame*." Griffe kissed her hand. "I trust that you have not met with any more trials *dangereux* since we last met at the exhibition hall, eh?" He pulled up a chair.

"No, thank heavens. When I told my niece, Miss Stonewall—"

Penrose stirred his coffee noisily.

"—how you had rescued me, Count, she was most captivated. She thinks highly of you, very highly indeed."

"That is flattering, *madame*, for your niece is a sparkling diamond, a rare flower, among women." Griffe cleared his throat. "What did she say about me?"

"Oh, it has simply flown from my mind. My memory, dear young man, is not what it once was."

Penrose took a loud sip of coffee.

Griffe studied Ophelia's face. She prayed her cosmetic crinkles were holding up.

"*Madame*," Griffe said, "they say that when one regards a young lady's elder kinswomen, one peers, as into an enchanted mirror, into the future. It seems that Mademoiselle Stonewall's future is bright." His voice dropped a half octave. "Even, may I say, *très belle*."

Penrose's cup clattered in its saucer.

"Oh! Well, I cannot even *think* what you mean," Ophelia said in a fluttery, matronly way.

The *maître d'hôtel* whispered something in Penrose's ear. Penrose frowned. He stood, threw his napkin on his chair, and said, "Excuse me Mrs. Brand, Count de Griffe. It seems I've a visitor in the lobby."

"I am greatly anticipating Prince Rupprecht's ball," Ophelia said to Griffe, as she watched Penrose's retreat. "Have you been to his château before?"

"*Oui*. It is a beautiful estate. You will enjoy it very much."

"And you have known the prince for many years?"

"Ten years. Perhaps more. We met in Rome. When he arrived in Paris several months ago, he looked me up."

"I'm told Prince Rupprecht plans to make a grand announcement tomorrow evening, at the ball. Some believe he intends to announce a bride."

"A bride! Prince Rupprecht is a sworn bachelor. And if he changed that and did take a wife, why, I would pity the poor lady who had become so entangled."

"Oh? I'm acquainted with more than one lady who would be delighted to marry Prince Rupprecht. He is titled, wealthy, handsome."

"You think him . . . handsome?" Griffe sagged. "*Oui*, I suppose he is. But he will never marry. Mark my words."

"Why not?"

"He is . . . *discontented* with ladies."

Ophelia frowned. "At the ballet, it seemed—I mean, according to my niece—that he rather enjoyed the dancers."

"I cannot think, Madame Brand, why you are so anxious to learn of the prince's marital prospects. Does Mademoiselle Stonewall wish to know?"

"No, no. You see, my youngest niece, Abigail, wrote to me and inquired about the prince. She is the prettiest of the Stonewall sisters, and her mama has high hopes that she will make a great match in Europe someday."

"Ah! Mademoiselle Stonewall's *sister*? *Je comprends*." Griffe brightened. "Write to your niece Abigail and tell her

that she should not give Prince Rupprecht another thought."
He lowered his voice. "He is a scoundrel. A cad. If Abigail is
anything like you and Mademoiselle Stonewall, then she is a
petite beauty. But for the prince, that is not enough. He is tired
of ladies. He would tire of her, for no lady is ever perfect enough
for him. He imagines he is like the Prince Charming, searching
for his Cinderella, but she will never be found. He grows impatient. He searches high and low. But every lady has a flaw—
too short, too tall, too fat, too thin. Big feet, small feet. A
crooked tooth. A donkey's laugh. *Non*, Prince Rupprecht will
never find a bride. And, eh! He does not deserve to."

Ophelia stared at Griffe. "Cinderella? Did the prince say
he is searching for *Cinderella*?"

"*Oui*, although I cannot think why a grown man has his
head in a muddle over a child's fairy story."

How could she have been so *blind*? Prince Rupprecht
was the murderer. He tired of ladies. He went through them
like racehorses, it seemed. And what did people do with old
racehorses who couldn't cut it anymore?

They shot them.

28

The *maître d'hôtel* led Gabriel out to Hôtel Meurice's lobby, with its marble floors and white-and-gold pillars. Gabriel wasn't certain if leaving Miss Flax and Griffe was a relief or a danger—because it was obvious that Miss Flax was attempting to get his goat by flirting with the chap. Griffe appeared ready to propose marriage to Mrs. Brand, Miss Stonewall, or both.

Gabriel couldn't complain. After all, he had his understanding (of sorts) with Miss Ivy Banks. Not that it had been the memory of Miss Banks kissing him that had kept him up half the night.

A handsome, olive-complexioned young gentleman stood against a wall, holding a bowler hat in his hands. A young nun stood beside him.

"This is the gentleman who summoned me?" Gabriel asked the *maître d'hôtel* in French.

The *maître d'hôtel* nodded and glided away.

"Well I'll be!" the nun shouted. "Professor Penrose! It really is you! What's happened to your ear?"

"Miss Bright! Good heavens! Are you all right?"

"star" B
"etoille"

"Fine as frog hair." She grinned.

"But why are you got up like a nun?"

"I was with the nuns. At the Pensionnat Sainte Estelle."

Sainte Estelle. Gabriel's breath caught. Sybille Pinet's landlady had said Sybille had come from a convent that had been named something to do with stars—and *Estelle* meant *star.* "Is that a convent orphanage?" he asked Prue.

"They've got a school, but it ain't an orphanage. The students there got families, it sounded like."

Gabriel cursed his own stupidity. He'd only gotten a list of all the convent orphanages in Paris, but Sybille hadn't been an orphan when she'd entered the school.

"Lord Harrington," the young man said in a refined Scottish accent.

Gabriel turned to him. "Good morning, Monsieur—?"

"Crawley. Dalziel Crawley."

Good God.

"Miss Bright," Gabriel said, "step away from this man. He is dangerous."

"Dangerous? Dalziel's my friend."

Gabriel studied Dalziel. He appeared to be intelligent, kind, and, most important, sane.

"I am my grandparents' ward," Dalziel said.

Ah. That explained quite a lot.

"I found your card, with this hotel's name jotted on the back, amongst Grandmother's things," Dalziel said. "I knew I could bring Miss Prudence to you. She cannot return to Hôtel Malbert."

"Of course not."

"I'd like to go and get Ophelia," Prue said, "back at the Malbert house."

"Miss Flax is here," Gabriel said.

"Madame Brand, I must go." The Count de Griffe stood, and treated Ophelia's hand to another smooch. As he bent, beads of sweat dripped from his brow.

Was Griffe sweating it out on account of what he'd revealed

about Prince Rupprecht? Or was it because of his peculiar passion for Miss Stonewall?

Griffe straightened. "*Madame*, I beg you, where is your niece now?"

"Oh, shopping for perfume. Or did she say she was going with friends to a panorama exhibition? I simply cannot recall."

"Edifying herself, eh? An intelligent young lady. I have the utmost regard for intelligent ladies. Please, *madame*, would you ask your niece to accompany me to Prince Rupprecht's ball on the morrow?"

"I really don't think she—"

"*Madame*, my very happiness depends upon it. Without her at my side tomorrow, I shall wilt in sorrow, decay like the—"

"Very well. I will ask her."

"Ah, *bon*. I shall leave here this afternoon for the countryside. I hope to have her answer by then."

Griffe loped away. Poor lovesick critter. If he only knew the truth about his soap and tallow heiress from Cleveland, Ohio.

The reunion of Miss Flax and Miss Bright was quite as noisy and teary—the tears were on Miss Bright's side—as Gabriel expected. They brought Miss Bright and the young Mr. Dalziel Crawley up to Miss Flax's suite of rooms and ordered food and drink for Miss Bright. She requested flapjacks and bacon; Gabriel told the waiter to bring strawberry *crêpes* and *jambon de Bayonne*.

It took a quarter of an hour to hear Prue's story.

"You ought to have told me about Hume," Miss Flax said to Prue.

Although Miss Flax's voice was scolding, Gabriel saw the tenderness in her eyes. Besides which, she was hand-feeding strawberries to a turtle. Apropos of nothing, it occurred to Gabriel that Miss Flax would make an excellent mother. Miss Ivy Banks would, naturally, always have regiments of nursemaids to help rear her offspring, and Gabriel supposed that was for the best. Miss Banks seemed to care more for her King Charles Spaniel than she did for her nieces and nephews.

Miss Flax set the turtle on the carpet, stood, and paced over to the windows.

"What is it, Miss Flax?" Gabriel asked.

She turned, holding her elbows tightly in cupped hands. "In all the excitement about finding Prue, I forgot to mention that I fancy I've worked out who the murderer is."

"I beg your pardon?" Gabriel said.

Prue took a large bite of whipped cream. Dalziel leaned forward in his chair.

"Prince Rupprecht," Miss Flax said. She recounted how Griffe had invited Miss Stonewall to accompany him to the ball, and what he'd said about Prince Rupprecht's discontentedness with ladies. "The prince is mad about the Cinderella story—we already knew *that*, right, once we learned he'd commissioned the ballet? Now, what I figure is, Prince Rupprecht became acquainted with girls from the ballet company—with Caleb Grant's assistance, probably—and dressed them up like Cinderella in the gown and such. That's why he wishes to have the stomacher tomorrow—to give it to whomever this *new* lady is. The one he means to introduce at the ball."

"You're suggesting that Prince Rupprecht is Monsieur Cherrien's client?" Gabriel said.

"Yes. And recall how spooked he was yesterday about ghosts, tossing that coin of his? And how he didn't wish me to peer into that chamber with all those . . . artworks? Well, I'd wager that chamber was where it all happened. Sybille was there, wearing the Cinderella gown and stomacher so she'd look the part for him. And then, something happened— an argument? Or perhaps she said she was leaving for New York?—and he shot her. Then he brought her to Hôtel Malbert and left her in the garden."

"What about the stomacher?" Gabriel asked.

"He lost it somehow, or someone took it. And he's desperate to have it back."

"Hold it," Prue said. "Prince Rupprecht was *at* the party that night."

"He could've placed Sybille in the garden before the party," Miss Flax said. "Or he might have simply stepped away—he could've said that he wished to smoke a cigarette outside—and then transported Sybille from his carriage to the garden."

"We should go to the police," Gabriel said.

"We *could*," Miss Flax said slowly. "Or . . . we might trap the prince into a confession ourselves."

"A trap?"

"Yes. I've just had a dinger of a notion. To begin with, Miss Stonewall must accept the Count de Griffe's invitation to accompany him to the ball tomorrow evening."

"The ball?" Gabriel asked.

Miss Flax nodded.

"Well, then, Miss Flax," Gabriel said, "you must have something splendid to wear."

Ophelia scrubbed off her Mrs. Brand face, but by necessity she still wore the bombazine gown and taffeta bonnet when she and Professor Penrose walked to Maison Fayette thirty minutes later. Penrose kept taking big breaths, as though he were about to say something. But he said nothing, and strolled beside her with his hands in his pockets and a creased brow.

They waited a long while after Penrose rapped on Maison Fayette's door.

"Sounds like no one's there," Ophelia said. "Wait. I hear something."

Footsteps came closer, and the door was opened by the seamstress Josie.

"Hello, Josie," Ophelia said. "Is Madame Fayette within?"

"Good morning, Mademoiselle Stonewall. No, *Madame* departed for her villa at the seashore in Deauville."

"The seashore? In November? Hasn't she ever so much work to do? Prince Rupprecht's ball is tomorrow."

"*Her* work is finished."

"All of the ball gowns are done?"

"*Non.* But as I said, *her* work is finished. The other seamstresses and I still have much to complete before tomorrow."

Ophelia hated heaping more work on Josie's plate, but they were attempting to trap a murderer. "Josie, is the ball gown you were to finish for me complete—or passable enough to wear in public?"

"*Oui, mademoiselle.* I did not know where to send it—Madame Fayette did not tell me—and it is waiting in a box in the shop. So, too, is the green visiting gown and the velvet paletot. Come in, please. Wait here in the foyer and I shall go fetch them."

Ophelia and Penrose stepped inside and waited in silence.

"Here you are, Mademoiselle Stonewall." Josie returned with two big, flat boxes. "The ball gown, the visiting gown, the paletot, and a hat and dancing slippers. Please do enjoy the ball. I am told that Prince Rupprecht's château is very beautiful, fit for a princess indeed."

Penrose took the boxes.

"Josie, forgive me," Ophelia said, "but has Madame Fayette ever mentioned Prince Rupprecht to you or, perhaps, to a customer in your presence?"

Josie's eyes filled with tears. "You ask me again, Mademoiselle Stonewall, to gossip. To risk my job. Poor *Maman*—"

"I know, Josie, but there is a murderer still at large."

Josie's eyes widened. "You believe Prince Rupprecht is the murderer?"

"Well, I—"

Josie hunched forward and whispered, "It is true. Prince Rupprecht, from time to time, orders clothing for . . . ladies. That is all I know. Please, *mademoiselle*, take pity on me and ask me nothing more."

Ophelia most certainly *did* take pity on poor Josie. And if Madame Fayette got caught in her blackmail scheme while they were trapping Prince Rupprecht, it would be fine and dandy with her.

Ophelia's plan was in place by eight thirty that evening.

Miss Stonewall had accepted, in writing, the Count de Griffe's invitation to accompany him to the ball. Griffe had responded with a rapturous reply, and an additional invitation to promenade with him in the prince's château gardens should she arrive by the afternoon. Miss Stonewall sent a terse acceptance.

Ophelia decided not to answer Griffe's second rhapsodic note; she didn't wish to make him late for his coach ride to the countryside.

Penrose, meanwhile, wrote to Inspector Foucher and informed him of their intentions.

"Do you suppose Inspector Foucher will come?" Ophelia asked Penrose.

"I certainly hope so."

Dalziel, who was eager to prove that he could be trusted despite his horrible grandparents, went to the Salle le Peletier just after the evening's performance of *Cendrillon* ended and endeavored to steal the Cinderella costume. He brought it back to the suite at the Hôtel Meurice, where Ophelia embellished it with supplies from her theatrical case.

In the morning, they would all travel by hired coach to Château de Roche.

29

❧

Château de Roche was a six-hour drive from Paris. By the time the hired coach turned down the château's drive, Ophelia felt crabby and her crunched toe felt close to popping. Prue, wearing her nun's habit, was asleep on Ophelia's shoulder—Ophelia's bear-scratched shoulder. Dalziel, on the opposite seat, gazed at Prue. Professor Penrose had been reading a book the entire journey. The book was called *Lectures on the Science of Language* by Max Müller, and although that sounded dull as dishwater, Penrose seemed awfully interested in it. Well, he might've only been pretending interest; Ophelia kept catching him looking at her.

What did he think of her forest green visiting gown and black velvet paletot? Probably, that it didn't go with her battered boots or the turtle on her lap.

Bare trees with gray, jigsaw puzzle bark edged the drive. They looked like sycamores, but earlier Penrose had called them plane trees. Beyond the trees farmland sloped, brown and muddy.

Prue snuffled awake and righted her wimple. Without a word, Dalziel took a packet of boiled sweets from inside his jacket and offered her one. Penrose closed his book. Their coach burst out into an open space ringed by white statuary and lawns like green baize tablecloths.

"Golly," Prue said, "another palace." The boiled sweet clacked against her teeth.

Château de Roche was preposterously large. Milky stone, tall, glittering windows, roofs shining with last night's rain. Several coaches queued in the drive. Folks in traveling costumes and footmen in yellow livery rushed up and down double front stairs that curved like crab's pincers. Their coach got in line.

"Ready, Prue?" Ophelia hefted her theatrical case onto her lap and opened it. "What will it be? Mouse-brown bun?" She lifted up a wig. Prue had to go in disguise to Miss Stonewall's chamber in the château or their plan would be foiled. Of course, she *was* wearing a nun's habit. Yet still.

"I've always wanted to wear this thing." Prue nestled the wig over her bright curls. "How about them specs, too?"

Ophelia passed spectacles over.

Prue put them on, and drew her wimple back around her face.

Dalziel stared. Penrose smiled.

Their coach rolled forward and stopped. Footmen darted forward to open their doors.

"We will see you presently," Ophelia said to Penrose and Dalziel. She clasped the turtle to her chest. "Keep your fingers crossed that this show goes off without a hitch."

Ophelia was handed down by a footman with yellow livery, a white curly wig, and a stubbly jaw dusted with face powder. Ophelia hooked her arm in Prue's, with the idea that the faster she got Prue hidden in Miss Stonewall's guest chamber, the better.

They were just climbing the steps when Ophelia spotted Malbert in the drive, arguing with a footman—or so it seemed—about a traveling trunk.

"We can't risk Malbert seeing us," Ophelia whispered.

There was something peculiar about Malbert's trunk. It was the usual size, with brass girding and a domed lid.

However, one side seemed to have . . . airholes. Ophelia could've sworn she saw a flash of motion inside.

Malbert glanced in Ophelia's direction. Ophelia turned her head away and dragged Prue up the steps and inside.

"Do you reckon the little doughball recognized us?" Prue whispered.

"I hope not."

What did Malbert need airholes in his trunk for? Ophelia didn't like it. Not one bit.

An hour later, Prue found herself sprawled on a divan alone in Miss Stonewall's guest chamber. Well, *almost* alone; the turtle paddled in a washbasin on the floor. Ophelia said she wished to set the little feller free in a country pond.

Prue had taken off the mouse-brown wig and fake spectacles, but she still wore the nun's habit. She reckoned *this* chamber had never seen a nun's habit before. Everything was blue velvet, gold paint, and plaster crustings of cherubs and seashells. The furniture was so fancy you could probably live in comfort for years just by pawning off the pieces, one by one.

Prue sighed. The clock on the mantel—gold flowers and enameled bluebirds—said it was headed towards five o'clock. Which meant she had to twiddle her thumbs in here for seven more hours. Seven!

Dalziel was supposed to keep her company, but he hadn't shown up yet. Ophelia had gone off for her promenade with the Count de Griffe, and Professor Penrose was to chaperone. Prue would've paid a quarter to see *that*. Penrose was just about as in love with Ophelia as a feller could be before he dissolved into a puddle on the floor.

Which reminded her. Prue got up, dug through a writing desk, and found a sheet of paper, pen and ink, and an envelope. In the past few days, she had realized a couple things. For starters, she had realized that Hansel wasn't exactly doing the right thing by her. He wouldn't claim her, and he wouldn't acknowledge her shaky position in life that didn't allow for waiting around for gents to make up their minds. But he hadn't set her loose, either.

Dalziel was right; she need someone to take care of her. So Prue was going to tell Hansel to cut dirt.

She dipped the pen into the bottle of ink and began writing.

Dear Hansel,

I have always wanted for a real family, and for so to find real people who wanted me, dearly. My ma is gone, maybe forever, and in late days I did spend some times with a cluster of nuns who were ever so good to me and took me under their wings. I wanted to tell you, Hansel, that everything between us or that I reckoned was between us, well, I am calling it off and you are free. I wont ever be a fine housewife like I fancied I might learn to be for you, I must face it now. But after all is done here tonight I will join a convent, see, and live amid ladys who want me, without making me wonder if it's true or not.

Sincerely,
Prudence Bright

A couple tears plopped on the page, but they dried quickly. Prue folded the letter and slid it into an envelope. She'd figure a way to send it first thing in the morning.

Then she took Hansel's letter to *her* from her bodice, the one she'd carried from Germany and all over Paris, and burned it.

The promenade with Griffe was interminable. Griffe practically wallowed in the pleasure of pointing out to Miss Flax (whom he of course addressed as Miss Stonewall) the beauties of the formal gardens behind Château de Roche. The great lout made even tall Miss Flax seem as dainty as a

Dresden doll. Gabriel was doomed to slouch behind them at a cousinly distance, hands in trouser pockets and irritation lapping over him in waves.

Gabriel watched as Miss Flax and Griffe bent their heads over a dormant rosebush. Miss Flax said something, and Griffe chortled.

Gabriel realized he must do something about this, once and for all.

Tonight.

"Why so grumpy?" Ophelia edged close to the professor. Griffe had been waylaid by two ladies and a gentleman of his acquaintance, who were also enjoying the sunset light in the formal gardens.

"Grumpy?" Penrose straightened his spectacles. "Whatever do you mean?"

"I figured you were getting peckish for dinner."

"Oh. No. Well, perhaps."

"I've been perishing to speak with you and I haven't had a chance." Ophelia glanced at Griffe. Still talking. She lowered her voice. "Did you happen to see Monsieur Malbert's traveling trunk in the drive?"

"No."

"Well, it had breathing holes in it."

"Breathing holes? Whatever do you—"

"And it was big enough for, well, for a *person*."

"Good God—but that is preposterous!"

"Henrietta's still missing. Malbert is mad. I've got to check it. I hope I've made a mistake, but I can't rest easy till I see with my own eyes." Ophelia paused. "So. Will you help me?"

"You mean, help you sneak into Malbert's chamber?"

"Yes."

"All right. But you've got to disentangle yourself from Griffe. Tell him you're having one of those fits you ladies have, why don't you?"

"I'll leave the fits to the grand ladies of the world. I don't have the time."

* * *

Ten minutes later, Ophelia hid behind a huge, blue-and-white vase in the corridor outside Malbert's chamber. They had learned the location of Malbert's chamber easily enough; Penrose had simply greased a footman's palm.

Penrose rapped on the door. It opened. Penrose and Malbert held a brief exchange in French, and then the door hit home.

Penrose came to Ophelia. "No luck."

"He didn't buy your line about wishing to borrow a cufflink?"

"I'm afraid not, and he was rather suspicious that I had asked. We've never met, you realize."

"Did you see the trunk?"

"He blocked my view."

"Then we must wait till he leaves, and then go in."

"You're determined to do this?"

"The last time I saw him he was waving a meat cleaver at me!"

"Fair enough."

They hid behind the vase for more than twenty minutes. At last, Malbert's door opened. They looked around the vase. Malbert waddled down the corridor in the opposite direction, pulling his traveling trunk behind him. Wheels were affixed to the bottom and Malbert held it by a hand strap. The wheels squeaked softly.

"What in Godfrey's green *earth*?" Ophelia whispered. "I knew he was up to something. I *knew* it!"

They crept along after Malbert, through a puzzle of richly decorated corridors and into a bare, spiraling stairwell. Malbert took great care to gently bump the trunk down each step. On the ground floor, a door led outside. Malbert had left it ajar.

He was setting off across a twilit side garden when Ophelia and Penrose dared to look out the door.

"Where is he going?" Penrose murmured.

"Hopefully not to bury anything." Ophelia swallowed. "Or anyone." She sure as sheep-dip didn't want to see *that*.

Malbert wheeled the trunk swiftly through the network

of low, geometrical hedges and sandy paths. Ophelia and Penrose skulked at a distance. The sun was below the horizon now, and Malbert was a black blotch. But if he were to turn around, there wasn't a place to hide.

Ophelia heard crunching footfalls behind them. She glanced over her shoulder to see two *other* black blotches, walking beside a fountain.

Penrose had seen them, too. "Keep on," he whispered. "I fancy they're only out for a stroll."

Malbert veered to the side and disappeared through an archway cut into a tall line of shrubbery.

"Bother," Penrose said. "We'll lose him. Hurry."

Ophelia and Penrose passed under the archway through which Malbert had disappeared, and emerged at the top of a terraced slope. At the bottom of the terraces, a ring of bare trees stood out against the purple sky. Behind the trees, a lake shone like a large, tarnished coin. Cold wind gusted up.

"There he is!" Ophelia pointed. Malbert was gently bumping his trunk down the steps.

Once Malbert reached the bottom, he headed towards the lakeshore and vanished into a dark clump of weeping willows.

When Ophelia and Penrose reached the shore, the sky had deepened to indigo. Frogs peeped, water lapped, and tall reeds rustled in the breeze. From the clump of willows came crunching sounds. Then the sounds stopped.

Ophelia and Penrose crept behind a thick willow trunk and peered around it.

At first, Ophelia saw nothing but blurs of gray and black. But she stared harder and made out the form of Malbert. He knelt before the trunk. He opened the lid, its hinges creaking.

"*Adieu, mes mignons,*" Malbert murmured in a singsong tone. "*Adieu.*"

Ophelia forgot to breathe.

Penrose shook with silent laughter.

Ophelia frowned. Malbert was placing tiny things onto

the ground. Tiny things that streamed away into the shadows, one by one.

"*Mice*?" Ophelia whispered.

"*Qui est là*?" Malbert asked, scrambling to his feet.

Penrose stepped out from behind the tree. Ophelia decided she may as well follow. Malbert wasn't a murderer. He was only . . . off his rocker.

"Lord Harrington, is it? Why have you followed me here? I knew you were not being honest when you said you wished to borrow a cufflink. And who is this young lady with you?" Malbert's spectacles shone like little moons.

"Miss Stonewall and I were merely out for a stroll, and we happened to notice you and your rather fascinating wheeled trunk. I confess that our curiosity got the better of us. I do beg your pardon. Releasing mice?"

Malbert dabbed his face with a hankie. "Please do not tell my daughters. They will laugh. But you see, my home is infested with the poor little creatures and I cannot bear to destroy them. I take away the poison and the deadly traps my servants set out for them, and catch them instead with traps of my own design and manufacture that will not harm them—"

Traps. Harmless mousetraps! That was what Malbert was forever tinkering on in his workshop. That was what those odd metal boxes were.

"—and I set them free, in the countryside. Usually in the evenings, when my daughters are out."

"Do you feed the cats, too?" Ophelia asked.

"How do you know of my cats?"

"Oh. Well, you must have mousers."

"I feed the cats, *oui*, I feed them amply so that they might not murder the poor little mice." Malbert bent over the trunk, scooped a mouse out, and placed it on the ground. "*Adieu.*" He closed the trunk. "That was the last one for today. Good evening, Lord Harrington, and Mademoiselle—"

"Stonewall," Ophelia said quickly. She ducked into deeper shadow.

Malbert, pulling his empty trunk, left.

* * *

Ophelia and Penrose waited for Malbert to get a nice long start back to the château. There was no point in crumbling the little fellow's dignity any further. He may have brandished a cleaver at Ophelia, but she *had* been a disguised stranger under his roof.

"We should have asked him about the feet in the pickling vat," Ophelia said.

"I cannot imagine how you might've woven *that* into the conversation, Miss Flax." Penrose smiled.

"It is not so humorous. I saw them with my own eyes!"

"There must be a rational explanation."

After a minute, they set forth along the curve of lakeshore. Several small rowboats lay on the gravel bank.

From somewhere beyond the rustling reeds came a rhythmic creaking sound. Not frog-peeping, and accompanied by hollow wooden thuds. As they stood watching, a rowboat slid into sight from behind the reeds. It edged towards the middle of the lake. The moon hung low in the ink-blue sky, and it shed a shimmering white line across the water. The rowboat passed through the moonbeam.

"Only a fellow with his lady," Ophelia said. "Mighty romantic. Let's go."

"Wait. Do my eyes deceive me, or is that . . . Prince Rupprecht?"

Ophelia squinted. "Certainly looks it." The prince's pale hair caught stray light, and even from this distance Ophelia saw the glimmer of his medals. The lady, seated across from him, wore a bonnet and some kind of veil. She held herself with ladylike stillness.

"I've got an awful feeling about this. The prince is the murderer. He ought not be alone with a young lady. And where's he taking her? Shouldn't she have a chaperone? If something were to happen to her, well, that'd be blood on our hands."

"I tend to agree."

Ophelia was already leaning over and shoving one of the

rowboats into the water. She hopped in. The rowboat wobbled from side to side and her skirts swayed, but she managed to sit without capsizing.

Penrose leapt into the boat just as it launched out onto the water. He clambered around Ophelia, sat, took up the oars, and began to stealthily row. Out they went, past the thicket of reeds and into the wide-open water. Because Penrose was rowing, his back was turned to Prince Rupprecht and his lady. Ophelia watched the prince as well as she could through the dark. He seemed to be making for the far shore. He was speaking to the lady; his rumbling voice reached Ophelia's ears. He did not seem to have noticed Ophelia and Penrose's boat.

Then a *third* rowboat nosed into Ophelia's vision. Off to the right and a little behind them. It must have been hidden in the reeds.

"Professor." Ophelia tipped her head.

"I had no notion the lake would be such a popular spot this evening." Penrose leaned into the oars, and they sped up.

The third boat was occupied by two narrow, hooded forms. Were they two ladies, or two slight gentlemen, or one of each? Impossible to tell. But they were plainly aware of Ophelia and Penrose, for two pale faces turned towards them. Ophelia's scalp crawled as she stared into the hollows of two pairs of eyes.

She'd never believed in ghouls, but she was thinking about giving it a try. "I fancy those two spooks are turning their boat towards us. Steer away, would you? I don't know who they are, but I don't reckon I wish to."

Penrose stole a quick glance. "Good heavens, it cannot be—no. Impossible."

"What? Who?"

"Don't laugh, but I would avow that is Lady Cruthlach at the oars."

30

"*Lady Cruthlach* behind the oars? How could that be? Her arms would snap like twigs if she tried to row a boat. And Lord Cruthlach can't sit up like that. Hume carries him around."

"Hume was concocting elixirs from that book. They might've had a revivifying effect."

"I couldn't believe that hogwash if my life depended on—"

CRACK! Something zinged past Ophelia's ear. One of the spooks had fired a gun.

"Get down!" Penrose cried. He rowed harder, and Ophelia threw herself to the bottom of the rowboat.

Another *CRACK!* Penrose stopped rowing and hunkered down. He patted at his jacket.

Searching for that revolver of his, no doubt.

"Let me row!" Ophelia said. "They're catching up!" The spooks' oars were splashing closer and closer.

"No. I could not live with myself if something were to happen to you." Penrose pulled the revolver from his jacket and checked the cylinder. He lifted his eyes and the gun's barrel over the edge of the rowboat. He aimed.

BANG!

Ophelia heard a *plop*. Penrose slid the revolver back into his jacket.

"That's it?" Ophelia asked.

"Shot it out of Lord Cruthlach's hand."

"Almost too easy."

"I've had a bit of practice."

"I'm afraid to inquire."

"Suffice to say that you and I, Miss Flax, could go into business together as a circus act."

"You'd shoot apples off my head?"

"Something of the sort." Penrose was on the seat and rowing again. "Do stay down, Miss Flax. They've drawn rather close, and they might have another gun."

Penrose rowed hard for a half-dozen strokes. His jaw was tight.

Suddenly, an oar splintered through the side of the boat, just in front of Ophelia's face. Water gushed in.

"Hang it," Penrose muttered. He patted for his revolver.

Ophelia tried to struggle upright, but the boat was already tipping. She dumped sideways into the lake. She knew how to swim, but one did not customarily swim in a crinoline, corset, boots, and four layers of skirts. Her bottom half swelled with water. She churned her arms but she could barely stay afloat. Penrose shouted to her, reached out. He wasn't watching Lord and Lady Cruthlach.

Lady Cruthlach, her face hidden in the shadow of her hood, pushed Ophelia under with an oar.

Ophelia screamed into the black, cold water. It filled her mouth, eyes, ears. She thrashed her arms, but the pressure of the oar bearing down between her shoulders was insurmountable.

She would die here.

A bright picture flickered. The swimming hole in New Hampshire, where she and her brother, Odie, had gone when the air was thick with damp summer heat and biting insects. The water there had been cool and sun-dappled, it had smelled of minerals. She saw Odie's smiling brown eyes, which she had not seen for years past now. She had always supposed, but never known for certain, that he'd died in the war, so seeing him like this now, did it mean *she* was dying?

The pressure of the oar lifted. Ophelia surged to the surface, her lungs burning for air. She fought against the dead weight of her skirts for a brief moment, and then strong arms were around her waist, pulling her through the dark water as she coughed and said good-bye to Odie's eyes. She was carried through the shallow waters to the shore. She was set down upon the gravel.

"Miss Flax," Penrose murmured. "You were almost—oh God."

Ophelia coughed again. Water poured from her mouth and nose.

"Lord and Lady Cruthlach are escaping to the other side. And the prince and his lady, too, have disappeared onto the far shore. But we shan't give chase. Come, now, are you able to walk?"

Ophelia nodded. She wished she could cry.

Arm in arm, they limped, dripping, back to the château.

When Ophelia entered Miss Stonewall's guest chamber, soaked and shivering, she found Prue and Dalziel hunched over a chessboard by the fireplace.

"Who taught you to play chess, Prue?" Ophelia asked, smearing water from her eyes.

"Ain't playing chess. Playing checkers with the chess set." Prue looked up. "Ophelia! What happened to you?"

"Suffice it to say that I'm in need of a hot bath." Ophelia glanced at Dalziel. He seemed a nice enough fellow, but he *was* Lord and Lady Cruthlach's grandson. "Will your grandmother and grandfather attend the ball this evening?" she asked him. She couldn't bring herself to admit that she believed the old codgers had nearly drowned her in the lake.

"They were invited, but no, they will not attend. They

are at home in Paris. You have not met them, Miss Flax, but it is rather difficult to picture them on a dancing floor."

Prue laughed. "Hume would have to do *all* the work. All right, Dalziel. Time for you to hook it. Ophelia needs her privacy. But won't you come back later and keep me company till midnight?"

"Of course, Miss Prudence. And I shall bring you something to dine upon."

"You'll make certain nothing happens to Prue, won't you?" Ophelia asked.

Dalziel studied her. "I shall guard her with my very life, Miss Flax."

Ophelia had no choice but to trust him.

"Quite a puppy dog, isn't he?" Ophelia said to Prue, once Dalziel had gone.

"It's only fair, Ophelia. You've got *two*."

After the incident at the lake, Gabriel bathed, tended to the bump on his head from Hume's wooden spoon, the other bump on his head from the automaton's champagne bottle, and affixed a fresh plaster to his bullet-nicked ear. Then he changed into evening clothes and went down to Prince Rupprecht's opulent gaming room, along with about half of the chaps in the château. After nine o'clock chimed, he went out to the ballroom to find Miss Flax. He brought his glass of Bordeaux with him.

What he meant to say to her would not be easy. But it had to be done.

At first, he did not see her. He was just about to wonder if he'd been foolish to leave her unguarded with Lord and Lady Cruthlach on the loose, when he saw her.

His heart wrung itself.

Miss Flax stood against a wall beside a row of glum wallflowers in gilt chairs. But Miss Flax was no wallflower. She wore a ball gown of eggshell blue, with an embroidered cream satin overskirt and a snug bodice with tiny tulle sleeves. Her hair was swept behind a cream satin band. Her cheeks were flushed and her dark eyes flashed.

She did not resemble the woman he'd been fretting over in the gaming room. The woman who would hang nappies out on a clothesline across Harrington Hall's rose garden, or instruct their children how to do the horseshoe-toss in the portrait gallery, or serve Indian pudding and molasses to aristocrats. No, Miss Flax looked like . . . a gentlewoman. And that was, oddly, a bit dismaying. Because for some reason, Gabriel did not wish for Miss Flax to be a gentlewoman; he wished for her to be simply *herself.*

He swallowed the last of his wine, set aside the glass, and waded through the crowd towards her.

"Miss Flax," he said when he reached her.

She lifted her brows. "What's the gruff voice on account of, Professor?"

"Truth be told, I've a blinder of a headache. Would you . . ." He swallowed. He felt like a bloody schoolboy. "Would you kindly come outside with me please, Miss Flax, and desist in peering into my mug as though you were looking through a spyglass?"

"You certainly do seem as though you require a breath of air." She took his proffered arm, but gingerly.

This was off to a dismal start.

Outside the ballroom, a terrace overlooked the formal gardens and, beyond, a great, shadowy park. A strip of starlit river shone behind black trees. Hanging paper lanterns lit up the gardens, a fairyland of topiaries, fountains, gravel walks, and white stone stairs.

Ophelia slipped her arm out of the professor's as soon as they got outside. He was acting shirty and she hadn't a notion why. Things had seemed fine enough when they'd parted after their dip in the lake.

Ophelia walked silently at Penrose's side down a few flights of steps and into the formal gardens. Ladies and gents were already up to some naughty tricks in the maze and behind statues. Ophelia and Penrose both pretended not to notice. A string quartet sat on a platform in the middle of a marble pool. The musicians sawed away—Mozart, maybe— by the light of candelabras.

"Feel better?" Ophelia asked Penrose. "Your headache, I mean."

He stopped, pushed his hands in his pockets, and scowled into the distance.

"Well. Perhaps you ought to be by yourself, because you seem mighty testy," Ophelia said. "I think I'll just go—"

"Miss Flax," Penrose said. He didn't look at her. "There is something I must say to you. Something rather important."

Her innards flip-flopped. "Oh?"

He paused. Gathering his thoughts. That didn't bode well. When folks had to gather their thoughts, it usually meant they were scrambling around for the nicest way to say something rotten.

"In recent days," Penrose said, "or, really, not precisely in recent days, but beginning in Germany, when and where I first made your acquaintance, but particularly in recent days, we have, at any rate, I believe we have, ah, become something of—well, we have formed a bit of a friendship. Have we not?"

"I reckon so. Yes."

"I am glad we are in agreement on that point. Now, there are certainly those who would argue that a lady and a gentleman cannot and indeed, by rights *ought* not, form friendships. In particular, young, unmarried ladies and unattached gentlemen."

"Unattached gentlemen? What about Miss Ivy Banks?"

"That is precisely it, Miss Flax. Precisely. It is with these social reservations, as it were, that I—"

"Hold it right there, Professor." Ophelia steadied the wobble in her throat. "I see where you're headed."

"You do?"

"You're about to remind me of Miss Banks. I don't require a reminder."

"Yes. I have a confession to make. You see, I admit that there was *some* truth in what I said about Miss Banks. My mother, for instance, wishes me to marry a lady of a certain . . . well, for lack of a better term, of a certain class."

Ophelia's heart frosted over.

"And Miss Banks is the very epitome of the lady I ought to marry. Do you understand what I am saying, Miss Flax?"

"You're saying we ought not be friends anymore. I couldn't agree more. You can have your Latin-spouting, fossil-digging, retiring lady *and* her perfect handwriting, because I don't give a hoot *or* a holler." Ophelia spun around and grabbed handfuls of slippery silken skirts. She ran up the stairs to the terrace, nearly losing her left slipper along the way.

Ophelia pushed into the ballroom and made tracks to the champagne table. The crowd was thick, the orchestra sounded shrill, and guests chattered and elbowed.

Why must the professor so cruelly rub her nose in things? Or was he only being honest?

Ophelia didn't know. She only needed to patch up this jagged wound. She wasn't a tippling lady, but there had to be *some* reason folks turned to tiddly when the times got rough. She reached for a glass of champagne. Thick, gloved fingers whisked it away. She opened her mouth to give someone a piece of her mind.

"Mademoiselle Stonewall," Griffe said over the din of flutes and oboes, "how is it that *la plus belle*, the most beautiful lady, is also the one with the so-sad face?" He passed the glass to her. "Come, *ma chérie*. Drink. It will do you good, eh? What has happened to your shoulder?"

The mechanical bear-claw marks showed on Ophelia's bare shoulder. "Cat scratch."

"Ah. What an enormous cat it must have been."

Ophelia drank the champagne down like water and held out her empty glass for more.

Griffe refilled her glass, tucked her arm in his, and led her out onto the terrace.

Ophelia scanned the gardens below. No sign of Penrose. Probably off composing a love sonnet to you-know-who.

"Deserve to have each other. Prigs," she muttered.

"*Pardonnez-moi?*"

"Did I speak aloud?" Ophelia looked into her empty glass.

"It is perhaps, *mademoiselle,* that you are unsettled by the crush. Perhaps they do not have such balls in Ohio, in the Cleveland?"

"Something like that." The champagne had already peeled off a layer of care. "I'm feeling much better, as a matter of fact." Griffe really was nice, in a burly, furry fashion. He was like one of those alpine rescue dogs who carried little casks of brandy around their necks.

"Better, eh? Then perhaps I shall take the opportunity to ask you an important question."

Oh.

"You must be aware, Mademoiselle Stonewall, how taken I am by you. How enchanted. You are a prize among women, a flower, a gem, a pearl, an *angel*—"

Ophelia parted her lips.

"Ah!" Griffe pressed a gloved finger to her lips. "Allow me, I beg of you, to finish, before I lose my—how do you say?—nerve." He dug in his waistcoat pocket. Extracted something. A small, sparkling something. "Your papa is across the sea so I cannot do this properly by first begging for his approval. I must ask you now and perhaps later, during our betrothal, your papa might make the journey to France—or we could sail, if you like, together to Cleveland." He knelt down on one knee. "Mademoiselle Stonewall, will you do me the very great honor of giving to me your hand in marriage? Of becoming the Countess de Griffe?"

Ophelia stared at the ring he held up. A berry-sized ruby glistened darkly. There were smaller diamonds, too, a constellation around the ruby, all set in dark gold. If a lady slid that onto her finger, it'd weigh her down like a ball and chain. Still, Ophelia had never, ever owned something so fine, or even *touched* something so fine.

Griffe held his breath, hound eyes pleading.

Penrose appeared at the top of the steps and passed across the terrace several paces behind Griffe. He didn't see Ophelia, but she felt again that stabbing pain, that plummeting sense of inadequacy. Penrose went inside.

Ophelia looked down at Griffe and said the rottenest thing she'd ever said in all her days. "Yes," she said. *"Yes."*

31

❧⟨✕⟩❧

The next two hours passed in a ruby-tinted, champagne-heated haze. Ophelia danced waltz after waltz with Griffe, who was tender, charming, and solicitous. She was having a fine time pretending she hadn't a care in the world, and the champagne quite numbed her sore toe. She ignored the awful thought that she would have to break things off with Griffe. Why had she said yes?

Professor Penrose was nowhere in sight, but Ophelia glimpsed Eglantine and Austorga seated on chairs against a wall. They were bickering, although Austorga's face was hopeful. Miss Smythe, beside them, gazed dully through her spectacles into the swirling throng. Mrs. Smythe read a book.

When Ophelia and Griffe sailed by a wine table, Ophelia caught sight of a pair of cunning, whiskey-colored eyes that she'd know anywhere.

She nearly tripped on her own feet. "I must go arrange my hair," she said to Griffe. She left him standing in the middle of the dance floor. "*Henrietta!*" she whispered at a cascade of chestnut curls.

Henrietta turned. She wore a pink brocade gown that

displayed her bosom like a bakery shop window. Her delicate eyebrows lifted. "My, my. Ophelia Flax. The things you see when you—"

"What're are you *doing* here? I ought to be happy, but I'm furious! I've searched Paris high and low for you! Prue thinks you could be *dead*." Ophelia snatched Henrietta's wineglass and took a gulp. Why not? She wasn't in New England anymore.

"Of *course* I'm here, darling. I wouldn't have missed this for the world. Goodness. I've never seen you looking so *feminine*, Ophelia." Henrietta's voice was the same as ever: silky, and clear enough to project to the uppermost seats in a theater. "You never used to be much for making an effort with your looks. I figured you were one of those girls who attempt to get by on cleverness."

"Do you know your daughter Sybille is dead?"

"Yes. I saw the newspapers. *So* sad."

"But you'd met her. You'd given her Howard DeLuxe's name."

"How did you dig that up? Yes. Sybille wished to leave Paris. Man trouble." Henrietta poked out her lower lip. "But *come* now, Ophelia. *Must* we speak of such rotten, gloomy things?"

"That tone of voice isn't going to work on me. I'm not one of your dullard gents."

"Speaking of which, who was that long-haired gentleman I saw you dancing with? He looked rich."

"He's my . . ." Ophelia swallowed. "My fiancé."

"Oh! Well done, Ophelia, well *done*." Henrietta clapped her gloved hands.

"Only, he believes I'm an heiress from Cleveland."

"A trifle. I once told a fellow my family owned a million acres in California. *That* tale was worth a Mediterranean yacht cruise."

Ophelia gulped more of Henrietta's wine. Was this what she'd become? Simply another opportunistic actress? Ugh. "I want a full story about where you've been, and why," she said.

"You've always been such a schoolmarm, Ophelia. Why don't we simply enjoy ourselves? This ball is magical! I—"

"*Now*," Ophelia said. She took Henrietta by the elbow. Henrietta swiped another glass of wine from the table, and Ophelia steered her through the mob and onto the terrace.

"Start at the beginning," Ophelia said.

"I met Malbert in New York. He swept me quite off my feet."

"Hard to picture."

"Well, you know. His title. And he mentioned a mansion in Paris."

"Did you know he was already married?"

"Goodness! You don't beat about the bush, do you?"

"No."

"At first, Malbert told me his wife was dead. When I pressed him for details, he confessed. I was rather relieved, because once we'd actually arrived in Paris it became quite, quite clear that he's broke, and those daughters of his did not take a shine to me. Nor I to them. I did, alas, make the error of confessing to that devious little *couturière*, Madame Fayette, that I was not truly a marquise, and that I had a daughter in the *corps de ballet* at the opera house, for which I paid a pretty price."

"Your diamond bracelet."

"My, you've been *busy*, Ophelia. Yes. At any rate, playing at marquise provided me with a splendid vantage point to scout out new opportunities."

"Is that where you've been for the last week and a half? Scouting a new opportunity?"

"Well, it didn't start *out* that way. I was simply visiting my dear friend, the authoress Artemis Stunt, at her château in Champagne."

Artemis Stunt? Now why did that . . . ? "Did Artemis Stunt happen to pen a book entitled *How to Address Your Betters*?" Ophelia asked.

"Ingratiating drivel, but she's earning buckets from it."

"And do Artemis's friends call her Arty?"

"Yes. But more important . . . we were in *Champagne*, darling. Do you understand what they've got locked up in their cellars? Champagne as far as the eye can see! It's like

paradise. It just so happened that Artemis's new husband—
some old Frenchman who looks like a scarecrow—had a
gentleman friend—"

"All right," Ophelia said. She could guess the rest. "Back
up a little. What about the lawyer, Monsieur Cherrien?"

A crease appeared between Henrietta's eyebrows. "How
do you know of him?"

"You are his client? But surely not for divorce—"

"Obviously not. I shall tell you, but you must keep mum.
Promise?"

Ophelia crossed her fingers. "Promise."

"Cherrien wrote me, out of the blue, three or four months
ago, and offered to pay a staggering sum for an ugly diamond stomacher kept in Malbert's bank box."

"You sold it to the lawyer?"

"It's a *hideous* thing, Ophelia. Only grannies would wear it."

If only that were true.

"The sum from Cherrien has tided me over quite nicely,
since Malbert cannot afford me. Cherrien wrote to me last
week and asked if there were any other antique items I would
be willing to sell. It seems his client is excessively interested
in the Roque-Fabliau estate. Inexplicably, of course. Those
mice! All the *droppings*."

That explained the half-burned envelope Ophelia had
found in Henrietta's grate. But Ophelia wouldn't tell Henrietta
just yet that Prince Rupprecht was Cherrien's client. She didn't
wish to stem the flow of Henrietta's confessions.

"I'm done with Malbert," Henrietta said. "And selling
off *one* piece of jewelry seemed my due. But two?"

"Malbert thinks you're dead, you know."

"But I *told* him, and his two ugly daughters, that I was
going to Champagne. Or, I told the daughters. Perhaps they
forgot to tell Malbert."

"Forgot? No. They've been keeping it a secret." One of
the stepsisters must have removed Artemis Stunt's book
from Henrietta's dressing table. They must have feared that
if Ophelia or Prue saw the book, they might deduce where

Henrietta was. "Why would Eglantine and Austorga neglect to tell Malbert where you'd gone?"

"Isn't it obvious? They didn't wish for me to come back."

"I'm mighty thirsty," Prue said to Dalziel. She'd polished off the entire roast fowl that a footman had wheeled into the guest chamber, along with a dish of the most luscious gravy. But the gravy had been as salty as the seven seas, and now she was absolutely parched. She eyed the turtle's swimming basin. Fresh water in there . . . no. She just couldn't.

"Take a glass of wine," Dalziel said.

"Can't. I've got my big performance coming up. Won't you get me a cup of water from somewhere? How about a whole pitcher? Maybe with some ice?"

"Your wish is my command, Miss Prudence." Dalziel headed for the door.

"Don't be too long," Prue called after him. "It's fifteen minutes till midnight."

Once Dalziel was gone, Prue changed out of the nun's habit and into her costume. It was tight in the waist, and since it was a ballet costume it exposed her bare feet and ankles. Luckily, Prue wasn't shy about her ankles.

A knock on the door. Dalziel was back already?

She swung the door open. No one was there. The long corridor, with its painted panels and elephant-sized furniture, was empty.

She was shutting the door when she saw a blue brocade pillow with tassels on the corners and a pair of sparkling shoes sitting on top.

"Hello?" she called down the corridor.

No answer.

Prue broke into a smile. *Dalziel.* He felt bad about her not having shoes for the ball. These were a little gift from him. She leaned over and wiggled her right foot into a slipper. It was awfully tight, but by golly was it pretty, with clear glass beads stitched all over in a flowery design. She had to cram her toes into the ends and then hook her finger around back like a shoehorn—but she got it in. Same with the left one.

Ouch.

She hobbled back into the chamber. The door had almost fallen shut when she heard a wheezing sound.

Her ticker gave up for a few beats.

Slowly, she pushed the door back open and stuck her head out.

"Cendrillon!" Lady Cruthlach said. "You naughty, naughty girl. You will be late for the ball! The prince awaits."

Prue took a step back. "Prince Rupprecht?"

"Whoever he is." Lady Cruthlach's face had more color than the last time Prue had seen her. She wore a small, pointy black hat, a lavender cape, and she held some kind of stick. A . . . *wand*? "It does not matter. The important thing is that the story continues without error."

"What story, ma'am?"

"The Cinderella story! Don't you know who you *are*, girl?"

"I sure do, but it seems like *you* don't." Prue moved to shut the door. Instead, it burst open and Hume shoved in, reaching out for Prue.

Prue dodged him and dashed across the chamber. Hume trundled after her.

"Hume shan't allow you to miss the ball, my lovely," Lady Cruthlach called.

Prue made it to the fireplace. She snatched up a brass coal shovel from a rack, and the rack crashed to the floor. She lifted the shovel high.

Hume smiled. One of his front teeth was missing.

He didn't think she was going to do it. "This is for all them kidnappings, you ogre!" Prue yelled. She took a mighty swing and smashed Hume across the side of his head with the shovel—*clang*.

To her amazement, he thunked to the floor.

"Oh!" Prue dropped beside him. Thank goodness. He was still breathing. She scrambled to her feet, tottered across the chamber, and pushed past Lady Cruthlach in the doorway.

"Cinderella did *not* do that," Lady Cruthlach said.

"Who cares, you old bat?" Prue set off down the corridor. There went that wheezing again, and a creaking-basket sound. Prue stole a look over her shoulder.

Lord Cruthlach bore down on her in a wicker wheelchair. He was just as scrawny as ever but his eyes had life in them now, and he spun the wheels with gusto. Lady Cruthlach wasn't far behind. Her little pointed hat hung on the side of her head, and her eyes looked mean.

Prue ran as fast as the tight, glass-beaded slippers could go.

At two minutes till midnight, the orchestra finished playing and shuffled offstage. The crowd watched and whispered as footmen cleared the dais of the musicians' chairs and stands. Fans flicked. Ladies giggled nervously.

Prince Rupprecht strode up onto the dais in his white evening jacket, crimson sash, golden epaulets, and medals.

Ophelia's palms sweated. Would her plan work?

Prince Rupprecht began a speech in French, and Griffe whispered a translation in Ophelia's ear.

"Ladies and gentlemen," Prince Rupprecht said, "at last the moment has arrived that we have all been anxiously awaiting. The moment when I, Prince Rupprecht of Slavonia, announce the identity of my cherished, my love, and, yes, my feminine intended."

Feminine yelps rang out. A glass splintered somewhere.

"At the stroke of midnight," Prince Rupprecht said, "I shall identify my cherished one, the only lady of flawless beauty, the only lady with a foot small enough to fit"— he extracted a tiny, shining shoe from his pocket—"this glass slipper."

The crowd erupted like a tree full of chickadees.

"Silence!" Prince Rupprecht boomed.

The crowd hushed.

"At the stroke of midnight, I shall fit this dainty slipper to my darling . . . Cinderella."

Ophelia craned her neck to see the huge golden clock on the wall. One more minute.

"Are you well?" Griffe whispered.

Ophelia nodded. She looked back to the dais and saw Colifichet standing up close, narrow arms folded, smug.

The crowd babbled. Ophelia stood on tiptoe to see a footman pushing something up a ramp and onto the dais. Shrouded in a white sheet, it glided as though on wheels.

"She arrives," Prince Rupprecht said, watching the thing approach with a look of boyish anticipation.

It *couldn't* be.

The footman parked the thing beside the prince. Then he bowed to his master and whipped off the sheet.

The crowd gasped.

Standing beside the prince was a beautiful automaton in a sumptuous gown of ivory tulle, embroidered all over with gold and silver threads. The Cinderella gown, except it didn't have a stomacher. The waist was plain ivory silk. The automaton's hair was heaped upon its head in a profusion of shining, diamond-studded cornsilk that looked too heavy to be supported by such a slender neck. Its demure lips and alabaster arms curved in permanent perfection.

"He means to marry a doll?" Ophelia whispered. "An enormous *doll?*"

Prince Rupprecht caressed the side of the automaton's neck. He must've touched some kind of spring, because it jolted into motion. It gracefully moved its head on its filigree neck. One hand lifted to touch its throat in a maidenly gesture of surprise, and back again.

The crowd was having forty fits, but Prince Rupprecht seemed to be deaf and blind to his guests. He knelt before the automaton. He gazed up at it, still holding the glass slipper.

"He truly seems . . . *jumpy,*" Ophelia said. "As though it were a real lady who might turn him down."

"I always suspected it would come to something like this with him," Griffe said. "He is not right in the head."

There was a delicate chime, and then another and another. The crowd fell silent.

The clock was striking midnight.

Where was Prue?

Just as the clock chimed twelve, the automaton kicked out a bare foot from under its tulle hem. Prince Rupprecht attempted to place the slipper onto the foot. He wiggled and shoved, but he could not get it on. All the while, the automaton went on swiveling its head and touching its throat. The prince leapt to his feet, cursing and ranting in French.

"What's he saying?" Ophelia asked Griffe.

"He asks if this is a joke. He demands to know who has tampered with his Cendrillon and replaced her foot with a larger one. He says someone will be punished."

Someone had replaced the automaton's foot? Yes. The feet in Malbert's workshop cupboard must have been the automaton's original feet. But how had they come to be in that brining vat?

Prince Rupprecht yelled and pointed at someone standing to the side of the dais.

"He says, 'You! You destroyed her, you ditch rat!'" Griffe said.

"Who?" Ophelia struggled to see. Her breath caught.

Prince Rupprecht was pointing at Pierre, Colifichet's apprentice.

32

Gabriel stood in a doorway to the side of the dais only a few yards away from Pierre. Where were Inspector Foucher and his men? Gabriel had received word that they were on their way from Paris, but he had not seen them yet.

Pierre had appeared downtrodden and flimsy the few times Gabriel had seen him before. Now he exuded a vicious power.

"Yes," Pierre said in loud, clear French, addressing the shushing crowd as well as Prince Rupprecht. "It was I who altered your automaton."

"You replaced her foot with another!" Prince Rupprecht yelled. "A large, ugly foot, like any *ordinary* woman's. You destroyed her—her *perfection*!"

"No lady is perfect," Pierre said. "Not even a clockwork lady, it seems. You thought you would destroy my sister for her imperfections, did you?"

Sister?

Understanding hit Gabriel. It hadn't been Lord and Lady Cruthlach on the lake. It had been Pierre—slightly built, vengeful Pierre. But who was his sister? Surely not Sybille.

"You thought," Pierre said, stalking forward, "you would

not pay the price for sullying my sister, for discarding her like a soiled rag? No, altering this automaton was only a little joke, Prince. Only the beginning of what we have in store for you."

The two men locked eyes, Prince Rupprecht large, opulent, and looking like he was about to erupt, Pierre cool and crackling with hatred.

Where was Miss Bright? Had she forgotten her role? Because an entrance on her part at this moment would be theatrical indeed.

The crowd parted for a figure barging towards the dais. Not Prue, but Miss Austorga in a puffy, pollen-yellow gown. She hitched her skirts and tromped up the dais steps. Redness mottled her upper lip, complexion spots dotted her forehead, and she was out of breath. "You say, Prince Rupprecht, that your intended, your bride, your true love, is the only one in the world who would fit that slipper?"

"Yes," Prince Rupprecht said with a scornful glance.

"And you promise to marry she who fits the slipper?"

"That was the idea, yes. But it has been ruined, and I—"

"But do you *promise*?"

"If her foot had been small enough, then yes, I would have promised to marry she of the tiny foot. But this grotesque thing"—Prince Rupprecht sneered at the automaton—"is *imperfect*."

Austorga dragged one of the musician's chairs to the center of the dais. She plopped herself in the seat, skirts puffing like a cheese soufflé, and pried off one of her slippers. She thrust out her foot. "I am ready."

"You cannot be serious," Prince Rupprecht said. He addressed the sea of faces. "*This* creature?"

"Her foot appears to be quite dainty," a gentleman near the dais said. "Why do you not make an attempt?"

"Try," another gentleman said. Then the whole crowd was urging him on.

Prince Rupprecht shook his head with disgust. He bent before Austorga and affixed the glass slipper to her foot. It slid on neatly.

The crowd cheered.

Prince Rupprecht's jaw went slack.

Lord Cruthlach, in a wheelchair, rolled up beside Gabriel. He was wheezing for breath. Lady Cruthlach, also wheezing, emerged beside her husband.

What had they been doing? Playing badminton?

"Where is she?" Lady Cruthlach whispered. "I cannot see her."

On the dais, Prince Rupprecht looked ill. Austorga looked like she'd just broken the bank at Monte Carlo.

The gas chandeliers sank to blackness. The only light came from paper lanterns on the terrace outside. For a moment, Ophelia was blind. Ladies yipped. Gentlemen made indignant noises.

A lady screamed, *"Un fantôme!"*

A lone figure stood outside on the terrace, staring through an open door. A young, fair-haired girl, lovely to see in her ivory tulle gown that seemed to shimmer with stars. But there was something wrong, very wrong, with her chest: her ivory bodice had a dark stain around a small, black hole.

The girl's face was expressionless. Slowly, she lifted a bare arm and pointed at Prince Rupprecht.

"Sybille?" the prince croaked. *"Mon Dieu*, Sybille!" His eyes were wild as he clung to Austorga's arm for support.

He'd fallen for it. "Translate for me," Ophelia whispered to Griffe. He nodded.

"I beg of you, have mercy," Prince Rupprecht said to the apparition. "I did not mean for it to—oh, Sybille, your grave is too fresh!"

The apparition did not move.

"You know that it was not I who pulled the trigger!" Prince Rupprecht said. "I only meant to lift you up from misery, to bring your beauty into the light, to polish it. I did not intend for you to—*mon Dieu*, say something, Sybille!"

The specter said nothing. Somewhere in the ballroom, a lady wept.

"I did not kill you!" the prince roared. "You cannot torment me so! You saw that it was that little wretch, Josie!"

Josie? Ophelia blinked. There was another fair-haired young woman, this one more willowy, in yet another ivory tulle gown. She glided through the dim ballroom. The crowd parted so she could pass. She ascended the dais, exuding a riveting power that belied her slight frame. The diamond stomacher on her bodice sparkled in the gloom.

A gunshot cracked out. Screams. A thud. Ophelia smelled gunpowder.

The chandeliers flared back up. Prince Rupprecht lay in a lifeless heap on the dais. Austorga wept over him.

Josie rushed out to the terrace, clutching a pistol, and the stunned crowd let her pass.

"I'm not going to let her get away after all of this," Ophelia muttered, hitching her skirts. She pushed through the staring guests. By the time she reached the terrace, Josie was heading down the steps into the formal gardens. Ophelia dashed after her, dimly aware that others were following.

She grabbed Josie's arm at the bottom of the steps.

Josie squealed and fumbled with the pistol. "I will shoot!" She aimed at Ophelia's face.

"No, you won't," Ophelia said. "You're done with murder, aren't you, Josie?"

"I thought I was finished already, but you! Whoever you are—"

"Miss Flax will do."

"You and your silly disguises, all your questions and prying and stirring of the hornet's nest! You could not let things be."

"An innocent derelict is in jail. Give me the gun." Ophelia held out her hand.

Josie hung on to the pistol, but her hands trembled.

Ophelia carefully plucked the gun from Josie's grasp, and Josie sagged in relief or defeat.

A few gentlemen guests arrived at the bottom of the steps. Ophelia held up a hand. "Please. Allow me to ask her a few questions. She cannot flee now. And, please, someone go and try to discover if Inspector Foucher of the Paris police has arrived yet." She turned to Josie, who had sunk to her knees on the gravel path. Her ivory skirts pooled around her. Her delicate head hung, and the diamonds on her stomacher glittered. "Josie, why? Why did you shoot Prince Rupprecht?"

"Why?" Josie jerked her head up. "Because he did not deserve to live! Because I have nowhere left to run, nothing left for me. I killed two people and would soon be caught— because of you. You!—by the police. I would not go to prison without destroying the prince, first."

"But did you know him?"

"*Oui.* Knew, yes, *knew.* I first encountered him at Maison Fayette four months ago, when he came to order a special gown to be made for one of his lady friends. He brought the stomacher. He wished to have a special gown made to incorporate it. The next day, Monsieur Grant came to the shop. I had never met him before, but when Madame Fayette could not hear, he offered me money. Money simply to dine with the prince. I thought of poor *Maman* and her fading eyes . . . I said yes. We dined, and the prince was so kind. He gave me flowers, and no one has ever done that. We dined again, and then he—his hands—" Josie's voice cracked.

"I think I understand," Ophelia said softly. Josie was a murderess, so was it right to pity her? "Did you sew the Cinderella ballet costume?"

"*Oui*, and another one very like it, but to my own measurements." Josie touched her gauzy skirts. "This. For him. To please him. He called me Cendrillon. But soon he grew tired of me, told me I was imperfect, cast me aside. My ears. My ears are too big, he said. But when the time came for Prince Rupprecht to order another Cinderella gown for his next girl, *I* had to sew it."

How humiliating.

"I decided to have my revenge. I stole Madame Fayette's revolver and went to the prince's mansion. I found him in that sickening chamber with his newest Cendrillon and, oh *mon Dieu*, I meant to kill *him* then, but I saw her in his arms, in the gown I had sewn, in the diamond stomacher he had given to *me*, and I . . ."

"Did you shoot Sybille?" Ophelia asked.

"I did not mean to, but when it happened I felt like a rotten tooth had been pulled out. The prince saw everything. I threatened to go to the police and say *he* killed Sybille, and he grew mad with alarm. He agreed to help me get rid of the body. I had overheard during a fitting at Maison Fayette that Sybille was Henrietta's daughter, so together, the prince and I placed Sybille's body in the garden of Hôtel Malbert to draw suspicion to the Malbert family."

Ophelia's pity for Josie faded. "You took the stomacher from Sybille's body?"

"*Oui*. The prince, he had forgotten it in his haste and worry."

"That was you I saw that night, riding back and forth in the carriage in front of Hôtel Malbert."

"I watched from a hired carriage to see when the police arrived. I wanted to be certain that the body was found." Josie's voice lilted with what sounded like . . . *pride*.

Well, murdering Sybille was probably the boldest thing she had ever done, and probably the first time in her life that she had stood up for herself. "Then you told your brother, Pierre, what you had done."

"After the police arrived, I asked the driver to take me to Colifichet's workshop. Pierre was working late. He devised the plan to blame a madman of the streets for the crime. Pierre went to the police and gave them his story about a madman fleeing the scene of the crime. The police seemed to know of a man who fit that description, and Pierre listened carefully as they spoke of him."

Foucher. The Insensible Man, indeed.

"After I shot Monsieur Grant," Josie said, "Pierre caught the madman, with blood on his hands, fleeing the opera house."

"But how?"

"Pierre had listened carefully to the police description of the madman they suspected. Pierre agreed that I should kill Monsieur Grant, and Pierre found the madman, gave him money, brought him to the opera house, spilled pig's blood on his hands. Then Pierre 'caught' him."

"That man is innocent!"

Josie lifted a shoulder. "He had to be sacrificed. Pierre and I would have been safe, we could have sold this stomacher and gone away, to America, perhaps. We might have begun a new life where there are no cruel masters, no princes. But you could not leave things alone, could you?"

"You put me off the scent time and again, Josie. To think I felt pity for you! You set me up to see Grant taking the parcel from Maison Fayette, didn't you?"

"You were so forthcoming," Josie said. "Stupid. And it was not even the stomacher in that parcel. It was a scrap of cloth."

"Grant never had the stomacher?"

"Never!" Josie's fingers spread across the stomacher.

"What about that note, threatening to kill for it?"

"I meant for Monsieur Grant to suppose that he might receive the stomacher by meeting me that night."

The wording of the note had been ambiguous. Ophelia realized she must have misinterpreted it. "Why did Grant desire the stomacher?"

"He had seen it before. He understood its value."

"But in the end, he was merely a pawn in your game, Josie. Why did you kill him?"

"For revenge. He procured me like a—a *whore* for Prince Rupprecht. He was responsible for my degradation."

"Why did you kill him at the opera house?"

"Pierre said we should have many witnesses when he caught the madman."

"And why on that particular night?"

"Because of you."

Oh, no.

"Once I became aware of your investigation—"

"How?"

"I could easily tell that Mrs. Brand and Miss Stonewall were one and the same. I saw you in both disguises. Once I learned that you were prying, I knew that Monsieur Grant must die. If I did not kill him, you see, you would sooner or later discover that he introduced me to the prince. I would become an obvious suspect."

Ophelia's belly sank. "Once you knew I was prying, you pointed fingers at Grant, Malbert, Madame Fayette—by delivering Miss Stonewall's gown to Hôtel Malbert. Pierre placed Professor Penrose and me in that trap in Colifichet's workshop in an attempt to have us arrested."

"Yes. And you, foolish lady, went off in the direction of each of my tricks like a cat after a clockwork mouse."

"I may have gone round and round a little, but each time I was getting a bit closer to the truth. Would you have come here tonight if it weren't for the professor and me?"

Josie's eyes shone with pure loathing. She puckered her mouth as though about to spit, but two gendarmes trotted down the steps, heaved Josie to standing, and hauled her away.

"That was by far your best performance," Ophelia said to Prue.

"Think so?" Prue forked a huge bite of cake into her mouth. "Never played a ghost before. That was the best scheme you've ever cooked up, Ophelia Flax. Where's Ma? Are you sure she's here?"

"I spoke to her."

"Probably met a new feller tonight." Prue's voice was careless, but her eyes were damp with hurt as they darted around the ballroom, searching.

Ophelia longed to tell Prue that her mother wasn't worth all that sadness, but how could she? After all was said and done, you only got one mother.

Prue wore the Cinderella costume that Ophelia had doctored with greasepaint and scissors to have a bullet hole and blood, but she didn't seem to mind. Neither did Dalziel, who had taken it upon himself as his sole mission in life to gaze at Prue while feeding her sweets.

"This cake is scrumptious, Dalziel," Prue said. "Hey, I

never realized your grandparents only wanted me to get to the ball on time."

"They wished you no harm. They only hold some rather peculiar beliefs about fairy tales—a sort of typology of fairy tales, if you will."

Prue chewed and blinked.

"They believe that the tales in those stories happen once every generation."

"But why were they acting so *pushy* about it? What's it to them?"

"It is shocking to say it, but to Grandmother and Grandfather, fairy tales are almost a religion. Making certain you arrived at the ball on time tonight was tantamount to acting as high priest and priestess at a sacred rite."

"*Nuts*," Prue muttered.

Dalziel looked hurt.

"I mean to say, I sure wish this cake had nuts in it."

"Oh," Dalziel said. "Shall I fetch you some cake with nuts?"

"Sure."

Dalziel hurried away.

"Are the police still questioning Josie?" Prue asked Ophelia

"I'm not certain." Ophelia looked around the ballroom. The crowd had thinned out and the orchestra had gone. A few determined merrymakers drank and ate, but when the host had been murdered it put a damper on things.

"Here comes Professor Penrose," Prue said.

Ophelia's belly sank. She hid her hand, with its cargo of ruby ring, behind her back. Thank goodness Griffe had gone off somewhere.

Penrose's face was taut. "Inspector Foucher has finished questioning Pierre and Josie—for now, at least. Pierre is silent and sullen, but all the strength seemed to have quite gone out of Josie once the stomacher was confiscated."

Penrose had gotten to listen in on the prisoners' questionings, since Inspector Foucher credited him with the trap. Never mind that it had actually been *Ophelia's* trap.

"Sugarplum!" someone said. Henrietta.

Prue shoved her cake plate and fork into Ophelia's hands, threw herself upon her mother, and started bawling.

Ophelia and Penrose inched away.

"Henrietta seems overjoyed," Penrose said.

"Don't forget she's an actress. She's about as maternal as a garter snake."

Penrose told Ophelia what he had learned in the police interrogation of Josie and Pierre. "Prince Rupprecht is—or, I should say, *was*—utterly fascinated by the story of Cinderella and more specifically, the character of Cinderella, who he took to represent the very pinnacle of female perfection. A beautiful girl ostensibly doomed to poverty and work, but lifted up by the love of a prince."

Not too loving, if you asked Ophelia.

"After Josie killed Grant, things began to come undone for her and her brother. They became desperate, and that is when Pierre began with his attempts to do you in. That was Pierre pedaling about on the velocipede and attempting to shoot us. It was he who pushed you at the exhibition hall, too—he knew you would be there because he'd followed you after delivering a parcel to Hôtel Malbert. And you do realize now, after seeing Pierre's trick this evening, what was in *that* parcel?"

"Pickled automaton's feet?"

"Yes. That little ruse killed two birds with one stone: it drew your attention away from Josie and once again towards Malbert, of whom you'd confessed to being suspicious to Josie, and it also gave Pierre a neat way to dispose of the feet he'd removed from the Cinderella automaton, to be replaced with larger feet."

"My sainted aunt."

"Indeed. The episode on the lake earlier this evening was their last-ditch attempt to stop us. After all of this, I daresay that we are fortunate to be alive."

"What about the lawyer, Cherrien? Why did Prince Rupprecht enlist him to locate the stomacher? Didn't Prince Rupprecht know that Josie had it?"

"Josie told the prince that she didn't know what had

happened to the stomacher after they left Sybille in the garden. He assumed, it seems, that someone in the Malbert household, or one of the other guests, stole it."

"And where is the stomacher now?"

"Foucher confiscated it. It will be returned to the marquis." Penrose paused. He adjusted his spectacles. "Miss Flax, would you come out onto the terrace with me? I have something else, of a rather different nature, that I would like to say to you."

33

Ophelia and Professor Penrose walked outside in silence, stopping at the marble balustrade overlooking the dark gardens and park.

"Miss Flax, you did not allow me to finish earlier," Penrose said, "and I insist that you hear me out before I—before I go. My students, my studies, await me in Oxford."

"I've heard quite enough of the charming Miss Banks, if you don't mind awfully. So you just go on back to your ivory tower and—"

"That's just it. Miss Banks is *not* charming. She is, in point of fact, somewhat horrid."

Ophelia frowned. "That's not very charitable, Professor." A wisp of hope arose.

"I oughtn't have spoken of her at all. She is really—well, it does not matter what I think of her. She will have her pick of suitors."

"Plucks them from the orchard, does she?"

"Miss Flax, I may not have been entirely accurate when I said that Miss Banks and I have an understanding."

"What?"

"I have never asked her to marry me."

"You scalawag! I've been tied up in knots on account of that I—that we . . ."

"I am very sorry. Please. There is something I must tell you."

Ophelia couldn't meet his gaze. She simply waited for him to continue.

"I cannot say why, or how, this happened," Penrose said. "How this has occurred. The revolution that has taken place in my mind—or, really, it is not my mind, for I find that the greater part of my mind rebels against the very idea of you. No, the change has occurred in my soul." He paused. "In my heart."

She felt his gaze upon her cheek. She couldn't move. She stared out into the star-studded horizon.

He continued. "I never could comprehend what people were going on about, speaking of their hearts in circumstances of sentiment. But I comprehend it fully, now. When I see you, Miss Flax—God, even in one of your preposterous disguises, that is how far this has gone—my very heart gives a wrench. When I attempt to sleep at night, haunted by fragments of your voice, the gestures of your hands, the singular gleam of your lovely dark eyes—my heart goes out of me, trying, I suppose, to find you. To bring you close. And when I try to think how I will live without you when I return home to England, well then, it is my heart that aches."

Ophelia noted, with great sensitivity, the way a breeze fluttered a tendril of hair across her forehead. Still more acutely, she felt the ruby ring on her hand. Cold. Heavy.

"I love you, Miss Flax. That is what I wished to tell you earlier, bumbling like a fool. It is really quite simple. But I see that you have nothing to say. That you cannot look at me—well, I daresay that speaks volumes, does it not? So. Good evening."

"Wait!" Her lungs were tight. "Wait."

He stood over her, looking, for the first time in her memory, vulnerable.

Why, oh why, did it have to unfold, to unravel, like *this*?

She brought out her ruby-ringed hand, stretching her fingers along the balustrade. "I might have made a mistake. But I must behave honorably."

Penrose stared down at the bloodred glitter in disbelief. "Griffe." His voice was ragged. "You will be a countess." He made a stiff bow. "I wish you and the count all the best."

Ophelia watched Penrose stalk away down the long, long terrace, pulling fragile threads of her behind him. His tall shape melded into the black night, leaving her alone, shivering, with her icebox of a heart.

In the blue light of dawn, Ophelia dressed in her fine, forest green visiting gown, which stank of lake water and was only half dry. She drew on her black velvet paletot, laced up her battered brown boots, and carried the turtle out into Château de Roche's park. She found a path that wound through misty woods and fields towards the river.

A turtle ought to be asleep in November, beneath dead leaves and mud in shallow, still water.

Ophelia took her time, despite how chilly she grew in her damp gown. At last, she found a stagnant little backwater sheltered by overgrown brambles, at the edge of a tributary stream. She crouched on the bank and held the turtle out. He flopped into the water and disappeared.

Two hours later, Château de Roche's front drive was a carnival of horses, trunks, coaches, footmen, and groggy guests. Ophelia and Prue descended the front steps. They would ride with the Count de Griffe back to Paris. After that, Ophelia wasn't exactly sure what would happen.

"Guess we aren't the only ones who want to clear out," Prue said.

"I allow, the ball did not end on an especially festive note," Ophelia said.

"I reckon your long face is about the professor?"

"The professor? What? No. Why would I think of him?"

"Maybe on account of you look like your hopes and dreams was just run over by a steam tractor?"

"He has gone," Ophelia said. "Last night, I was told."

"He's a mutton-head to leave you."

"He has his pride. Can't blame him for that." It was also true that if a lady was responsible for breaking her *own* heart, she really had no right to complain. "Sybille's killer has been brought to justice. That is the most important thing. And we've found your mother."

"Don't sound so *glum* about it, darling," Henrietta said, sailing down the steps behind them. She wore a smart traveling costume and a plumed hat, and her eyes darted about from guest to guest. Tallying up their titles and economic wherewithal, no doubt. "Go on. Look at that ruby on your finger. Doesn't *that* cheer you up?"

No. It did not.

"Hey!" Prue said. "Ain't that Seraphina Smythe? Over there. Getting into that wagon-looking thing."

"Goodness. I fancied she was a prim and proper English rose," Henrietta said, squinting. "Whatever is she doing in that rattletrap?"

It *was* Seraphina. But she'd removed her spectacles, and her cheeks were flushed. Driving off in a hay wagon with—

"*Henri*," Prue said. She whistled. "I'll be. That's why the carriageway gate was always open. On account of Seraphina and Henri and their amorous rendezvous."

"Prue!" Ophelia said.

"What? I'm learning French."

"What about the lost key?"

"I reckon Beatrice really *did* lose it at the market. Don't know how she could see straight half the time, what with all that wine she glugs."

They were helped up into Griffe's carriage by a coachman. Griffe bounded down the steps and climbed into the coach, all smiles.

"Good morning, ladies," he said. "Mademoiselle Stonewall, how lovely you look this morning. I am most glad to convey your friends to Paris. The friend of Mademoiselle Stonewall is the friend of mine, eh?"

This was going to be an awfully long journey.

They set off.

About half an hour later, Griffe was snoring with his head thrown back against the seat, mouth open.

Prue piped up. "Ma, I've got something to tell you. I ain't going back to America with you."

"I had no intention of going back to America, sugarplum. The grass is *so* much greener here in Europe. The gentlemen are more innocent, somehow."

Not wise to Henrietta's tricks, more like.

"I'm going to be a nun, Ma."

Henrietta burst out laughing.

"It ain't funny."

"What about that young gentleman, Dalziel? He's smitten with you."

"I'm through with fellers. I already mailed off a good-bye letter to Hansel this morning."

"You did?" Ophelia said.

"Who is Hansel? Sounds like a peasant," Henrietta said.

"I'll say good-bye to Dalziel when we get to Paris," Prue said. "I couldn't do it last night on account of he was in a stew trying to help Lord and Lady Cruthlach find their stolen spell book."

"It was stolen?" Ophelia asked.

"Right out of their château chamber last night."

Professor Penrose would be mighty interested in that. Come to think of it, maybe *he* had stolen the spell book himself . . . but Ophelia realized she ought never think of the professor again.

"After I break the news to Dalziel," Prue said, "I'm shutting myself away."

"What has gotten *into* you, Prudence?" Henrietta turned to Ophelia. "Prudence never made a peep as a baby. I put her in a drawer in the corner of my dressing room—"

"A *drawer*?" Ophelia said.

"Well, of course I *cracked* it. And it was filled with old bits of costumes and such, and she would sleep through everything. *Such* a little bonbon." Her eyes went hard, and she poked Prue with the toe of her shoe. "Allow Mommy to take care of things, all right?"

Prue sighed.

Griffe snorted himself awake. *"Quelle heure est-il?"*

"Count," Ophelia said. "I've got something important to tell you."

"Eh?"

"Don't you *dare* muddle up my plans," Henrietta hissed in Ophelia's ear. Henrietta smiled sweetly at Griffe.

Griffe beamed at Ophelia. "I have been meaning to say, Mademoiselle Stonewall, I do hope your delightful aunt, Madame Brand, might come to our wedding. I have just had a dream of her, all in white."

Mercy.

The coach joggled along. Ophelia looked out at the stretching brown fields and rows of bare trees, and wondered exactly how she was going to pry herself out of *this* one.

Keep reading for a preview of
Maia Chance's next Fairy Tale Fatal Mystery . . .

Beauty, Beast, and Belladonna

Coming February 2016 from Berkley Prime Crime!

1

Beware of allowing yourself to be prejudiced by appearances.

—Gabrielle-Suzanne Barbot de Villeneuve,
"Beauty and the Beast" (1756)

The day had arrived. Miss Ophelia Flax's last day in Paris, her last day in Artemis Stunt's gilt-edged apartment choked with woody perfumes and cigarette haze. Ophelia had chosen December 12, 1867, at eleven o'clock in the morning as the precise time when she would make a clean breast of it. And now it was half past ten.

Ophelia swept aside brocade curtains and shoved a window open. Rain spattered her face. She leaned out and squinted up the street. Boulevard Saint-Michel was a valley of stone buildings with iron balconies and steep slate roofs. Beyond rumbling carriages and bobbling umbrellas, a horse-drawn omnibus splashed closer.

"Time to go," she said, and latched the window shut. She turned. "Good-bye, Henrietta. You will write to me—telegraph me, even—if Prue changes her mind about the convent?"

"Of course, darling." Henrietta Bright sat at the vanity table, still in her frothy dressing gown. "But where shall I send a letter?" She gazed at herself in the looking glass, shrugging a half-bare shoulder. Reassuring herself, no doubt, that at forty-odd years of age she was still just as dazzling as the New York theater critics used to say.

"I'll let the clerk at Howard DeLuxe's Varieties know my forwarding address," Ophelia said. "Once I have one." She pulled on cheap cotton gloves with twice-darned fingertips.

"What will you *do* in New England?" Henrietta asked. "Besides get buried under snowdrifts and Puritans? I've been to Boston. The entire city is like a mortuary. No drinking on Sundays, either." She sipped her glass of poison-green cordial. "Although all that knuckle-rapping *does* make the gentlemen more generous with actresses like us when they get the chance."

"Actresses like us?" Ophelia went to her carpetbag, which sat packed and ready on the opulent bed that might've suited the Princess on the Pea. Ladies born and raised on New Hampshire farmsteads did not sleep in such beds. Not without prickles of guilt, at least. "I'm no longer an actress, Henrietta. Neither are you." And they were *never* the same kind of actress. Or so Ophelia fervently wished to believe.

"No? Then what precisely do you call tricking the Count de Griffe into believing you are a wealthy soap heiress from Cleveland, Ohio? Sunday school lessons?"

"I had to do it." Ophelia dug in her carpetbag and pulled out a bonnet with crusty patches of glue where ribbon flowers once had been. She clamped it on her head. "I'm calling upon the Count de Griffe at eleven o'clock, on my way to the steamship ticket office. I told you. He scarpered to England so soon after his proposal, I never had a chance to confess. Today I'm going to tell him everything."

"It's horribly selfish of you not to wait two more weeks, Ophelia—two measly weeks!"

Not this old song and dance again. "Wait two more weeks so that you might accompany me to the hunting party at Griffe's château? Stand around and twiddle my thumbs for two whole weeks while you hornswoggle some poor old gent into marrying you?"

"Not hornswoggle, darling. Seduce. And Mr. Larsen isn't a *poor* gentleman. He's as rich as Midas. Artemis confirmed as much."

"You know what I meant. Helpless."

"Mr. Larsen is a widower, yes." Henrietta smiled. "Deliciously helpless."

"I must go now, Henrietta. Best of luck to you."

"I'm certain Artemis would loan you her carriage—oh, wait. Principled Miss Ophelia Flax must forge her own path. Miss Ophelia Flax *never* accepts handouts or—"

"Artemis has been ever so kind, allowing me to stay here the last three weeks, and I couldn't impose any more." Artemis Stunt was Henrietta's friend, a wealthy lady authoress. "I'll miss my omnibus." Ophelia pawed through the carpetbag, past her battered theatrical case and a patched petticoat, and drew out a small box. The box, shiny black with painted roses, had been a twenty-sixth birthday gift from Henrietta last week. It was richer than the rest of Ophelia's possessions by miles, but it served a purpose: a place to hide her little nest egg.

The omnibus fare, she well knew from her month in Paris, was thirty *centimes*. She opened the box. Her lungs emptied like a bellows. A slip of paper curled around the ruby ring Griffe had given her. But her money—all of the hard-won money she'd scraped together working as a lady's maid in Germany a few months back—was gone. *Gone.*

She swung towards Henrietta. "Where did you hide it?"

"Hide what?"

"My money!"

"Scowling like that will only give you wrinkles."

"I haven't even got enough for the omnibus fare now." Ophelia's plans suddenly seemed vaporously fragile. "Now isn't the time for jests, Henrietta. I must get to Griffe's house so I might go to the steamship ticket office before it closes, and then on to the train station. The Cherbourg–New York ship leaves only once a fortnight."

"Why don't you simply keep that ring? You'll be in the middle of the Atlantic before he even knows you've gone. If it's a farm you want, why, that ring will pay for five farms and two hundred cows."

Ophelia wasn't the smelling-salts kind of lady, but her

fingers shook as she replaced the box's lid. "Never. I would *never* steal this ring—"

"He gave it to you, darling. It wouldn't be stealing."

"—and I will never, ever become . . ." Ophelia pressed her lips together.

"Become like *me*, darling?"

If Ophelia fleeced rich fellows to pay her way instead of working like honest folks, then she couldn't live with herself. What would become of her? Would she find herself at forty in dressing gowns at midday with absinthe on her breath?

"You must realize I didn't take your money, Ophelia. I've got my sights set rather higher than your pitiful little field-mouse hoard. But I see how unhappy you are, so I'll make you an offer."

Ophelia knew the animal glint in Henrietta's whiskey-colored eyes. "You wish to pay to accompany me to Griffe's hunting party so that you might pursue Mr. Larsen. Is that it?"

"Clever girl! You ought to set yourself up in a tent with a crystal ball. Yes. I'll pay you whatever it was the servants stole—and I've no doubt it was one of those horrid Spanish maids that Artemis hired who pinched your money. Only keep up the Cleveland soap heiress ruse for two weeks longer, Ophelia, until I hook that Norwegian fish."

Ophelia pictured the green fields and white-painted buildings of rural New England, and her throat ached with frustration. The trouble was, it was awfully difficult to forge your own path when you were always flat broke. "Pay me double or nothing," she said.

"Deal. Forthwith will be *so* pleased."

"*Forthwith?*" Ophelia frowned. "Forthwith Golden, conjurer of the stage? Do you mean to say *he'll* be tagging along with us?"

"Mm." Henrietta leaned close to the mirror and picked something from her teeth with her little fingernail. "He's ever so keen for a jaunt in the country, and he adores blasting at beasts with guns."

Saints preserve us.

* * *

Ophelia meant to cling to her purpose like a barnacle to a rock. It wasn't easy. Simply gritting her teeth and *enduring* the next two weeks was not really her way. But Henrietta had her up a stump.

First, there had been the two-day flurry of activity in Artemis Stunt's apartment, getting a wardrobe ready for Ophelia to play the part of a fashionable heiress at a hunting party. Artemis was over fifty years of age but, luckily, was a bohemian with youthful tastes in clothing. She was also tall, beanstalkish, and large-footed, just like Ophelia, and very enthusiastic about the entire deception. "It would make a marvelous novelette, I think," she said to Ophelia. But this was exactly what Ophelia wished to avoid: behaving like a ninny in a novelette.

And now, this interminable journey.

"Where are we now?" asked Henrietta, bundled in furs and staring dully out the coach window. "The sixth tier of hell?"

Ophelia consulted the Baedeker on her knees, open to a map of the Périgord region. "Almost there."

"*There* being the French version of the Middle of Nowhere," Forthwith Golden said, propping his boots on the opposite seat next to Henrietta. "Why do these Europeans insist upon living in these godforsaken pockets? What's wrong with Paris, anyway?"

"You said you missed the country air." Henrietta shoved his boots off the seat.

"Did I?" Forthwith had now and then performed conjuring tricks in Howard DeLuxe's Varieties back in New York, so Ophelia knew more of him than she cared to. He was dark-haired, too handsome, and skilled at making things disappear. Especially money.

"You insisted upon coming along," Henrietta said to Forthwith, "and don't try to deny it."

"Ah, yes, but Henny, you neglected to tell me that your purpose for this hunting excursion was to ensnare some doddering old corpse into matrimony. I've seen that performance of yours a dozen times, precious, and it's gotten a bit boring."

"Oh, do shut up. You're only envious because you spent your last penny on hair pomade."

"I hoped you'd notice. Does Mr. Larsen have any hair at all? Or does he attempt to fool the world by combing two long hairs over a liver-spotted dome?"

"He's an avid sportsman, Artemis says, and a crack shot. So I'd watch my tongue if I were you."

"Oh dear God. A codger with a shotgun."

"He wishes to go hunting in the American West. Shoot buffalos from the train and all that."

"One of those Continentals who have glamorized the whole Westward Ho business, not realizing that it's all freezing to death and eating Aunt Emily's thighbone in the mountains?"

Ophelia longed to stop up her ears with cotton wool. Henrietta and Forthwith had been bickering for the entire journey, first in the train compartment between Paris and Limoges and then, since there wasn't a train station within fifty miles of Château Vézère, in this bone-rattling hired coach. Outside, hills, hills, and more hills. Bare, scrubby trees and meandering vineyards. Farmhouses of sulfurous yellow stone. A tiny orange sun sank over a murky river. Each time a draft swept through the coach, Ophelia tasted the minerals that foretold snow.

"Ophelia," Forthwith said, nudging her.

"What is it?"

Forthwith made a series of fluid motions with his hands, and a green and yellow parakeet fluttered out of his cuff and landed on his finger.

"That's horrible! How long has that critter been stuffed up your sleeve?" Ophelia poked out a finger and the parakeet hopped on. Feathers tufted on the side of its head and its eyes were possibly glazed. It was hard to say with a parakeet. "Poor thing."

"It hasn't got feelings, silly." Forthwith yawned.

"*Finally*," Henrietta said, sitting up straighter. "We've arrived."

The coach passed through ornate gates and rolled between naked trees casting shadows across the avenue. They clattered to a stop before the huge front door. Château Vézère was three stories tall, rectangular, and built of yellow stone, with six chimneys, white-painted shutters, and dozens of tall, glimmering windows. Bare black trees encroached on either side, and Ophelia glimpsed some smaller stone buildings to the side and the rear.

"Looks like a costly doll's house," Henrietta said.

"I rather thought it looked like a mental asylum," Forthwith said.

Ophelia slid Griffe's ruby ring onto her hand, the hand that wasn't holding a parakeet. Someone swung the coach door open.

"Let the show begin, darlings," Henrietta murmured.

A footman in green livery helped Ophelia down first. The Count de Griffe bounded forward to greet her. "Mademoiselle Stonewall, I have been restless, sleepless, in anticipation of your arrival—ah, how *belle* you look." His dark gold mane of hair wafted in the breeze. "How I have longed for your presence—what is this? A *petit* bird?"

"What? Oh. Yes." Ophelia couldn't even begin to explain the parakeet. "It's very nice to see you, Count. How long has it been? Three weeks?"

Griffe's burly chest rose and fell. "Nineteen days, twenty hours, and thirty-two minutes."

Right.

Forthwith was out of the coach and pumping Griffe's hand. "Count de Griffe," he said with a toothy white smile, "pleased to meet you. My sister has told me all about you."

Ophelia's belly lurched.

"Sister?" Griffe frowned.

"I beg your pardon," Forthwith said. "I'm Forthwith Stonewall, Ophelia's brother. Didn't my sister tell you I was coming along?"

The *rat*.

"Ah!" Griffe clapped Forthwith on the shoulder. "Mr. Stonewall! Perhaps your sister did mention it—I have been most distracted by business matters in England, *très* forgetful . . . And who is this?" Griffe nodded to Henrietta as she stepped down from the coach. "Another delightful American relation, eh?"

It had *better* not be. Ophelia said, "This is—"

"Mrs. Henrietta Brighton," Henrietta said quickly, and then gave a sad smile.

Precisely when had Miss Henrietta Bright become *Mrs.* Henrietta Bright*on*? And . . . oh, merciful heavens. How could Ophelia have been so blind? Henrietta was in black. *All* in black.

"Did Miss Stonewall neglect to mention that I would chaperone her on this visit?" Henrietta asked Griffe. "I am a close friend of the Stonewall family, and I have been on a Grand Tour in order to take my mind away from my poor darling— darling . . . *oh*." She dabbed her eyes with a hankie.

Griffe took Henrietta's arm and patted it as he led her through the front door. "A widow, *oui*? My most profound condolences, Madame Brighton. You are very welcome here."

Ophelia and Forthwith followed. The parakeet's feet clung to Ophelia's finger, and tiny snowflakes fell from the darkening sky.

"You're *shameless*," Ophelia said to Forthwith in a hot whisper.

Forthwith grinned. "Aren't I, though?"

2

~~∞~~

Ophelia's conscience demanded that she call off the entire visit *now*. Because, well, the gall of Henrietta and Forthwith, springing those fake identities on her at the last minute! On the other hand, she didn't have a *centime* to her name. Griffe would surely kick her out on her ear when he learned she was a fraud. She needed a little more time to cook up a plan.

She was led upstairs to a chamber with a canopied bed, walls painted with dark forest scenes—trees, rivers, castles, wild animals—and a carved marble fireplace. Footmen brought up the two large trunks of finery borrowed from Artemis Stunt, and then a maid arrived.

The maid, a beautiful blond woman of about thirty years with the full, sculptured figure of a Roman statue, tapped her chest and called herself Clémence. As Clémence hung the finery in the wardrobe, she furtively inspected Ophelia. Then she led Ophelia down a creaking corridor to a small bathing chamber. Marble from floor to ceiling, with a tinned copper tub and gold water spigots shaped like ducks' heads.

Clémence ran the bath, gave Ophelia a cake of soap and a parting glance of disdain, and left.

Awkward, having people tend to you. Especially when they made you feel that *you* ought to be waiting on *them*.

After her bath, Ophelia returned to her bedchamber, dried her hair before the fire, and arranged it in a frivolous braided knot. Then she squirmed and laced herself—she would *not* ring for Clémence—into corset, crinoline, evening slippers, and Artemis's green velvet dinner gown.

After that, she checked on the parakeet. Griffe had sent up an unused brass birdcage from somewhere, and Ophelia had hung it near the fireplace with a saucer of water and a little bowl of breadcrumbs. The parakeet puffed up its feathers, its eyes mostly shut. "Are you all right?" Ophelia whispered.

The parakeet ignored her.

Outside the windows, snow blew sideways through blackness. The Baedeker claimed that it never snowed in the Périgord.

A rap on the door.

"*Entrez*," Ophelia called. She was picking up bits and bobs of French.

Clémence had returned, carrying an envelope. She gave it to Ophelia in sullen silence and left.

Ophelia looked at the envelope—it read *Mademoiselle Stonewall*—and sighed. She knew that sloped, smeary handwriting. Although she hadn't seen the Count de Griffe since the day after she'd accepted his marriage proposal, he'd written her daily rhapsodic letters from England. Luckily, she'd been spared the need to reply because he had been traveling.

She tore open the envelope and read,

Dearest Mademoiselle Stonewall,

It is with a swollen heart and fevered brow that I welcome you at last to this, my ancestral home. How ardently I dream of showing you every inch of this sacred place, the formal gardens by moonlight, the riches housed in the library, the Roman statues alongside the ornamental canal, the fruits and blooms in the orangerie. How I long, too, to show you the more intimate features of your future home.

Ophelia's palms started sweating.

For instance, my late mother's own wedding gown, preserved in delicate tissue in a box in her bedchamber, and the nursery and schoolroom where I once romped and studied and where, God willing, our own children will romp and study, too.

Ophelia hurried to a side table, where she'd seen a decanter of red liqueur. She poured herself a small glass and drank it down. Cherry. She coughed. She wasn't really a tippling lady, but the image of a half-dozen hairy baby Griffes crawling around in diapers required blurring.

She turned back to the note.

We did not enjoy even one minute alone upon your arrival today. Could I beg you to join me at half past eight this evening—dinner will be served at nine o'clock—in the ballroom? There is so much in my heart I must convey, ma chérie—may I call you that?—and a pressing question I must ask.

> *Your most humble and obedient admirer,*
> *Griffe*

Oh, mercy.

Ophelia glanced at the clock on the mantel. Almost half past eight already. She stuffed the note in a dressing table drawer and sat down to wallow in guilt until nine o'clock. She'd rather stick her hand in a beehive than be alone with Griffe. She could tell him she'd fallen asleep.

At two minutes till nine o'clock, Ophelia slid Griffe's ruby ring on, over her satin elbow glove. The ring was heavy, and too tight. Probably served her right. She trudged downstairs for dinner.

At the bottom of the stairs, she turned left and found herself in a long, dim gallery with a checkerboard marble floor and tall windows. Snow piled up in the corners of rattling windowpanes. Gleaming suits of armor lined the gallery, along with a couple of cannons and glass cases displaying swords, bows, and arrows.

Ophelia hugged her elbows and picked up her pace. Griffe's voice boomed from beyond the far doorway. Drat. She didn't relish the notion of meeting Griffe in here. Too dark.

His voice again. Closer.

Ophelia dodged behind a suit of armor, one of four standing close together. She was hidden in shadow.

Griffe speaking. She caught the words *perhaps* and *dinner* . . . wait. Ophelia held her breath. Her eyes slid sideways.

Someone *else* was hiding behind the suits of armor, not three feet away. A tall, shadowy male form—

The man cleared his throat.

Hold it. She'd know that *ahem* anywhere. Yet how could it—? Why—? What was he doing here?

"Professor?" Ophelia whispered. "Professor Penrose?"

"Ah, it *is* you, Miss Flax," Penrose murmured. "How good to see you."

"What are you doing, hiding back here?" Ophelia's eyes had adjusted to the faint light. Penrose held a wineglass and wore evening clothes. She saw the glow of his spectacles, his square shoulders, the line of his clean-shaven jaw. Her heart skittered. "I thought I'd never—"

"I merely wished to inspect the mechanism at the back of this helmet." Penrose tapped one of the knight's helmets. It clanged softly. "Fascinating sort of hinge."

"In the dark? Stop fibbing. Who are you hiding from?"

"Who are *you* hiding from?"

"Griffe said nothing of you being here." If Griffe *had* said something, Ophelia would never have come. Penrose had told her *I love you* three weeks ago, right after she'd impulsively promised her hand to Griffe. She fancied she'd broken the professor's heart. She'd broken her own heart, too, and since broken hearts must be let alone to mend, she'd banished Penrose from her thoughts.

Another disaster.

"It was a last-minute invitation," Penrose whispered.

"Professor, if you happen to notice . . . anything odd. I mean to say, well, I still haven't gotten the chance to tell Griffe that I—"

"That you aren't Miss Stonewall, the Cleveland soap heiress?"

Ophelia swallowed. "Well, yes. And Henrietta is here, too—"

"Henrietta Bright? On the husband hunt, I suppose? Not to worry. Your secrets are safe with me."

Griffe said loudly, "He cannot be far, my dear." He was inside the gallery now. "Shall we seek for him in the gaming room? It is just through the armor gallery here."

"I suppose so," a woman's voice said in a crisp British accent. "I can't think why he would simply disappear like this just before dinner."

"Penrose is a scholar, Mademoiselle Banks," Griffe said. "Scholars become engrossed in their studies, I understand, to the point of sheer distraction and forgetfulness. Perhaps he has gone, not to the gaming room, but to the library? Come along. We will find your mislaid fiancé."

Fiancé?

Oh.

Griffe and Miss Banks passed by in a breeze of *eau de cologne* and silken rustles. Penrose didn't move a muscle.

"Dreadfully rude of him." The woman's voice was sulky. "Once we are married, I'll insist that he remedy his ways."

"You may insist," Griffe said, "but gentlemen rarely undergo change. Particularly after matrimony."

Their footsteps receded.

Ophelia whispered to Penrose, "I recall you speaking of Miss Banks with great enthusiasm last month in Paris. Congratulations on your engagement. Your *swift* engagement."

"Miss Flax. What I told you three weeks ago . . . I beg your pardon about all that." Penrose adjusted his spectacles. "I was rash and, indeed, mistaken. Paris had gone to my head, I suppose."

Ophelia swallowed. "I see." He'd taken that *I love you* back. Well. What an absolute *relief*.

"I do hope I did not cause you a moment of unease," he said.

"Unease? No. Certainly not. I will see you at dinner, I reckon." Ophelia stepped out from behind the suits of armor and hurried out of the gallery, in the opposite direction that Griffe and Miss Banks had gone.

And this lump in her throat? Well, it must be that she was thirsty from traveling all day.